PRAISE FOR *FINDING RAMANATA*

"Robyn Dabney does it again! *Finding Ramanata*, the second book in Dabney's Daughter of Summit and Sea feminist fantasy series, is an intense, emotional, brilliant novel. We follow Klarke Ascher as she continues her quest, scaling mountains as she works to free her country from a cruel dictatorship hell-bent on destroying her. *Finding Ramanata* has everything I loved in *The Ascenditure*—unnerving political intrigue, thrilling action, rich characters and world building, and lyrical prose. Readers will find enormous inspiration in Klarke's determination and passionate resolve to uncover the truth despite the personal cost, anguish, and peril. I can't wait for the final installment of this series, because of this I have no doubt: Klarke will not fall. She will not fail. She will not betray the truth. A must read."

—Adriana Allegri, author of *The Sunflower House*

"In this dazzling, whirlwind of a YA fantasy novel, the second in a series, Robyn Dabney once again immerses us in the troubled kingdom of elite alpinist Klarke Ascher, a young woman bent on not only scaling the most treacherous mountains but on freeing her country from ruthless dictatorship through quests that could destroy her life."

—Janet Goldberg, author of *The Proprietor's Song* and fiction editor of *Deep Wild: Writing from the Backcountry*

"The Daughter of the Summit and Sea series is an absolute delight to read! These novels feature characters with great depth and a plot that is exhilarating. I couldn't put the first book down, and the second one is even more thrilling. Somehow these novels contain the most exciting and compelling details of *The Handmaid's Tale*, *The Hunger Games*, and *Into Thin Air*.

The protagonist, Klarke Ascher, is an amazing Young Adult character who fights the patriarchy and climbs mountains with the same fierce courage, dedication, and aplomb."

—Zackary Vernon, author of *Our Bodies Electric*

"If you've read *The Ascenditure,* you'll want—no, you'll need—to read *Finding Ramanata*, Robyn Dabney's second book with climber Klarke Ascher. The reader witnesses Klarke's naivete and uncertainty turn to rock solid conviction when startling turns of events make her question everything. The story builds like a snowball rolling down a very steep, glacier-covered mountain until the reader is speeding along toward revelations that make the wait for the third installment in the series seem agonizing. As always, Dabney's deft touch with language and world building is evident throughout, but nowhere is it more apparent than when she describes climbing and mountaineering. You'll be right there with Klarke until the final page. I couldn't put it down."

—Jill Murray, author of *The Glimmering Sea*

"Though a formidable character, Klarke's real power isn't in her literal strength or stunning defiance, it's in her quiet, determined insistence that the world can be made better if only people are willing to face the truth, even if it means confronting themselves. Klarke isn't a Mary-Sue. She's strong but flawed. Complicated yet earnest. Wounded yet hopeful. And she's a heroine we should all root for."

—Stephanie Scott, author of *Daughter of Wrath*

"In the gripping sequel to *The Ascenditure*, Klarke Ascher's quest continues as she heroically navigates political intrigue, forbidden love and epic dangers, through a brilliantly crafted world designed for her to fail."

—Laura Reeves, author of *Otherworldly Secrets*

"Our very own Katniss Everdeen with the climbing ropes, Klarke Ascher, returns in this makes-you-want-stand-up-and-cheer next installment in Dabney's feminist historical fantasy series. I was ecstatic to return to Ectair and go with Klarke as she navigates multiple mysteries abound with adventure! Not only is Dabney an obvious master climber, but a master of intrigue as well. You won't be able to put down this twisty turny adventure until the last page. Then you'll be waiting on the edge of your seat, like I am, for the next in the Daughter of the Summit and Sea series!"

—Samantha Schinder, PhD author of *The Deliverance* Series

"Daring, dazzling Klarke Ascher is a timely heroine for the ages. Leaping from the brilliant world and characters created in the first book, the second installment builds and climbs to deliver one of the most satisfying fantasy series since *Throne of Glass*. Sure to become a classic to read again and again. It's that good!"

—Claire Bethke, author of *That Summer in Monaco*

FINDING RAMANATA

Daughter of the Summit and Sea
Book Two

Robyn Dabney

Fitzroy Books

Published by Fitzroy Books
An imprint of
Regal House Publishing, LLC
Raleigh, NC 27605

https://fitzroybooks.com
Printed in the United States of America

ISBN -13 (paperback): 9781646036219
ISBN -13 (epub): 9781646036226
Library of Congress Control Number: 2024951380

Cover images and design by ©studiochi.art
Maps by © Adam Bassett

Printed in the United States of America

Regal House Publishing, LLC
https://regalhousepublishing.com

For all who dream of forbidden summits

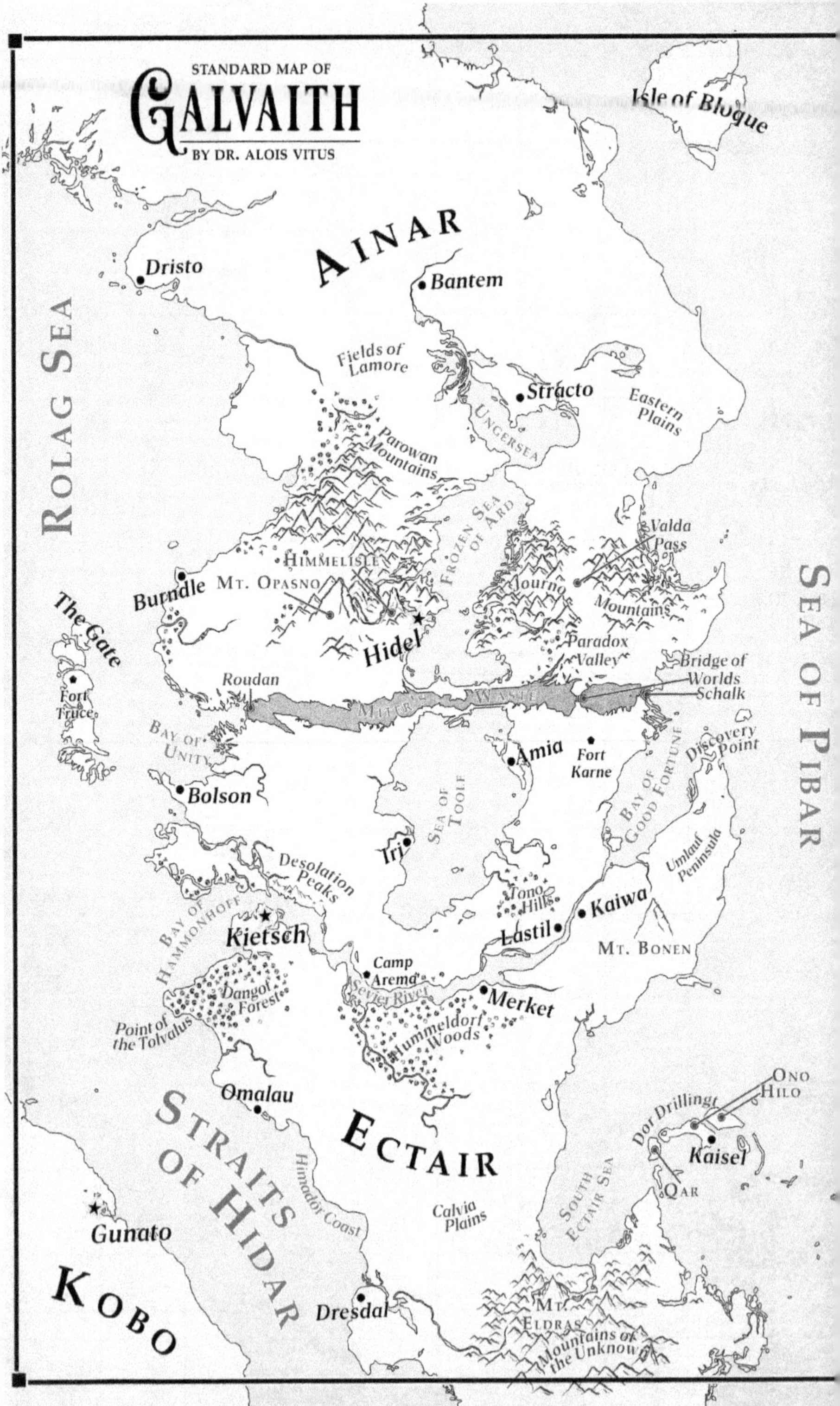

STANDARD MAP OF
GALVAITH
BY DR. ALOIS VITUS
Isle of Bloque
AINAR
Dristo
Bantem
ROLAG SEA
Fields of Lamore
Stracto
Eastern Plains
Ungersea
Parowan Mountains
Frozen Sea of Ard
Valda Pass
Himmelisle
Mt. Opasno
Burndle
Journo Mountains
The Gate
Hidel
Paradox Valley
Fort Truce
Roudan
Miter Waste
Bridge of Worlds
Schalk
SEA OF PIBAR
Bay of Unity
Amia
Fort Karne
Discovery Point
Bolson
Sea of Toolf
Bay of Good Fortune
Umlauf Peninsula
Iri
Desolation Peaks
Tono Hills
Kaiwa
Bay of Hammonhoff
Kietsch
Lastil
Mt. Bonen
Camp Arema
Sever River
Dangol Forest
Merket
Point of the Tolvalus
Hummeldorf Woods
Ono
Hilo
Omalau
Dor Drillingt
STRAITS OF HIDAR
ECTAIR
Kaisel
Himador Coast
South Ectair Sea
Qar
Gunato
Calvia Plains
KOBO
Dresdal
Mt. Eldras
Mountains of the Unknown

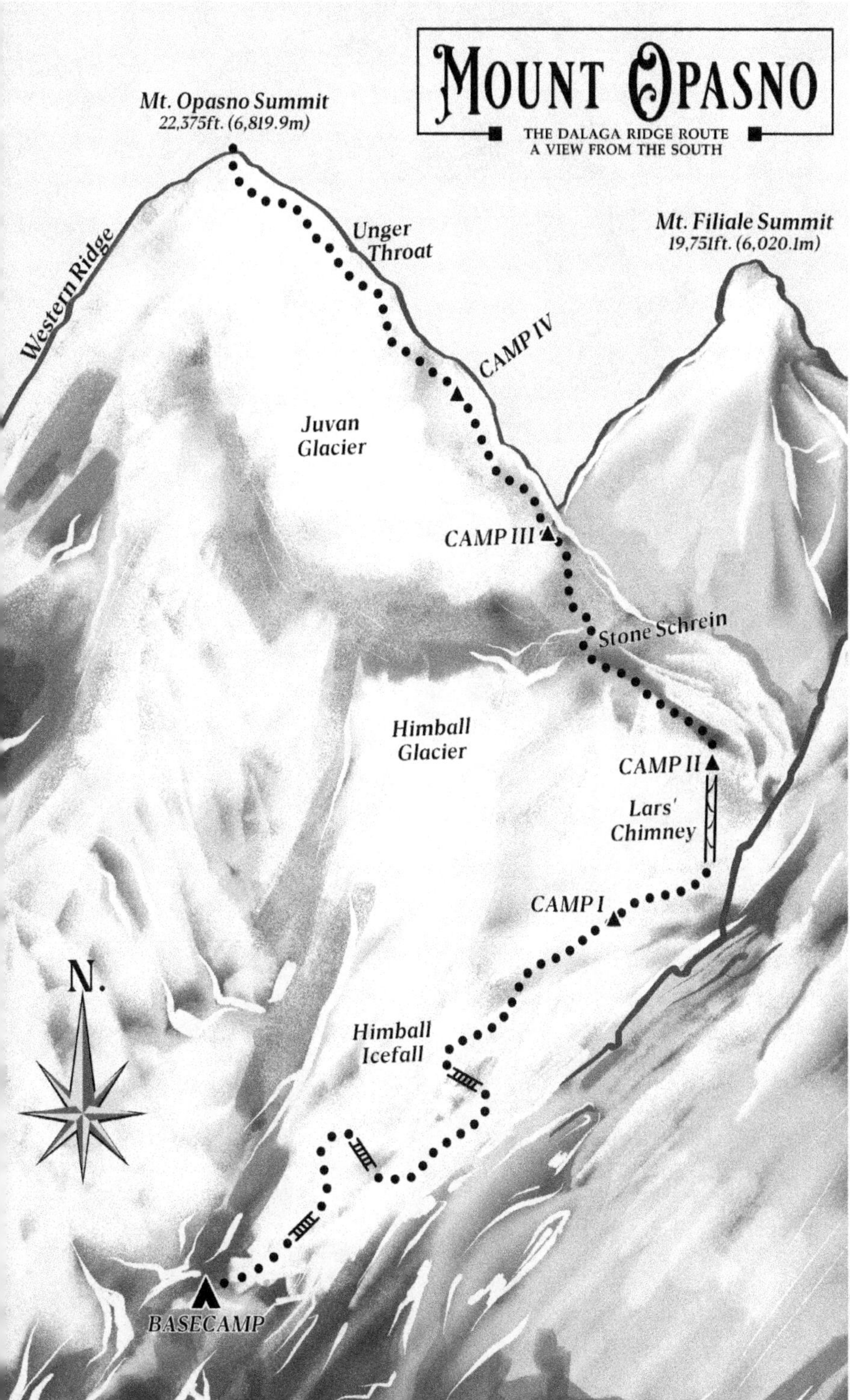
MOUNT OPASNO
THE DALAGA RIDGE ROUTE
A VIEW FROM THE SOUTH
Mt. Opasno Summit
22,375ft. (6,819.9m)
Mt. Filiale Summit
19,751ft. (6,020.1m)
Western Ridge
Unger Throat
CAMP IV
Juvan Glacier
CAMP III
Stone Schrein
Himball Glacier
CAMP II
Lars' Chimney
CAMP I
N.
Himball Icefall
BASECAMP

1

Serrated rock cuts into my fingers as I grip the small fissure with one hand and a sharp flake with the other. Below, a bed of straw, pine needles, and decaying leaves lies stuffed into a stitched lump of fabric.

"You've got this, Klarke!" Russet shouts.

"Use your feet!" Aedan, the lead climber of the Ascenditures, calls out. "Hook that heel."

I lift my leg and secure the heel of my new leather climbing boot—a gift from my betrothed, Prince Otto—over a fold of dark igneous. The old shoes that accompanied me through years of trials and defeats, growth and survival, went to Gerd's little sister, Marike. They are too big for her now, but she will grow into them. I couldn't bear to throw them out. The faded leather holds too many memories. Too much sweat and blood. And joy. I remind myself that climbing is also something I love. Something I fiercely love. I've sacrificed everything for it.

"Good. Now use your arm and shoulder in the crack," Aedan says. "No one person climbs a route exactly the same. Make this yours!"

I nod, hang from a good jug hold with one hand, and shake out the tension in my free arm. I switch hands and do the same with the other. Then I stretch my arm up to my elbow into the crack, make a fist, and add tension to my shoulder. The pressure is enough to secure me into the rock.

I'm climbing Veber's Split, a bouldering problem hidden in a lava tube in the hills just west of Vether's Fel that only Aedan and Burkhart have been able to complete. The route is named after Lars Veber, Ellias's grandfather and the father of mountaineering. He pioneered this sport we love so much.

They killed Lars for treason. They killed Ellias because he knew too much.

There is only one fate for those in Ectair who don't hoist the proper sails.

I close my eyes and take a deep breath. I can't think of Ellias right now. Or of fear. I can't concentrate on the climb and remember what his broken body looked like on the moraine at the base of Fitzhan.

"Head up, darling," I whisper to myself. "Always head up."

A red spider covered in golden spots crawls from the crack near my face, and I take a deep breath. It is a gluspider, a rare creature we believe comes from Laren's realm that occasionally slips through into the world of the living. According to our omies, she brings fortune to the ones who see her and hardship to those who squash her. Maybe Ellias sent her.

I watch her scurry from the route and plot my next move. Veber's Split is a series of splitter cracks marked by white dust from previous climbers' hands. It winds up the side of an ancient lava tube, arcing over the cavernous floor twelve feet below before descending the other side. It is like climbing the underbelly of a bridge or the violet edge of a rainbow. I have no protection, no rope. Just my strength and the straw-stuffed mat Russet is adjusting below as I climb. I press against the rock to gain traction and stretch my other arm to the next crack. I've reached the crux of the route, the hardest part. Here the crack, and the associated holds, disappear entirely.

"There's a flake about thirteen inches from your right hand." Aedan moves into my periphery until he is standing directly below me. "If you dyno, you may be able to reach it."

"If I jump on this rock, I'll have no skin left on my hands," I pant through a grunt. My arms and clenched fingers tremble.

"Not if you do it correctly," Burkhart says. I still wouldn't consider us friends, but ever since I accompanied him on Gio's rescue mission and ever since he witnessed Gio try to kill me, he has at least been cordial.

My mind floods with images before I can stop it—the tightening cord around my throat, Gio's decapitated head rolling beneath a bush, Rayna's bruised arms, Ellias, broken and bloodied on the moraine.

Please, not now, I beg. *Leave me be.*

"I'm here to spot you if you fall." Aedan's arms are raised as if to catch a tossed sack of saltz. "You won't sustain any injury you can't heal from."

Won't I? I'm not afraid to fall. Not really. I fall often. I've fallen my whole life. It is violence at the hands of others, of narrowly escaping with my life, of which I have a lingering dread.

I tilt my head back, searching for the flake Aedan mentioned. I find it, but all four of my limbs will have to leave the rock in order to reach it. I will have to fly like a flitchen.

"Do it!" Veit shouts, his words echoing through the dim tunnel. "Quit being a girl and jump."

That's all it takes to vanquish my fear. I'll show them what being a girl actually means. I bend my knees, pushing with every muscle as I fling myself forward, fully airborne, reaching for the hold. Instead of landing lightly, my body swings violently beyond the flake. Skin tears against sharp stone. Momentum rips my fingers from the rock. There is a split second of confusion before I slam into Aedan's outstretched arms and then more gently onto the ground.

Kiel crouches next to me, taking my bloodied hand in his own and cleaning the cuts and scrapes with water. "It was a good try." He gives a soft smile. His touch sends jolts that sear like bacon in an iron pan through my body.

I cringe as the liquid seeps between skin fragments. Blinking rapidly, I try to focus on the immediate pain. This is the first time we have touched since Gio's death, since Kiel's betrothal to Lady Gelta. I've stuck close to Dieter or Russet at practice so that Kiel and I are never alone. I avoid him whenever I can and refuse to meet his gaze, but sometimes, before I can look away, I see his smile falter and his shoulders droop.

Aedan brings a clean scrap of wool and ties it around my

hand. I lie on my back, staring at the ceiling of the lava tube, and endeavor to ignore my overwhelming desire to flee to Kobo with Rayna and Kiel.

"Fantish effort, Klarke," Aedan says. "Truly. It took me a long time to bag this one." He smiles, a flash of white teeth against his leathery skin. He wears his long, mattlocked hair tied back with an old piece of climbing rope.

Veit leans over me, his face blocking my view of the jagged ceiling. "That was terrible."

"I think it was a brilliant try." Dieter encourages me with a wink as he prepares for his climb. "Just wait till it's your turn, Veit, and you miss the dyno. Then we'll be able to make a comparison."

The others laugh. I stand, dazed, and move to the wall as Dieter begins his climb. Kiel chews the corner of his lip and slightly shakes his head, but doesn't look at me. My heart tightens, and I let out a deep, slow breath. I can't handle his touch, but the absence of it hurts too.

Dieter follows the same route as me, until he reaches the crack's end and must decide whether to jump. He hangs for a few seconds before dropping to the ground. "Not today. I'm not feeling strong," he acknowledges as he moves to stand by my side.

"You better not have dropped for my sake." I glare at Dieter and rub a knot on my neck.

He laughs and leans against the rock. "I would never insult you like that. If I babied you, I'd never hear the end from Otto."

Prince Otto, my betrothed and Dieter's secret lover, is fully on board with my mission—our mission, actually—to change Ectair's punishing treatment of women, gleibels—the term for people who love others from their same gender—and those with features signifying they come from other lands.

I punch Dieter lightly on the arm, feeling a surge of happiness to enjoy a friendship with one who also has pursued a path contrary to society's wishes. He necessarily lives a secret life, trying desperately to survive in a world digging in its heels against the wrench of change. He carries blood from Ainar in his veins but has kept himself from the labor camps by dedicating his life to climbing and being one of the best. I could imagine King Adolar's rage, should he discover his son's love for another man, let alone one descended from his sworn enemies.

A thump echoes as Tizian hits the ground following his failed attempt at a dyno. I smile at him and shrug. "Nice try."

He grunts and pretends he doesn't see me. While Burkhart's ice has thawed a little, Tizian seems to have doubled down on his loathing.

Veit opens his dust sack, buries his hands inside, and then rubs them together. A shower of fine white powder mists to the ground and dusts his tan hosen. "Watch, Klarke," he says. "These boys might go easy on you, but you know I won't. Not ever."

"It's one of your only endearing qualities," I reply.

Veit begins his ascent, working his hands smoothly up the crack, his weight shifting gracefully as he moves from one handhold to another. He is the tallest of us, which affords him the advantage of a longer reach but also the difficulty of added weight and in some cases less stability.

Despite Veit's dismissiveness, despite his derogatory comments about women, I don't hate him. I have a fondness for him that is hard to explain. Perhaps it was the horrific journey we shared on the slopes of Mount Bonen, where six other climbers were murdered. Or maybe it's that, deep down, he doesn't loathe me as much as he pretends. Doesn't understand why he's supposed to.

"Come on, Veit!" Aedan yells, clapping vigorously. Aedan is a strong leader who cheers for us all, wants the best for our team, and doesn't see my gender as a weakness. Veit reaches the end of the crack and eyes the flake, taking his time to plan the next move.

"Quit being a boy and jump!" I can't help myself.

Veit smirks, bites his bottom lip, then bends his knees for the leap. He thrusts himself off the rock and is airborne, arms outstretched as he reaches for the flake; grasping it, his body sways slightly as he jams his arm into the crack, bracing a palm against one side and an elbow against the other. He swings his legs upward and jams his left foot into the crack. Veit swaggers through the rest of the route with ease and steps onto the ground with enough confidence to challenge King Adolar to a duel. We cheer—even me. My hollering helps to quash the jealousy swirling around my stomach like spoiled kuhka meat. When a teammate accomplishes something tricky, the idea of enemies and individuality dissipates. We become one.

"In your face!" Veit shouts, yanking his woolen coppola from his head as he thrusts a finger toward me.

I slap his hand away. "Beginner's luck."

He rolls his piercing blue eyes, and I roll mine back and laugh. "Good job, Veit. I'm proud of you."

He opens his mouth to speak, but nothing comes out. Instead, he backs up slowly, nodding. But I see the softness in his eyes. I see the struggle between needing to despise me and wanting to accept my evident goodwill.

"You're up, Drich. Show us what ye' got." Tizian pushes the newest recruit who filled Gio's empty spot toward the wall.

Haydrich Malte is my age, of average height, and incredibly strong. He wears his hair shoulder-length and messy, and his eyes are the color of unburnt coal. A short beard covers his chin, making him look older than he is. I'd thought, initially, that he'd come from Merket in the Hummeldorf Woods, but Russet told me he'd traveled from Qar in the Dor Drillingt Islands. Dieter, however, insists he hails from Omalau on the Himadôr Coast. Haydrich finally told us the truth of the matter—he'd been born in Dresdal, a city beyond the Calvia Plains where an endless sea of dense grass and hidden sinkholes cover the southern lands.

Haydrich steps forward, his expression unreadable, almost bored. Not smug. Not cocky. He reaches for the rock and moves as if no amount of effort fatigues him. With the poise of an adel at court, he floats in and out of the crack, holding his body weight with just the tips of his fingers; then, he twists in one swift circular motion, somersaulting to the crack's end. He is a rock dancer. A stone poet. I realize I'm barely breathing.

"Why did we let this guy join? We're likely to lose our jobs to him," Tizian mutters with a chuckle. Following Gio's death, he has been named as a team lead. Haydrich is the rear climber for his kletshot. His team.

Haydrich shakes out his arms and then grasps a nub of rock in the gap between the crack and the flake. Bracing his boot against an awkward corner, he moves across the ceiling of the lava tube as if weightless, reaching the flake without leaving the wall. It is climbing perfection.

The cavern is silent as he finishes the route. He steps softly onto the ground, and we erupt in jubilant chaos.

"What in Miter's holy grave was that?" Russet rubs his eyes as if that will help him better understand what he just saw.

"Best damn climbing I've ever seen," Burkhart muses. "Think I'll quit now."

"Don't think he's coming for your job, Tiz." Aedan laughs and claps Haydrich's shoulder. "Pretty sure he'll take mine."

Veit's lips tighten, and I bite back a smile. It must be hard for him to have his victory shadowed.

I nod politely at Haydrich, but feel the sharp pang of jealousy prick at my heart. I realize then that Veit and I have the same stew boiling in our pots. I'm envious of Haydrich's physical skill, of his focus, of the praise lavished upon him and the awe surrounding his feat. There have always been climbers stronger, faster, more agile than me. I wonder why Haydrich's ability affects me so deeply.

Aedan waves, and we gather in a circle. "That's it for today, team," he tells us. "Since we are no longer collecting solans and ulrind due to inclement conditions on Miter's Backbone, we will spend a lot of time in these tubes, at the factory, or working jobs. Busy season is upon us. Take care of your hands. Cold weather and dust will crack them so painfully that you can't even wipe your arsch. Use the klettecreme morning and night and get some rest. Dieter, Russet, and Kiel. You three will join me early at the north gate to head to the Roudan. Someone reported a leak in the dam a few stars past, and they need us to fix it. Pack for a few days. I'm not sure how long we'll be out."

"Apparently, the guy who reported it claimed he saw Hildegroth's tentacle rise above the dam, and that when he went to check it out, the great sea beast seized the man's pony and pulled it into his swirling jaws." Tizian, with eyes wide and arms outstretched, lurches toward Veit with a shriek; Veit flinches and shoves Tizian away.

"That's what happens when you overdo the veisel." Veit shoves Tizian away and straightens. "Too many brain-rotted sods wandering our streets now."

"Here's hoping that guy is wrong," Kiel says. "I'm excited to work on the Roudan, but not keen on being swallowed by Hildy."

"I second that," Dieter says.

"Scouts were sent and, of course, there was no sign of the beast." Aedan packs his dust and boots into a rucksack and wipes chalky hands on his pants. "It will, I am sure, be a straightforward dam repair."

The Roudan, the dam that prevents the sea from entering Miter's Waste, was jointly constructed by Ectair and Ainar after the great monster Hildegroth's destructive rampage through the Unity Canal many years before. Hildegroth, King Adolar claims, is controlled by King Gyalzen of Ainar, who sends the fearsome beast to do his will.

Gyalzen can't control that beast, Obid, the ship's cook and friend of my parents, had told me. *No man can. But a woman. Might be that a woman can. Might be that a woman's what set off the great beast in the firs' place. That's why ya mum worked so hard to get her out of there.*

His words remind me of the many secrets and lies infesting Ectair, lies that have shrouded my entire life in a dark confusion. I have to find Obid and discover the truth about my mother, my father—all of it.

Peering at Kiel, I try not to let Tizian's antics affect me. Hildegroth is gone. My mother and Obid succeeded in smuggling Lady Genalt to Ainar. She is now either safe or dead—if, indeed, she ever truly wielded the power to control the monster. Besides, what reason could there be for Hildegroth to return now, after all this time? Kiel will be fine. It is just a routine repair.

I pull on a sweater and yank heavy sheepskin gloves over my hands. Knocking my dark braid over my shoulder, I don a green woolen coppola like the men wear and reach for my gear. While climbing—so long as there are no spectators or palace guards in the vicinity—I wear pants instead of my regularly required garb of a long woolen skirt and tight blouse.

The rest of the team have eyes only for Haydrich as they continue to banter, slap him on the back, and congratulate him on his climbing feat. I pick the skin at my finger and observe their camaraderie. I don't care for the envy that swallows me whole; I don't want to treat him as others have treated me. I've always prided myself on being able to control my emotions, and as fear has already slipped free, I decide to wrangle jealousy, before it, too, becomes too powerful to control.

As Haydrich moves past me, I grab his arm. He stops to stare. I think frantically of what to say but words elude me.

"Good climbing," I manage finally. "It's nice to have you on the team." Is it nice? Yes, I tell myself. It's fantish.

"Tanks." He pulls his arm free.

"How did you learn those tricks?" I ask. Maybe if I chat with him, get to know him better, my jealousy will subside. All climbers, at star's end, compete against nobody but themselves.

"My uncle."

"He must have been excellent. Did he ever want to be an Ascenditure?"

"Nide," he says curtly.

Is he shy or purposefully not giving me better answers? Or perhaps, like Tizian and Burkhart, he is disgruntled at having a female climber on the team. "Is there good climbing in the Calvia Plains?" I ask lamely.

"If you know where to look," he says.

"So I guess you know where to look?"

"I always know where to look." To my surprise, he winks, quirks a smile, and walks away. I stare after him, dazed. The wink felt familiar, but everything else about our newest climber feels strange in a way I cannot quite pinpoint. I roll my shoulders back and follow the others out of the lava tube and across the clearing to the forest's edge.

Frigid air blows down from the icy lands of Ainar to the north, whips my braid across my cheeks, and sends my skirt flapping about my legs. Slushy rain wets the back of my neck and trickles in cold rivulets beneath my collar. At the edge of the forest, standing patiently beneath the dripping canopy, my other new gift from Prince Otto waits—Ixy, a mare almost entirely black in color with white ankles, a white chest, and streaks of red in her dark mane.

Ixy greets me with a friendly nicker, nudging me with her velvety nose. Closing my eyes, I bury my face in her neck, trying to harness the joy I felt while climbing to take back to the palace. My wedding night approaches, and, although Otto has become an invaluable friend, I feel consumed by loneliness and an ache for what I can never have.

Is that all that life holds for me? A dark void of life without love? Consumed by a nasty envy of the skills of others? I have finally become an Ascenditure, a goal for which I have fought and struggled my entire life. Why is it not enough?

"Klarke, please stop avoiding me. Just talk to me."

There it is. The alpenstock hacking into my heart. I open my eyes and take in Kiel's tall figure, draped in a heavy wool coat. He also has a new pair of leather boots that lace up over his dusty brown hosen. His dark eyes carry a weight, an intensity—a message—that only I can interpret.

"I..." My gaze drops to Ixy's hooves, shifting restlessly in the sodden ground. Despite myself, I imagine Kiel with his betrothed, Lady Gelta, dancing across the ballroom at the vintazite festival. I foresee the arid stretch of my own life ahead, where my love for him exists only in the peripheries of the world, in silent, unspoken thoughts packed away into crates in the hulls of ships bound for the unknown lands to the west. These thoughts pain me more than any physical injury I have suffered, and I feel the weight of my misery like stone-filled baskets upon my shoulders.

"I can't right now. I'm so sorry." Emotion clogs my throat as I step into the stirrup and climb onto Ixy's back.

Kiel grabs my ankle, gently holding me in place as he glances up at me. The anguish in his gaze stops my breath. "It'll always be you, Klarke. Always. No matter the chasm between us. The mountains we must climb. The endless valleys and harsh wastes we must toil through. At the end of it all, at the summit. For me, it's only you."

My heart splits like the cracks in the lava tube and the pain of it breaking nearly knocks me from the saddle. Tears fill my eyes before I can compose myself. Reaching down, I rest a gloved hand on Kiel's and give it a light squeeze. Our eyes meet, and I tell him what I must in a wordless glance, words I cannot say aloud. He rests his forehead against the leather covering my shin. I let his touch warm me until I see Veit glaring at us from across the clearing.

"I have to go."

Kiel takes a step back. I kick Ixy's side, and she lopes into the forest. The limb of an elderpine scratches a gash into my cheek. The trees break at the top of the ridge, giving me a full view of Ectair's crowded capital city of Kietsch. Factory chimneys belch dark plumes of smoke into the sky, and it is impossible to tell where the smog ends and the sea mist begins. My kreison, a province of the kingdom, is known for its saltz production. Our factories also process the resources from the other eight kreisons, which means our air always smells of burning tar, boiling vats of glue, and the stink of unrelenting poverty.

I look west, toward the sea. Red-brick buildings dot the Westlich, the respectable part of town where I grew up. Decorative metal birds sit atop their shingled roofs, weather vanes that spin and creak in the wind. Intricately carved wooden balconies, draped in vines and flowers, ornament their facades. The Bay of Hammonhoff stretches liquid fingers up to the wooden planks of Pohle Pier, where merchants and sailors struggle to scrape up a living. Ships with brightly colored triangular sails float upon a momentarily placid sea. Their canvas is not orange, like my father's; those tattered sails washed ashore without him long ago, but I think of those sails—bright as garsip fruit—whenever I see boats returning.

I avert my gaze from the sea and its drowned memories. Dingy tenements and crumbling brick-and-mortar storefronts crowd the other districts. From my vantage point above the city, I am too far to smell and hear, but I know the fetor of destitution and the sound of souls slowly dying from pulmonosis as well as I know how to tie tight knots on a cliff.

At the heart of it all rests the Rektburg—an old stone gargoyle in a city scraping its way into a future of steam and iron. Ten stone towers jut into the sky like accusing fingers, and inside each lie secrets and falsehoods it would take centuries to unravel. I have only one lifetime—a precious, fragile thing—in which to accomplish it.

I take a deep breath and channel my melancholy into rage. King Adolar, like his palace, is dated, old, and at risk of becoming obsolete. He represents the patriarchal hierarchy that will do anything, risk anything, to keep us in our place, to keep women subservient, to keep those of the wrong blood—or who love the wrong people—downtrodden and despairing.

I gently nudge Ixy, and we gallop down the hill toward the bridge that crosses the Sevier River. I must find Prince Otto. Uncovering the truth cannot wait. King Adolar may be the stone, but I am the iron. I am the steam. And it is time for the rock to crumble.

2

Revolution Square lies mostly empty. There are no Ascenditures to swear in today, no women to hang for treason. No bodies to send to the sea. The wealthy have not ventured from distant cities to watch whatever drama Kietsch has concocted. The women have given up their cries for equality, lulled into a false sense of progress by the smokescreen of my unfolding life.

Only the peasants mill about, hawking half-rotten fruit and mealy grains to absent patrons. Toshers encourage hollow-bellied ponies to pull carts burdened with fish heads, cow dung, and whatever other detritus they've pulled from the gutters. A light rain mingles with the smog, and yesterday's slushy snow melts into muddy puddles that stink of sewage. It is too cold now for the flies and maggots, so the filth remains until it is slowly washed away, from gutter to gutter and into the sea.

A bell rings in the crooked tower of Hadrian's Monastery. The seven summits of Miter's Backbone rise behind the castle, behind Vether's Fel and the lava tubes, towering over us all. The summit of Fitzhan, Ectair's guardian mountain, lies shrouded in clouds. If only it could have protected Ellias against betrayal.

I bring Ixy to a trot, and we make our way through the narrow streets to the palace stables. A stable hand takes Ixy to her stall. "Take good care of her," I tell the hand, rubbing Ixy's sweat-dampened neck. I toss an extra dracal into his palm, and he bows deeply. "She loves the little oat rings."

"Only the best, Fram Ascher."

"Tanks ye."

I jog up the stone steps of the Rektburg, the old palace King Miter built long ago, to the platform where I swore my oath as an Ascenditure. It still feels strange that not only am I responsible, with the rest of the Ascenditures, for maintenance of the Rektburg's towers, but also that I now reside within its walls. I glance up at the massive stone bulwarks. The Rektburg comprises three parts—the outer fortress called the Pentengen with five towers forming its corners, the most prevalent being Miter's Tower, which juts out onto the platform. Four great towers—Prince Otto's, the late queen's, and the towers of Laren and Orna, our two gods—form the diamond-shaped inner structure called the Geistich. Within the Geistich stands the lone Nied Tower, the beating heart of the castle, its inner sanctum—or, as I often think of it, the belly of the beast—where King Adolar resides.

Guards patrol the shadows of the ten great turrets, icy raindrops dripping from their metal helmets and darkening their green tunics and dun-colored pants. They barely glance up as I pass, bantering as they are about their conquests in the brothels at Pohle Pier.

Silias, however, is not so lax. He waits for me under the eaves of a columned walkway, his guard uniform dry and crisp, his helmet gleaming, the leather band of his satchel crossing his chest. "Welcome back, Fram Ascher," he says, with a slight bow.

"Silias." I nod at the guard who has been assigned to report my every movement to the king.

"How was practice? I trust you went?" His icy-blue eyes narrow. One of the furry creatures he calls an eyebrow rises.

"Would I lie to you?"

We stare unblinking. Ten seconds pass. I barely swallow. Then I burst out laughing. He snorts and shakes his head. "You are an imp, Fram Ascher. How have I so earned Laren's wrath to be assigned watch over you?"

"Whatever your sin, I am grateful for it."

Silias retrieves a bundle of fabric, a climbing skirt, from his satchel, and inclines his head toward the small door behind him. "Tread lightly." He nods at the pants I am still wearing. "Loud footfalls of mice draw the attention of cats."

"Tanks ye." I feel a surge of gratitude—spy he may be, but he also feels like a friend, and I have few of those. I fight the impulse to give him a quick hug. But such displays of affection are not customary, and he would reject it. He might even be removed from my guard if the king had any inkling of Silias's kindness. Instead, I shoot him a grateful smile before making my way through the door to the vacant guardhouse beyond. I change from my dust-covered pants into the long climbing skirt and set off through the palace in search of my husband-to-be.

I find Otto in Walburga's Library, named for a long-dead queen whose love of reading, Lena tells me, anchors her spirit to the space. I've never seen her ghost myself, but the cleaning women will often find books stacked haphazardly, moved from one location to another, and hear deep groans through the walls.

I breathe deeply the scent of leather and old, brittle parchment, of burnt candle wax and incense. The library is massive, with shelves that reach up two stories or more, accessed by wrought-iron ladders that can be wheeled from one section to another; arched ceilings tower far above, with endless rows of books stacked from the dusty floor to the cobwebbed rafters. I sympathize with Queen Walburga—I wouldn't want to leave either.

Otto is bent over a thick tome, *Odabei dei na Odabei*, by the Galvaithian scholar and philosopher Ebhard the Stout. The binding is as thick as the decking on a ship and looks as old as Walburga herself. An open book of translated Galvaithian runes sits on the table beside him, a sheaf of parchment with scribbled notes resting on its pages.

"Find anything useful?" I pull up a chair to sit beside him.

"Not yet." Otto turns the book so I can see the writing. I recognize the letters, but they mean nothing to me. "It's all written in Galvaithian," he says. "I have to translate everything I read. The title means *Urspra of the Urspra*. Origin of the origin. Seems like a good place to start."

I glance over the book he is reading and sigh. "You will join Walburga's ghost before you finish translating that. There must be a better way to do this."

He carefully turns the page, peruses the scrolled writing,

then jots a few notes on the parchment. "I don't think complicated matters, such as these, are ever easy to unravel," he says, glancing across at me with a wry grin. "People who weave deceit tie tight knots. Perhaps patience is the great weapon of the righteous."

"What exactly do you think you'll find in there?"

"No idea. Perhaps a reference to Death's Whisper or the purple ferns. Or details of the creation story that can help us figure out what my father and the päters are up to. We should also go through Dr. Vitus's journal again in case we missed something."

I give a theatrical groan, and Otto laughs, takes my hand, and kisses it. "Shall we try something more immediate then?"

"I need to speak with the prisoners from Ainar. The young man, I know him. I'm certain of it." I have focused on little else since the vintazite festival when the two strangers—the dark-skinned woman who leads Ainar's climbing team, the Parvanatari, and the young man who flung fish guts at me, just as my old friend Losan used to do in jest—arrived with an offering of a peace climb to reunite our two fractured kingdoms, Ectair and Ainar.

"My father will never allow it," Otto says.

"Could you speak with him? Please?" I recall Losan, as a boy, and then the gaze of the man who had so recently tossed fish entrails my way at the party. Was the twinkle in his eye the same as that of the boy I had once known? Was there some resemblance in the curve of an eyebrow, in that shock of dark hair? Much of my childhood had been spent chasing Losan around Pohle Pier, laughing at his jokes, getting pulled into his schemes. He had been the closest thing to a sibling in the years before I met Rayna. I feel a certainty in my bones, in the beating thrum of my heart, that the imprisoned man in the dungeon far below is that same friend I knew so long ago. Impossible as it is for the dead to reappear. "The Ascenditures must be allowed to go to Ainar for the climb," I insist, pressing Otto's hand.

"My father's reign is built on animosity with Ainar. Can you imagine him admitting he was wrong?" Otto places the book on the table and leans back in his chair, eyeing me sadly. "I thought your friend was aboard your father's ship when it sank?"

"I know it sounds crazy, Otto. But I'm telling you, it is him." I chew my lip and stare at the wooden tabletop. "But this is not just about Losan or about climbing. Damn the climb. Everything leads to Ainar. Our mothers, Obid, your twin sister, Lady Genalt if she is somehow still alive. Your mother's journal describes my mother smuggling your sister out, right? Obid took her north. She's there. I know it, and I have to find her."

Otto sighs and rubs his forehead. "I don't know why I'm afraid to broach the subject with him."

"Because it's him, and he's a savage worse than the demon Ignaz."

Otto chews at a finger until I knock his hand away from his lips.

"So much of me hates him. But some pieces love him. Some parts remember him reading stories, or clapping me on the back after a successful hunt, or sitting by my bedside all night when I was ill. I..."

I take his hand and squeeze it. He turns glassy eyes to me.

"Am I a monster for being unable not to love one?" he asks.

"Of course not," I say gently. "He's your father. It's always more complicated than either love or hate. Especially when it comes to family."

I'm lucky I don't have to carry such a burden. My father was kind. Gentle. I bear the grief of his loss, but I can love him fully in that grief. My mother, too, I recall as loving—even though I am just now discovering there was more to her than I knew.

"If I can find your sister, Otto, and bring her back, we can expose the king's pretense. He bore twins, fulfilling the prophecy of a doomed lineage, and then concealed it from everyone. He will have to step down. I loathe the king, Otto, but I do not want him to die. I know what it is to miss a father. I just want him to lose his power."

"I am part of that pretend lineage, too, Klarke. If my father has to step down, so will I. According to the prophecy, as the son in this doomed lineage, I will bear no children. I will be the end of the line. And then who will take my place?"

Our conversation is interrupted when the library door opens, and six dark-robed päters file silently into the room. We quiet as they pass our table. The candlelight from wall sconces throws a gleam into their eyes behind their white masks. These men honor our gods Laren and Orna by the keeping of secrets, secrets that consolidate power and preserve the repressive regime, secrets gathered like ill-gotten gains from between the pages of old books. I imagine them as spirits from across the darkened sea, sucking the life essence from the pages over which they pour.

Apparently, our gods sent messages to the päters long ago, warning of twins, a girl and a boy, that portend a dynasty's end. But it is not just royal dynasties that fear the arrival of twins; peasants and adels, too, have become convinced of the evil associated with such twin pairings and opt to throw the baby girl into the sea, in a pretense that the infant son was the sole one birthed. King Adolar may be a wicked fool, but the päters are the source of that evil; and, if such prophecies are to be believed, then the great god Laren is the nastiest of them all.

The päters glance briefly at us as they pass, the cold white of their masked faces sending a chill down my spine. I struggle to keep my face impassive, to contain my rage, my hate, my sense of powerlessness. The religious men seat themselves at a table in a dark corner, too far away for our conversation to be heard.

"What if we fall, only to usher in a ruler even worse than my father?" Otto asks.

"We have to risk it," I say to Otto. "What choice do we have? I believe the people will give you a chance."

"It's not up to the people. It's up to them." Otto inclines his head toward the päters, and I wish Walburga would make an appearance and knock a flaming candle-sconce onto their scattered parchment. I recall the ash and bone they gave me before my ascent of Mount Bonen; of the glass shards from the queen's tower they provided as an offering on Fitzhan; of the black diemants and purple ferns they secretly harbor in the Geistich; of the purple ferns Gio collected on their behalf.

Ellias died because he discovered Gio's activities on Fitzhan. Perhaps King Adolar gave the order to cut Ellias's rope, or perhaps it was the päters—I don't care either way. They are all implicated in one way or another, and when I uncover the truth, anyone who had a hand in Ellias's death will burn.

I clear my throat and refocus. "Why not tell the king it would be good for morale? He could spin the opportunity, present himself as a just and fair ruler who cares about his people but is constantly thwarted by evil Ainar. I don't care what you say. Belittle me if you must."

"Okay," he says. "I can't promise anything, but I'll try."

"Tanks ye." I let out a heavy breath. I am on the edge of understanding, so close to gaining clarity about so much that has been obscured. But the edge is precipitous, and I am unsure if I'm attached to a rope or if I've leaped without protection.

"And if he says no, we'll figure out a way to break into the dungeon and speak with them anyway," I suggest.

Otto raises an eyebrow and chuckles. "The dungeon isn't a stone wall you can climb. It's deep underground. Guarded by men who would cut off their own hands if my father requested it."

How can people so blindly follow a tyrant? Heed the bidding of a man who cares for only himself? Because they are not the objects of his cruelty. And their humanity only goes as far as their own well-being.

"Let's say the king says yes to my request. What then?" Otto asks. "We know nothing of my sister's whereabouts. Searching for her in the vast expanse of Ainar will be like seeking a minnow in a lake."

I have seen a map of Ainar only once in my life. It is a sprawling land of mountains, lakes, and rivers—an endless wilderness that could easily swallow a child whole.

"I want to find her, Klarke. I want to help you succeed. But we also have to be pragmatic. Without Obid, or a name or location, it could take years, maybe a millennium, to find her. And even then, our chances of failure are great."

A name.

A name helps. More than just a face blending into a crowd. A name gives identity to a person. Humanity. Agency.

Rosalie. I close my eyes and remember the pink noose tightening around her neck, her feet knocking against the wooden gallows. A name. Ramanata.

It's the only name I have.

Find Ramanata.

At least, I think it's a name. Is my mother's final request to me, stitched into the fabric of the handkerchief she made bearing the orange sails of my father's ship, a plea to find Otto's sister? Are these the concise instructions to ensure King Adolar's downfall once and for all? It's poetic, really, that his downfall could be his blood kin. A daughter born of his loins that he then attempted to kill.

"Bring your books. I have a plan," I say.

"So much for patience. Where are we going?"

Together, we make for the door, studiously avoiding the steely gaze of the päters as they turn to watch us leave.

"I want to visit Dr. Helmut," I whisper, "and ask him where I can find Dr. Vitus. If I am to find your sister, I need to know everything I can about the day you two were born."

The infirmary consists of a small stone room, dominated by a blanket-covered platform in the center. An assortment of jars, filled with strange-looking ointments, salves, and potions, line the walls; candles flicker in iron wall sconces, and dim light filters in from the courtyard window. The acrid stench of burning tar and occasional hints of lavender fill the room, coming from behind a dark curtain at one end of the infirmary. A thin trail of smoke wafts from beneath the fabric.

"Dr. Helmut?" I call out. Otto holds up a jar of green

liquid and shakes it slightly, startling as an eel-like creature within slams against the glass container, open jaws revealing razor-sharp teeth. With a grimace in my direction, he places the jar back on the shelf.

"Hello?" I pull the curtain aside to find Dr. Helmut bent over a smoke-belching pot hanging above a hearth fire. I cover my mouth and nose with the sleeve of my blouse.

"Two drops of Haven tonic," he mutters. "That must be it." Dr. Helmut tips a vial into the pot, allowing two shimmery drops to fall into the bubbling mixture. The stew hisses, the smoke dwindles, and the smell dissipates.

"Dr. Helmut," I whisper.

He spins around, slipping the vial in his pocket. "Fram Ascher. Are you fine? And my prince," he says to Otto, who has appeared behind me. "What might I do for you?"

"I'm fine, yes. We have some questions, Dr. Helmut." We step back into the main room of the infirmary. The doctor washes his hands at a stone basin. I nudge Otto to begin.

"Doctor," Otto says, "I'd like to know about Dr. Vitus. He delivered me, at my birth, is that correct?"

"Good man, Dr. Vitus. Such a pity what happened." Dr. Helmut dries his hands on his robe and sits on a rickety wooden stool, gesturing for us to take up the other two.

Anyone who knew the truth of Otto's birth, and of his twin sister, would not have been allowed to live, no matter their rank or prestige. King Adolar had my mother killed. He had his own wife, the mother of his child, murdered. And if women such as these had been killed, there is little chance a lowly doctor had been allowed to live. But I understand the power of information, no matter how small. "What happened exactly?" I ask.

Dr. Helmut shifts on his stool, eyeing us uncertainly. "Dr. Vitus failed a critical surgical procedure on the king's sister, now deceased, Laren rest her soul, shortly after she returned home after having moved to the Dor Drillingt Islands following Hildegroth's destruction. I took on his position after he was dismissed."

"He wasn't dismissed after Otto's birth?" I ask, confusion clouding my thoughts, my heart beginning to race.

Dr. Helmut's gaze narrows as he ponders my question. A horseshoe of hair circles his otherwise bald scalp. "No, no," he concludes. "He was dismissed after the catastrophe with Lady Genalt, though it was not long after the prince was born."

"My aunt?" Otto leans forward, pinioning the doctor with an intense gaze of his own. "But she—"

I squeeze Otto's arm. The story told at court, one encouraged by the king, was that Lady Genalt had gone mad and killed herself.

Obid revealed that she had been tortured for her powers before my mother had been able to smuggle her to Ainar. Had she come back to Ectair at some point? And why? While Dr. Helmut seems like a kind man, I have been cut to the quick by enough kind men to know that they, too, can wield knives beneath their smiles. The truth of what happened to Otto's aunt must wait.

"The king was devastated by his sister's passing. He couldn't bear to look at the doctor who had, he determined, caused her death. Last I heard, Dr. Vitus was one of the many on the streets of Kietsch, with eyes as green as the veisel that floods his veins."

"He's alive?" I lean forward, riveted by Dr. Helmut's recital. This time, Otto's soft touch cautions me.

"Alive," Dr. Helmut muses. "Is anyone alive when they no longer know themselves from an eel in the sea? I couldn't say. He had a marvelous mind, and now it is as murky a soup as the potions I brew."

I glance at Otto, his expression reflecting the same thoughts that are racing through my mind. Even if we are able to find Dr. Vitus on the streets of Kietsch, what could he tell us? Victims of veisel are rarely capable of coherent thought beyond where they might get their next fix.

A knock sounds at the door.

"One moment, please!" Dr. Helmut retrieves the vial from

his pocket and, opening the doors to a wall cabinet, carefully places the Haven tonic between a jar of pink liquid and another of red. I have seen little pink around the kingdom lately. People are afraid to wear it or have tired of caring for something that will not come.

"What exactly was it you wanted to know about Dr. Vitus, my prince?" he asks.

"I want to speak with him about the day I was born. About my mother."

Dr. Helmut takes Otto's hand in his, his eyes filling with pity and compassion. "I am afraid even if you find Dr. Vitus, you will not find the answers you seek."

"But he's in Kietsch?" I demand.

"If you find him," Dr. Helmut says, "it will not be a pleasant encounter."

Unpleasant encounters are so common we could practically be friends. Dr. Helmut opens the door to a dark-robed päter with his white-masked façade, carrying an object wrapped in burlap. I shudder. Such cowardly men to hide their identities behind such childish masks. Absent of expression, of any appearance of humanity, they resemble vacant spirits, haunting our kingdom with lurid threats from vengeful gods. And vile men.

I glare at the päter, but he does not look my way. The päter waits silently, evidently expecting us to leave.

"Tanks ye, Dr. Helmut," I mutter, seizing Otto's arm as I pull him toward the door.

"I hope you find what you're looking for," he calls, despite my warning glance. "Best of luck to you both." Then, I hear him say to the päter as the door drifts to a close behind us: "I have not yet perfected the tincture you've requested, blessed one. I will need more time."

What kind of tincture do the päters want from Dr. Helmut?

Otto and I walk swiftly down the hallway, through the corridors of the Pentengen, until we get to my room. My heart races and my breath comes short and quick in my throat.

Otto sits on the edge of my bed, and I drop beside him, falling back on the intricately woven duvet that covers my bed. Green and gold threads depict images of bessils soaring over the lofty peaks of the Mountains of the Unknown in southern Ectair, each bird carrying an ulrind flower in its beak. Lena had this made for me to replace the old one that had belonged to Lady Genalt. This room used to be hers. Before she…before whatever happened to her.

"The päters frighten me," Otto says. "I never thought much about them before, but now that I know what they are capable of, I'm more afraid of them than I am of my father."

"They are your father."

A knock at the door reveals Lena, a dress over one arm and a measuring ribbon and roll of parchment over the other.

"Dress fitting, my lady. For the wedding."

Oh, right. My wedding. When I think of wedding dresses and celebrations, I think of Kiel—I cannot help myself. Then my mind turns to him dancing with Lady Gelta; and then, of myself, of being a wife and not just a climber. No longer free. Otto kisses my cheek.

"I will leave you to your preparations and will go speak with my father about the…matters we discussed," he says, closing the door behind him.

Lena lays the dress over the chaise in front of the fire. The satin skirts are the color of the sea during a fierce orkansturm, a blue so inky it could be black.

"Now you must try it on."

Lena helps me into the dress, shimmying the satin skirts up my legs and helping thread my arms through the lace-bodiced top. The skirts shimmer as though the stars have dropped from the sky into the night sea. The lacy bodice is threaded through with patterns of ferns, heidel flowers, ulrind, and vines that wind around the torso in threads of gold, green, and blue. Two panels of light gauzy fabric, as sheer as lecal wings, fall from each shoulder to graze the floor.

"We will finish the look with a black pearl ilice from Kaisel,"

Lena says, as she finishes fastening up the tiny satin buttons at my back. "Extra pearls will decorate your hair, and the metalsmiths are fashioning a matching crown." Lena grins as she takes hold of my shoulders and steers me toward the mirror. "I think you'll like the design."

"Miter's arsch, Lena. How could I not?" I stare at the young woman gazing back at me from the mirror. She doesn't look like a captive, a cowering wife, or a caged bird. She looks like someone who wields all the power of the summit and sea.

"I feel…" I caress the satin fabric and stare at my toes peeking out from beneath the skirt's hem. "I feel…"

"Like a goddess?" Lena moves around me, tilting her head as she examines the fit, pulling on this piece or that, adjusting something at my back. "I designed this as if I were creating it for Orna herself. I asked myself, what would the goddess of the mountains wear to her wedding?" She pulls a pin from the pocket of her dress and adjusts the fabric under one arm. "Because that's who you are. You are Orna reborn."

"I could almost believe it, in this magnificent dress."

Lena spends the next ten minutes making minor adjustments, and I stand patiently, letting the master do her work. I think of the wedding. Of what we will eat, how I will dance, and who will be there. The Ascenditures will come, of course. King Adolar will want me to see Kiel's face as I promise myself to another man. Despite that particular pain for us both, I welcome the company of friends.

I think, with a pang, of Rayna.

My heart fills with longing and my belly with acid. Guilt trickles through me. My lies forced Rayna to choose her violent husband over me, and we have not seen each other since. I hope she has not suffered further because of me. Even though it has been forbidden, I yearn to see her again.

"Lena?" I ask before I can help myself. "Do you know Martus Meats, down on Fleeker Street?"

"Of course, my lady."

"Can you deliver a message to Rayna, the woman who works

there? I would like to extend an invitation to the wedding from Prince Otto and myself. And to her husband as well, of course. I…I need her there."

"I will go as soon as we finish here."

"One more thing." I move to the bedside table and rummage through the drawer crammed with an assortment of objects: a writing quill, hairpins, a copy of the *Laren Fealties*, the metal-knotted Ascenditure pin. *I will not fall. I will not fail. I will not betray my kingdom.* And under a sheaf of parchment, scrawled with a poem I liked, I find what I am searching for. It is the coin my father brought me from Kobo, engraved with the head of a hozierleon. I gave this coin to Rayna before I climbed Mount Bonen, only to have it flung in my face by King Adolar when he hit me in the throne room.

"Here." I hand the coin to Lena and close her fingers over it. "I need Rayna to know I'm sorry." My voice breaks.

"You may tell her that yourself," Lena says, tucking the coin into her pocket. "I will make sure she is there."

After Lena has completed the fitting, I pry up the loose board next to the dormer window molding; inside the shallow cavity behind the board, I store my most precious and secret items—the Death's Whisper crystal Gio gave to me before his death and the solan from Fitzhan. The bumpy red tuber has now grown a forest of tangled roots and will eventually spoil. I am afraid to dispose of it, however, as the tuber is the only known antidote to the Death's Whisper poison.

Also in my secret stash is my mother's handkerchief and the small painting of my mother with Queen Eleonora—the one I took with Dr. Vitus's journal when I broke into the queen's tower. My mother looks to be about my age in the painting, and it is a strange feeling, knowing I will outlive her. That someday I will pass the age she was when she drew her last breath. I was only eight when they took her from me. Tears fill my eyes and spill down my cheeks.

My mother remains a mystery to me, even more so now that

the lies about her have been revealed. And the truth, whatever that is, is equally elusive. While the memory of her has faded over the years, I have always kept the feeling of her love. Now even that has started to dissipate.

I rub the thin fabric of her handkerchief between my fingers, examining the intricate stitching of my father's ship with its bright orange sails, at the lettering sewn along the hem in old Galvaithian, which I now know how to read: *Death is no accident. Someone always has a hand. Be it the gods' own might or the traitorous will of men.* And then, *Find Ramanata.*

"I intend to, Mother," I say, brushing the tears from my face with the back of one hand. "I will find her, and she will set us all free."

A knock comes at the door. "Klarke, it's Otto."

"Hold on." I stash my precious belongings back into their compartment and cover it with the loose board. "Come in."

"No luck," Otto mutters as he enters, frowning. "My father said even Laren himself couldn't make him send the Ascenditures north."

My heart sinks, even though the answer is precisely what I expected. "You'll have to try again. He has to agree."

"It is my father we're talking about, right? A man who is pretty much only disagreeable?"

I chew my lip and try to think of a solution. King Adolar can't keep the prisoners locked up forever; the people of Ainar will eventually come looking. But that could take months. "I have to go," I whisper.

"I'm not sure you're hearing me correctly," Otto insists. "My father will not allow it, and if I were to ask again, he would become suspicious. What if he concludes that we are conspiring?"

I glance at the portrait hanging over the fireplace of Lady Genalt, a dainty woman with soft features and dark hair. Delicate. She looks familiar, as if we've met. It must be that I see the familial connection with Otto and King Adolar.

"It's not just about finding your sister." I think of Naisae, the leader of the Parvanatari, Ainar's climbing team, who is currently in chains in the Rektburg's dungeon. I need to know what it's like to be her. To be free. To be in my own power. "I need this for me, Otto. I need to know there is air to breathe somewhere in the world. That what we're fighting for here isn't for nothing. Do you understand?"

"I do understand," Otto says gently, squeezing my hand. "But instead of you rushing out to take on the world all by yourself, no doubt risking life and limb with all the kingdom's soldiery after you, perhaps there is another way we can persuade my father to send the Ascenditures north. My father is fond of Aedan. Could be he'd listen to him; it's worth a try. Perhaps he could appeal to Father's vanity, persuade him that this is an opportunity to prove Ectair's climbing superiority. But *you* must be nowhere near these matters if we are to see any success."

"You're right," I acknowledge reluctantly. "The king must believe this is only about climbing and the prestige of Ectair. I will speak with Aedan."

"Maybe he will agree if his most loyal supporters on the Ascenditures also make their voices heard," Otto muses.

"What about Veit?" I ask. "His family, the Obeldorfs carry great pull in the kingdom. They are personal friends of your father." A smile slowly curves my lips as I think through this new scheme. With a little push and pull and a subtle bit of maneuvering, I can get what I want. I must put aside any qualms I have about using underhanded wiles to manipulate the Ascenditures, my climbing family, my friends. I must use Veit to my own advantage. I must become more like King Adolar than I ever thought possible. A voice inside warns me against this logic, but I ignore it.

"Otto, I think that will work!" I say, my smile widening to a delighted grin.

3

Marike stops in the doorway, wide-eyed, mouth dropped, taking in the colorful routes that stretch across the climbing walls, that ascend through dark nooks and crannies, up and out of sight into one of the four smokestacks featured in this old wax factory that is now a climbing gym. The main room smells of sisal rope, dust, and leather, and is bustling with men—including the Ascenditures, as well as stand-by climbers, part of kletshot four led by a man named Bastian, who train in the event that they are required to assist with repairs and construction should the Ascenditures be occupied—as well as wealthy elites who have recently taken up climbing as a leisurely pastime. Several climbers are sweating on the ropes, their muscles bunched and gleaming, while others shout, berate, and urge them on from below, their voices echoing through the cavernous space.

Marike looks small in her oversized dress and lumpy boots as she enters the gym. She is eleven but looks no older than seven or eight. Many of us who are undernourished in the early years look that way. She glances furtively about the room, shifting uncertainly from one foot to the other. Is that how I appeared to Ellias when I walked through those doors after my parents died? Lost and afraid, but somehow also at home. Somehow, exactly where I needed to be.

The men notice her arrival and turn to jeer and laugh.

"Laren's arsch, now there's two of 'em," one snorts.

"How many fozies does it take to bring down a kingdom?" another calls to general laughter.

"Go home, foze kid!" someone behind me shouts. I glance at Marike—she flinches slightly; she has heard the insult, but she squares her shoulders and plants her feet firmly on the ground, ignoring the man's jeers. I silently applaud her courage as Veit, on a central route, begins his climb. He has not offered any crude gestures or derogatory comments. He doesn't look at us. Perhaps his memory of Gerd is sufficient to refrain from tormenting his sister.

"What was King Adolar thinking? He must be getting weak," a new voice mutters.

That last comment startles me—criticizing the king is enough to get any man or woman hanged. Glancing over my shoulder, I see two spectators—elegantly attired in elite climbing gear—whispering together, but not so quietly that I cannot hear every word. Being only occasional visitors to the gym, they do not understand the acoustics here the way I do.

"Seems there might actually be room for the Dark Promise," one mutters.

"So you've heard too?" the other says under his breath. "The leader is calling himself the Schaeter. I don't know what to make of it all."

"Not just heard. I've met with them. Not the Schaeter but with his faction here in Kietsch."

"And?"

"Not here."

The men move toward a route at the far end of the gym, and I am left pondering their cryptic conversation. What the hüle is the Dark Promise, and who, in Miter's deepest hole, is the Schaeter? And if the Schaeter commands the loyalty of men such as these, men so willing to throw women to the volves and babes into the sea, how afraid should I be?

Marike makes her way toward me, and I smile encouragingly, but I feel a lingering unease from the conversation I just overheard. "Ignore them all," I tell her as we make our way toward one of the easier routes. Despite my new worries about the Schaeter, Marike deserves my attention. "I wish I could say that the taunts will go away, but they won't. It will get worse. It doesn't matter how hard you push yourself, how many routes you climb or how many cuts or sprains you muscle through.

These men will be the most painful and perpetual obstacle you will face."

Marike glances over her shoulder. Some men have gone back to climbing. A few have gathered and moved closer. One makes a crude gesture, which I ignore with some difficulty.

"I'm not here for them. I'm here for Gerd and for me." She shrugs and gestures toward the sisal rope we will use to fashion our harnesses. "Can you show me how to do this? I forgot."

Smiling, I pick up the sisal rope and show her the basic knots to form the harness, and how to tie a sling onto an anchor along the route. I hope she will always be able to train her focus on her love of climbing and the memory of her brother. Was I ever like that? Or have I been jaded from birth? Regardless, I had Ellias to train me, to protect me. I will be the same for Marike.

The pang of Ellias's loss washes over me again. The best way to hold him close is to honor him and his legacy. To memorialize him in what he loved most—climbing and sharing that love with others.

Marike and I move on from knots and harnesses to ascend the first route. I teach her how to belay me when I'm lead climbing, and then I have her top rope each route, ascending with the rope already securely in place high up. She moves up the wall with fierce passion and determination, her jaw clenched, her gaze fixed on the next handhold above, sometimes slipping, but never asking to come down, never giving up.

"This skirt is dumt," Marike seethes, slipping as the bottom hem of her climbing skirt becomes entangled in the toe of her boot. "Why won't they let us wear pants like the others?"

Marike's climbing skirt, while secondhand, is stiff and relatively new. The hem of my skirt is threadbare in patches where my boots have dug fabric into footholds, worn thin by the constant abrasion of stone against fabric. As a result, I slip more than the men, the skirts entangling my boots and enveloping my legs in a manner the other climbers do not have to contend with. "We will wear pants someday," I tell her. "I promise you that, but right now, we must accept what we can get. You'll be a better climber because of your skirt, though it is unfair."

She glares at a leering adel and returns to the wall. "Klettag," she says, letting me know she is ready to climb, skirt and all.

"Klettag und," I reply, giving the response that indicates she is safe to ascend.

Marike's confidence grows with each route she masters, and I grin, delighted, each time her feet touch the ground. I've had to fight every day to belong, to create space for myself in a world that doesn't want me; this battle has left me exhausted, without the capacity or inclination to give my energy to someone else. But as we climb, as I point out different techniques or congratulate Marike on her accomplishments, as I watch her learn and thrive, an energy surges through me. What a relief it is to let go of myself for a bit and to share this world with another. To pass to her the gift of climbing that had once been given to me.

After Marike's sixth climb, we rest, leaning back against the wall as we drink water. My thoughts turn to Kiel, repairing the Roudan dam, and I worry for a moment about the sighting of Hildegroth. Could Kiel really be in danger from that tentacled beast? With an effort, I shake my fears away. I have enough monsters to contend with in Ectair.

Across the gym, Haydrich moves gracefully through a difficult overhanging route. He climbs with such elegance, such ease, as if holding himself against the rock wall is as natural to him as breathing. Will I ever be able to climb like that? Perhaps, if I spend more time training and less time scheming to outmaneuver King Adolar.

"I really miss him," Marike says beside me. Tears well in her eyes, and she dashes them away with the back of a dusty hand. My heart aches with hers, and I reach an arm around her shoulder and pull her in for a hug, hoping to block her tears from the scrutiny of observers. I wish I could protect Marike by letting the world see her truth. The only way I know to protect myself or someone else is to become a shield.

"Will you tell me about him?" I ask, taking her hands in my own. "I knew Gerd on the mountain. He was kind and strong, but I know nothing about his life off the slope."

"He was always happy," Marike says, her voice catching. "Even when we were hungry or when Mama was angry. Or when the roof leaked."

"Yeah?" I smile as I remember Gerd's tender efforts to comfort the wounded men we'd had to leave in tents, and his words of encouragement as I lay, despairing, on the Snag, ready to give up. "Was he funny?"

"No," Marike replies with a laugh. "But he thought he was. And that was funny."

Unbidden, the image of Gerd at the bottom of the crevasse comes to mind, his leg broken, his cries for help echoing on the icy wind. Images of blood, shockingly red against the white snow, and of a man in black garb dragging bodies into the path of the avalanche, follow. I shudder, my hands trembling like dying leaves in an orkansturm.

"Are you okay?" Marike asks.

"Yes, sorry." I curl my fingers into fists to still the trembling and force a smile to my lips. "Tell me more."

"Gerd never got cross with me or my sister. We could do anything, and he let us. Pull his hair. Put worms in his shoes…" She trails off, her gaze falling to her boots. At only eleven, she has already learned to be a shield, and my heart aches for her.

"Now Mama is always mad or crying. And my sister and I are too." She chews at the corner of her thumb. "And now Mama has the cough. It just started, but it won't stop. Day and night she hacks and retches."

"Oh, Marike." I wish I knew of something to comfort her. The inhabitants of Ectair seldom live long lives. Pulmonosis, a disease of the lungs that plagues our factory workers, kills so many of us. Once the cough begins, the victim has only a few years of life left. The ulrind flower the Ascenditures gather from the Celebern Fields on the summit of Fitzhan is the only known cure, but the flowers are scarce and expensive to procure, and each flower yields only minuscule amounts of the precious medicinal powder. Apothekers, as a result, charge so much for the medicine that those afflicted often choose death over a debt that can take their families generations to repay.

"I know how pulmonosis works," Marike says through gritted teeth. "I know she's going to die."

I shake my head and fix her with a fierce stare. "I won't let that happen, Marike. I am an Ascenditure, and I live in the palace. I will get your mother the medicine she needs."

"Tanks ye." Marike whispers, squeezing my hand.

I accept her gratitude, but we both know that the medicine is not always effective. And in Ectair, once you've opened the door to rage and grief, they do not readily depart. Like unwelcome guests, they perch themselves in your home and make themselves felt any time you discover a thread of joy. Misery and squalor are the unavoidable destiny for most Ectarians.

"Marike, you have every right to be angry. What happened to Gerd on the mountain, the pulmonosis your mother is struggling with, the taunts and jeers of these narrow-minded dumtkofs"—I gesture toward the men crowding the gym around us. "None of this is fair. But your anger is now a part of you. You have to decide what you will do with it. I was so angry when I lost my mother and father. So furious when I was evicted from my home to survive in the streets. And when I didn't get a spot on the Ascenditures, even after I had more than earned it, my rage grew. My fury was fed when King Adolar sent us up Mount Bonen and when your brother died. And now, now I am furious beyond measure that in a few moonrises I must marry a man I did not choose. I live so closely with my anger, Marike, that it could be the moss that covers the face of my rock or the familiar feel of the sisal rope across my shoulder. It lives with me, and I with it. I know it better than I know most people. But if you are to survive it, you must not let it consume you. Anger unchecked becomes a deep and poisonous bitterness, and that will destroy you. It will roil within you like the fiercest orkansturm. And if you don't govern it, it will drown you."

"Ash and wave for us all," Marike whispers through indignant tears.

"Don't let it win, Marike. I keep my rage in check by climbing," I tell her. "You must leave it at the base of the pitch. There is no room for anger on the fel. Only focus. Anger can't reach you when you hang over the moraine. It is afraid of heights. It is afraid of courage. And if you escape it long enough each day, you will not drown. Do you understand?"

Marike nods, and I give her a reassuring smile.

"We got a job," a voice interrupts us. I look up to see Burkhart frowning down at us. "Bridge repair, Klarke. You're on it."

Burkhart's dark hair is pulled into a tight bun, accentuating his receding hairline and the sharp edges of his cheekbones. He is only in his mid-twenties, but already grooves of care and worry line his face where scars do not. I wish I could ask him about the scars—which cover his face and arms and, perhaps, more of his body that cannot be seen. He grew up near Merket, enlisting in the lumberjack trade, felling the giant trees of the Hummeldorf Woods. That is almost all I know of him—and that he does not believe women should climb.

"When do we leave?" I ask, rising to my feet.

"In an hour. Should be a quick job with four of us." He glances again at Marike, then returns a steely gaze to me. "Don't be late." He moves across the gym to Haydrich.

"You were great today," I tell Marike. "You're going to be a fantish climber. Next time, we'll skip the basics and get to work on the harder stuff."

We stand and gather our gear, and I walk her out to the front of the gym. Beyond the arched doorway, it is raining, and a thin mist winds through the streets. I can just make out the seven ghostly peaks of Miter's Backbone looming above the city.

"One more thing," I say. "Maybe the most important thing I will share with you. My mentor Ellias used to say this to me, and I repeat it to myself every time I feel pulled under by the storm."

"What?"

"He would say to me, 'Head up, darling. Always head up. For that is the direction in which the mountain grows.'"

"I like that," Marike says softly.

"Repeat it anytime you feel angry or sad or scared." I slip a small sack of golden dracals into her bag. "See you in a few days."

"Oleg, Klarke." Marike smiles, waves, and then turns into the rain-soaked street toward home.

In the gym, I collect my rucksack from my cupboard, filling it with a harness, several slings, a doubleacht—which I will use to rappel from the top of the bridge down to the repair site—a rope, a pair of leather gloves, and the bag of tools Aedan gave me.

This is the first time I have been called out on a repair project, and I am determined to learn as much as I can. Haydrich, Veit, and Burkhart, my repair team today, will insist that because I've never fixed bridge masonry, I should not be a climber. I fight a surge of anger. After surviving the avalanche on Mount Bonen, after excelling at climbing route after route, when do I ever get to stop proving myself to these dumt men? Recalling my advice to Marike, I resolve to work through my anger, whatever nervousness I feel. I will spend the day with Veit. I have not given up on my plan of having him use his family connections to persuade the king to let us go to Ainar.

We meet out front and load our belongings and ourselves into a carriage that takes us south of the city to a bridge that spans a yawning, dry gulch, the boundary that separates the southernmost edge of Kietsch and the Dangof Forest. After the carriage rattles to a halt, we unload our gear—three sacks of mortar powder, three sacks of gravel, two barrels of water, a shovel, and an empty barrel in which the components will be mixed. As if to assist in the mortar-mixing, a light drizzle of rain begins to fall, darkening our clothes and running in rivulets down our faces.

"There are several compromised areas we need to address," Burkhart tells us. "One on the abutment on the far side and two places where the bridge deck meets the second pier cap. We'll stabilize the pier cap first, then the abutment. With this rain, the surfaces will be slick. Work carefully. One of us needs to stay up top to mix mortar and send it down."

They all glance my way. I scowl, fixing my unwavering gaze on Burkhart. Veit chuckles as he begins to prepare his harness.

"No." I give Burkhart the look I'd give a dog about to steal mutton from the table.

Burkhart holds my gaze, his expression unreadable. I want to shake him, to remind him that it had been me who accompanied him up Fitzhan in the freezing rain to find Gio. Me who had the strength remaining to do what others could not. Me who fought off a murderer while the rest of them drank ale and danced. "It will *not* be me," I say, arms crossed over my chest.

"You." Burkhart points to Veit, and I almost fall to my knees.

"What?" Veit and I say together. Veit looks inclined to throw me off the bridge. Burkhart with me.

"That's not my job," Veit protests, glancing between Burkhart and me. "That's not my job, Burk."

"Mix the mortar, Neuba," Burkhart says, a sharp edge to his voice.

Neuba is our name for novice climbers. Veit's mouth thins. A smile twitches at the corner of my lip, but I keep it in check. I am not quite sure what just happened, but it feels monumental. Burkhart hands Veit the shovel, then ties a harness of sisal rope that he loops around his chest.

"Klarke's probably not strong enough to mix the mortar and lower it," Burkhart adds, without meeting my gaze. He straps a bag of tools around his waist, and the rest of us, minus Veit, follow suit.

I don't let the edge of his words close enough to cut me. Not so long ago, he would have given me that job even if he thought I wasn't strong enough, just to watch me fail. To revel in my inadequacy. That I could never do what a man could. I will take snide words any day, so long as the associated actions send a different message.

"This is absolute scheiz," Veit mutters under his breath as he pours a bag of mortar powder into the barrel. He adds gravel and water, then stirs the mixture with the shovel. "Such scheiz. Such foze scheiz."

I roll my eyes but don't engage. Let Veit call me what he wants. Even a foze—the most contemptible word a man can use to describe a woman. I need him now for a purpose far more significant than my bruised ego.

Haydrich has already tied his harness, strapped on his gear, and is now hammering in three anchors to the side of the bridge from where he, Burkhart, and I will rappel. I watch closely, not trusting that Haydrich won't deliberately place mine to fail. I have no reason to mistrust him, but that, in itself, is a source of concern. He does not make his feelings known, and I don't know what to make of him and his uncanny ability to defy gravity with such ease. He makes no effort to befriend any of the Ascenditures, so it seems we must all be in the dark when it comes to the mystery that is Haydrich. Beneath his dusty scrabble of beard, his jawline is sharp, as are his dark eyes. He is what a knife would look like if a blade could be human.

"You sure you know what you're doing?" Veit has left his mixing and is inspecting Haydrich's work. "Do they even have bridges down in Dresdal? I hear it's a wasteland with a few squatters who find just enough food to scheiz on their scheiz piece of land."

Even Burkhart stops working and looks up. Is this really happening? Is Veit taking his anger out not on me but on Haydrich? Perhaps I am reading too much into everything, but in the last few minutes, two men who loathed me have, in their own crummy ways, shown me some minute amount of respect.

"Aye, we have bridges." Haydrich turns inky eyes on Veit. "We have bridges and villages and men who don't rely on Daddy to do everything. Our people have the strength to withstand the things that come up from the south, things that would make you wet yourself. So, to answer your question, aye, I know what I'm doing." Haydrich turns his back to Veit as he hammers the next anchor into the wall. "Mind if I get back to it, then?"

"You think I can't withstand the elements?" Veit demands hotly. "You think I don't know fear? I survived on Mount Bonen last year when no one else did."

"She did," Haydrich replies, his attention fixed on his work as his hammer smashes the anchor with a metallic clang. That might be the first time he's acknowledged my existence.

"I survived an avalanche. I survived…" Veit continues, flustered. He glances at me, and I look away. I won't help him use the deaths of good men to salve his ego. Besides, he never believed me before when I told him of our friends' murder.

"I don't care about bloody Bonen," Haydrich snaps, turning from his task to thrust his hammer under Veit's chin. "I've climbed Eldras, mate. A mountain you've probably only heard about in your omie's stories. A mountain ten times deadlier than Bonen. I've climbed every peak in the Mountains of the Unknown in the south and have survived encounters with creatures you could not even begin to imagine. Have you ever been chased across a glacier by a risant and his unger? Didn't think so. So why don't you mind your scheiz and get back to work."

There is a moment of shocked silence—this must be the most that Haydrich has ever spoken and as much as he has ever revealed of his past. It's almost a comical relief to sit back and watch someone else deal with the antagonism normally reserved for me.

"Enough." Burkhart finally speaks. "Those anchors look fine, Haydrich. Let's get to work."

I attach myself to the anchor using my harness, the doubleacht, and the extra rope I brought, and the others do the same. Veit leans against the mortar barrel, his lip curled, his eyes narrowed.

"I'll just be here waiting for the mortar call," he says.

"Good lad," Haydrich responds. Veit's crimson cheeks and throbbing neck veins are the last I see before lowering myself over the edge of the bridge. The three of us drop in tandem, like a trio of spiders on a fine silver thread. We descend about fifteen feet before Burkhart uses his body weight to swing himself over to the bridge pier. Once there, he pulls a hammer and an anchor from his tool belt, beats it into the bridge, and then attaches his harness with a long sling to the bolt so that he can move freely.

Haydrich does the same, positioning himself on the opposite side of the pier to Burkhart. I similarly rock my body in the air until I have enough momentum to swing to the far side of the bridge pier. Once I'm anchored on the wall, I notify Burkhart that I am ready.

"Fertaag," I call out. This is a part of being an Ascenditure I haven't yet gotten to enjoy. I smile, feeling even more real now.

"We're going to tuckpoint this." I hear Burkhart call from the other side of the pier. "Clean out the damaged mortar, and when that's done, we'll backfill with fresh material from Veit."

Ellias taught me how to undertake repairs when I was ten. All Ascenditures and trainees learn the practical elements of construction and repair, in wood and stone, using mortar and nails. But this is the first time I have mortared a bridge pier. Burkhart will oversee my work, and I am determined it will be perfect. I don't want him to regret choosing me over Veit.

I remove the saw from my belt and dig out the crumbling sections of rock. Rotating between the hammer, saw, and brush, I clear out cracked and crumbling mortar, splintered rocks and pebbles, ash, and dust. Sheltered from the rain by the overhead arch of the bridge, I brush out the last of the debris and prepare the crevices for the mortar. Poor Veit stands above us, soaked and angry. Thinking he deserves to be here because Gio didn't kill him on the mountain.

My thoughts drift to Mount Bonen and the men who died on its icy wastes. Gerd should be alive, training Marike and taking care of his ailing mother. Tristan could have become a friend, and I still grieve his loss. They still haven't found his body. But that is not unusual. Mountains can be jealous of their victims; cracks and crevasses and hungry ice could easily have swallowed him whole. King Adolar claims Tristan was in league with Gio and has fled to avoid being hanged for his crimes. It is bad enough that Tristan died, that he was another victim of Adolar's scheming, but to further darken his reputation—of what use is that?

Mount Bonen—and the evil machinations of King Adolar—has taken good men from us, even those who were at first hesitant about me. I would take them all as teammates, every moonrise, over a team of Veits and Haydriches. Of Gios.

I wonder, still, about the identity of the *other* Gio alluded to before he died. Was it merely an attempt to torment me? Or is there another I should be worried about? Petrus warned me, just before he died, that the eyes of the other would give him away. I need to find the päter with two different eye colors who sent me up the mountain with ash and bone. He fits somewhere in this puzzle.

Gerd and Tristan are never coming back. All I can do for them now is continue to unravel the spool of thread until I reach the end. I made a vow at their funeral to find every last person who had a hand in their deaths no matter the cost. I will have the truth.

"Mortar!" Burkhart shouts, interrupting my reverie.

Burkhart lays the first layer of mortar, and the next batch descends on a rope to me. I remove the joint trowel from my waist belt and apply the mortar, smoothing it flat across the space. Occasionally, Burkhart swings around, glances at my work, grunts, and then swings back. We rotate the mortar bucket between us, building layers and allowing them to dry as we go until all the holes are filled. It is slow work, but it gives me time to think and breathe.

"Goin' on then?"

I turn and see Haydrich leaning around the corner of the abutment. "The mortar? Yeah, it's going on."

"Nide," he says with a laugh. "That's what we say down in Dresdal for *how are you?* or *all good.*"

Why is he now speaking to me? I cannot help but wonder as I search for a response. "Oh. Yeah, it's goin' on then. And you?"

"Goin' on."

"Good." I fiddle with the trowel, pretending to have something to do, even though we are both waiting on Burkhart to finish so we can apply our final layers of mortar.

"Sorry about earlier." Haydrich offers what seems to be a genuine smile. "I have to play a game too. And part of that game is fitting in here. And part of fitting in here means not being friendly with you."

I narrow my eyes and make a disgusted noise. "Half of this team, more even, are my friends. Being cold to me won't endear you to them."

"I'm not worried about them." Haydrich pushes off from the pier and swings around until he lands so close to me that his face is inches from my own, and I can feel his breath on my cheek. "I need the king to like me," he whispers.

I lean back, even though there is no place for me to go. "Cocky jerk with the right dangly bits," I say, looking him up and down. "Pretty sure you're a boot in."

How has Burkhart not finished, and why has Veit not sent my last bucket of mortar?

"We want the same things, you know," Haydrich continues, pulling back slightly to hold my gaze with his own.

"I highly doubt that," I reply.

"We both want a new leader."

My eyes widen, and my breath stalls in my throat. Does Haydrich have a death wish? "You mistake me," I say evenly. "Our king is a wise and just man." I seize the collar of his shirt and yank him to me so that my mouth brushes his ear. "Why are you telling me this? How dare you put me in danger."

He wraps his fingers around mine, his voice dropping to a whisper. "Our king is weak and knows nothing of the world. A power grows in the shadow of the Rektburg. Beneath his arrogant nose. A power originating from the Mountains of the

Unknown, my home. I would see this power on the throne over the spineless worm that is Adolar."

"Are you speaking of the Dark Promise?" I ask, thinking of the conversation I overhead at the climbing gym.

Fear flashes across his face, before he quickly controls it. "How do you know of the Dark Promise?"

"Why are you telling me this?" I ask again, my hands clammy, sweat beading across my brow. I could be hanged just for listening to this seditious talk.

"Because I know you are working your own plan, and I need you to not interfere with mine."

"I just want the women of Ectair to be free," I tell him.

"I will assure your freedom when Adolar is toppled. You have my word."

"And what is your word to me? What is any man's word to a woman in this place? I know what your leader thinks of women."

"Klarke! Bucket!"

I let go of his shirt and he lifts a finger to his lips before swinging back to his side of the pier. I don't actually know anything. My stomach twists. Not even how dangerous lying to Haydrich might be.

I patch the last layer of mortar, mulling over what I have learned. Haydrich came from the south and joined the Ascenditures not for the love of climbing or to repair bridges or collect the ulrind flower, but to get closer to the king. To overthrow him. Is Haydrich an enemy or an ally? While I, too, want King Adolar gone, I have no wish to see one tyrant replaced by another. Otto is the king we need and deserve. Why would Haydrich trust me with this confidence? He has just given me the power to ruin him.

No one would believe me, a woman. That's what he's counting on.

We finish the pier repairs and prepare to move on to the abutment. Only two rappellers are required, so I volunteer to assist Veit before Burkhart can assign me to the task. I watch

Burkhart and Haydrich rappel over the edge, hands on my knees as I take in a few deep breaths.

"New guy's a total arsch, right?" Veit grumbles as he pours a sack of gravel into the mortar mixture. "He needs a good whoppin' to learn his place."

My vision swirls. I try to stand, but the world spins, so I sit and lean against the stone rails. I don't want the dangerous gift Haydrich handed me.

"This is why they should have sent me. You can't handle this job."

I don't care what Veit says. I close my eyes and take a few deep breaths. Rain patters lightly on my forehead. The coolness helps to soothe my mind. I open my eyes and watch Veit pace angrily. Forget Haydrich and his plan. I have my own, and the only thing I need to worry about now is getting to Ainar.

"Yeah, he's a total arsch," I agree. "All this talk of summiting Eldras, as if that's impressive. Everyone knows that the only measure of a climber's worth is if they make it up Mount Opasno."

"Exactly!" Veit spits, stirring the shovel in the thickening mortar with a violent jerk. "No way Haydrich could beat me up Opasno."

"Not a chance," I agree. "You were so quick summiting Bonen. Haydrich may have some fancy moves, but I doubt he could maintain that pace."

I wish I could say I feel guilty for manipulating Veit, but he makes it too easy.

"Some arsch kid from the south? Impossible," he mutters, scooping mortar into a bucket.

"It's a shame King Adolar won't grant us permission to go to Ainar with those climbers. It would be gratifying, once and for all, to see who on this team belongs on the mountain and who does not."

A candle flickers behind his eyes. I see the conversation in his mind unfolding through the minute twitches and movements on his face.

"I'd love a chance to prove myself. Scheiz. I'd love to show those heathens from Ainar that Ectair is the home of the best climbers. They probably speak of us as we speak of Haydrich. Southerners. They probably think there's no way this team of southerners could keep up."

Veit pauses to wipe his brow, his gaze thoughtful on the forest beyond the bridge. I wait silently, leaving the line cast, the bait wavering tantalizingly in the current, waiting for the fish to bite; he will either want what I've set or will swim on—I have done what I could.

"I should speak with my father," Veit muses aloud. "He holds the king's ear. Those northerners will mock us if we refuse to show. It is a humiliation we must not abide."

"We've worked too hard to hide our talents beneath bridges," I say, hardly daring to believe how easy this was.

"Too hard," he repeats.

"Mortar!" Burkhart shouts from below.

Veit offers me the bucket to hold while he attaches the sisal rope. "Looks like you aren't my enemy, Fram Ascher."

"For now." I wink and grab the handle of the bucket.

We lower it over the edge and watch it descend toward the two figures anchored to the abutment below. Haydrich stares up as Veit chuckles at my side.

I stand with nervous excitement at the prospect of going to Ainar and with cautious fear of being let in on a plot to overthrow the king. I embarked upon this day hoping to move the tides of my life, but I ended up with my feet on two opposing ships, each steered by a different demon. The currents are flowing. Wind rushes into the sails. The doldrums are finally over, but I must decide—and soon—with which fiend to entrust my fate.

4

After practice, I make my way toward Pohle Pier, hoping to discover some sign of Obid, or perhaps even Dr. Vitus, if he is still alive. I pass beneath the great stone archway that marks the entrance to the pier. The columns soar above me, the words *Ash and Wave* carved into the front face remind all that our time here is precious, and, eventually, we will all return to Laren and the darkened sea, to be pushed into the waves on a floating bier that is then lit by a flaming arrow.

I search every side alley and peer into every storm drain, looking for a man of Dr. Helmut's age, sixty or so, stricken by veisel. Veisel addicts are often reduced to skin and bone, with mouths dark and rotted, empty of teeth, and pale, patchy hair. A person of eighteen could look eighty with enough use.

I set my course on finding Obid. That feels like a more manageable task. With what I know of the cook, he has his finger in every pie, an ear in every corner. If anyone might know where to find Dr. Vitus, it would be Obid; besides, I have a score to even with him. He knows more of my parents and my life before their deaths than he has so far let on, I am certain of it. And he has shared only a thin layer of oil floating atop the deepest of waters. What else does he hide in the bowels of his galley? What else is he not telling me?

I move down the hill toward the docks, the dark and frothy waters of the Bay of Hammonhoff coming into view. Submerged beneath the confluence of the Sevier River and the bay lies Pieter's Uplift, an underwater ridge of peaks that mirror Miter's Backbone. Many a ship has smashed against these underwater summits, their hulls splintered by razor-sharp rocks. The ridge may be dangerous, but it is also our greatest protection. During Hildegroth's rage, these submerged mountains kept the beast from Kietsch and all cities that dwelled along the Sevier

River. Legend says that Orna created Pieter's Uplift after Laren gifted Hildegroth to King Miter, to protect her people from Laren's call for death and destruction. The distance from the sea floor to the top of Kimbu, the tallest peak of Pieter's Uplift, is higher even than Mount Opasno, or so Ellias used to tell me.

"Fresh thund fish!" a merchant hollers, brandishing a woven basket of gold-scaled fish.

"Seagrass from the Gate." A man in a tattered coat shoves a handful of seagrass, wrapped in dirty linen, into my face. "Healing properties, fram. Cures pulmonosis. Only two dracals per pound!"

Two dracals for a lie, I think, pushing his arm aside. Ulrind is the only cure for pulmonosis. This man would rob his fellow poor, selling them false antidotes to fill his pockets. I take in his greasy face, the broken veins that thread across his wrinkled cheeks, his one clouded eye. I hand him two dracals, take the bundle of seagrass, and move away.

Another vendor hawks stones he claims come from Pieter's Uplift and carry within them the power to control Hildegroth. *Only a woman can do that*, I think, but I leave him to his efforts, which perhaps, after all, keep his children in bread, and weave my way through the canvas-covered stalls to the berthed ships that lie beyond.

Vendors call out their wares: fresh fish, seaweed, hairk-teeth necklaces, and other trinkets. I pass the massive wheeled krane where I last saw Obid loading his ship. The krane is occupied today with lifting pallets of lumber onto a waiting vessel, with eight sweaty men grunting at the effort of turning the wheel to maneuver the winch high above.

I pass the statue of Layal—King Miter's daughter, whom he pushed into the sea as a gift for Laren in exchange for harnessing the services of Hildegroth, Laren's great tentacled sea beast. The sculptor has provided her with a peaceful, happy expression, as if she had never been betrayed by her own flesh and blood and forced into marriage with a violent god. Her arm reaches toward the sky as birds light upon her fingers, and her gown spills into a stone sea where tûndles and fallow fish swim among the swirls of granite fabric.

Help, I imagine her calling.

The air smells of rotting fish, drying seaweed, and men who only bathe in the rain and the sea. The evening Cleos, our star, sets to the south, his light visible as a dull glow through the mists over the Dangof Forest. I pause at a ship offloading cargo. A man almost twice my height, his skin dark with tattoos, one brow gleaming with a brass ring, hauls a bulging sack over one shoulder. "Geitsê," I greet him, attempting to look apologetic, "and sorry to bother you."

"Out a muh way," he snarls. "Ain't the time for a romp."

"I am not working. I am looking for someone, a man by the name of Obid who frequents these docks."

"Ain't seen Obid in nigh a full mooncycle," he mutters, spitting out a long thread of yellowed saliva before striding toward a waiting wagon. I ignore the spittle, and trot to keep up with his long stride.

"You have heard nothing about him? Like when he'll be back?"

He drops the sack onto the back of the wagon with a thump and stretches his neck with a loud click from side to side. "Why would I know a man's business? We come, we go. Sometimes we die. And right now, I've got work to do." He pushes past me, back toward the ship.

I throw my hands up and search for someone else to question. I used to know these sailors; my father had once been a sea captain, after all. But that had been many moons ago. The men I once knew have either weathered beyond my recognition or have passed beyond the darkened sea. These sailors, these new men, have no loyalty to the name Ascher. And none to a dead captain's orphaned daughter.

"You are the future queen," a voice in my head reminds me. I harden my resolve and walk with renewed purpose down the dock to where a group of sailors haul barrels of dried flowers and berries from Kobo, destined for the dye factories on the south side of town. I grab the shirtsleeve of the nearest sailor and gift him with a regal stare.

"Do you know the whereabouts of a man named Obid? He left a mooncycle ago on a ship bound for Ainar, and I urgently need to speak with him."

"Innt he dead?" The sailor passes his tongue over the black stumps of his front teeth and stares thoughtfully at the sky. "Ors that Obda?" He nods and meets my stare. "Musta been Obda. He fell on his own harpoon. Ash and wave for us all."

"Yes." I take a deep breath and fight the urge to roll my eyes. "Such a tragedy for Obda and his family. But what of Obid? The cook?"

"Obda ain't got no family. Wife was barren an' then died of pulmonosis."

"All very well and good," I say. "Praise Laren. And Obid?"

"Aye, praise Laren." The sailor puts three fingers over his heart and bows his head in silent respect.

"And Obid?"

"Obid?" another sailor interrupts. "Are you askin' 'bout Obid the cook? Terrible cook, he is. Served nothin' but burned biscuits. He got off in Burndle an' didn't come back. It happens. Too much kimmeron an' a man forgets where he lies."

"Tanks ye," I tell the seaman, and then make my way back to Layal's statue. I lean against her stone skirts and ponder my next move. Did I really expect that finding Obid would be simple? Answers could take time, years even, but I had none to spare.

I stare out at Haradön, the ruins of the old castle, older even than Miter, clinging to a rocky peninsula paralleling the pier. Waves roil about the stone foundations and the tower of the inner wall, all that remains now of the once-mighty structure. It is said to have been built by our ancestors, the first men to settle Galvaith; perhaps it had been intended as a fortress to keep marauders and foreigners from Kobo and the other western lands at bay. We know little about where it is we have come from, only that our forebears sailed to Galvaith on ships from the east.

Exploration beyond the Gate in the west and beyond the

Dor Drillingt Islands in the southeast is forbidden, and has been since before King Adolar's days. No one knows what lies beyond our maps. Some claim that if one sails straight east for a year and a day, they will reach the darkened sea. I've heard tell of black stone sentinels there, rising from the sea, arms outstretched to welcome us home.

My omie used to say that all the creatures from her stories—Ignaz the statdamen, Hobar the child eater, Wilda the four-legged krone—come from the unknown lands, and that it is safer for us in Galvaith. We have no business chasing monsters, Klarkey, she used to say. I didn't seek to become a monster hunter, Omie, I reflect now. They came to me, giving me no choice.

Maybe after Otto takes the throne, we can open up the realm to exploration. How interesting it would be, to know from where we come. Who we truly are. The monsters beyond our maps can't possibly be worse than the ones within our borders.

The sound of retching draws my gaze, and I turn to see a figure crouched at the base of the statue, shuddering convulsively as he brings up the contents of his stomach. As if sensing my attention, he looks up, his hair matted and his skin dark with patchy grime, but it is his eyes that hold me riveted—they are a neon green so vivid they could light up a cave. "You should not be here," he hisses.

He looks somehow familiar, and these are words I have heard before. "Do I know you?" I ask. "Have we met?"

"You should not be here…you were meant for the sea," he mutters weakly.

A jolt of recognition hits me—this was the man who emerged from the crowd the day King Adolar announced I would join the Ascenditures for the ascent of Fitzhan; he had approached me with the same message before Ellias had instructed someone to take him away.

I bend down to the man's eye level but keep my distance. "Who are you?"

He stares at me vacantly, spittle dribbling down his chin;

when he opens his mouth to speak I see rotting gums where teeth used to be. He frightens me, but I also feel a swell of pity. His fate is such a common one among the Ectarian people. How easily that could have been me. Perhaps if Obid hadn't brought Rayna and me together. If Ellias hadn't taken me under his ropes. I have always been a few misencounters away from ending up like this man. "You—" he begins again.

"Klarke! There she is!" I turn to see Silias charging down the dock toward me, trailed by a small group of greencoats carrying muskets.

"We must go," Silias barks as he approaches. "For your safety. Riots have broken out at the Rektburg. The king has requested your presence." He seizes my arm and propels me forward down the dock toward the city.

"Wait! Who are you?" I shout at the man crouched by the statue.

His green gaze follows my departure, but the man remains motionless. *You should not be here*, he mouths again, before he is swallowed by sailors and merchants. By carts of fish and barrels of mead.

I shake my head as Silias moves me briskly along. No doubt the man was just some raving lunatic ramped up on veisel. But what if he knew of Dr. Vitus's whereabouts? Perhaps addicts had a common source to feed their veisel addiction. And couldn't he also be Dr. Vitus?

"Rioters have set fire to four homes flanking Revolution Square," Silias tells me as we maneuver our way through the stalls and vendors that crowd the pier.

I shiver. The last time we had riots…an image of Rosalie floods my mind; Rosalie, with a noose around her neck and her legs kicking helplessly before becoming horribly still. "We have to stop them."

"Only you can do that."

This is a pressure I do not want, and a power I don't know how to wield.

A horse and carriage waits for us by the stone arch. I climb into the carriage and Silias follows. I hear the greencoats shouting to clear the street to allow passage for the carriage.

"What are they protesting?" I ask Silias as the carriage jostles along the cobblestones.

"The wedding." He pulls back the canvas curtain with one finger and watches the street. Armed greencoats walk ahead, to the sides, and behind us.

"If they are protesting on my behalf, why do we need so much protection?"

"One cannot trust fanatics." Silias drops the canvas and sits back, fixing me with his icy stare. "Perhaps someone, in their quest to liberate you, moves to snatch you from this coach or to set you free permanently by casting you into the darkened sea."

"You think someone might try to kill me?" I ask with a shiver.

"I think many someones might try to kill you."

I release a single dry laugh. He gives me an understanding look. "What must I do?" I ask.

"King Adolar wishes for you to speak with the crowd. To let them know you are happy and that this is what you want and that no one is forcing you into this marriage."

"Does he think they are stupid?"

Silias raises an eyebrow, and I look away, sinking back into my seat. The images of the women swinging from the gallows haunt me still, and I close my eyes against the sound of musket shots that echo in my memory, and the sight of dirty pink ribbons being trampled underfoot by an enraged mob.

"I will say whatever I must."

In the street, I hear someone shouting, but I cannot make out their words. A guard in front calls a warning, before the shouts are stopped by a *thunk*, then silence. My stomach drops. I shift back the canvas to see a man lying sprawled on the ground, blood pooling around his head, a pink ribbon tied around his upper arm. He moves slightly and a figure from the crowd comes to his side as the carriage turns the corner and they are lost to view. Sickened, I turn away.

"Be cautious up there," Silias barks to the driver, his fist white-clenched around his club, which rests on the seat beside him. While I like to think Silias is different from the greencoats he commands, I know that, ultimately, he is one of them—Adolar's minion, who would kill me if the king demanded it. It had been Silias, after all, who swung the blade that killed Gio before he was able to share the truth.

"And you, too," he tells me, turning his icy-blue gaze my way.

"I am always cautious," I say defiantly.

The rest of the ride takes place in silence. I try to govern my emotions, to adopt a façade that is strong, composed, and passionate—that is how I must appear before the crowd. But the suppressed rage that boils below—my inner furnace that protests oppression and disease, the subservience of women, and the variety of personal slights and injuries that I have endured—those flames burn brighter and with much greater ferocity than anything else.

Once at the Rektburg, I am ushered in a side entrance, away from Revolution Square and the waiting mob. Prince Otto, Lena, and a host of guards and soldats await me. The greencoats, stoic beneath their helmets, grip their muskets tightly, as if they might begin shooting. Prince Otto envelops me in a hug.

"Are you okay?" he asks.

I nod, reluctant to confide, even to him, how I truly feel, for I might burst into tears, and this moment requires more than that from me.

"Lena is here to ready you," Otto says, gesturing Lena and her assistants forward. In a private antechamber, Lena runs a comb through my hair, dusts blush across my cheeks, and paints my lips with a rosy hue of insect wax. Two of her assistants help me into a simple ankle-length blue skirt and a cream-colored blouse that buttons up to my chin and around my wrists. A rustic straw hat is placed on my head—elegant in an informal way, but not so fancy that it separates me from the common folk outside. And in a moment I am transformed from a climber to an adel, the nobility. Lena squeezes my hand and gives a reassuring smile. Outside again, I loop my arm through Otto's and follow the guards through the palace to the base of Miter's Tower. King Adolar and his host of personal bodyguards arrive shortly after us.

"Make them leave, or I will hang them all, do you understand?" the king hisses in my ear. Cords form at his neck. His nostrils flare.

I nod, my knees weak as we pass through the main entrance in the tower's base. The roar of the crowd as I emerge onto the platform overlooking Revolution Square is thunderous.

People, horses, and carts cram into every inch of the square, and the wailing, shouting cacophony rises like the noise of some terrible beast. I step back, horrified to see protestors on the ground, held down by the boots of greencoats with muskets pointed at their backs; others have been tied, tethered, and bundled into the back of a justice wagon. Smoke billows over the far side of the square, where houses still burn, feurmenn shouting to one another as they blast the flames with long streams of water drawn from the harbor.

A sick world, akin to an infected body, will burn to eradicate the disease. I try to swallow through the lump of fear that has lodged in my throat and grip Otto's arm tightly as the king impatiently prods us forward. The ferocity of the mob frightens me, as does the king to my rear. I feel trapped between two steadily closing walls. Soon I will be squished, pressed into a piece of parchment on which both sides will scribble their versions of the truth: Klarke Ascher was a climber. She was a princess. A revolutionary. A rebel. She minded her manners. She was a hero. She was nothing.

I did not seek to chase monsters, Omie.

I close my eyes and inhale. I imagine grasping a small flake of rock; my arms tremble under the strain, my legs quake as they stretch for the next foothold. Ellias, smiling up at me, belays from below, feeding me lengths of rope each time I secure a sling to an anchor point. It is my first lead climb, I remember, and I am afraid. Afraid to fall. Afraid to hurt myself. Afraid to not be enough. I glance down at him, tears filling my eyes.

I'm not ready. I can't do it, I tell him, my voice breaking.

Don't look down at me, he calls. *I stand in the wrong direction. Where do we look when we are afraid?*

Up, I whisper, gripping the rock tighter.

Up, he repeats, his voice a font of calm and reassurance. *Why do we look up, darling?*

I lean into the rock, trying to feel its vital force, its connection to the life that surrounds it. *For that is the direction in which the mountain grows.*

I open my eyes and step forward, out from under the canvas awning and into the rain. The mob roars, and I can feel King Adolar seething beside me. Guards below beat their clubs against the raging tide of people that swells forward. I raise my gaze, staring up at the darkly clouded sky. Tilting my head back, I hold my hat and let the vintazite rain drum against my face. The drops feel cool and calming, as if medicinal spring waters were dousing my internal flames and leaving me calm and sure; as if Ellias had returned from the darkened sea with a soothing benediction.

I take another step forward so that my boots are poised on the edge of the platform. Cheers surge from the crowd, and I raise my hand. Quiet descends, and I take in the crowd of men and women, but it is the women to whom I turn my attention—unmarried women in their green dürmels; women, already brideprizes, attired in white dürmels; the adels in intricately stitched dürmels of silk and wool; the poor, their bodices dark with soot and tar, tears and patches. They stand together again, side by side, battered by the winter winds, each seeking a better life. Many of them wear shades of pink—a rosen apron covering their dürmels, a pink ilice adorning their necks, or a rose-colored ribbon woven in their hair.

A woman in the front of the crowd lifts an old piece of driftwood above her head, *Climb Like A Girl* scrawled in pink paint across its side. Another hoists a pink flag with a graceful white bird holding what looks like a small flower—ulrind—in its mouth stitched in the middle. A mountain bessil.

I smile, then bite my bottom lip to force it away.

My army dons the color of the ulrind flower. The flower we climb Fitzhan to gather. The flower that provides the only source of salvation for those who suffer from pulmonosis. Pink is a color not just for me but for the people.

"Please," I call out, hoping I can convey gratitude while still encouraging them to peacefully disperse. The crowd will not quiet, and as the cheers resound through the square, I wait, with a smile, for them to cease.

To my side, the giant wooden pyramid stands, the largest in all of Ectair. The holzenschrein to honor Orna, our goddess of the mountain, of life, and of Azura and Cleos, our moon and star. Each of the four sides is carved with images representing the nine kreisons or regions. Saltz mining, lumber, tar, pearls… We have had our differences, she and I. But I need her strength now.

Be with me, I pray, resting a hand on the polished wood. *Help me know what to say.*

I don't know if she listens. I don't even know if she is real.

"My friends!" I shout as the cheers finally die away. "I know why you are here, and I am grateful for your continued support. I—" I turn and glance at the king. His eyes wield a fiery whip. I want to speak truthfully, but I know he will not strike me if I do; he will strike them and make me watch.

"I want you all to know that I am happy. I am an Ascenditure, a great achievement that I could not have made without all of you, and I climb our sacred peaks not against the wishes of the gods and our king, but with their full support. I am to wed a man whom I have grown to love. A man who is good to me and who will, someday, be a great king. But I promise, I will work tirelessly to support all of you, to push, always, for a better Ectair."

The king takes a step forward, standing just behind me, so close I can feel his breath on my neck; he grips my arm in warning. I fight the urge to scream, to shriek that injustice and tyranny are alive and festering within the walls of the Rektburg. I quell my desire to urge the crowd to storm the platform, to kill our king, and to torch the old ways. My own fires of rage come to life in the depths of my belly, and it is as if my soul is hewn from straw. I exhale in the effort to extinguish them before the whole of Kietsch sees my hair ignite.

"Revolution!" a voice screams.

"King Adolar must step down!"

"All hail King Otto!"

In the crowd, guards again raise their clubs against the defenseless people as they rush the steps to the platform.

"Wait! Wait, my friends!"

I recognize the growing sensation inside me. It is the feeling I had when I said Eugen Martus attacked and kissed me in the alleyway. It is the sickness of lying but justifying it because it meets one's needs and the needs of the greater good.

"Before you attack our king, I want to share with you his enlightened progress over these past few moons. Do not yet cry for his abdication!"

The shouting gives way to murmurs in the square below, and the guards, too, stop their violent battering to hear my words. I take another deep breath and place my bet. I cannot wait for Veit to persuade a stone to turn into a feather.

"As some of you may be aware, an envoy from Ainar arrived the night of the vintazite festival. They requested that our Ascenditures join the Parvanatari for a unity climb in Ainar. King Adolar discovered that the Ainarians had been mistakenly incarcerated in the dungeons beneath the Rektburg and not only has ordered their release, but has also accepted the offer from Ainar's King Gyalzen to this historic climb of peace. After all, our king fears no one, and he seeks peace for the betterment of his people."

A collective gasp rises from the crowd. I don't look back. In his mind, I know the king is murdering me in a thousand different ways.

"I am climbing, my friends. To new heights. And that is all thanks to our generous leader." I turn to King Adolar, red-faced and fuming at my side, and politely clap my hands as I bow my head in pretend homage. I will pay for this. I see the violence of his intended retribution in every bulging vein and in the depths of his glittering eyes. "I am going to climb Mount Opasno," I yell, turning back toward the crowd, "and I will be the first woman from Ectair to stand on top of the world!"

The mob joins me in thunderous accord, the entire square reverberating with the strength of our collective enthusiasm. Women in the crowd wave pink ribbons, handkerchiefs, and scraps of fabric triumphantly in the air. An ilice of river clay, polished stones, and wood chips, all strung together on a piece of rosen twine, is thrown to the platform. I stoop to pick it up and drape it around the tip of Orna's holzenschrein. The bells of Hadrian's Monastery begin to toll, sounding the fourth hour, and the clanging adds to the joyful chaos.

I did what was asked of me. I hope this rejoicing will be enough to spare me another strike to the face.

King Adolar steps forward, and waves to his people, beaming. He does not speak, refuses to corroborate my story. Then he turns, his green robe billowing behind him, his face the same reddish hue of his beard, into Miter's Tower. Silias beckons me to follow, and we all return to the tower.

Once inside, Otto grasps my hand, and together we make for his tower in the Geistich. In the privacy of his room, he turns to me with a barely controlled anger of his own. "What in the name of Laren were you thinking? Do you have a death wish?"

"I did just as instructed." I shake his hands from my shoulders and storm to the window. "I appeased them, didn't I? I made them love him again. I had no choice."

"You always have a choice, Klarke," Otto insists. "I need your help to change things in Ectair, but sometimes I wonder whether you really care about making a difference for all those people out there or if you are obsessed only with climbing, with proving yourself."

"I'm doing this for change, Otto!" I reply, stung. Rayna's accusation runs through my mind—that I am selfish, that the chip on my shoulder will someday sink me to the bottom of the Rolag Sea. "We agreed that I need to go to Ainar to find your sister. To find proof of your father's treachery. I cannot grant King Adolar the time and opportunity to have Ainar's climbers murdered. Revolution doesn't come from waiting around for things to get better."

He slumps onto his bed and pulls a pillow over his head. I lean against the window and stare at the Nied Tower. I'm certain Adolar is in there now. Plotting his next move.

"You're right," Otto finally acknowledges. "I'm afraid to lose you, Klarke. But of course you are right. What you did was a brilliant piece of political maneuvering, and I hope you live long enough to see it come to fruition. I want nothing more than for you to find my sister and your glory."

"It's not about glory, Otto. We have nothing right now. Nothing. All I can do is grasp every lihtbug that flies by and hope it leads me somewhere in the darkness."

He relaxes and throws the pillow at me. I catch it, smiling.

"I'm sorry," he says. "It just makes me nervous when you're reckless. I'm afraid to lose the ones I love."

"I'm a climber, Otto. Why is everyone so surprised when I take risks?" I throw the pillow back at him and join him on the bed. "But I appreciate your concern, really."

"Always," he says, leaning into me.

"But tell me," I ask gently. "I have been all in my own head about our upcoming wedding. How are you and Dieter feeling about everything? It is all moving so fast."

"We've been arguing a lot lately." He drops his gaze. "Dieter has proposed we end things; he says that after we are married the situation becomes more dangerous for all of us, but particularly for him."

"Your father would have him killed if he knew," I say quietly.

"Yes."

"I'm so sorry, Otto. What did you say?"

"Absolutely not. I can't just end things. I, I love him."

"What did he say to that?"

"Nothing. He's terrified and brokenhearted. And I am too selfish to let him go. And he is too caring to force me to."

I rub Otto's knee, feeling sick inside. King Adolar would order the death of anyone who shamed the crown, who smeared his reputation. Kiel was hardly immune; he may be getting married to another, but I could well imagine Adolar ordering his death simply to spite me. And then, with such evil glee as only Adolar could summon, he would pass the bloody knives on to Otto and me to bear for the rest of our lives.

"Dieter's right," Otto continues. "He's Ainarian; he cannot hide his bloodline. That he was allowed to climb is a miracle we can attribute to Ellias. But he's always had to toe the line, to be perfect. He is one false move away from being sent to the labor camps. If a single word got out that he was…that we were…"

"I know." I take his hand. "We will be careful, Otto. No one will find out. You and I must play our parts well. We must show the world how madly in love we are. Make them believe we could never have eyes for another."

He laughs and pulls me into a hug. "I am madly in love with you, Klarke Ascher. You are my best friend."

I poke his side, and he jumps. We laugh and he reaches out to tickle me. I squeal and dive away. It's so easy with Otto. How lucky I am to feel so safe. To be treated with so much respect. He is my best friend too. With a pang, I think of Rayna. I hope to have the chance to explain myself at my wedding, to repair the bridge I have burned between us. The burden was mine to protect her and I failed. Now I sleep in the comfort of the palace, betrothed to a man who is kind to me, while she slumbers in a grimy butcher shop, abused by a violent husband from whom she cannot escape. Yes, I have failed her, but I aim to make it right.

I walk briskly back to my room, the fine hairs at the nape of my neck prickling at every imagined creak in the wooden floor or gusty billowing of a window drape in the breeze. Surely King Adolar would not seek my death now; this would prompt a revolution that would consume even him. No, he would arrange for something quiet that could not be traced back to his hand. Turning the corner, I collide with a solitary päter and leap back. His face is impassive, concealed entirely behind his white mask. I can see only the gleam of his eyes as he turns to watch as I back away, fighting the urge to break into a run as I retreat down the hall to my room. I fling open the door, stumble inside, and slam it closed behind me.

I lock the door and move wearily to the bed. The strain of the day weighs down my limbs. I shift out of my blue skirts, tossing them on the chair. Then, drawing aside the bed curtains, I fall onto the duvet and close my eyes. I don't notice the pain at first, just something hard, like pebbles scattered over the comforter. I raise my hands and cry out. Blood blooms in long welts through the thin fabric of my blouse and across the palms of my hands. I whimper as I pull a jagged shard of glass from my thigh, staunching the wound with the apron from the skirt.

It is window glass, I notice, turning the shard over in my hand. Window glass from the queen's tower, the tower I infiltrated in a covert, unsanctioned night climb. The same glass the päters added to my offering to Orna on my last journey up Fitzhan.

I move to the washbasin and wipe the cuts clear of blood. I stare at the nicks covering my trembling fingers. My hands are my livelihood. The bridge to my dreams. I don't think the cuts are too severe, but I could have lost everything if they had been.

"Head up, darling," I whisper.

I startle at a knock on the door.

"Klarke, it's Lena. I have news from Rayna."

I unlatch the door and open it to let Lena in.

"My gods. What happened?" she asks, seeing the bloody skirts and the washbasin crimson with my blood.

"The bed," I say.

Lena pulls aside the bed curtains. I hear her gasp, then return to my side. "How could they do this to you? How could a human being torture another in such a cruel way?"

"I'm afraid I got off easy today," I say. "It could have been worse." I sit in the chair as Lena pulls small pieces of glass from my arms and legs. "The people tied up in the square today, the ones piled in the wagons. They will be killed. It has to stop, Lena. I'm trying so hard, but I can't make it stop."

"You are doing all you can," she says fiercely, even as tears trickle down her cheeks. She dabs my cuts with ointment that she retrieves from her satchel, her voice as soothing as the ministrations on my wounds. "You are so certain, Klarke, that keeping the people safe falls to you, but tasks of this magnitude cannot belong to any single person. You must let go of your guilt and shame. The people who will die today do so willingly as powerful fighters advancing the cause. You are not responsible for everything that happens in this kingdom. That would be an impossible burden. Now, I'm going to clean up this glass, and then I will ensure that one of my ladies is always stationed in the hallway outside your room. Just to keep an eye so you can rest easy."

"Thank you," I say, gratefully pressing her hand.

Lena helps me into a nightshirt, settles me in the chair with a fur throw, and then prepares a fire in the hearth. She is only a few years older than I, but seems so much more capable in ways I have yet to understand. Perhaps it is because she is already a mother. She has a daughter. She knows what it is like to take care of girls in a world like Ectair.

"Rest here while I clear the bed. We will say nothing of this. We will give them no satisfaction. Isn't that right? They get nothing from you."

I nod and pull the fur around my body, wishing it were my mother's arms, wishing Lena were right. Unfortunately, the people who did this have already taken so much from me.

5

I linger outside Dr. Helmut's chambers, reluctant to knock. I don't want him to see me. Don't want him to ask why I look as if I have fallen on knives.

"I will be outside when you finish," Silias mutters, then he bangs on the wooden door for me. "Suertgût."

Dr. Helmut opens the door. "Fram Ascher," he greets me with a smile, motioning for me to enter. The door closes behind me, and I exhale.

"Please change into that smock and lie on the table. We will accomplish this necessary task quickly. Please do not be afraid or embarrassed."

Dr. Helmut retreats to his curtained alcove to afford me some privacy as I undress. I unbind the bodice of my dürmel, untie the apron, drop the dress from my body, and don the smock. Chilly and feeling uncomfortably exposed, I step up onto the slab of rock and lie on my back.

A clatter draws my gaze. Dr. Helmut walks toward me, carrying a wooden tray with a variety of sharp instruments. My eyes widen, and I flinch away from him on the stone.

Dr. Helmut places the tray at a side table and moves to my head so he can meet my eyes with his own. "This is a customary examination," he says kindly. "One I must do for all adels who wish to marry. I am only checking to see that you are pure and fit to marry the prince." He takes my cold hand in his own and squeezes it. "I am sorry for it."

I shudder and stare at the ceiling, where large river stones have been cemented together between thick wooden beams. I eye the edges of the rocks and try to figure out how I would climb them. Where are the holds? What is the best route across the sky and out of this place?

"I will examine your womanhood and then collect a blood

sample to test for parasites, pulmonosis, and black blood. Just try to be calm and breathe." I tense in expectation of pain, but instead, I feel gentle fingers brushing against my limbs. "Fram Ascher, what happened to you? Have you been attached by that wicked statdamen Ignaz?"

"Climbing accident," I mutter, my gaze fixed to the ceiling.

"So many wounds, Fram Ascher. It grieves me to see," the doctor murmurs. He retrieves a soft fabric from a drawer behind him, douses it in a stringent liquid from a jar on his desk, and brushes it gently across several inflamed cuts. "To prevent infection," he tells me. Dr. Helmut is a kind, tender man, and I trust him. Which is why I cannot hand him the dangerous gift of the truth.

"I fell on igneous in the lava tubes," I say. Another lie. So easy for me. Always for the right reasons. Don't all liars feel that way?

"I see. Well, next time you have such a *climbing accident*, you must come to me. Some of these needed stitches. They could have gotten infected."

"Of course. I promise."

After cleaning the worst of my cuts, the doctor performs his examinations, and I endeavor to remove my mind from all that is happening down below. He finishes his first task, the one I most dreaded.

"You may sit up now, Fram Ascher. You are doing very well."

I prop myself upright as he retrieves a scalpel and a thin slice of glass.

"For the blood," he says. "This will hurt only a little and only for a moment."

He proceeds to nick the smallest of cuts on my arm and tilts my elbow to spill a few drops of blood on the glass.

"I will analyze your blood and get back to you, but for now, I think it is safe to say you are a healthy young woman capable of bearing children for the future king. Now, I will give you some privacy so you can dress yourself."

I am a child myself. I shiver at the notion and slide from the stone slab. It doesn't matter. Otto and I will not have children, no matter my duties. Otto will be the last heir to this kingdom.

"Thank you, Dr. Helmut." I shift out of the smock and pull on my dress. "Can I ask you something? In confidence?"

"Please understand, Fram Ascher, that I am obliged to share anything of revolutionary import with the king. Not that I assume you are about to tell me such, I just offer the information in a general fashion, yes?"

"I understand." I hesitate for a moment, then forge on. I made a promise to Marike, after all. "This is not about me, and it is not a matter that would be of interest to the king."

"Proceed, then, if you wish," he says.

"I have a friend whose mother is dying from pulmonosis. I promised to help her obtain medicine, and you're the only person I know who can help me do that."

"Ulrind powder is closely regulated and very expensive," Dr. Helmut says, emerging from his curtained alcove.

"I know." I pull a small velveteen money pouch from my apron pocket. "I can pay. I can give you everything I have. Just please help me."

He glances uneasily at the money pouch and then at the closed door. I meet his gaze with pleading eyes. Dr. Helmut turns to a wooden cabinet carved with a scene of Azura and Cleos in human form, frolicking across a sky full of stars.

He unlocks the cabinet and rifles through the contents, then turns to hand me a small wooden box. "This should be enough to last three mooncycles," he says. "If it does not clear her of the disease, then it has progressed beyond help. I cannot do more for you than this."

I throw my arms around him in a hug. He pats my back, then gently pushes me away. "You must speak of this to no one. As must I."

"You have my word, Dr. Helmut. Tanks ye." I offer the bag of coins, but he waves it away.

"Ah, but one thing before you leave. Could you bring me the bottle on the counter marked Azleanium?"

I examine the labels affixed to the bottles that cover the counter surface—Hexafran. Pentadas. Menagal. What the doctor has in kindness, he lacks in organization. I push aside a stack of papers and search beneath a pile of burlap. Then I spot the small brown bottle labeled Azleanium in faded white letters. Beside it, to my shock, sticking out between the pages of a book, are the leafy fronds of a purple fern.

I think of the cave atop Fitzhan. Of Gio emerging amidst white stones and purple ferns. And these ferns were, somehow, precious to the päters—I had spied them carrying bundles of purple ferns between Orna and Laren's towers. The same occasion on which one of the päters wore a black diemant.

"Dr. Helmut?"

"It should be there," he calls. "Sorry for the mess. Check behind the book on medicinal algae from the Dangof Forest."

"I've got it, but what's this?" I reach for the fern and accidentally knock over the bottle of Menagal, whatever that is, but right it before the contents can leak out. I remove the dried fern and hold it up.

Dr. Helmut turns, eyes widening. "Ah yes, the mysterious plant. My apprentice found it in the hallway outside of Orna's tower and brought it here. He'd seen nothing like it, and neither have I. Come." He beckons me to an overstuffed bookshelf, his finger tracing the spines of the books. "Here."

I take the dense tome and stare at the cover. *Herbalism in Galvaith.*

"Flip to page 423."

I place the book on the stone slab in the center of the room and turn to the suggested page. A faded painting depicts the goddess Orna on a throne made of jagged stone, bathed in the blue light of Azura. Surrounding her is a dense grove of purple ferns. I glance over at the doctor, eyebrow raised. "What does this mean?" I ask.

"I am not sure," he says. "That is the only reference I've seen to this specimen. The title of the painting is *Urspra*, which translates in our language to *Origins*. Make of that what you will."

Origins. I finger the fern thoughtfully. Origin of what?

"I know where they grow, Dr. Helmut. I've seen them."

"Where?"

"These ferns grow in the mouth of a cave atop the summit of Fitzhan." I hesitate, reluctant to endanger the doctor with information. But if I am to solve this mystery, I will need his help. And has he not already proved himself by providing the ulrind medicine for Marike's mother? "I saw the päters, once," I tell him, "carrying the ferns from Orna's tower to Laren's tower. I do not know what they are."

"The cave atop Fitzhan. The center of the world," he whispers, scratching his chin thoughtfully. "Creation."

"Creation of what, though? What do the päters do with these, Dr. Helmut?"

"I don't know," he says. "But they've instructed me to concoct a tincture that, when poured onto rock, will mimic the effects of subjecting the stone to immense pressure."

"They're creating diemants."

His head whips to me, and his eyes widen. "We mustn't speak of such things," he exclaims.

"Is that what it could be, though?" I persist.

"Doubtful. There are more effective ways to create diemants."

"The päters already have diemants," I tell him. "At least one. I've seen it. I think King Adolar does too."

"Impossible," Dr. Helmut refutes, shaking his head.

"Say they do have one. What would a diemant, a pressure-inducing tincture, and a purple fern be used for?"

"I imagine they would be trying to create something," Dr. Helmut says slowly.

"What?"

"Well, our origin story describes the emergence of life when lightning struck the first diemant, releasing Orna, Laren, and the other minor gods. Perhaps—and this is supposition only—the päters wish to create something…big."

"A god?" I gasp.

"By the darkened sea, no," Dr. Helmut says with a laugh, tucking the fern back between the pages of the book. "Of course, this is all just silly talk. Legends and superstitions. I am sure it all means nothing, but nevertheless, I think we must keep this quiet, Fram Ascher. I suspect we are meant to remain ignorant of such matters."

"Agreed." Although the thought is now unraveling in my mind. What in the known world could the päters be creating? Icy dread runs through my veins. "I do have one more matter I would like to briefly discuss with you."

Dr. Helmut again glances nervously at the door. Sharing what I know could be dangerous for us both, but the doctor has access to information and people I do not. Otto and I need his help.

"Death's Whisper," I say. "It is not a disease, is it? It comes from the mineral flüstodapul, which is ground from a clear crystal."

"How could you possibly know this?" he demands.

"I found Dr. Vitus's journal," I tell him, omitting any mention of my breaking into the queen's tower, or the time Gio stuffed the crystal in my mouth—the first time he tried to kill me. "I also found a history book he wrote in the library. He wasn't just a doctor, was he?"

"Dr. Vitus was a brilliant man. An inquisitive man. A budding agitator."

"He knew too much," I whisper. Those who know too much don't last long in Ectair. Ellias. My mother and father. The queen. "There is an antidote to the poison," I tell him. "Dr. Vitus didn't mention it in his journal, so I don't know if he was aware of it. I don't know if you know. But someone other than me and the evil men who walk these halls should."

"Go on."

"The solans. Everything to create life, to take life, and to save life, apparently resides on the summit of Fitzhan."

Dr. Helmut leans back against the counter, as if in need of it to support his weight. "Of course," he breathes in astonished understanding. "Orna would have created a life form to fight back against Laren's weapon. This is powerful information, Fram Ascher."

"I know."

"You must be careful who you share this with. As we both know, knowledge is a dangerous item to carry in your rucksack."

"Yes, you are right, Dr. Helmut." A cold trickle of dread flushes through my body.

He pats my shoulder and gives me a reassuring smile. "Do not fret. Your secrets are safe with me. Like you, I only want the truth and what is best for this kingdom. I do not involve myself in petty politics."

"Tanks ye." I match his smile and glance toward the door. "I must go, but I'll let you know if I discover anything else. For medical reasons, of course. If you believe it safe, please do tell me if you learn anything."

"For medical reasons. And for the truth," he adds in a whisper. I leave feeling strangely euphoric and optimistic; I have gathered valuable information this day and perhaps found an ally—more than I could possibly have hoped for from the embarrassment of a pelvic purity test.

When I emerge into the hallway, Silias is engaged in a heated conversation with a päter. I cannot hear their words, and while the päter's expression is hidden behind his mask, Silias's lip is curled, his hands form white-knuckled fists at his sides, and his face, reddened by anger, is too close to the päter for polite conversation.

I approach slowly, feigning interest in a tapestry of King Adolar planting the flag of Ectair atop Mount Bonen.

Silias notices me and turns abruptly from the päter, coming over to block my view of the hallway and the man behind him.

"Did all go well?" he asks with forced calm.

I spy the hem of a black robe swishing around a corner as the päter departs. What were they arguing about? I wonder. And were the päters responsible for placing the glass shards in my bed? And did Silias know of the plan?

"Yes, all went well," I say with a calm equal to his own. "I am ready and poised to bear an heir." I raise one hand in sarcastic triumph.

"The king will be pleased to hear this."

"The päters, too, I assume. What were you speaking about just now? You seemed upset."

"My business is not yours, Fram Ascher," he replies shortly, his tone a cool rebuke.

"And yet mine is yours?" I demand.

"And yet it is."

We stare at each other, neither breaking gaze until I can stand it no longer. I roll my eyes, sink a hand into my pocket with an exaggerated sigh—feeling Dr. Helmut's little wooden box there—and move around him to proceed down the hallway toward my room.

As I stride briskly down the corridor, my thoughts return to the discoveries of the morning. The päters are creating something from an illegal diemant, a strange tincture, and an elusive purple fern. But what? And to what end?

On an empty strip of beach, just outside of Kietsch, I hold Ixy's reins as the wild sea wind whips my skirt about my ankles and presses my blouse against my torso. I button my woven jacket tightly across my chest and cross my arms. A silk hat is tied tightly under my chin; the night aiwl feather that protrudes from one side flaps and flutters in the rising wind as if it longs to attach to the bird again and fly free across the darkened sea.

In the bay I can see the Stone Päters, a series of four jagged rock pinnacles that rise fifty feet into the sky, white-capped waves frothing at their base. Atop each pinnacle, blood red in color, sits a flat white stone resembling the white masks worn by the päters. The spires remind me of nails hammered partway into a board, shanks and heads still visible. I've never climbed them, but some of the Ascenditures claim to have done so.

Ixy stomps her foot and lets out a whinny as I dismount.

Glancing down the beach, I see Kiel striding toward me. Exhaling slowly, I steel myself for the coming conversation. Unlike Otto, I have become proficient at saying goodbye to those I love. The atmosphere within the palace grows ever more tense with each passing day, and, with all that I have learned, my imperative must be to keep Kiel safe. To which end, I must now end all associations—and all hope of such—between us.

A dark-bellied, pregnant sky looms overhead, but the rain holds its breath. Waiting, perhaps for when I break Kiel's heart. Are the gods so dramatic? Or perhaps they are kind, leaving the rain to disguise my tears.

Upon reaching me, Kiel pulls me into a hug. I breathe deeply of his skin and tremble. He feels warm, safe—and I feel that I am home. I am about to set fire to my only shelter, so that I might sleep out in the raging storm.

"I've missed you," he says into my hair. "And I've worried about you. We haven't really spoken since…"

Since Gio tried to kill me. "Yes. I…I haven't known what to say."

"Are you okay?"

I shake my head but can't bring myself to speak, not yet. I take his hands.

"So much is happening, Kiel. I don't know where to start."

"It's not over, is it? Whatever this is didn't die with Gio?"

"Gio was only the single peak of an underwater mountain range we cannot begin to comprehend."

"What do you mean?"

It all spills out of me, as if in a flood. I tell him about what I overheard in the climbing gym. About the Dark Promise and the Schaeter. I tell him of Haydrich's plot to overthrow the king, and I roll up my sleeves to show him the healing cuts across my arms. He stands, wide-eyed, hands on my shoulders, as I tell him of Dr. Helmut and the purple ferns and my theory that the päters are using these items to create something, something suggested in our origin myths. And then I share my proclamations from the platform, about the king's supposed ambition to send the Ascenditures to Ainar and for my plan to discover Otto's sister there. It feels good to share what I have learned. Too good. My stomach lurches at the thought of ending this relationship.

"How in the deepest hüle are you supposed to handle all of this, Klarke?"

"Gods only know," I say with a hollow laugh. "Rather like running up an avalanche or trying to swim in snow before it buries me."

"Haydrich is interesting though," Kiel says. "Might he be a useful ally if he, too, wants to be rid of Adolar?"

"I don't think so. These cryptic references to a Dark Promise and this mysterious Schaeter make me nervous. What if we end up with someone worse than Adolar?"

"I could see what can be learned about the Dark Promise in Kietsch," Kiel says. "I could go undercover. Pretend to join them."

"That sounds incredibly dangerous."

"I want to help, Klarke."

My heart clenches, and I look away at the Stone Päters rising ominously from the wind-tossed water. Being with me, I am well aware, is the most dangerous place to be. How can I warn him of threats when I hold a knife to his throat?

"Dieter wants to end things with Otto," I say. "He thinks it's too dangerous for them to continue a relationship after the wedding."

Kiel raises an eyebrow and stares at me. "And what does Otto think?"

"Otto doesn't want to. He says he knows it's selfish but doesn't want to let Dieter go."

"I see. And what do you want?"

"I…"

He touches my cheek with his hand, gently turning my chin until we are looking into each other's eyes. "I want to help, Klarke, but I also want you. I know the risks. Remember when I free-climbed the lower half of Hansba with Aedan in the rain? Incredibly stupid and dangerous, I know, but the risk of death is a daily occurrence for an Ascenditure. And what is the point of all that risk and danger if one cannot also strive for some measure of happiness in this life? You, Klarke, are my happiness."

"You're crazy."

"What Ascenditure isn't a little crazy?" He smiles, and I can't help but smile back. "Please don't end things between us because you are afraid for me. Allow me the agency to decide what risks I will endure."

How can I argue with agency? I chafe under my own restrictions—being monitored by Silias and forced into a role I did not choose for myself.

"All right," I say finally. "But please be careful. I need to get back to the Rektburg for tea and training."

"Training?"

"Apparently, I still have much to learn about being a lady."

We laugh together. Kiel leans forward and plants his lips on mine. I wrap my arms around his neck and pull him closer. It is a stolen moment of freedom, and it will fuel me in the hours to come.

Kiel takes Ixy's reins in one hand, my hand in the other, and we walk down the beach toward a sheltered path surrounded by fizhte trees that will lead us to the outskirts of Kietsch. Once we leave the beach, we will also have to abandon our public affections.

"What happened with the Roudan repairs? Any sign of the fearsome Hildegroth?" I tease.

He chuckles and shakes his head. "No, no sign of a giant sea beast, but we got the cracks repaired. Aedan worries about the dam's structural integrity, but the leaks were small. I don't think we'll have anything to worry about for a long time."

"Maybe Hildegroth is dead," I muse.

"Maybe."

A light rain begins to fall, dampening my coat and dripping from our clasped hands.

"And what about your wedding?" I ask with a forced lightness. "What of your betrothed, Lady Gelta?"

"They have not yet set a date."

"She's very pretty."

"She's very not you."

I nudge him, smiling sadly. "It's simple at the moment because Otto knows about you. But once you're wed, the danger for us both will grow exponentially. What will we do then?"

"We deal with it then," he says. "I know it's silly, childish even, but we must simply make the most of each day together, then pivot when we are forced to do so. Just take it one moment at a time."

"It's how I survived on the streets after my parents died. One moment at a time," I muse.

"Maybe I'll just tell them all no," Kiel says, coming to a sudden halt. "I will refuse to marry her."

"You can't say no, Kiel," I protest. They will hang you."

"Only if they can catch me." He winks and lifts my hand to kiss it.

"That's not funny. I can't lose you."

"You're right. It's not. And I'm sorry."

We reach the bend in the path where it turns toward Kietsch, and I let go of his hand.

"You go first." He hands me Ixy's reins and kisses my cheek. "I'll follow in a few minutes, and then I'll see you at the wedding."

The wedding—words that make me feel sick.

"It's okay, Klarke. It's all going to be okay."

I nod through sudden tears. Otto is a good man, and I will be safe, but I didn't get to choose this. None of us gets to choose this. Once girls turn seventeen, they are told whom they must serve for the rest of their lives as if they don't have imaginations, aspirations, dreams of their own.

How do I seize control of my own life in such a place?

I glance ahead at the forested path and behind at Kiel as an idea forms in my head. I pull him close and whisper in his ear.

"Seriously?" he asks, eyes wide.

"Seriously," I say. "Small acts of rebellion, no?"

"You truly are one of the bravest people I know," he says, the corner of his mouth lifting in a smile.

"Or the most reckless."

"We're Ascenditures. It's what we do." He winks, and I am warmed by his grin, by the twinkle in his dark eyes.

We sneak one more joyful kiss before I climb onto Ixy's back and ride down the path to my prison and my prince.

Instead of setting Kiel free and keeping him safe, I have set a plan in motion to take back my power on my wedding night. Otto might be furious. Dieter most certainly will be.

It could be a wonderful night, or it could end in tragedy.

6

I mince across the room, flitting on tiptoes, knees slightly bent, trying to keep my back straight and my face relaxed.

"Remember, you must float like moss on a quiet lake!" Misha, my etiquette teacher, calls out. "You are lumbering like a pregnant bosete! Delicacy, my lady!"

I clench my teeth, forcing a nod as I mutter beneath my breath. Again, I take up the train of the silk gown, hold it aloft, and slide along the waxed floor with what I hope is a floating delicacy.

"That was better," Lena calls from the sidelines.

"Better?" Misha demands in scowling disbelief as she folds her arms across the breast of her dürmel. She is married to Hannar Hahn, a senior member of parliament, and is as welcoming as a herchfly on pudding. "A fontanl stomping through the forest has more grace than her. What a disastrous bride for our esteemed prince."

"Are you questioning King Adolar's judgment?" I ask with pretend astonishment. "Do you think him a fool?"

"I meant no such thing!" Misha replies indignantly. "Our king is gracious and gifted with Laren's wisdom. I am simply saying that you are a most undeserving bride. My daughter—"

"My lady," Lena interjects. "Your daughter is betrothed to Hannar Karmine. Perhaps we should focus on matters that are under our control."

"The wedding comes on the morrow and still she moves like a drunken sailor. I fear that it is, indeed, a hopeless task," Misha concludes with a disdainful sniff.

"Well, we certainly appreciate your help, my lady," Lena says with a slight bow. I marvel at Lena's poise; while she loathes the self-important adels as much as I do, where my odium leaks through like saltz from an overstuffed sack, hers remains safely contained on the shelf.

"Pretend you are on a rock." Lena places her hands on my chest and back to straighten me. "I know you are graceful and balanced there. Don't think of this practice as foreign. You are an expert at poise, just in a different way. Channel the manner in which you move on the fel to how you move here."

I try again, stepping forward on my toes as I imagine inserting the tip of my boot onto a jib, a small foothold. I let my arms swing forward as I would when balancing and reaching for a high crimper. Slow with intention.

"Yes, that's the way. That movement is softer, more graceful. Can you feel that?" Lena exclaims with a clap of her hands.

"Hmph." Misha sniffs again but has nothing else to say, which I take as a compliment.

The creaking hinges of the wooden door announce a visitor, and I turn to see a black-robed päter with a white-masked face. My stomach twists with revulsion and a thread of fear.

"A word," he says in a deep, monotone voice, turning to Lena. A metallic gleam at his neck is suddenly illuminated by a shaft of muted light that streams in through the eastern window. Is it a chain like the one worn by the päter with the two-toned eyes? The päter who sends me up climbs with death threats for an offering?

"Yes, your heliness. Misha, please continue with the training. I will be right back."

I watch Lena leave with the päter, disquiet filling me. What word would the päter require with Lena? Since when has she interacted with them? Since when have the paths of servants and helimen crossed?

"Move," Misha says sharply. "I will make you worthy of Prince Otto, whatever it takes. You will not dishonor the crown on the morrow."

I swallow and tear my gaze from the door. Training my eyes on the window, to the view of the wall of the Geistich beyond, I imagine I'm perched on a sheer cliff face and move as delicately as I would on a climb. One toe in front of the other.

"Again."

I refocus on the rock wall outside. Misha knocks my back with her hand. I straighten. She taps the top of my head. I bend my knees slightly.

"Again."

I go into a trance, floating in and out of walking like a princess, climbing like an Ascenditure, and wondering why all the people nearest me keep having private conversations with the päters.

"Again."

Misha pokes my stomach. I suck it in. At one point, I no longer hear my footfalls. The only sound in the room is the slushy rain pattering the glass pane. I stop at the window, press my hand against the frigid surface, and take a deep breath.

"That could have been much worse."

"Thank you for teaching me," I tell her, knowing that I must endeavor to not entirely alienate the adels; while Misha might not appreciate the change I hope to bring, perhaps her daughter will. "I know that wasn't easy."

"I am a woman of Ectair," she says sternly. "I respect my duties."

"You are an honorable woman. Hannar Hahn is lucky to be served by you."

"Well," she says briskly, "be that as it may, we are now finished for the day." She pauses at the door and, over one shoulder, says, "Blessings to you and the prince. I wish you both a contented marriage and hope that you can honor your prince in the way he deserves."

"Tanks ye."

Misha nods once, then is gone, the heavy door swinging to a close behind her.

After a further ten minutes of waiting fruitlessly for Lena, I also leave, heading for my room two floors down. I still manage to regularly get myself lost in the palace, even though I've walked the Pentengen many times, circling the five sides to learn the hallways, the floors, the rooms, memorizing who lives where. The outer structure of the Rektburg feels safest; I prefer to keep my distance from the two towers of the gods in the inner Geistich, and as far as I can from the Neid Tower, where King Adolar resides. The adels who live in the Pentengen tend to ignore me or content themselves with casting withering looks as I pass.

The long corridors with their arched windows are shadowed and gloomy, the sky outside a dull gray. I cannot recall our last star day, when the sky was blue and Cleos showed his searing face. It had been bright atop Fitzhan the day Ellias died—perhaps that was the last time the world was radiant.

Lost in my thoughts, my gaze drifts to the wall to my right where dusty portraits of King Adolar's regal ancestors hang in heavy gold frames. Stern visages of dark-haired men scowl down at me, their heads heavy with the weight of the crown. How much longer must we endure this tyranny? My attention is then drawn to a small alcove, within which, in the shadowed recesses, a strange sculpture sits. Bending to take a closer look, I realize that the statue is unfinished, only partially carved out of a block of granite. Half is roughly hewn stone, and the other half depicts the figure of a climber in old-fashioned attire. Hanging from a rock outcrop, he holds the wall with one hand and lifts a rope in the other. He looks rather like Ellias.

I trace my fingers along the base of the stone, searching for a title or an artist's name.

"That is Lars Veber. Carved by the famed Ectarian sculptor Navaris Umbol."

I turn slowly, a frisson of fear stopping my breath.

"Navaris also crafted the sculpture of my grandfather, King Hammonhoff II. His portrait is on the wall here somewhere as well. It's a magnificent piece, truly. It rests in the hallway between my son's tower and the late queen's. Have you seen it?" King Adolar asks, leaning nonchalantly against the wall, crossing his booted feet, one across the other. He is casually attired, in dark hosen, a white overcoat, and wrapped in the luxurious fur of the bergbear. All I see when I look at him is a creature from my omie's stories.

I swallow and let out a shaky breath. We haven't been alone together since he struck me in the throne room and accused me of being just like my mother. "No. I haven't had that pleasure," I say steadily.

"You must the next time you visit my wife's tower. One cannot appreciate the history of Lars Veber without also appreciating King Hammonhoff II. Many considered Lars to be a direct son of Orna. Gifted by the goddess of the mountains herself with supernatural abilities to thrive at great heights. And my grandfather, well, he did what he had to do."

"Why was Lars killed?" I ask.

"Treason. He betrayed his king."

"What treason did he commit?"

King Adolar traces one hand along the stone carving of Ellias's grandfather, so close to me I smell the cured leather of his furs. I fight the instinct to turn and flee. "He refused a marriage summons. To my aunt, the king's niece."

"Why?"

"He was an arrogant fool who had forgotten his place. This statue should have been destroyed years ago. But *you*, you know your place, Klarke Ascher, don't you?"

King Adolar smiles as he steps closer, placing a cold finger on my face, tracing the curve of my cheek before he lets it linger on my lips. "You are ready for the wedding tomorrow?"

"I am filled with joy at the prospect of being Otto's brideprize," I whisper, hands trembling and clenched behind my back.

"I bet you are," he says with a slow smile, his hand moving from my lips to my hair. "You are beautiful, aren't you?" he continues, gripping the back of my head so that I cannot turn away from his glittering gaze. "Just like Mina. Why did I give you to my son?"

A scream rises in my throat, and I want to wrench my head away from his grasp, but my body feels leaden with fear, as heavy as the block of stone upon which Lars Veber climbs. Hysteria grips me—my mother's name in his mouth is like screaming pigs in a slaughterhouse.

"You gave me to your son because you hate me," I hiss, tears filling my eyes despite my every effort to blink them back.

King Adolar laughs, then, to my immense relief, steps back, disentangling his hand from my hair.

"A man needn't like his wife to take her. Hate renders a marriage infinitely more exciting, sûssa. If I've raised my son correctly, you'll soon find that out."

With an icy smile, he turns and leaves, striding down the carpeted hallway before he turns the corner and is gone.

Exhaling, I sink to the ground, skirts puddling around me as I attempt to calm my racing heart. The breath comes quick in my throat.

We want the same things, you know. I remember Haydrich's words. *We both want a new leader.*

Placing my palms flat on the flagstones, cold to the touch, I struggle to regain my composure, to stifle my fear and bury the rising sobs that threaten. Maybe I need an ally after all. Perhaps the enemy of my enemy might also be my friend. Perhaps it is time to trust Haydrich. How could the one he supports be any more vile than our current king?

7

Three chandeliers, each filled with a hundred flickering candles, provide the light Lena needs to craft my hair into an elaborate work of art. An army of women bustle about the formal antechamber in Hadrian's Monastery, laying out my dress, unraveling numerous strings of pearls, and mixing colorful pigments to delicately dab upon my face. Today I will become the crown princess of Ectair, and I must look perfect. I would rather be dangling in an icy crevasse on Mount Bonen.

Lena threads a number of black pearls through my hair, and then several assistants join her to help me into my gown. As I step within the circle of skirts, I notice the dark pink stitching that threads the inside hems of the bodice, the waist, and the skirts. Invisible to the outside observer, but very much there, snug against my skin. This is Lena's protest, her way of supporting me, of giving me strength.

The dark lace clings to my torso, wrapping my skin in swirling patterns of ferns and flowers. The blue silk skirt falls from my waist like a waterfall, the trail rippling on the floor behind me. Two sheer panels of azure-colored fabric, affixed to my shoulders, billow like the sails of a ship. My dress, I realize, contains the essential elements of Mount Bonen, the Sevier River, and the Dangof forest. I am dressed as the very best part of Ectair, the beauty of its wild and natural world.

Lena's assistants powder my cheeks and brow and dab elegant colors across the lids of my closed eyes. When they finish, they step back, and Lena presents me with the ilice that I will offer to Orna. It is fashioned from black pearls harvested from the Dor Drillingt Islands, interspersed with polished sections of driftwood and shiny shards of smooth sea glass. I lift the ilice over my neck; the string of the ilice, like the stitches in the lining of my dress, has been dyed pale pink, the color of alpenrose, a hue so light it could almost be mistaken for the whiteness of snow. Lena bows slightly, a smile curving her lips.

"Take this." She hands me a blue sachet tied closed by a silk ribbon. "It contains all you will need for the ceremony."

I nod, blindly, as if my head is no longer properly attached. Like a child pretending to understand the meaning of the stars.

"Leave us," Lena instructs her ladies. They oblige, and she guides me toward the window where the Rektburg, with its dark granite stone towers, looms over Revolution Square.

I am surprised to discover that I am not afraid, despite all that is to come. To fight this would be fruitless, a waste of my energy and resources. I am not afraid because it is Otto I am marrying. Today, I become an Adolar. And what better way to destroy my enemy than from within?

"I want you to remember, Klarke," Lena tells me, "that you are not alone out there. You are the lighthouse. The captain. And your sailors are here."

"Tanks ye," I whisper and lean into her strength, taking a few deep breaths in an effort to calm my nerves. Shortly, Silias will usher me from this room, down the tower's stair, where I will be paraded before a hall crowded with curious adels. My heart tightens at the thought of Kiel watching me swear my love and service to Otto. I was not born in Ectair to be happy, I remind myself fiercely, blinking back tears. I was born here to fight so others can achieve peace and happiness. I am the sword to their flower, and the means by which we can bring justice to Ectair. It is a most lonely destiny.

"What did the päter want with you yesterday?" I ask Lena, suddenly remembering that strange interruption to our training session.

"Oh, just details of the wedding," she says dismissively, her fingers fluttering over my hair and tucking in a stray ribbon here and there. "Unfortunately, working with our helimen has been a necessary part of the preparations."

The door opens to reveal Silias and a cluster of guards milling in the hallway behind him.

"They are ready for you, Fram Ascher," he says.

Lena kisses my hand, and I touch her cheek in gratitude before moving toward Silias and the hallway beyond. We descend the staircase, moving down through several floors to a subterranean chamber, from which a tunnel leads to another staircase.

"The rest you do alone." Silias gestures toward the stairs. "Should you require my services, I will be down here."

I glance up at the stone stairwell that circles up and up in a seemingly never-ending spiral, as if to the himmelorbs themselves. Lena has instructed me as to what I must do on this day, but now I have forgotten everything. My legs shake beneath the skirts of my dress, and my mind is a dark whirl of confusion; my sweaty palm slips on the stone banister as I make my way up the stairwell to the floor above. The stairway proceeds into an intricately carved wood-paneled foyer, with images of vessels at harbor and birds flying high in the sky above, all brushed with gold foil—Ectair's industry lit to a golden sheen in the light of Cleos. The stairs rise through an opening above my head, from where I can hear the low rumble of voices murmuring. I take a deep breath and try not to throw up.

Steeling my nerves, I ascend those last few steps into what appears to be a giant holzenschrein. I see hundreds, maybe thousands, of faces staring in my direction through the delicate filigree of a carved wooden screen that separates us. Three unlit candles in different shades of green have been placed on a table inside the holzenschrein. Light green, like sea foam, on the left. Bright green, like stone moss, in the center. On the right, dark green, like the depths of the forest where light cannot pierce the canopy.

Exit through the door in the back and join your prince. Lena's voice sounds in my head as I find the door and make my way through. Otto stands on the chancel, looking dashing in a light-green jacket with golden epaulets, dark-green hosen tucked into polished boots, and a golden sash snug across his chest. A saber hangs at his hip, the blade etched with old Galvaithian runes, and on his head rests a humble copper crown decorated with finely wrought tree limbs interspersed with gold leaves and set with polished river stones. In one hand he holds a green silk sachet identical to the one I carry. Otto smiles at me, mouthing, *Wow* as he takes in my dress. I smile back, and my creeping fear fades, until I notice the line of nine päters that stand behind him in the gloom.

One of the päters steps forward, a heavy golden ilice around his neck. As my eyes adjust to the dim light, I see that the other eight päters each hold a different sacred object—a bowl of incense, a gold-painted knot of rope, a green candle with a black flame, a broken oar with runes carved into the blade, a pitcher filled with clear and blessed helivater.

Which one put glass shards in my bed? The thought comes unbidden to mind as I scrutinize their masked faces.

"Beneath the moon and star of Orna and alongside Laren's waves, we gather in this holy house of goddom to bind two souls in eternal unity," the gold-iliced päter intones. I rarely hear the päters speak. It is like suddenly hearing a lamp say your name or a bookshelf laugh.

"Prince Otto Ewald Adolar and Fram Klarke Verena Ascher come to us today as individual boats floating in Laren's great bay, and they will leave here a united vessel that will sail henceforth, delivering life as Orna intended until the pair cross the darkened sea. Ash and wave for us all."

"Ash and wave for us all," Otto and I repeat.

"Before this union can be sanctified, we must first honor our gods. In the name of our goddess of land, life, the himmelorbs, and the mountains, you will each present an ilice to Orna, your offering for her blessing. Once you have draped the ilice, you will enter the holzenschrein and light the three candles. One for fertility, promising the goddess that you will bring life into the world. One for her protection from death, her commitment to your life until it is time to hand you over to Laren. And one for loyalty and commitment to each other and to the gods."

Otto climbs a wooden ladder built into the side of the great holzenschrein to drape his ilice across the summit of the pyramid, then I do the same with mine. We enter the dim interior of the schrein, lit only by the light of the candles filtering in from the ceremony hall. Inside, surrounded by carved paneled walls, the details of which I cannot make out, sit the three unlit candles.

Together Otto and I strike a match and light the three wicks. Around us the wooden panels of the holzenschrein are brought to vivid life in the sudden gleam of light—one panel depicts two gods, Laren and Orna, bursting forth from the first black diemant on the ocean floor; the second shows Laren in his glory, erupting from the waves as lightning strikes a ship in the distance; the third is of Orna giving birth to Azura and Cleos, our moon and star. Behind us, around the opening of the door, I see a boat sailing toward a horizon, crossing the darkened sea.

"Am en ah," the päter says. *It is done.*

"Am en ah," the other päters repeat.

The first part of the ceremony complete, we return to the chancel, now on display for the thousands of adels to gawk at. The hall is dim, however, and I can scarcely make out individual faces in the crowd. I ignore the murmur of voices that rise like the tide when we appear. The chamber is majestic, and while the hall is dim, the ceiling is lit to brilliance. I tip my head back to admire the ceiling high above and the exquisite painting that covers its surface. At the mural's center sits Orna, on an igneous throne atop a mountain's summit, cradling her children, Azura and Cleos, in her arms. Laren is beside her, his gaze directed toward a dark and frothing sea where a boat, filled with the corpses of the dead, sail to his realm. Around the two gods, life and death coexist. For every man leading a cart of kuhkas is a man building boats to send the dead across the darkened sea. For every child consuming an ear of corn is a child dying of pulmonosis. While half of the ceiling is bright, enveloping Orna and her offspring, the other half is dark, representing Laren's domain.

"In the name of our god of death and the sea, you must now present your sacrifice to Laren," the päter intones behind me, drawing my attention back to our tasks below.

On a small table at the front of the chancel rest two stones, two blocks of wood, two matches, and two crystal chalices. Lena has instructed me well, and I can remember my tasks. Otto and I open our sachets. Inside are three glass vials, each containing a kefir beetle, a splash of seawater, and a small dried leaf.

I upend the beetle onto my block of wood, then smash it with the stone, crushing it into a paste. Then I strike the match and burn the leaf until ash rains down upon the crushed beetle paste. Otto silently does the same beside me, until, together, we scrape the beetle and the ash into our goblets and pour the seawater over.

"In the great wisdom of our gods, Orna is provided with the power to create life, so long as that life always returns in death to Laren and his kingdom across the darkened sea. Ash and wave for us all."

"Ash and wave for us all," the congregation repeats along with us.

"You must now drink of the holy mixture you have concocted as a promise to Laren to one day return to him, and as an acknowledgment to all present that you do not belong to yourselves or to this world, but to the great destroyer. Drink now and find peace in submitting."

Eyeing the mixture dubiously, I think of Kiel's fierce kiss on the beach, hold my breath, and then tilt the goblet into my mouth. The saltwater burns. The ash tastes bitter, and the legs of the beetle cling to my tongue. I try to swallow, but my throat tightens to a gag, and all I can do is cough. Otto drinks without a murmur, as if the concoction were the finest of Ectarian wines. Apparently, I'm not good at finding peace in submitting.

As we move back to the center of the chancel, ladies moving throughout the hall light wall sconces to illuminate the crowded congregation. The front row of witnesses is now clearly visible:

King Adolar lounges on a heavy throne, intricately carved and decorated in gold leaf. Six of the Ascenditures are seated toward the middle of the front row. Haydrich and Tizian, I notice, are absent. Kiel's gaze is tilted downward, as if he is sleeping, but I suspect he just does not care to watch the proceedings.

"Klarke."

Otto's whisper draws my attention as the päter hands us two lengths of rope.

"You must tie these around the other's wrists to symbolize your allegiance to Ectair, to each other, and to our great king."

I tie an intricate figure-eight knot around Otto's right wrist, a knot used on the fel to anchor a line, to keep me safe. With a self-deprecating shake of his head, Otto ties a simple square knot around my left wrist. "My knot is scheiz," he mutters.

"It's perfect," I whisper with a smile. "Though it wouldn't keep me safe on the rock."

"Quiet," the päter hisses. "Now, lift each other's knotted hands in the air."

My left hand finds Otto's right, and we clasp our fingers together, then lift our hands toward the crooked spire atop the monastery.

"I am but a humble servant of the gods," the päter says. "A mouthpiece for Orna. A puppet for Laren. In the name of these two great gods, I pronounce you one pair, one knot. Once you have walked the line of päters and touched the sacred objects, you will go forward as man and brideprize. Prince Otto, your task is to protect the new princess and keep her healthy so she might bear you many sons. Princess Ascher, your task is to serve the prince and bear him many sons. You will teach them to be kind and honest members of our kingdom, faithful to the gods and to the rule of law. Go forth now and forge your bond. Go forth now and be one."

We walk the line of the päters, touching each object they hold. The last päter carries my crown. Glancing into his eyes in the candlelight, I startle to see that one is brown and the other blue. This is the päter I saw wearing the black diemant, the päter who sent me up the mountain with the death wish of ash and bone. *Look for the eyes*, Petrus had told me. Otto clears his throat, bringing me back to the present moment. I glance down at the crown, resting atop a green silk cushion; it is forged of a dark, unfamiliar metal, with a circular band twisted to resemble a rope. The diadem is cut to resemble the jagged peaks of Miter's Backbone, with a colored gem inset at the summit of each peak. Atop the central summit is a polished rosen diamond. A perfect adornment for an Ascenditure princess.

Otto lifts the crown to place it on my head.

We are ushered back to the front, splashed with helivater, and I am declared, to the applause of the crowd, Otto's wife. We are escorted out the door, across Revolution Square—packed with people and animals, cheering, yelling, whooping, and whistling—and through the castle doors to the balhalle, the large banquet hall.

Long rectangular tables surround the perimeter of the great room, with the central space reserved for dancing. White and yellow flowers decorate the walls and cluster in bouquets down the length of the tables. The air smells of honeysuckle, hugal, and pine—what a fortune it must have cost to acquire fresh flowers this time of year. Ribbons and banners, in varying shades of green, drape across the ceiling and through the archways and doors. Garlands of fizhte limbs, interspersed with beads, bartlenuts, and carved wooden figures hang from the walls. A massive ice sculpture chiseled in the shape of two intertwining knots, representing our marriage and the flag of Ectair, command pride of place on the dais, sparkling in the flickering light of surrounding candles. One knot represents our sailors, the other our climbers. We are all children of the summit and sea here.

Gaily dressed minstrels, in tunics dyed with special pigments from Kobo, fill the hall with music as we enter. The bellowkord player gives me a quick wave, and I smile in return. The music of the bellowkord always signifies a festive party.

Shelving adorns the walls to a height of twenty feet or more, and from each shelf, hundreds of flickering candles glow; and, in company with the numerous chandeliers, it is as if we stand beneath an endless sky of burning stars.

King Adolar and his court sit on the elevated dais, and we take our seats at a table to one side of the platform.

"That wasn't so bad," Otto murmurs. "Was it, wife?" He snorts slightly, and I smother my giggle with one hand.

"No, husband. It was not." I cough delicately. "Although I never want to drink dead bugs and seawater again."

"Not your favorite?"

"Blech! Although you did very well with it. I embarrassed myself."

"Everybody gags at that part in the ceremony," Otto reassures me, reaching across to give my hand a squeeze. "I've sat through many adel weddings, and trust me, you aren't the first to get beetle legs stuck in your throat."

"And why would Laren demand that of us anyway? It's not as if we have a choice as to whether we cross the darkened sea."

"What's the point in any of it?" Otto whispers. "It's all a charade to make us believe we have any power over anything."

A servant arrives with a chalice of mulled wine and fills our goblets. We both gratefully sip the steaming liquid, the sweet strength of the wine a relief after our ordeals of the day. The wine is spiced with zimtammon, clove, and hünich. Holding the glass, I let the mulled drink warm my belly and my hands.

Kiel and the other Ascenditures enter, and I see that Tizian and Haydrich have joined them. Kiel glances up at the table, and I meet his gaze. We exchange soft smiles before each of us looks away.

"Did you notice one of the päters has two differently colored eyes?" I whisper, leaning over toward Otto. "It's what Petrus warned me about. We have to find out who he is and speak with him. Perhaps you can uncover his secrets while I am in Ainar?"

"Sounds like a plan," Otto whispers back. "You find my sister, and I will learn what I can of Hannar Double Eye."

"You make him sound like a pirate."

"Isn't he our villain? Gio said there is another, yes? Another what? Another murderer?"

Swallowing, I glance over at King Adolar, who laughs with one of the adels, and then look to Haydrich, who sits silently, his gaze on the king, his drink untouched on the table before him. How many villains live in our kingdom? There may be those present who have yet to show their faces.

We are served a feast of baked fish, seasoned potatoes, and crusty bread with vinegared peppers and olives. All washed down by endless glasses of mulled wine. For dessert, we are presented with gleaming mounds of orange-tinted solan pudding. How long will the king's hoard of the sacred tuber last, now that we are no longer climbing Miter's Backbone to retrieve them? It is, as far as I am aware, the only antidote against poisoning by Death's Whisper. Why would Adolar waste this precious resource on a thousand guests?

I pick up a delicate silver spoon and hover over the pudding. I have eaten solan only once before, raw atop Fitzhan when Gio attempted to poison me; but tonight, I dip the spoon into the orange pudding and close my eyes as the sweet, buttery taste coats my tongue. Many have died retrieving this stupid vegetable, yet my refraining from it won't bring them back. Perhaps the greatest act of protest I can manage tonight is to enjoy myself.

A jester, wearing a cap hung with bells and dressed in poofy green hosen and a frilly top, gives Otto and me objects to distribute to our guests. Otto receives three ulrind flowers to gift to young women, symbolizing that they, too, will soon be blessed with a happy marriage. I have been given three dark rolls of bread, which I must pass out to bless the men with a future brideprize who, I suppose, will, in turn, make them tasty bread.

We dance, we drink, and I avoid watching Kiel twirling around the dance floor with his betrothed. I cannot think of the future; it hurts too much. Unless those thoughts formulate plans of justice and revenge. As Kiel said, we must exist in the here and now. And the here and now consists of wine and minstrels.

Despite the festive energy, I keep thinking about my mother and father and wish they were here. What would my life have looked like if they hadn't been taken from me? Warmth spreads through my body as I imagine the bedtime stories they would have read to me while I lay beneath a pile of feather-down blankets. Of the stews that would have filled my belly. Of the hugs that would have comforted me. Of my strong and powerful father, who wouldn't have let King Adolar anywhere near me, who would have done everything in his power to fight the monsters on my behalf.

I obligingly dance with Gustl Scharm, a member of parliament from Omalau. Then I twirl around the floor with another before taking respite against the cool stone column at the edge of the hall. "Klarke," a soft voice says.

I turn slowly, and my heart both tightens and swells. Rayna wears a simple white dürmel, her hair tied in many small braids and looped around the top of her head. She is alarmingly thin, and she carries a darkness in her eyes that terrifies me.

"Rayna." I pull her into a tight hug, tears filling my eyes. "Rayna, I'm so sorry. I'm so sorry that I lied about Eugen. I was trying to protect you, and it backfired. Please forgive me."

"Of course I forgive you, Klarke. I know your intentions were good." Rayna brushes one hand across her own wet cheeks. "I'm sorry, too, that I called you a liar. I'm sorry I chose myself over you."

"No, no," I plead. "You had to protect yourself. I have not forgotten about you. I've just given you space because I don't want to put you in any more danger."

"I know." She pulls away from me and smiles through her tears.

"I'm glad you came. Is Eugen here?"

Her face tightens, and she inclines her head toward a far table where I can see her husband, Eugen Martus, drunkenly laughing with a group of men.

"I see."

"Never mind him. How is all with you?"

"I'm good, Rayna. Otto is a kind man. Together, we hope to make many positive changes in Ectair."

I take Rayna's hand and draw her through the crowd to where Otto sits with a group of adels. "I want you to meet him. And I want him to meet you."

Otto sees us approaching and rises to his feet.

"Otto, I want you to meet my dearest friend in all the worlds. This is Rayna."

Otto beams, and Rayna blushes. "My lord," she says with a bow.

He kisses her hand and then bows to her. "It is my pleasure, Rayna. I have long wanted to meet you. Any friend of Klarke's is welcome in our home. I hope we will see more of you."

"It is difficult, my lord. My husband is…we have much work that occupies us at the butcherii."

Otto glances across the crowd at Eugen, his lip curling slightly. "I know how important your friendship is to Klarke," he says, turning bright eyes back to Rayna. "On days when you visit, I will send a house woman to take over your duties."

"Oh…that is so kind…but I wouldn't wish that on my worst enemy…" Her hand covers her mouth, and she steps back, eyes wide with horror at what she has revealed. "Apologies, sire. That was inappropriate."

Otto's face darkens. "You would not wish that work on your worst enemy, why?" he asks softly.

Rayna is silent, but her shuttered expression, her suddenly pale face and trembling lip reveal more than words ever could.

I am struck by how much of life's torments Otto has been spared. Yes, his life in the palace is a charade, and he cannot love whom he chooses, but he also knows nothing of the struggles in the slums. Of what it means to be a brideprize to most men in the kingdom.

"We will address this, Rayna. I promise you," Otto says finally, inclining his head in a slight bow. "Now, please excuse me.

I see Hannar Schmidt is hailing me, no doubt to confer about the explosion of squirrels in the Hummeldorf Woods that are destroying his nut crop."

"Gods," Rayna whispers. "Am I a fool? To insult my husband to a total stranger. I could be hanged for that."

"It's okay," I say, wrapping an arm around her narrow shoulders. "Otto is safe. Ignorant of your plight, growing up as he has. But safe nonetheless." We move to a dimly lit corner bench beneath a hanging drapery, and I motion to a server to bring us drink. Soon we are sipping wine and laughing, and I want to cry at the joy I see on Rayna's face. I relate all that I have discovered in the past weeks, and her face grows somber.

"Klarke, this is so dangerous."

"I know, but I understand now that my mission is bigger than just climbing. I have the power to do something about this."

"I would ask you to promise to be careful, but I know that would be a waste of breath."

I smile and request more wine. "And how are you? How are you really?" I am afraid to hear her answer.

She takes a breath so deep I worry her fragile chest might shatter. "I am alive."

"I can't tell if you think that's a good or bad thing, and that worries me."

"Some days, like today, it's a good thing." She smiles and squeezes my hand.

I take a sip of wine and feel sick. She is clearly not eating or not eating enough.

"It's like when my pa fell off the pier and drowned, and then ma was killed," she says. "Things feel so hopeless. I'm sure just like then, it'll pass. I'll find the will again to exist."

"How can I give you hope?"

She leans her head on my shoulder, and I lean on hers.

"Do you remember when Obid introduced us?" Rayna asks. "Without thinking about whether you wanted the responsibility of another kid, you said, 'Well, come on then. Let's find some food and a place to sleep.'"

I smile and nod, watching Kiel slip away through the crowd and out the entrance doors.

"That bread you gave me," she continues. "It was the first food I'd had in days. It filled me. *You* filled me. As long as you are in the world, Klarke Ascher, I will find my way back to hope."

I squeeze her hand and pass her one of the rolls that is supposed to be given to three men this evening. "Well, come on then. Let's find some food." She laughs and takes a big bite from the roll. "Tell me more of your life, Rayna," I say. "It has been such a long time since we had the opportunity to talk."

"Well, we've been traveling to Iri a great deal, and I've enjoyed that," she says. "I'd never traveled anywhere before, and while Iri isn't exactly exotic, I like the briny smell of the Sea of Toole."

"What's in Iri?"

"Kuhkas. Eugen has made a deal with a farmer there who offers a good price for the cows."

From across the room, a trumpet sounds. The dancing stops, and all eyes turn toward either me or Otto.

"I have to go now, but we will speak soon. Eat another potato dumpling. They're delicious!" I kiss Rayna's cheek before I am pulled away to join Otto.

"My kingdom!" King Adolar's voice booms as he joins us in the center of the dance floor. "It is now time for the prince and princess to bind their union and make whole the promises which earlier they laid before the gods. While they will now leave us, our festivities don't have to end. Let the celebration continue, my friends. More wine!"

As clapping and cheering rise from our guests, I take Otto's hand and smile at them. He waves. We look like the perfect happy couple.

Six guards escort us from the banquet hall to the Geistich, and then they leave us to climb the spiraling stairway to the top of the prince's tower. Unlike the rest of the palace, the walls leading up to Otto's chamber are not decorated with gilded paintings or theatrical tapestries. Occasional portraits hang from the stone walls, all paintings of his late mother or the pair of them. None features the king.

"Klarke," Otto says as we reach the top and enter his room. "I'm glad it's you." He draws me into a hug. "I know this is weird," he says, his voice muffled in my hair, "but I'm glad it's you."

"I'm glad it's you too." I squeeze him back. "I couldn't have asked for a better partner."

"Why do I have a feeling our first year of marriage will be incredibly dramatic?"

"I have a feeling you could be right." I laugh and remove my crown, placing it carefully on the table in front of the fire. His room, much like the stairwell, is modest in its adornment. A grand bed, stripped of its canopy, stands as the centerpiece, accompanied by a simple table and chairs. A bookcase, heavy with leather-bound volumes, dominates one wall, while a velveteen chaise lounges near the fire. There is no trace of gold leaf, no elaborate draperies, no portraits of ancestors flaunting their triumphs over exaggerated prey.

A sharp rapping comes from the window. Otto startles and reaches for his sword.

"No need, Otto," I say with a smile, lifting the window latch to allow Dieter and Kiel to crawl in.

"What in the himmelorbs?" Otto asks, mouth agape. "Really?"

With a wide grin, Dieter unties the harness from his chest and smooths his formal garb. "Surprise!"

Kiel kisses me, clasps Otto on the shoulder, then removes his harness and pulls up the long rope they used to climb the tower. "Let's celebrate the happy couple, shall we?"

8

So, which part of the drink was the worst?" Dieter asks idly, his head resting on Otto's lap.

"Definitely the water," I say from a mound of velveteen duvets and down pillows. Kiel, stroking my hair, chuckles, and I feel the warmth of his chest vibrate beneath my cheek. It is as if we are four friends in the Westlich, enjoying a routine evening of social entertainment. For us four, however, it is something special and completely forbidden.

"I would have to disagree with you there, darling wife," Otto contributes. "It was definitely the smooshed bug guts."

I laugh and flutter one hand in his direction. "As you will, my liege," I say with mock gravity. What I do not say is how the mouthful of saltwater had reminded me of my father, and those moments before he drowned, flailing in the water, desperate for breath—how much must he have swallowed before he crossed the darkened sea?

"Of course you could not abide the bugs. You grew up a spoiled prince in a palace." Dieter squirms and shouts with laughter as Otto attacks with a playful growl.

"And how exactly does that factor into it?" he demands.

"If you're starving, worms are tasty cooked in helrin oil, and kefer beetles, if you can catch them, are good toasted on coals..." Kiel says.

"Yes, kefer beetles are not bad," I acknowledge with a lazy yawn. "I've had worse. My best friend Losan and I would dare each other to eat fish guts. Raw, stinking, star-marinated fish intestines."

All three turn to me with horrified expressions.

"You didn't?" Kiel pleads.

I twist around and shift my body so my lips hover a few inches from his. "Oh, but I did." He pushes me away, laughing.

We lie before the dying fire for hours, reminiscing and drinking from a bottle of kimmeron Kiel brought. The smoky liquid burns my throat and sets my belly afire, but it brings a languid contentment to the evening. I deliberately push thoughts of päters, purple ferns, and black diemants from my mind, determined to enjoy the evening.

"To men in love!"

I raise the bottle to the cheers of the men and take a long glug.

The kimmeron bottle grows lighter with each toast we make.

"To the future king and queen!"

"To Kiel's biceps!"

"To Veit's mother!"

"To the overabundance of squirrels in the Hummeldorf Woods!"

"What are you going to do about that?" I ask Otto, chuckling.

"As if that would be anyone's priority. Hannar Schmidt should be able to manage his own woods."

"That's hardly a kingly thing to say," Kiel says. "You have to manage everyone's woods once you are king, not just the ones you want to."

Otto sighs and shakes his head in mock disappointment.

"So I have a question for each of you," Otto says. "What made you want to be Ascenditures?"

"Easy," Kiel chimes in. "My father is head of Ectair's northern forces. I was intended to become a soldat, but I had no love for fighting or for the march. Then Gio's father, who formed part of my father's legion, took me climbing once near Camp Arema, and from then on I could think of nothing else. Fortunately, my father was pleased with my choice, so long as I was dedicated, worked hard, and excelled at it. Climbing began as a way to avoid a certain life and turned into an absolute love for the sport."

"Well," Dieter begins, "with my Ainarian heritage, I was either going to be sent to the labor camps or end up shoveling dung in some rich adel's stable. I could never own a business, but I could not reconcile myself to being a doormat for the rest of my life. I saw the Ascenditures training once at Vether's Fel; it seemed they had no master other than the gods themselves. And certainly, being able to move into the granhaus kept me off the streets. We are working under orders, of course, but on a climb, we are free."

A silence follows, and then the three turn inquiring faces to me. "I don't remember that I ever thought about it," I say, shrugging off the weight that has descended upon my heart. "I was just a sad little girl mourning the loss of my parents when Ellias tied a harness around me and stuck me on the rock. 'You can climb your way out of a lot of dark places,' he said. And so I went up. And I kept going up. I didn't stop. And when I am on the rock, I feel closer to my father. I feel a bridge to what I've lost. Then, as I got older, it became a way to avoid becoming someone's brideprize."

"Ah, sorry to have ruined those plans," Otto says with an apologetic smile.

I shake my head and laugh, tossing a cushion at him. "You're the exception. You're like climbing, Otto. A way to escape."

"I'll take it."

Dieter seizes the bottle and raises it for another toast, his voice slurring with drink. "To a kingdom where people are really free and don't have to fear for their lives every time they sneak off to find a moment of happiness!"

He gulps down the last of the kimmeron, then wipes his mouth with the back of one hand. "So I have to ask," he continues into the sudden quiet, "how is it exactly you two are going to produce an heir to the kingdom?"

"We don't have a plan," Otto says stiffly. "For all they know, Klarke is barren. It could take years."

"It can't take years," Kiel warns. "You know what will happen if it does."

I do know what will happen. Should the princess not produce an heir within a certain period of time, she will be removed to allow Otto to remarry a more fertile candidate. I can imagine several ways in which Adolar might choose to remove me.

"We have time," I say with forced cheer. "Not forever, but we don't have to figure this out now."

A pall has been cast over the room, and I fear the evening is near to over. But I have one more pressing question I need their thoughts on.

"What are the chances of Adolar actually letting the Ascenditures go to Ainar?" I ask.

"Aedan has said nothing of plans yet," Kiel says.

"I hope we go," Dieter mutters gloomily. "It would be best for me to be away from here for a while."

Otto frowns, and I ache for him. Truth be told, I can hardly blame Dieter. I know what it is to live half a life in shadows, haunted by the threat of discovery. The noose will tighten—it is irrevocable; I will lose Kiel to Gelta, Otto will lose Dieter to rigid tradition, and we will both be heartbroken and alone in this godsforsaken palace.

"I think, as dangerous as Klarke's platform speech was, the king has to be considering the prospect, if only to save face," Kiel says. "Klarke has planted the seed, but perhaps we need another gardener to now ensure its growth."

"Veit," Dieter and I say together. "Assuming we can trust him," Dieter muses.

"We can trust Veit to do what's best for Veit and no more," I say. "However, he's envious of Haydrich and desperately wants the opportunity to summit Opasno to prove that he is the better climber."

"I will push the issue tomorrow," Kiel says. "Best that you stay clear of this, Klarke. For now."

"Yes," I say quietly. "For now."

"But before we delve too much into serious plans," Kiel says, rising to his feet. He offers me his hand, then, when I take it, he pulls me to my feet. "I'd like to request some alone time with your wife, Otto."

"Oooooo, finally!" Dieter calls with a muffled laugh.

"How dare you," Otto exclaims with pretend outrage. "How dare you request to leave me alone on my wedding night with the most handsome man in all of Ectair? No offense, Kiel."

Dieter grins, his eyes alight with merriment.

"You poor thing." I laugh and wink at Otto. Kiel grabs a lantern from a side table, seizes my hand, and pulls me from the room.

"Don't make an heir!" Otto shouts as we step over the threshold. Convulsed in giggles, I shut the door, and we descend the staircase to the study below. Kiel places the lantern on the table, dims the light, and pulls the drapes tightly over the solitary window.

A nervous energy thrums through my veins; my heart picks up its pace and the palms of my hands dampen. Kiel smiles calmly, running the tips of his fingers lightly down my arm. I take a shaking breath and look up into his eyes. His lips meet mine and then travel across my neck onto my shoulder. "We don't have to do anything you aren't comfortable with," he says earnestly.

"Can we just talk?" I ask.

He laughs into my ear and kisses my forehead. "Of course we can."

"Sorry, it's just there are so many expectations for me tonight, and I don't like the pressure."

"You never have to apologize for taking care of yourself."

"Tanks ye."

We move to a green velvet sofa below the window, and I curl up beside him. He drapes his arm around my body, and I snuggle close to his broad chest, feeling the steady beat of his heart beneath my cheek. My world spins slightly, courtesy of the kimmeron, but I feel safe and free, loved and cherished.

"I found the Dark Promise," Kiel says.

"What?" I demand, struggling to right myself on the sofa. "I thought we agreed that was too dangerous."

"Agreed?" He laughs and fixes me with an amused stare. "*You* mentioned it might be dangerous, and I agreed. But I never agreed to do nothing." I open my mouth to argue but cannot find the words. "Anyway, it was just a preliminary meeting, and I didn't learn much."

"Wait, you attended a meeting?"

"Yes, we met in the basement of the Gorganch alehouse. I'd say there were around two hundred men. A couple of hannar spoke, mainly about the rising costs of fish and whores. It seemed more like a meeting of grumpy men airing grievances than a political gathering of powerful rebels."

"So you didn't see the Schaeter or Haydrich? There wasn't talk of an impending coup?"

"At the end of the meeting, we raised our glasses to the Dark Promise and the Schaeter's health, and then we left. I don't know, Klarke. I think whatever Haydrich is up to, perhaps it isn't as dangerous as he makes out. Perhaps he exaggerates the mystery to impress you."

I wrap one arm across his chest and rest my chin on his shoulder, my gaze resting on the leather bindings of the books that line the walls. I feel an inexplicable sense of disappointment. Isn't it good news that I don't have to worry about the Dark Promise?

"You wanted them to be something, didn't you?" Kiel asks into the silence.

Damn Kiel, the mind reader.

"I wanted there to be someone else out there also striving to overthrow the king."

"I wanted it too," Kiel replies softly.

I squeeze his arm. The stakes are high for both of us; should Adolar fall, there is a glimmer of a chance we could have a happy future together. I lean over to kiss Kiel's cheek, then move to his forehead, trailing kisses across the hollow of his neck, then, finally, up to his waiting mouth.

Forget Haydrich. Forget King Adolar and the Dark Promise. Forget everything that is not Kiel and me on this couch in this tower. At least for one night.

9

The buildings in Southlich are repaired and extended with salvaged boards and rusted tins from cargo barrels; they bulge out over the street, crooked and swollen like pregnant giants. In the narrow streets beneath, wagons stacked high with burlap sacks of saltz jam the thoroughfare. Saltz is our lifeblood, the biggest export from our kreison, and the richest export in Ectair. During vintazite, when the ice and snow descend from the mountains, men move from the farms and fields into the saltz mines, where they work underground, protected from the elements. For a few months of the year, the streets are so clogged with saltz carts, en route to the harbor—where ships wait to ferry the saltz to Kobo and the lands beyond The Gate—that there is scarcely room to walk.

I squeeze between a cart and a crumbling brick wall, slick with moisture, nodding to the saltzfram whose cheeks are dusted with the white powder of her trade. She hoists a sack of saltz to the top of her wagon, then tightens a canvas cover over the top to protect it from the rain. The men work the mines, but it is the task of their women to haul the saltz.

I make my way through the narrow streets to the climbing gym. Marike waits, and I dig into the depths of my satchel as I hurry along—the ulrind powder is buried beneath a climbing skirt and a coil of rope. My heart lightens at the prospect of the hope I am carrying to her, the hope that her mother's pulmonosis might yet be cured.

Marike's climbing skills are progressing remarkably well, but she still needs to learn to use and trust her feet. I've created a list of drills to help her build strength and confidence, but I try to steer her away from talk of becoming an Ascenditure; she has much yet to learn. Also, an Ascenditure must die to provide a space for a new recruit. And that new recruit, as I found so often, will most likely be a man. While I root for her success, I cannot wish for the death of a teammate.

"Halt, Fram Ascher!" A palace guard materializes from the crowded street. "You must come with me."

"I don't think so. I have training…" I start.

Before I can say anything further, he grabs the waistline of my skirt and yanks me toward an adjacent alley. Our booted feet splash through stagnant puddles of rotting food and mule piss.

"I am the future queen of Ectair, sir," I gasp, attempting to pull away from his grasp. "How dare you? When the prince hears—"

"I got orders," he barks, yanking me along after him. "Git down there, or I'll make you wish you was high enough on veisel not to feel a thing." The gloved hand rises and points once more down the alley.

I glance frantically around, but the street has quickly emptied of its citizens, the saltzfram's wagon abandoned in the road. The appearance of palace guards is enough to send everyone scuttling within doors; certainly, the saltzfram will not risk her neck to save mine. Not while there are children to feed.

The guard comes to a halt at a door set into the brick wall, opens it, and shoves me inside. The dark room within is filled with smoke from a fireplace with a blocked flue. Blinking against the acrid haze, I make out the figure of someone sitting before the hearth.

"Daughterbride."

I cough, choking on the smoke as a sliver of fear dances down my spine. I grip the band of my satchel tightly as I move reluctantly forward.

King Adolar would not venture from the safety of his castle to kill me in the Southlich, where rebellion rumbles behind closed doors. While he might want to close his hand around my neck and squeeze until the life leaves me—and I have seen that desire in his eyes before—this inclination would battle with his own cowardice. It is so much easier, after all, to simply order the death of another. And he would be careful to protect his throne, his crown, his power. But this care would not extend to those I love. To Kiel and Dieter. To Dr. Helmut. Oh gods.

"My king," I murmur with a slight bow. The guard hovers behind me to prevent any retreat.

"I received an interesting letter yesterday from Bertrand Obeldorf," King Adolar continues. "Can you imagine what he might want from his king?"

A flood of relief courses through me—I had been so afraid that the king had discovered my confidences with Dr. Helmut, the ulrind powder in my satchel, or the thwarted wedding night when Otto and I had spent the evening in the arms of others. I had no notion of what I might do, should any of this come to light, but I knew I would cross the darkened sea before I let anything happen to Kiel, Dieter, Otto, or Dr. Helmut.

"I wouldn't know," I say carefully. "I do not know the Obeldorf family."

"Of course not. Why would you?" he says with a slow smile. He stands, and I involuntarily take a step back. "Veit, it seems, is desperate to prove himself on the slopes of Mount Opasno and to represent our kingdom on the streets of Ainar. Apparently, the Obeldorfs agree with you, Fram Ascher. They insist I make a formal proclamation on the matter and that preparations begin immediately for the journey."

I hardly breathe, the smoke stinging my throat and bringing tears to my eyes. The king steps toward me, and I feel riveted in place by the intensity of his glare. It is as if I were a jeltmouse being stalked by a harrincat; the harrincat has acute eyesight for movement and a deadly aim, but only if the jeltmouse panics. If it remains immobile, with scarcely a quiver of its whiskers, if it can outwait the predator, there is a chance of survival.

King Adolar drags a ringed finger across my cheek, where a small scar remains from his last blow, cut from the rings that adorn his fingers. He caresses the scar, then drops his hand. "I have agreed."

My breath catches as I stare up at him. A million thoughts tumble through my mind. A million questions whose answers lie in the frozen north.

"Under one condition."

I release a slow breath and wait for the axe to fall.

"You will stop training that girl immediately."

It takes a moment for me to realize he is speaking of Marike.

"But—"

He seizes my face with such punishing force that I steel myself for another blow, but he grips my chin, forcing me to look into his eyes. "If you disobey this order, I will marry her off, regardless of her age, to the most vile sailor I can find. Stop her training or be responsible for what comes next." My mind freezes at the thought of such a fate for Marike.

He drops his hand and moves to the door, where the guard holds it open. "Take your warmest coat, Fram Ascher," he says over one shoulder. "It would be a shame for you to freeze to death once you leave these lands."

The door closes behind them, and I collapse into the chair, sucking at the smoke-laden air.

Thinking of Rayna, I know that I must do as the king demands. I can no longer train Marike. As much as I want to put women on the mountain, help lift them from poverty and abuse, I cannot put Marike's life at risk so that she can climb. I can't carry that burden.

When my composure has returned and my hands stop shaking, I return to the streets that are, again, busy with trade.

As I weave haphazardly through the city, hoping to lose anyone who might tail me, I spot a street boy selling dried cow dung for fuel a few blocks west of the gym. His eyes gleam beneath a layer of grime and soot, and his hair, bleached by Cleoslight, is shiny with grease; the ragged remnants of a tunic hang about his scrawny frame as if shredded by galing winds. Glancing at him, I shiver in recollection of the years I lived on the streets after my parents died. There's a certain level of poor one can be that tugs on the heartstrings of the privileged. Once one falls beneath that, they might as well be the pigeon who poops on one's head.

"What's your name?" I ask, approaching the boy.

"Who wants to know?" he asks suspiciously, leaning over his dung pile protectively, as if I intended to run off with his livelihood.

"I come with a job offer, but first I want to know who I'm dealing with. I come in good faith," I say gently but firmly.

"Helkin," he replies, eyeing me dubiously.

"I will pay you more for this one task than you will make all month selling your dung."

"Was kinda job?" Helkin asks distrustfully, eyeing my clean skirts with a narrowed gaze. He looks as if he'll just as quickly stick a knife in my guts as take a favor from me. Scrappy kid.

"I have a message I need delivered. But it has to be secret. Nobody can know anything of it other than the person to whom I want it delivered. Can you do that?"

"Depends. Was you gonna pay?"

I retrieve two golden dracals from my pocket—a ridiculous, even dangerous, amount of money for this child. "This. But you must use it sparingly. You would not wish to draw attention to yourself or to me. Do you understand?"

He laughs and throws a cow patty at me. I duck to avoid it. "Crazy fram. Was else you wan for that?"

"Nothing. It's important. So important, I'm willing to pay handsomely for it to be delivered in secret. If you don't want the job, I will find someone who does."

He glances at the throng of people and wagons making their way down the street, then at his small pile of dried dung. "Can you watch this for me? They eash go for a pentus, or two for adels, in case anyone asks."

"Fine, I will keep an eye on your dung." I place one gold coin in his grubby hand. "One coin now, and the second when you return with proof that the message was delivered."

"How'm I gonna do that?" Helkin protests.

"Ask the girl to whom this message goes the name of her brother. When you tell me her brother's name, you get another gold coin."

"All right," he agrees.

I pull him close, telling him what Marike looks like and where she can be found. He scampers off into the crowded street, and I lean against the brick wall of a dilapidated storefront, the pile of dung neatly arranged for sale, a hand-scrawled sign at my feet.

Someone scoffs, and I glance up. A group of ladies walk past, casting me horrified glances and staring between me and the dung.

"That's the princess," one says.

"Imagine poor Otto, having to lie with a woman who collects animal feces."

"What a waste of royalty."

They giggle and continue on. Before I can stop myself, I reach for a patty and lob it down the street. It hits one woman in the rear. She whirls around and glares. I wave and tilt my head. "Poor Otto indeed," I laugh to myself.

Within half an hour, Helkin returns. "Gerd," he says, holding out his hand. "He's dead now."

"Gerd," I say, dropping the other coin into his hand and a few extra pentus from the patties I pretended to sell and to cover the one I tossed. "There's power in a name. Don't forget that."

He looks at me like I'm crazy again. I smile at him sadly, hoping he can make it through the winter, and then I head off down the street to meet Marike for the last time.

❧

The coast, where the streams from the Dangof Forest meet a finger of sea, are riddled with tunnels and caves that spill out onto the beach in a series of brackish pools. Massive boulders are draped in moss and lichen, food for the picnin birds that cluster on their surfaces and leave behind streaks of white scheiz.

I wait by a boulder pile—one that Ectarian children claim resembles a saltz mine troll and have nicknamed Bagnaz—hoping

Marike will soon appear. I half hope she will not, and I will not have to tell her the dreaded news that her dreams are fruitless, that she will never climb. Had the king spoken such to Ellias when it came to my training? Or was my mentor simply more courageous than me? Whatever the case, Marike is eleven, and I cannot condemn her to a life of misery such as the one Rayna already endures.

"Klarke?" Marike whispers from the dark mouth of a tunnel leading into one of the caves behind the boulder pile.

"Here," I say, moving quickly into the dark to join her.

She is not alone. Another girl waits with her, nervously fiddling with the waistband of a surprisingly clean green apron, her eyes wide in the glimmering light that reflects off the water beyond the cave.

"Who are you?" I ask the girl.

"That's Winola," Marike says. "She wants to learn to climb too. And there's more. Five of us, but the others had to work. Nola's from the Westlich, so she doesn't have to work. We want to form our own team."

A team of girls? Of five girls who want to band together to learn to climb? For a moment I am astonished, impressed, and proud. I have always been alone. Always the only woman. What I wouldn't have given to have had comrades such as these! Not that it matters. What they ask for is impossible.

"I can't," I whisper, the words a bitter taste in my mouth.

"Why not? If you can train one, why not more?" Marike demands. "We can pay. Not sure how, but we'll figure it out."

"Oh, Marike, no." I wave my hand, feeling like a fraud, like the worst kind of mentor. "It's not the money. I can't train anyone anymore, including you."

"Why not?" she asks.

"If I keep training you, the king has threatened to make you a brideprize before you're even a woman. I can't do it. I won't do that to you. To any of you."

Marike hesitates, glances at Winola, and then finally looks back at me, her face set and determined. "I don't care," she says.

"I do. And you would, too, if you knew what it meant."

"I don't care," she repeats, her gaze blade-sharp and insistent in the dim light of the cave. "You said you'd make me matter. You promised."

"I won't risk your life for climbing. It's not worth it."

"Gerd was allowed to risk his life climbing," she insists stubbornly. "I want that same chance."

I grab her shoulders and fight the tears filling my eyes. "And it killed him, Marike. This isn't some game. They killed Gerd, and they'll do worse to get to me. I can't do it. I can't carry that responsibility. There's already too much blood on my hands. I'm so sorry. You deserve better. You deserve your freedom. But I can't give it to you. Not yet."

The three of us stand silently in the dim cave. Angry tears fall from Marike's eyes. I have let them down, I know. But I have also saved them. Someday they will see that.

Marike wipes her nose on her sleeve; then she straightens and, turning to Winola, declares, "I'll train you then. I'll train all of us."

"Marike don't—"

"I thought you were brave. I thought you were the bravest person in all the worlds. But you're a coward."

"You're going to get someone hurt."

"Come on, Nola." Marike grabs Winola's hand, and they turn to leave. "We don't need her."

"Wait." I pull the small wooden box out of my satchel. "It's ulrind. For your mother. Have her take it every day for the next three months. If the pulmonosis clears, she'll be okay."

Marike hesitates, her eyes glimmering with tears before she grabs the box and dashes out of the cave, Winola in tow.

I breathe deeply, feeling the weight of failure deep in my bones. I let them down. I bowed before a hateful king. But I have so many glass spheres that I am juggling, so many lives already to account for, to protect, I will not see Marike consigned to an abusive marriage because of me. And there will be time, I console myself, once we remove King Adolar from power;

there will be time for a female Ascenditure team. Marike just needs to be patient a little while longer.

"Everything will be fine," I murmur aloud as I return to the beach, which is strangely quiet. The picnin birds have returned to their nests, the wind has stilled, and the bay is a placid gray beneath the darkly rising cloudbank in the skies above the Bay of Hammonhoff. A storm is coming. I shiver as the temperature drops and start briskly back to town.

10

The Rektburg's throne room is crowded to capacity with curious onlookers, mainly adels in their silks and furs standing on tiptoe and elbowing their neighbors for a better view of the dais. King Adolar lounges on the throne, one leg casually crossed over another, a habitual sneer curling his lip. Guards, rigid in their green tunics, line the outer perimeter of the room and flank each exit. I stand with the Ascenditures, twisting my hands together behind my back in nervous anticipation. A low rumble fills the room as Ectarian citizens murmur among themselves—it is a monumental occasion, after all; it is not often that Ainarians are granted an audience with King Adolar or that the Ascenditures might be permitted to compete against their climbers.

A wooden panel slides open to our left and two guards stride into the room, followed by a man and a woman dressed in worn red cloaks and travelers pants. Naisae walks, proud and erect, exuding the confidence and grace I would have expected from the leader of the Parvanatari. I feel a pang of envy at a northern kingdom where women are so elevated in rank and prestige. What would I not have given for such a chance? Or Marike and Winola? The man who accompanies her—might it be Losan? I fidget, shifting to peer around Aedan's shoulders to get a better look. My breath catches when I realize the Ainarian man is looking right at me. He grins and blows me a quick two-fingered kiss.

The two captives are brought before King Adolar and forced to their knees.

"It seems your king's wish for a peace climb will be granted, Naisae of Ainar. I have agreed to send my climbers north, but I will require assurances they will return. While this boy may accompany you, your remaining companions will remain in Ectair until my Ascenditures arrive back in Kietsch."

"Understood," she replies. The candlelight gleams in her eyes, gives her skin the appearance of dark satin and throws her intricately braided hair into elegant relief. "And I am Naisae of Ubana, not of Ainar. Kobo is my heart home," she says, holding the king's gaze with her own. "King Gyalzen has also sent an offering of goods, which we have stored outside the city—gold and jade from the Parowan mountains; silk thread from the Eastern Plains spiders. And, lastly, and perhaps of greatest interest to your lordship is information regarding a traitor."

The murmur among the adels—chatting as they were about these two unexpected arrivals—stills to absolute silence as the king leans forward, eyes narrowed and hands gripping the armrests of his throne. "And who might that be?" he demands.

"A man who goes by the name of Obid," Naisae replies.

My heart lurches. Is Naisae an enemy of Obid? If so, she is an enemy of mine as well. Kiel and I exchange worried glances. Has Obid been captured? Does Naisae intend to turn him over to Adolar in exchange for some other provision?

"I will require more specific information, Naisae of Ubana." The king waves one hand in irritable dismissal. "My kingdom is vast, inhabited by individuals who go by all manner of names. We will speak further of this matter in private. I will have my guards retrieve your gifts and we shall discuss your departure. Now, Aedan Pfaller, step forward."

Aedan steps forward, and I notice Haydrich intently watching all that unfolds just as a bellsnake fixates upon its prey. Veit, scowling, looks like a petulant child who has been sidelined in favor of one less deserving.

"Naisae, this is Aedan Pfaller, the lead climber of the Ascenditures. Aedan, you will introduce Naisae to the Ascenditures and work with her to coordinate this challenge. Naisae, we will speak later."

King Adolar moves toward the paneled exit to one side of

the throne room, guards flanking him, then pauses, turning to me. “And how is my dear daughterbride? When can we expect a princeling?”

He glances toward my belly, and I feel as if my guts curl and shrivel in loathing. Nevertheless, I force a demure smile to my lips and incline my head in a bow. And then he is gone, and I can breathe again. As is customary, the adels reluctantly file out of the throne room after their king has left, glancing over their shoulders at the foreign climbers and muttering amongst themselves as to what this unusual alliance might mean for Ectair.

Once the hall has quietened, with only the guards standing still, to rigid attention, Aedan moves toward Naisae. “You are most welcome in our home,” he says. “Please, come meet our team.”

Aedan proceeds to introduce us by name, detailing briefly when we each joined the Ascenditures and particular routes at which we have individually excelled. “It is a pleasure to meet you all,” Naisae says graciously after Aedan has finished. “Especially the famed Fram Ascher,” she adds with a warm smile in my direction.

“I am, as you are aware,” she says to us all, “Naisae of Ubana, the captain of the Parvanatari, and this is Nopsan Janbo, a member of our climbing team.”

Nopsan? I glance at the dark-haired man who stands behind Naisae. My heart sinks. It had been foolish to believe that he could have been my childhood friend returned miraculously from across the darkened sea. I know as well as anyone that people don’t return from the dead. If they did, I wouldn’t be so alone. I blink and say goodbye to my friend once again.

“King Gyalzen invites you all to join us in a unity climb to the summit of Mount Opasno,” Naisae continues, her voice clear and strong, filling the room and echoing from the rafters, “the highest and most challenging mountain in all of historic Galvaith. Our king believes the rift between our two lands has festered for too long and that the best way to forge a new alliance is to climb together, an undertaking of great skill and accomplishment that both our kingdoms value."

I notice Tizian scowling his displeasure; while he revels at the idea of a climb, I know he hates the idea of a woman in charge—and not just a woman but a foreign woman with skin and hair darker than those within our borders. She is me, but worse. She is his nightmare, and I welcome her reign of terror if it shakes the foundations of his narrow-minded soul. Burkhart and Veit look similarly scornful; only Russet offers her a genuine smile. But I am sure none of this is unexpected to Naisae.

"We have a long road ahead; we travel first to Hidel, and once there, we will take a little time to train and acclimate before tackling the mountain. Opasno is not only the grandest mountain in Ainar and Galvaith, but also the deadliest. The mountain claims the lives of one in every fifteen who climb it."

I cannot help but think of Mount Bonen, where only a quarter of our team survived. Six of our eight had been left behind on its icy slopes. I think of Otto's sister unknowingly hiding out in the north and of Obid on the run. Of my mother, who smuggled unwanted baby girls into the frozen lands above us. Before, I had risked everything to climb. Now, I will risk it all for the truth.

"Bring what gear you have with you. We will provide proper mountaineering equipment when you get to Ainar. And we will train you to climb as a mountaineer, not just a rock jock. If you live and stand on top of the world, breathing air that tastes like Orna's breath, you will return home as more than heroes. You will return as children of the gods."

These are seductive words for climbers who already consider themselves to be an elite few blessed by the gods with skills and abilities that so few can claim. Veit is nodding in agreement, and I, too, feel a thrill—a sense of divine power that is as archaic and as old as the first diemant.

"The king has ordered our departure, and so each of us are expected to go north. However, as the leader of our team, I also require your assent. While we may be subject to royal decree," his voice drops slightly so the guards are unable to hear, "on the mountain, we act as one, one team together; and for this all of us need to want this for ourselves, for our team, not just for our king. Do I have an *aye*, Burk?"

"Is the backup team ready to step in?" Burkhart asks.

"Bastian has lined up eight of the best climbers to fill in while we're gone. Repairs to Ectair's critical structures will continue in our absence."

"Then aye," Burkhart says.

"Aye," Russet contributes.

"Aye," Veit adds.

"Aye," Tizian grumbles. "Though I'm not sure this isn't an ambush."

"If we wanted you dead, friend, we would have climbed the walls to your bedchamber and slit your throat in the night before you even knew we were there," Nopsan says matter-of-factly.

Tizian opens his mouth to protest, but Kiel speaks first.

"Aye, I'm in," he says.

"And me," Dieter says.

Haydrich has yet to speak—I would have thought he'd be the first to chime in, to declare his support for an opportunity to exhibit his climbing superiority. His words of rebellion and regicide, confided to me as we hung under the bridge, come back to me. How does several months' absence from our kingdom play into his plans? Perhaps Kiel is right, and the Dark Promise is nothing more than a blustery pretense by men who wish for importance.

Kiel elbows me, and Haydrich turns and fixes his cool gaze on me. Is Haydrich waiting on my commitment?

Naisae smiles encouragingly. I need to find out if she is friend or foe, but I also want to hear her stories. I want everything this adventure offers.

"Aye," I say.

"Aye," Haydrich says quickly, almost before I finish speaking. What game is he playing at? I muse, glancing over at him with narrowed eyes.

"We will meet tomorrow at the gym and review final details," Aedan says.

"We will need to leave very soon," Naisae adds, "in order to meet our climbing window on Opasno. Once vintazite has fully set in, we will lose the opportunity."

As the climbers disperse, I pull Haydrich aside. "I know you're up to something. Whatever it is, I want no part of it."

"Of course you know I'm up to something. I told you about it," he replies with a sly smile. "And this is bigger than you and me. It's bigger even than this supposed peace-climb with Ainar. It is all in motion now; I could no more stop this than drink all the water from the Rolag Sea. Naisae said that when we summit Opasno, we'll feel like gods." He leans closer so his lips brush against my ear, and I feel the heat of his breath. "I don't need a mountain peak to feel like that. I'm already almost there."

"You're insane," I exclaim, stepping away from him.

He laughs. "See you tomorrow, Klarke," he says quietly. "My offer still stands if you're interested."

I watch him stride away, feeling a rising foreboding about what lies ahead. Unpredictability, generally, can be terrifying. Unpredictability on the deadliest mountain in the known worlds is often fatal. I remember the terrors of Mount Bonen and send a quick prayer to Orna that Opasno will be different.

❧

I rifle through my trunk at the gym, building a small pile of ropes, slings, and karabiners. I add my climbing skirt and blouse to the pile, wondering if the Ainarian women climb in skirts. Doubtful. Naisae had mentioned providing us with climbing gear upon arrival. I think of Naisae's dusty traveling pants and hope that my gear, too, will be befitting of a climber, irrespective of gender. I jam my belongings into a rucksack and fasten it closed.

"Ever climbed an actual mountain?" Nopsan asks, lounging against the doorframe. "One with glaciers that will swallow you whole and avalanches that will bury you so deep in Orna's bosom you'll never find your way out."

"I know well what you mean," I say, rising to my feet. "I pulled two friends out of a crevasse on Mount Bonen and watched as an avalanche swallowed the others."

"So you're not just a rock jock then?" he replies, twisting a length of sisal rope between his fingers. "Good to know."

"Why did you throw fish guts at me during the vintazite festival?" I ask.

"Did I do that?" He glances down at the butterfly knot he's just tied. "I don't know. It seemed amusing at the time."

"You yelled *fischbomb*."

"Well, that's what it was, wasn't it? A fischbomb?"

"So we have never met before, you and me?" I persist.

He ties the rope into a goosetail and tosses it to me. Catching it, I glance down at the manner in which he's threaded the rope—he's good.

"How would we possibly?" he asks, with the arch of a brow.

"I guess we couldn't. You just reminded me of someone I used to know."

Nopsan paces the room, glancing idly around at the stacks of climbing gear, the ropes and harnesses, all being readied for the journey. "You're very pretty, you know," he says casually. "It's a shame you just got married. I'd love to court you."

I peer up, glaring into his dark, narrow eyes that twinkle mischievously. "You don't even know me."

"I have a good feeling for people," he says with a slow smile and a wink. "And I think you're one of the good ones."

"Look around you," I snap. "There is an overabundance of self-bloated, pompous men. I have neither the time nor the patience for you or your games." I heft my traveling bag across my shoulder and stride out of the room, satisfied at his downcast expression.

I drop my bag on the gym floor next to the others. For a moment I take my fill of the old place, of the giant smokestacks, the crumbling bricks, the dust and leather—which reminds me, still, of Ellias. His words are always with me, encouraging me to take the jump, make the reach, and trust my feet. I wonder if any of us will return to see our climbing gym again. How many victims will Opasno claim, and will I be among them? Despite my fears of the future, I know Ellias will offer guidance from beyond the darkened sea, his voice a source of wisdom.

"How are you feeling about all of this?" Kiel asks, dropping his bag next to mine.

"Do you remember my first climb up Fitzhan? When you showed me Ainar through the clouds and told me not to trust what I had heard about them?"

"Of course."

"I am not afraid of Ainar," I tell him. "But I am afraid of the mountain. And," I drop my voice to a whisper, "I'm afraid of what might happen if we can't find Otto's sister. If we are unable to remove Adolar from power."

Kiel opens his mouth to answer but is interrupted by Dieter, who throws his bag on the pile.

"Everything okay?" he asks.

"Yeah, all good," Kiel says loudly. "Just a pep talk for the climb ahead."

"And our immediate objectives?" Dieter asks, his voice low. Climbers bustle around, laughing and talking as they test their harnesses, coil sisal ropes, and replenish their dust satchels. There is little chance our furtive conversation will be overhead.

"Our plan is simple, with three goals," I say. "The first is to find Otto's twin sister; the second, to find Obid. But we must be wary of the Ainarians; it seems they are ready to sacrifice Obid to King Adolar. If we can find him, he will have answers for us."

"And the third?" Kiel asks.

"Survive the climb," I say grimly. "I need you both for this and for everything to come."

We join hands, the three of us—a gesture of determination, of the love that binds us together, and of the work we must do on behalf of those we leave behind. For you, Marike, I muse. And for all the girls who want to climb.

Aedan calls the team to attention as Naisae and Nopsan join us.

"We leave in one week. That gives us time to ready the ships and gear and for Naisae to send a letter to Hidel, so that they may prepare for our coming. It will be a long and difficult journey." On a center table he unrolls an old Galvaithian map, one that features both Ectair and Ainar, and even a portion of Kobo to the southwest. I gasp to see the scrolled writing in the upper corner. *Standard Map of Galvaith by Dr. Alois Vitus.* A doctor. A historian. A map maker. The man holds as many secrets as my mother.

"There is only one remaining bridge by which to cross the Waste." Aedan points to the Bridge of Worlds, north of Fort Karne in the North Inland Sea kreison. "We will travel down the Sevier River to Lastil and then journey by coach to the crossing. Once we cross into Ainar, we will make the rest of the journey by foot, except for the dangerous crossing of the Frozen Sea of Ard to Hidel, which we will make in ice boats."

As I examine our route, my excitement grows. These are places I have never seen, places my generation has only heard of in stories. And now, for me, they will become real—new mountains, new plants, new animals…all inhabiting a strange and new terrain.

"We look forward to welcoming you to Ainar," Naisae says with a smile. "The journey will be long, but once we have reached our destination, you will all be our honored guests."

"But whatever ye do, friends," Tizian growls, "don't eat Ainarian meat. Unless ye like children's liver and old man's tongue!"

Veit and Burkhart laugh, as much as Burkhart can laugh. It sounds more like rocks tumbling down a hill in a metal barrel.

"Enough!" Aedan barks. "This is a serious journey, Tizian, for serious climbers. There is no room for that scheiz. Do you understand? Any more of that talk from any of you, you're out. Not just from this climb, but from the Ascenditures."

"You don't have that power," Burkhart mumbles. "We answer to only one person, and it is not you."

"It is me," Aedan hisses, stabbing a finger in Burkhart's chest. "Test it again, friend, and find out."

In the uneasy silence that follows, Tizian glares at Naisae, who smiles back.

"We only feast on the flesh of our enemies, Tizian," she says. "Not that of our children and our respected elderly."

There is a ripple of laughter as Tizian's face turns deep red with embarrassment. Whatever happens in the frozen north, I reflect, one thing I am certain of: I am very much looking forward to spending time with Naisae of Ubana and learning what it truly means to be an indestructible female climber.

11

I clasp Rayna's hand as we make our way down the subterranean corridor that connects the Geistich to the Nied Tower. I glance over at her face and delight in the simple happiness I see there—an afternoon stolen away from her domineering husband so we may escape to the Maja Grotto. A basket slung over my shoulder is crammed with rolls, cheeses, jellies, ham, and a bottle of fresh hugalberi juice. The walls here, like the palace corridors above, are lined with massive paintings, intricately woven tapestries, porcelain vases, and elaborate sculptures. Silias trails several feet behind us, sufficient to provide a small measure of privacy.

"Why would they keep such exquisite art underground?" Rayna asks, stopping before an oil painting of the Celebern Fields. The flowers are lit to brilliant pinks, yellows, and purples in the dying light of Cleos. The bright pillowed white of clouds scuddle across the sky.

"The fields really look like that," I say, staring at the artwork. I remember Ellias crouched next to me in the field, showing me how to harvest solans. His bald head shining in Cleos's rays. My fingers buried in the dry dirt, searching for roots. "Unbelievably beautiful."

"I envy you, Klarke. To have seen such sights. The painting looks so real; I feel as if I can reach out to touch it, to feel the velvet petals of the ulrind flowers under my fingers, the soft brush of grass under my feet." Rayna closes her eyes, a smile crossing her lips as if she has managed to transport herself to that magical place.

I want to touch the painting, to feel close to the meadow's heat and Ellias's memory, but I keep my hand at my side. "I can teach you how to get there, if you'd like," I offer.

Opening her eyes, Rayna laughs, girlish and carefree—a

sound that I had almost forgotten she could make. "Oh, you're serious," she asks, mouth open in astonishment. Then, laughing again, she says, "Do you remember that time when we were thirteen and you took me to Vether's Fel?"

I grin and look at the arched ceiling. "Maybe."

"I made it ten feet before I was screaming for you to let me down." She shudders theatrically, and we continue walking. "I'm not sure there's anything I fear more than heights. Perhaps Hildegroth."

"Then I will bring you back a bundle of fluset grass next time I go. You can hold it next to a roaring fire, close your eyes, and pretend you are sunning beneath Cleos's rays."

"I'd settle for that," she says with a warm smile.

I feel a pang of heartache for her miserable marriage, and I wish I could just steal her away; I'd give her a room in the palace filled with flowers, artwork, and all the delicacies she could possibly eat. Otto and I have already decided—the first royal decree he will make after ascending the throne will be to allow the dissolution of all marriages, should the wife so request.

We enter the Nied tower and descend nearly one hundred steps to the Maja Grotto. The stairs continue down to the lower levels—cellars for wine, dried herbs, and root vegetables stored in large wooden casks; then below those, in the dark and damp, far from the light of Cleos, lie the dungeons where Naisae and Losan were imprisoned, and where the other Ainarians still reside. They must feel as if they've been buried alive, I think with a shudder.

Shaking off these dismal thoughts, I lead Rayna into the circular foyer at the base of the tower. A velveteen bench is positioned against the wall beneath the stern portrait of an aged adel in a hideous wig. A door of fizhte wood on the far wall, its exterior decorated with a simple series of etched Xs, announces the entrance to the Maja Grotto.

"You may wait here," I tell Silias.

"I have been instructed to keep you in my sights, princess," Silias insists.

"Well, I am going to be entirely unclothed in there, and I am not sure my husband would approve. Shall we request his permission?" I ask, unable to suppress a smile as Silias's face, usually so frustratingly impassive and taciturn, turns a deep shade of red.

"Very well," he mutters. "I shall sit here, risking the king's wrath, so that you might have your frolicking fun."

"We appreciate your sacrifice, Silias," I reply with mock seriousness as Rayna giggles beside me.

Passing through the wooden door, we enter a tunnel carved out of dark granite. A hanging lamp at the entrance illuminates six feet or so, and beyond, in the darkness, we see small red lights flicker on and off, casting a warm glow upon the walls.

"Are these lihtbugs?" Rayna exclaims in wonder, reaching out her hand. "It is like something from a lecaltale!"

"Yes," I reply softly. "They live only underground. And in caves. Sometimes we see them in the lava tubes." The tiny insects drop and rise from the tunnel floor and settle upon the small ferns that grow from crevices, spilling in delicate green fronds like little waterfalls. Their light flickers like a thousand tiny red candles.

"I've only ever heard of them," Rayna says. "A friend who works in the mines told me how the lihtbugs saved his life after a cave-in. He was alone in the dark for six days before his crew could dig him out. He said the lihtbugs, with their little red lights, were sent by Orna to keep his spirits up."

"Yes, I can see how one might believe such a thing," I say. "It is almost as if Orna has lit the stars on fire and sent them to light Laren's darkest regions."

Ahead, we hear the rush of water and feel the cool mist of the falls against our cheeks. Rayna runs a hand across the cold stone where water collects and drips to the floor beneath.

"Come," I say. "The grotto is just ahead."

The tunnel veers slightly to the right, and we see a lavender glow that exudes from the pool.

Rayna comes to an abrupt halt as we turn the corner. Three

waterfalls cascade from mossy crevices into a pool the size of the Rektburg's throne room; the water is lit to a glowing turquoise by algae that float upon its surface. A small rocky outcrop in the center of the pool showcases a statue of Laren holding a sculpted torch from which a bright blue flame emerges. A fishing net hangs from his other hand. A small pathway winds its way around the edges of the pool beneath archways festooned with ferns, ivy, and purple flowers with broad-leaved plants below that absorb the light emitted by the algae. The roof of the cave rises to a hundred feet above, and we hear the sweet song of the brimbas bird amid the red constellation of flickering lihtbugs.

"This is breathtaking," Rayna says, casting her gaze around as if in disbelief that such magical places might exist.

"Otto told me that King Berengar Schmultz III added the grotto to the Rektburg in honor of his beloved queen, Lady Maja from Kobo."

"His queen was from Kobo?" Rayna's eyes widen.

"Apparently, a few hundred years ago people didn't care so much about where you came from."

"Wouldn't that be nice? To not have to worry about where you are from and what rights that might deny you?" Rayna sighs and stares at the pool. The dark complexion of her smooth hair and narrow eyes are clear signs of her Ainarian blood—an ancestry that has subjected her to ridicule and hate. She might well have ended up in the labor camps should Obid not have brought us together when he did.

"The water here comes from underground thermal vents, so the pool is warm enough to swim in," I say, hoping to cheer her up. Rayna's face lights up like the flowers.

Dropping the basket and our pile of clothes under an archway, we dive into the pool. The warm water sluices over my skin, and I revel in the freedom of being able to swim unrestricted by clothing. As water people, Ectarian parents teach their children to swim in the Sevier River as soon as they can walk. The purpose, however, is not for leisure or fun, but to know how to survive should you fall off a boat or pier. It is hard to muster enthusiasm for swimming in the polluted waters downriver of the glue-factory runoff.

But now, Rayna swims in circles, her eyes closed in blissful appreciation of the clean, warm water. It is as if she is a tolvalus, diving and ducking beneath the surface with a kick of her pale feet, then emerging with a wide smile, her hair sleek against her head. I am content to float on my back and gaze at the dark cavity of the cave filled with an abundance of flickering red stars.

A little later we retrieve the food, pull out a small wooden lakboat from under the reeds—the kind small boys commandeer when learning how to sail—and paddle to the small island. I steer the boat between lumps of glowing blue algae that float upon the surface, tiny minfish beneath nipping at the luminescent clusters. At Laren's feet, we unroll a blanket and unpack our lunch.

"This is my favorite day ever," Rayna declares as she chews on a fig. I pass her the hugalberi juice and slice some cheese onto a hunk of bread. I hand it to her with a napkin, grateful that her appetite has returned. Perhaps the lihtbugs have reawakened her desire to live and to thrive, just as they had done for her miner friend in his days of darkness.

"Mine too," I mumble through a mouthful of hagenjelly cheese.

A brimbas bird lands on Laren's foot and eyes our bread with gleaming black eyes. I toss it a pinch, and the bird leaps into the air, its feathers transforming with its movement from black to blue to a shimmering orange. It seizes the nub of bread in its beak and flits away, the underside of its wings dotted in white. "I haven't been in water since my father drowned," Rayna muses.

I nod in quiet understanding—while my father's ship sank at sea, Rayna's father fell off Pohle Pier in a drunken stupor. "Did you like being in the water?" I ask, seeking to divert her thoughts to more cheerful topics.

"I loved it," Rayna exclaims with a smile. "I thought it would scare me, reminding me of all that I have lost. But it did the opposite. It makes me think of all the wonder the world has to offer, all of life that is yet to be experienced. And you, Klarke? I can tell you were enjoying it!"

I cock my head and purse my lips. "I love that it is so quiet, that nobody is watching me. I love the warm feel of water against my skin. I feel completely, utterly, and wonderfully free."

"Yes!" Rayna agrees, nodding vigorously. "It is all those things." She grows quiet, her face pensive. "Are you afraid to climb Opasno?"

"It's hard to explain," I reply after a moment, pulling the blanket around my shoulders. "I wish I could say I wasn't afraid, but I think every time I make a summit, where the mountain is steep and the way is treacherous, I feel a buzzing in my heart. A thrumming of my soul. And I think that movement inside of me is a kind of fear.

Not overwhelming, but present. I imagine my body will hum when I stand at Base Camp and stare up at the summit."

"I am afraid for you."

"I know." I lean into her and rest my head on her shoulder. "I'm sorry to put you through this."

"I feel like your mother," she says with a laugh, dropping her head atop mine. "Always worrying."

"Thanks, Mum."

"Anytime, sûssa," she says. "You'll be gone for many moons."

"I will."

"Do you think you'll be able to find Otto's twin?"

"I don't know."

We fall silent again. I am reluctant to admit to Rayna that I'm embarking on an impossible mission. The kingdom of Ainar, home to millions of people, stretches all the way from Miter's Waste to Dristo, and even beyond the edges of any known map. Otto's twin could live anywhere, go by any name—for it certainly won't be Adolar—and look nothing at all like her sibling.

"I don't think the gods care about twins at all," Rayna says sharply. "I think it's a stupid story created by men to bolster their own political and social power. It just makes no sense; if twins of the opposite sex represented Azura and Cleos, the children of the gods, then why would the gods demand we destroy one of them? And how convenient for all the men that it is the baby girls that are murdered, not the boys. Orna would never abide such a monstrous waste of life and potential."

Considered ill omens sent by Laren, different-gendered twins serve as harbingers of doom, foretelling the end of a family's lineage. The discovery of the birth of twins exiled the family to a commune in the Mountains of the Unknown in the southern reaches of the Calvia Plains; the newborns, however, are not so fortunate—they are both killed in a ritualistic sacrifice, intended to keep the taint of doom from their Ectarian neighbors. Parents with newly born twins of different sexes will frequently dispose of one—invariably the girl child—immediately after birth in secret, so the kingdom never finds out.

"If my brother hadn't died at birth, my parents would have thrown me into the sea," Rayna says.

Like Otto, Rayna was a twin. *She was meant for the sea*—the words thrum through my mind like an echo; an echo of what? Then I recall the words of the man from the pier, the grimy addict with the green-streaked eyes. *You were meant for the sea,* he said. Could he have mistaken me for Rayna?

"I need to get going," Rayna says, interrupting my thoughts as she rises to her feet.

"I will miss you." My heart lurches painfully to think of leaving her behind, and I make a mental note to ask Otto to check in on her regularly.

"I will miss you too, Klarke. Take care of yourself, and come back to me."

"I will. I promise."

"One last swim before we leave?" Her eyes twinkle, and before I answer, she's splashed into the pool. I follow, chasing her through the water, but she's too fast. Rayna's little body is full of unseen strength.

"Are you sure Laren isn't your father?" I laugh as we dry ourselves off and pack up the picnic. "You swim like a sea tûndle."

She shakes out her hair and climbs into the lakboat. "I mean, aren't we all technically Laren's children?"

"I guess so." I peer back at the towering statue as we row away, missing my real father. Wishing he would be on the climb with me, teaching me how to arrest a fall, showing me better ways to tie knots, standing on the summit of Mount Opasno cheering as I kiss the top of the world. All I have left of a father is an angry god and ever-slipping memories of a man whose hugs made me feel safe in this world of monsters.

12

Before leaving the palace, I wind a pink ribbon through my braid, vowing to carry with me all the women who have sacrificed themselves to the cause as well as the many who struggle through each day just trying to survive. The women of Ectair have paid the ultimate price for me to climb, for me to now journey to Ainar and stand on top of the world—they have rallied in the streets, burned buildings, even hung from the end of a noose. I wear this ribbon for all of us; I make this climb for all of us.

A young boy lugs my gear onto the boat, and I am gripped by a sudden flashback of boarding another boat for Mount Bonen, when I dropped some of my equipment, and Gerd bent to help, offering a smile, friendship, and trust. I mishandled all those things as much as I did the gear I dropped that day.

We travel on just one boat this time, for it is only the Ascenditures, the two climbers from Ainar, a cook, and a crew of three. Most of the other Ascenditures have already arrived and lean over the deck railing, joking and laughing in the excitement of our upcoming journey. The docks are crowded with excited citizens ready to wave us off; conspicuous are the women with pink ribbons threaded through their hair and tied in bows about their wrists. Aedan lingers over his farewells, hugging his wife and two children. He is the only Ascenditure with children. I said my farewells to Otto at the palace. I kissed Rayna's cheek and promised to be safe when we left the grotto. My list of nearest kin is short.

Tucked away in the depths of my bag is the Death's Whisper crystal Gio gave me before he died. It seems safer, somehow, to keep it in my possession always. I toss my bag on a bunk that folds down from the starboard side of the boat; an oil lamp hangs from the rafters alongside. I won't rock in a hammock listening to my friends grow ill on this trip, though I imagine I will still hear the cries of Petrus and Ingo in the wind and creaking wood. If only the darkened sea were far enough away that it kept the ghosts at bay.

Later that evening, after the ship has departed from the dock, I find a quiet spot at the bow and lean over the railing. Starlight washes the waves to silver and occasional sistphins leap alongside the boat, their orange-spotted backs gleaming. The breeze caresses my skin and plays with my hair, and for the first in a long time, I feel that I am inhabiting a small patch of peace—free of King Adolar's schemes, Silias's stern presence, and even the expectations set by a court, and a kingdom, for their princess. Perhaps, for a time, I can just be Klarke Ascher, an Ascenditure, a climber, a girl with a dream to summit Mount Opasno.

I reach into my pocket and retrieve my mother's handkerchief, rubbing the stitched cursive with my fingertips. *Find Ramanata*, it says. Ramanata must be Otto's sister. This quest is not just mine but also my mother's. I will find Ramanata to set the kingdom free and also to set my mother free.

Dieter and Kiel cross the deck, each taking a place at the rail beside me. I lean my shoulder against Kiel for a moment, appreciating his presence, and send a smile Dieter's way.

"May I?" Dieter asks, gesturing toward the handkerchief. "What happens to Otto when we find his sister, when we find Ramanata?"

"I don't know," I admit. "But they won't hurt him."

"How can you know that?" Dieter asks, staring out across the river. Softly rounded hills appear on the port side, dark on the horizon beneath the wash of stars. "I know you want him to be king, Klarke, but if the Adolar line is compromised, they will not let him rule."

"King Adolar will hang," Kiel says softly. "For his lies and his treason. Otto is innocent of his father's crimes. The parliament might banish him rather than make him king, but he will not face a hangman's noose."

"I would leave with him," Dieter says softly, passing the handkerchief back to me. "I won't let him go alone."

"You could go to Ainar," I say, covering Dieter's clenched grip on the rail with one hand. "You could climb for the Parvanatari. Otto is smart and capable. I bet he could get a position in King Gyalzen's parliament."

"Perhaps," he says. "But who would be king in Ectair, then? King Adolar could be followed by a successor far worse."

We stand in silence for a moment, each of us contemplating the horrors of a reign worse than Adolar's. Could such a thing be possible?

"Do you know what lies beyond The Gate?" Dieter asks. "What lands lie in the farthest stretches of the Rolag Sea?"

"I've heard it's entirely uncharted," Kiel says. "Nobody knows what lies out there."

"I could chart the western lands," Dieter says. "Why not? Perhaps Otto might come with me."

"What an adventure that would be," I say with a smile.

"We should probably get some sleep," Kiel says, one hand gentle on my back. "We can't solve it all tonight."

As we leave the rail, we hear voices and heavy booted steps on the stairs ascending to the main deck. A finger to my lips, I motion to Kiel and Dieter to move behind the small cabin structure that rises from the main deck. From this vantage point, we see the heads of Tizian and Burkhart emerge from below.

"—he'd pay me royally to do it, Burk," Tizian is saying, his voice quick and furtive in the dark. "Come on, man. I need your help."

I glance over at Dieter and Kiel, the whites of their eyes gleaming in the starlight. Kiel shrugs, with a slight shake of his head.

"Sorry, Tiz, but my loyalty is to Aedan," Burkhart replies steadily.

"To Aedan? To that spineless foze lover? I wish Gio had told me what he was up to. I could have helped him then, and this would all be over."

I hear a thudding sound and peer around the corner of the cabin to see Burkhart shoving Tizian up against one of the smokestacks, his forearm thrust against his throat. "I don't care for either of the fozies on this boat, but I care less for treason."

Treason? Has someone offered Tizian money to murder me? Or Naisae? The climbers from Ainar?

"Take my advice, Tiz," Burkhart mutters, his voice low. I strain to hear him over the creak of the deck, the whistle of wind, and the wash of water against the hull. "Climb the fieckin mountain and go home." Then we hear booted feet crossing the deck and descending the stairs; after a moment, the other follows, and above-decks is again quiet.

I turn to Kiel and Dieter. "What was—?" I begin, before a dark figure slips over the side of the cabin roof above and descends with soft footfalls to the deck beside us.

"Haydrich, what in Laren's name are you doing?" Kiel asks.

"Klarke," Haydrich says, ignoring Kiel and Dieter, his gaze locked on mine. "I can tell you exactly who will take Adolar's place, and I can guarantee the safety of your sweet prince if you join me instead of getting in my way. I can also tell you where to find them."

"Find who exactly?" Dieter asks.

"Them?" I say, one eyebrow raised. Certainly, Haydrich overheard our earlier conversation, and certainly he would twist the information to his own nefarious purpose. It was just a matter of figuring out his game before he could use us all as pawns in it.

"The girls, of course," he replies.

Girls? Shock skitters up my spine. Could there have been two? Or was this all just trickery to divert our attention and allow Haydrich freedom to pursue his own agenda?

"I'm not your enemy, Klarke," Haydrich adds, clearly reading the skepticism crossing my face. "At least not yet. You'll have time while in the north to consider your options. The Dark Promise grows stronger every day; soon, a line will be drawn in the dirt, and anyone on the wrong side will be deemed an enemy." He pauses a moment, his sweeping glance taking in Kiel and Dieter—Kiel standing protectively at my shoulder; Dieter leaning against the starboard railing, arms crossed, a dubious expression on his face. "I am prepared," he continues, his voice low but steady, "to dispatch Tizian to the darkened sea to prove that I can be trusted."

"What?" I exclaim. "No!"

"I can also tell you who was behind the death of your friends on Mount Bonen. All we ask is your allegiance to the Dark Promise. Think about it." Moving closer, he taps my arm with one finger, his gaze narrowed and intent. "But don't wait too long." And then he is gone, across the deck and down the stairs to the cabin below.

"Klarke, he is a liar and clearly not far from being a murderer as well, as ready as he was to kill Tizian." Kiel wraps me in his arms and kisses the top of my head. Despite the warmth of his embrace, I feel my body shaking. "Anyone he believes should be our leader will also be a liar. Don't trust what he says, Klarke. Do not go to him for salvation."

"Kiel's right," Dieter contributes. "We have a plan. And we have people we trust. We must stay the course, retain our honor, and look after one another."

I nod, breathing deeply of the salty night air in an effort to slow my racing heart. "You are right, of course. But what if Haydrich can tell us of the 'other' Gio referred to before he died? What if he really can tell us who Ramanata is and where she can be found? If Haydrich can identify our enemies, wouldn't that make us safer on Opasno?"

"Klarke," Kiel says firmly, gripping my shoulders. "Trading one psychopath for another is not our mission. And of what use is any information he can provide if you do not trust the source?"

Of course Kiel is right, I reflect as I lie sleepless in my bunk later that night, the snores and snuffling of my fellow Ascenditures filling the night air with a familiar sound. Regardless, I cannot help but dwell upon the intelligence Haydrich offers and his intriguing use of the plural—*them.* What could he have meant?

In the days that follow, I spend as much time as possible above deck, watching the forested hills slip by the port side. We pass Camp Arema on our second day at sea, where Kiel's father, Imre Abel, is stationed. The metal roof of the barracks, nestled amidst the trees, flashes in the muted Cleoslight creeping through the clouds, as if signaling to ships at sea. Like a lighthouse, I muse, guiding the way to keep us from the perils of the darkened sea. If only life offered such surety; we are heading into the unknown without compass or guidance, without knowing who is friend and who is foe.

Imre Abel is the general of Ectair's northern forces, commanding a royal military unit one thousand strong. Kiel has told me a little about his father, of how he was his son's fiercest critic and greatest advocate during his youth. He worked ceaselessly, had little tolerance for fools and much for those who had earned his loyalty; he expected the same of his men—and his son.

Gio's grieving father, Severin Vincenz, is also stationed at Camp Arema. My thoughts turn to Liselotte, Gio's young sister, held captive by King Adolar. Might the king have allowed her to return home now that Gio is dead? Or has he kept her for some awful purpose in the depths of the Rektburg's dungeon? I promised Gio that I would find her, that I would ensure her freedom. I feel the weight of all the promises made like a heavy yoke about my neck and fervently hope I might live to keep them.

"You like to read?" A voice interrupts my dismal reverie, and I look up to see Nopsan's smiling face by my side.

The book, forgotten in my hand, is one that details the medicinal plants of the Dor Drillingt Islands.

"It keeps my mind occupied so I don't have to think about…

things." I place a pink ribbon in the book to mark my spot and close the cover.

"May I join you?" He nods toward the railing.

"Please," I say with a smile.

Nopsan joins me at the railing. His hair is the color of a diemant, his skin a dark copper from Cleos's rays; he offers me a wide grin, his teeth a white gleam in his dark face. "I think your boy Tizian is starting to like me. He sure spends a lot of time staring. You think he's obsessed?" he asks cheekily.

"Tizian stares at everyone he hates," I say with a laugh. "I wouldn't take it personally."

"Perhaps I should start my own intimidation campaign. See if I can outstare him. What do you think?"

I cannot help but chuckle, impressed at how Nopsan uses humor to make light of our situation, surrounded as he is by Ectarians who might willingly throw him overboard at any given time.

"I like your laugh," he says. "You don't do it often."

"There's not a lot for me to laugh about these days."

"That's a pity. When was the last time you remember laughing so hard you cried?"

"Not since I was a kid." I grin, recalling the memory. Losan sprinting down the pier, a fishmonger chasing him. Losan slipping on a strand of seaweed and sliding into a table stacked high with fish. The pyramid of fish crashing down, burying him in slimy scales and bringing down the wrath of two fishmongers. I'd hidden beneath a saltz cart, watching the whole thing, tears spilling down my face as the fish toppled from the table and bounced off his body. My stomach hurt the next day from laughing so hard.

I suspiciously turn toward Nopsan. He's so much like my old friend. Even the way he finds joy in mischief.

"Nopsan. Come!" Naisae stands at the other end of the deck, motioning for him to join her. Her face is serious, and her body is tense. I hope this has nothing to do with threats from the men on board.

He pats my shoulder and moves to leave. "Talk to you later, then. Watch for me in Tizian's shadow." With a wink, he strides across the deck and disappears behind the far steam stack with Naisae.

On the way to Lastil, we pass the Tono Hills, and I remember my wish when coming this way before to the Lecals, the fairies who live in these hills. I sought their blessings to grant me safety in the months ahead, and, in their wisdom, answers to who orchestrated the death of my fellow climbers on Mount Bonen. I am still alive, I muse, gazing at the soft hills that roll away toward the horizon in various shades of green. So at least the Lecals honored that part of my request.

"I'm back," I whisper. "Might you consider granting my second request?"

A light rain rolls through, dousing the hills in a misty shroud, but there is no sign of life—either of fairies or otherwise. No matter. I will not rely upon wishes or dreams or the magical creatures who grant them.

We pull into the Lastil harbor, and I can't help but peer east. The city of Kaiwa sits just downriver from the bustling port. I cannot look upon the city without thinking of Petrus and his father's face, red with rage, as he accused me of all but murdering his son. I feel a swell of shame, despite knowing full well that it was King Adolar who had been responsible for Petrus's death, not I. But the responsibility of acquiring justice for Petrus, of revealing Adolar's treachery, that burden is mine. And I silently send a prayer to Orna that Petrus's father might have found some semblance of peace.

Mount Bonen, too, lies in that direction, concealed now by thick clouds. I turn my gaze from the south side of the river to the north, toward Lastil and beyond. For ahead lie two formidable challenges: ascending Mount Opasno and surviving the effort; and unveiling the truth of what has happened in such a way that protects my loved ones and safeguards my soul. I shiver in the quickening breeze as we drift into the harbor. Is it possible, I wonder, to meet both such challenges and survive? And is it possible to maintain my honor and integrity when it seems that those around me have long since abandoned their own?

13

The journey from Lastil to Fort Karne is made in wagons and is joltingly uncomfortable on our hard wooden benches as we lurch through potholes in a poorly maintained road. Then, from Fort Karne, we progress on foot, each supplied with a fifty-pound rucksack filled with rocks.

"Training for Mount Opasno begins now," Naisae informs us.

Unlike Mount Bonen, where our training comprised a single day of technical instruction, our summit of Opasno will be well planned and, if Naisae has anything to do with it, well executed. The differing objective here, I acknowledge with grim satisfaction, is for us *not* to die.

The first day progresses smoothly, and we make our way amid laughter and easy conversation; we are all delighted to be traveling north, visiting the fabled Ainar that we have all heard so much about. At midday Russet entertains us with a stanzl-lied his mother used to sing, and we follow up with a popular marching song that sets us upon our way after the mealtime is over

Climbing mountains high and bold,
with hearts of courage, we are told.
Through rugged paths and icy snow,
To reach the summit, we will go.

It is an old song, written by climbers who lived in the Umlauf peninsula. No one knows the identity of the author, although some have claimed Lars Veber crafted the tune; Ellias, though, used to tell me his grandfather had learned it from a local farmer in whose company he ascended Mount Bonen.

The wind may howl, the skies may gray,
But onward, we will find our way.

Each peak we conquer, we'll proclaim,
In nature's beauty, we'll find our fame.

Kiel tells me that soldats also sing this tune under march. And I understand why—my feet feel lighter as I sing, and so too does my spirit. Dieter claps Russet on the back as both belt out the song in raucous accord. Burkhart's deep rumbling voice joins in and is surprisingly sonorous. His contribution to the music is soothing, if not his presence.

We all join in, except for Haydrich; Naisae and Nopsan, too, are silent—the words are unfamiliar to them. Nopsan contributes to the levity with a quick dance step now and again, and even Naisae allows herself a smile or two.

So march with purpose, climb with pride.
On this adventure, Orna is our guide.
With teammates by our side we'll see,
The world's grand beauty, in unity.

I share a tent with Dieter and Kiel. We talk late into the night, the comradery of the team lifting our spirits. Kiel and I fall asleep holding hands. I trace a finger around the center of his palm, and the next thing I know, it is morning.

Yesterday's strength becomes today's leaden burden. My shoulders ache, and my legs tremble under the weight of the pack. Today's march takes eight hours but I find some diversion from my aches and pains while watching Nopsan torment Tizian.

Nopsan meanders easily along, the rocks in his pack mere feathers, it seems. He hovers close to Tizian, deliberately bumping into his pack several times, then staring wide-eyed and shrugging when Tizian turns around. At rest stops, Nopsan positions himself right next to Tizian, gazing fixedly at him as he gnaws on a piece of rankar jerky.

"What's your problem, Azi?" Tizian finally asks.

There is a sudden silence in the chatter of the group; there is not a name much worse for a citizen of Ainar than Azi. It is a derogatory curse of a word, a name uttered right before men come to blows, before men die. I admire Nopsan's composure—his expression remains impassive, his gaze unblinking.

Aedan moves forward until his face is inches from Tizian's; his eyes are narrow, and his mouth is a tight line. He says quietly, "If I hear that word out of your mouth again, you are gone. Do you understand me?"

"The freak is after me," Tizian mutters. "He won't leave me alone."

"Just eager to get north again," Nopsan contributes, shifting the pack across his shoulders. "I miss the taste of manflesh," he adds mournfully, patting his belly as he winks in Tizian's direction.

"Did ye see that?" Tizian demands, gesturing toward Nopsan. "What the fiek, man?"

"What?" Nopsan asks innocently, biting into a boiled potato he's pulled from his pack.

"Nopsan, please," Naisae says. "Manners."

I laugh every time, and Nopsan smiles each time I do. A smile that lights up his face and brings me joy. He is so much like Losan. Or maybe I just want him to be.

After three days we reach Fort Karne, our final stop before crossing the Bridge of Worlds. I have struggled even to maintain the most basic of conversation these past two days, as overcome as I am by fatigue, the rocks seemingly heavier with each passing day. My sole focus has been to move forward, one step at a time, endeavoring to ignore the wrenching pain in my shoulders, the bone-deep ache in my legs, and my yearning to sleep for a week.

The approach to the bridge is concealed by a twenty-foot stone wall, with a pathway wide enough to accommodate a single horsecart, the only access. The entry is flanked by two stone watchtowers, the crumbling mortar thick with gray chickweed, the top platforms each occupied by a sentry who trains his musket down on our approaching party. Two additional soldats stand on either side of the bridge entrance below, a snarling rechtdog chained to a rusted ring embedded in the stone tower. It's hard to believe Miter's Waste was once called the Unity Canal.

Between the towers I see the narrow expanse of the bridge extending out, only to disappear after a hundred yards or so in a thick cloudbank of fog. With a shiver, I recall a story my omie told me about the mists of Ainar, fine droplets that, like acid, could melt flesh from bone. I smile grimly at the thought that Ainar's myths could hardly be worse than Ectair's reality.

Aedan approaches one of the guards, keeping his distance from the salivating rechtdog that lunges at his chain, and hands him our scroll of travel that bears the insignia of King Adolar. The guard glares at all of us, spits a wad of gray chew tobacco to the ground, then leisurely unrolls the scroll. The second guard saunters over, reading the scroll over his colleague's shoulder.

"What business do you have in Ainar?" he asks Aedan.

"We are climbers, all of us, from Ectair and Ainar together," Aedan replies, one hand sweeping toward the rest of us. "We are to summit Mount Opasno on a peace climb."

"A peace climb?" the second soldat scoffs. "Do Ainarian savages know peace? The only peace you will find once you pass through that gate is that across the darkened sea." He rolls up the parchment and returns it to Aedan. "Ash and wave for us all."

"Ash and wave for us all," we murmur in reply. Naisae, I note, makes unflinching eye contact with the guard, a smile lurking about her mouth, as if she is in on some secret of which the guard is unaware. Clearly she has endured far worse, and the scorn of the watchtower guard does little to disturb her equanimity. She is made of stern stuff indeed.

After the guards make careful note of our names in a massive ledger, they wave us through. Silently, we proceed in a single file. It is an eerie feeling, walking into the mist, with the path ahead and the Waste below entirely hidden by gently swirling clouds of white. Even Veit is silent, and I cannot help but wonder if we are all thinking of the guard's words, of the certainty that only death awaits us on this side. Fear has been a familiar friend my entire life, and this is where I have the advantage over my male counterparts. After all, they do not fear being given away as brideprizes, like a fatted calf or a bolt of jistsilk; they are not forced into dürmels of a particular color to advertise a position of subordinance; they can choose their path. But I know fear well, so I can tap it on the shoulder, give it a grin, and be on my way. What is the worst that can happen? I could be reunited with my parents across the darkened sea—a fate that comes for us all sooner or later. I speed up, passing my teammates until I am walking next to Naisae and Nopsan.

"How is the journey for you so far?" Naisae asks.

For a moment I feel the need to impress her by making light of the journey, pretending it has all been an easy undertaking, but she would see through that. And I have no desire to insult her.

"Really hard, actually," I reply.

Naisae laughs as she adjusts her pack. "But getting easier, no?"

"I suppose you could say that," I say with a smile.

"You interest me greatly, Klarke Ascher," she says. "You have accomplished something in Ectair that we northerners thought impossible. Your father would have been so proud."

"How did you know him?"

"We worked together to dam the waste, a long time ago now. I was a climber for Kobo, and Anselm was overseeing the stretch of construction I was assigned to. The great Anselm Ascher and his assistant Ellias Veber. They were quite the pair." She smiles, her expression softening in fond remembrance.

"What was he like, my father?" I ask eagerly. "I don't remember so much of him as I'd like."

"Powerful," Naisae says thoughtfully. "And charming. And incredibly kind."

Naisae, I realize, would have met my father before he married my mother and well before I was born. It is odd, thinking of him as having a life before me, before he became my father.

"Why didn't you go back to Kobo?" I ask.

"I did for a while," she says, glancing at Nopsan. "But the glories of climbing in Ainar was a siren call that was impossible for me to resist."

"How did you become captain?"

"We all voted," Nopsan says. "Naisae's the best climber in Ainar."

A woman, and a foreigner, rises through the ranks to become captain of the Parvanatari based entirely on merit. I struggle, still, to comprehend such a world where women have such liberty. Why did I ignore Obid's offer to smuggle me out of Ectair when we had the chance? But I know the answer to that, and it has always been the same—those I love who depend on me. How could I abandon them?

"What role do the Parvanatari play in Ainar?" I ask. "In Ectair, we climb for sport and glory, of course, but we also undertake construction and repair work and gather medicinal plants from the high summits." And Death's Whisper. And purple ferns. And who knows what else. I shudder.

"We also work in construction and repair," Naisae says. "But the Parvanatari are concerned with so much more than just the practical. We represent and uphold a lasting legacy of Ainarian climbers. The act of climbing is one of almost religious devotion, one that gives our people something to believe in, to connect with."

"And what about you?" I ask Nopsan. "What is your story?"

He slows to loop around behind Naisae's back, then slips over so he is walking at my side. "I grew up in the shadow of Himmelisle," he tells me with an engaging grin. "I could not get enough of the Parowan mountains and was climbing almost before I could walk. A scout from Hidel encouraged me to join the team a few years back, and here I am. Not much to it really."

"You remind me of someone I once knew," I tell him, my mind flashing back to my childhood friend Losan and his expression that day when we watched his mother's funeral box sent to sea—he never cried, I realize now. Had I ever seen him cry, even once? Even during those long, wracking years of his mother's slow decline from pulmonosis? He had been a mirthful trickster, always quick with a flashing grin, but I had never seen a tear. "Do you see your family often?" I ask.

"No, my parents are in the Parowans now, and I am in Hidel. We don't see each other often. And you, are your parents in Ectair?"

He speaks of his family with so much confidence I believe him. I wanted so desperately for Losan to be alive. Did I imagine him throwing fish guts at me during the vintazite festival? I was under a lot of stress. And I had been drinking.

"My father died at sea," I tell him, "and I believe my mother was murdered."

Nopsan's eyes widen, and Naisae starts—just a subtle hitch in her step, but I catch it. They glance at each other, then back at me. My revelation has triggered something for them, I know, but what?

"That sounds like a lot to bear," Naisae says gently. "When the news came to Ainar that Laren had claimed the great Anselm Ascher, it was a great loss to us all."

"Yes, thank you. Many people tell me so. My mother, too, was a hero, in her own way. People compare me to my father, but I also want to be recognized as my mother's daughter."

We walk the remainder of the bridge in silence, and I am struck again by the great depth and width of Miter's Waste that lies so far beneath us. And how massive the two dams must be that block the sea from entering the Waste—they must be architectural marvels. Finally, we emerge from the fog and arrive on the far side. We are greeted by two soldats, who smile from beneath rounded fur caps, their long capes the stormy gray of volcanic rock.

"Tashta," Naisae says with a smile, lifting her hand in greeting.

"Tashta," they reply, stepping aside to let us pass.

I take my first step onto Ainarian soil—and nothing happens. I am not seized by convulsions; my flesh does not melt from my bones; I am not overcome by the urge to consume

Russet's brain. Perhaps Ainar has more in common with Ectair than King Adolar would have us believe.

"Welcome to Paradox Valley," Naisae says, gesturing toward the snow-covered valley before us. Codal trees line the path ahead and carpet the entire valley below, their distinctive bark a snowy white, their conical canopy of lush green far above our heads. Tipping my head back, I marvel at the impossible height of these trees, trees that used to decorate the hillsides of Ectair before they were harvested to extinction.

Interspersed between these ancient giants stand jagged pillars of black rock from which curling wisps of steam arise. Red tongues of flame flicker from cracks in the rocks, and sulfur pools bloom in curious shades of pink and yellow at their bases. White and green, red and black. It is a landscape of life and death—a paradox.

Naisae leads us down a narrow path that twists along the side of the cliff face, with a breathtaking view of the forested valley below. The path opens up into a massive cave, inside which we stop, awestruck, and stare at the crumbling ruins of what seems to be an elaborate temple structure. Columns, ten feet in width, rise to the roof of the cave, and sacred alcoves, home to small statuary, line the walls. Massive stone lintels have collapsed into various piles of rubble, and all is overgrown with dead vines and thorned chickweed.

"What place is this?" I breathe in wonder.

"This is a temple to the Sleeping God," Nopsan tells us. He points toward the valley, at the fiery columns breathing smoke. "And those are the Sleeping God's fingers. I'll grant one hundred dracals to the climber willing to ascend one of them."

"Sleeping God?" Veit sniffs in disdain. "Didn't your päters teach you anything? Everyone knows Orna and Laren are the only true gods."

Russet drops to the cave floor, his rock-filled pack thudding to the ground beside him. "I've never heard of the Sleeping God," he says, pulling a handful of bartlenuts from the pocket of his pack.

"That's because ye were raised right," Tizian mutters, tipping his water flask back as he takes a long gulp.

"But you were taught only part of the truth," Nopsan says. "There are many gods, including Laren and Orna."

"Rubbish," Burkhart mumbles.

"When the first diemant was created," Naisae says quietly, "and the gods emerged from beneath the sea, countless life forms were birthed from the stone. Orna and Laren were the most powerful, drawing the allegiance of the Galvaithian ancients. But there was a third being, one even more powerful than Orna and Laren, who transcends all that is human and divine. The Sleeping God, as is their name, slumbers yet, and we have but little understanding of their power; but when they awaken, they will set a brave new course for our world."

"And does your Sleeping God eat the flesh of man? Is it he who turns you to cannibalism?" Veit asks derisively.

"The Sleeping God is no he or she, man or woman," Nopsan explains with exaggerated patience, as if to a fidgeting child. "As Naisae says, they transcend all that is human. And when they awaken, if they tell me to roast your eyeballs in your blood and feed them to a goat, I am afraid I will have to obey, friend."

Veit's lip curls into a dangerous smile as Nopsan slaps him on the back with a hearty chuckle. I vaguely recall our schoolteachers telling us of other beings who had sprung from the diemant, but all, they said, had been destroyed in the chaos that followed or had been subdued and buried by Orna and Laren. The Sleeping God and the gods of Kobo, our teachers said, were no more real than the tales of giant lizards in the Calvia Plains.

"There is another theory about your Sleeping God," Haydrich says quietly.

I glance his way, startled by his voice. He has been so quiet this trip, I almost forgot he was still with us.

"If you are referring to Gildamer, you are mistaken," Naisae says.

"There are those who believe Gildamer and the Sleeping God are one and the same," Haydrich responds.

"Only misguided fanatics and those who follow a dark path," she tells him, her expression fierce.

The two of them face off until Haydrich turns away and moves off to the shadows on the far side of the cave. I know the name Gildamer only from the old stories. A stone creature Orna created and was then forced to destroy because it became too unruly, too destructive to her other creatures. Stone and rock must be used only for immovable creations like mountains, so they cannot wreak havoc. Gildamer was like an avalanche released on the world.

Curious about this new world and religion, I move toward the dim back of the cave where the dull gleam of gold shines in the shadows. It is the trunk of a codal tree, fashioned into a totem and carved with a variety of strange symbols and figures. The central motif, however, is recognizable as Cleos, our star, positioned above Azura, our moon. Underneath, beneath a tangle of chickweed, I see a symbol of a pyramid with a round object balanced on the peak. Fresh sprigs of sweet-smelling lavender are strewn around the base of the totem, accompanied by small bowls of saltz and other unknown minerals. While the temple lies in ruin, the totem is tended to.

"When our god awakens, the Chada sticks will ignite across the lands. We will know they are here, and we will be ready," Nopsan says quietly, glancing over at me with a strange, pained yearning.

While he may not be Losan, he—and Naisae—know something of me, of my past, that they are yet unwilling to share. And it is knowledge that I am determined to uncover. But I know, too, that the alliance between Ainarian and Ectarian climbers is a fragile one, fraught with distrust and suspicion, and I must proceed carefully and with a patience I fear I do not have.

"We must be on our way. We have rested here long enough," Naisae says, shrugging back into her pack. "The welcome ceremony awaits, and we must be safely inside before night falls and the temperature drops. Paradox Valley boasts the hottest fires but also the coldest nights."

We descend into the basin, skirting bubbling sulfur pools and the piles of snow at the bases of the codal trees. Cleos has dropped beyond the edge of the world by the time the flickering lights appear on the horizon. As we draw closer, we see the lamps illuminate a cluster of stone-bricked buildings with reed-thatched roofs. Naisae leads our weary group to the arched doorway of one such structure, unlocks the thick wooden door, and ushers us silently inside.

A spacious room accommodates a long rectangular table of polished black stone, with long benches to either side. I drop my pack to the floor with a grunt of relief, and collapse onto the bench to catch my breath. As the other climbers follow suit, a number of fur-clad men and women enter through a side door, each bearing a tray of tea and a steaming bowl of noodles, fragrant with chile and sarsroot. Each server places a tray on the table, and Naisae gestures for us to sit and eat.

"Where is the meat?" Burkhart asks.

"We don't eat meat here," Naisae says. "The Sleeping God forbids us to sustain our own existence through consuming the flesh of another."

So much for cannibalism in Ainar, I reflect. The teachings of Ectair, it seems, are all about sowing division, about manufacturing difference where perhaps there is none. To what end? For what purpose? King Adolar has dark plans afoot, and I have no doubt that palace intrigue infects the schoolwork of even the youngest Ectarian.

We devour the noodles, ravenous after our day's march. Servers with copper-colored skin and dark, hooded eyes bring in trays of sidhbeans, lentils, rice, and cooked greens. They communicate to one another in Ainarian, a fluid melodic language filled with soft clicks and intonations I can't follow. Ectarian, in contrast, is guttural and harsh. I glance across the table at Dieter and wonder what it must be like to finally find others who look like you.

As we finish our meal and the servers clear away our plates, a deep, rumbling horn sounds from outside. Each of us is provided with a small bundle of clothing.

"Please join us for a traditional sweat ceremony," Naisae says, rising to her feet. "This ritual purges you from toxic influences that may have trailed behind as you crossed the bridge. Dress in these garments and bring the towel with you. You may leave your belongings here. Then, please follow the sound of the drums to the inner courtyard. I will await you there."

The horn sounds again, joined by a rhythmic drumbeat, its sound primal and ancient, like the heartbeat of the mountains and the sea.

Naisae taps my elbow and gestures toward a door at the end of the hall, where I dress in privacy. In my bundle I discover a pair of short pants and a breast band, which I tie around my chest. Wearing the robe over the top, I take the towel and return to the dining hall, where the rest of the team are in the final stages of dressing.

Through a series of narrow hallways lit by lanterns, we follow the drums to the interior courtyard, where a large leather-skin tent is surrounded by ten tents, identical to the first but smaller in size. Behind the circle of tents, a series of black stone pillars rise precipitously, one hundred feet or more from the ground, terminating in small fires flickering through cracks in the summits. I tilt my head back to gauge the height, invariably looking for possible footholds in the sleek rock face. I can see few cracks or crevices with which to sustain a grip, and those that can be found are bright and flickering with the heat of an internal flame.

The flap to the central tent is lifted, and a stream of light appears in the dark, silhouetting a figure who ushers us inside. Within, the air is sweltering, heavy with heat. A circle of stacked wooden benches rise toward a taut leather ceiling. In the center, a large curved bowl, cut from stone, holds a pile of smoldering volcanic rock. At the far end of the tent a wooden throne sits high above the ground, accessed by a ladder built into the scaffolding of the legs. The Ainarians, who earlier brought us food, are now attired in woven hosen similar to our own; they sit on towels on the far benches, glancing toward us with friendly smiles.

"Take a seat." Naisae motions toward the benches. "And if one of you is feeling sufficiently brave enough, take your place on the Fury Throne and see if you can survive the breath of the Sleeping God."

"I will take that bet," Veit shouts with a laugh as he leaps from the bench and clambers nimbly up the ladder to the throne. Atop the wooden seat, he reclines with an air of regal majesty, crossing one leg over the other, grinning triumphantly back at us.

Naisae and Nopsan join their fellow Ainarians, spreading their towels across the bench beneath them. As they sit, one of the Ainarians begins to stomp their feet, and before long, others join in until the tent is filled with a thunderous accord. The stomping grows to a rhythmic fury, and the bench beneath my bare feet vibrates with the deafening sound. The tent flap opens to reveal a man and a woman dressed in simple hosen, their torsos painted in spirals of charcoal and ash, their faces covered by white-bark codal masks festooned with antler-like branches. The woman holds two flags aloft, each affixed to a wooden spear—one, with white mountains and purple hills beneath a black sky, the symbols of Cleos, Azura, and a rock schrein stitched in gold in the top left corner. The flag of Ainar. The other is red in color, with a white codal tree at the center. On the woman's back, two large branches of feathered pine are strapped. The man carries a bucket in each hand: one sloshing with water and the other mounded with snowballs.

The stomping slows, then ceases as the voices of the Ainarians rise in song. The woman deposits her pine boughs at the base of the Fury Throne and holds the flag staff aloft. Her masked companion ladles water onto the lava rocks, which emit a hissing steam. Then he holds a snowball up and turns as the Ainarians resume their stomping in tune to the song which fills the tent. He flings the snowball onto the volcanic rocks, and the tent fills with the scents of rosemary and orange. He detaches one flag from the woman's staff as the singing and stomping rise to new heights of enthusiastic fury. They are now singing in Ectarian, I realize, and the words become suddenly comprehensible.

In the depths of my soul, an orkansturm roars.
Battling demons on the darkened sea's shores.
With a heart of iron and a spirit bold,
I'll conquer the darkness, as the legends foretold.

The masked couple begin to dance, snapping the flags in rhythmic waves that send hot air cascading toward us. Sweat beads at my hairline and trickles down my face. I wipe my brow with a corner of my towel and wonder what toxic Ectarian influences might be purged by such a ritual.

In the darkest abyss, where Hildegroth dwells,
I'll forge my oath, break the darken mages' spell.
With an alpenstock of purpose, and a rope of might,
I'll conquer the darkness and bring forth the light.

Glancing up at Veit, I see his body slumped sideways on the throne, head lolling backward—he has fainted. Kiel smirks beside me as two burly Ainarians climb the ladder to revive Veit with strong-smelling minerals and assist him down. They escort him from the tent, Veit stumbling between them in a cloudy confusion.

A brisk series of chants ushers in a new song, and the masked man places a fresh snowball on the rocks and douses the bowl in water. In the fragrant clouds of steam, I recognize the scent of pine, clove, and ligon blossoms. The masked duo place their flags against the base of the throne tower and take up the pine boughs. Burkhart rises from our bench and strides confidently toward the throne to take Veit's spot.

In the realm of ancient dreams,
Where the Sleeping God in slumber schemes,

Their power lies in patience's hold,
In the shadows of time, their secrets unfold.

The masked duo wave the pine boughs with frenetic energy, swirling hot air in gusts; it is as if they are dancing through a wildfire. The sweat pours from my pores, drenching my hosen and darkening my chest band. The Ainarians' chant rises in intensity until I feel that I am living a fevered dream.

Before the song has ended, Burkhart staggers down the ladder and collapses against the far benches, head between his knees. Before I have time to think, I am on my feet, making my own way across the tent floor to the Fury Throne. Climbing the ladder to the top, the rising heat hits me like a slap across the cheek, and I feel suddenly dizzy, the edges of my vision a darkening whirl. Gasping, I manage to clamber up to the seat and collapse upon it. The air scalds my lungs and makes breathing difficult—it must be twenty degrees hotter at this height. The song cycle finishes, and the masked man begins anew, flinging a snowball that emits the fragrance of mint and barberries. A new song rises from the Ainarian benches:

To the hidden mountains in the northern mist,
where legends are born and warriors exist.

The heat at the Fury Throne is a monster fiercer than Hildegroth, but I take deep, slow breaths in an effort to ease my rising panic. I refuse to descend the ladder. If I fail, it will be the way of Veit—where the body can withstand no more despite the will of the mind. But I will not entertain the notion of failure. I must become one with the heat—let it course through me until my blood boils, until my bones heat to a scalding fury; I think of a steel blade forged in heat and cooled in the hiss of steam, and I channel that strength. Closing my eyes, I stomp my feet in rhythmic accord with the Ainarian chanting. Nausea rises in my throat, and my peripheral vision darkens in a dizzy whirl. I steel my thoughts to dwell upon those who are determined to see me fail—King Adolar and Haydrich. Gio, Veit, and Tizian. Burkhart. My rage lends me strength to withstand the heat, even as sweat pours from my body and pools in my seat. Shielded by my wrath, I feel as if I could climb even higher, ascend to the dizzying height of one of the Sleeping God's fingers without so much as a flesh burn.

The song ends, and I remain upright on the throne. The masked man raises one palm toward me—a motion to stay seated—then flings another snowball onto the embers. In the hissing steam, I see Burkhart, Russet, and Dieter stagger toward the tent flap and disappear. Only Haydrich, Aedan, Kiel, Tizian, and I are left. Haydrich sits rigidly upright, staring, unblinking, at the smoking rocks. Perhaps he, too, is protected by a defiant rage.

The melody of the next song is slow and deep, the voices hypnotizing in a harmony that is almost haunting. Seeking to distract myself from the furnace that seems to be building in my body, I fix my gaze on the masked figures who swirl and dance around the ember pit. As the song comes to an end, a hush falls over the room, and all heads turn toward the Fury Throne where I am trying not to wilt into the puddle of sweat on my seat. The masked woman steps forward and raises her arms to me. "A true Ainarian!" she shouts in accented Ectarian. "A woman with fire in her veins and rock in her blood. Welcome to Ainar!"

A thunderous sound fills the room as the Ainarians pound their feet on the wooden benches in collective approval. I startle, then smile—I could even feel what might be the rise of a blush in my cheeks, but who could tell? My face must be redder than a bloody starrise.

The masked man climbs swiftly up the ladder to help me down; with legs trembling beneath me, I am grateful for his support. Exiting the tent, we stand in the frigid darkness of a Paradox Valley night. Azura's blue light casts us in an eerie haze as steam rises from our flesh and mingles with the fog of our breath. Beyond the lights of the tent I can see the dark, looming profile of the Sleeping God's fingers against a sky bedazzled with stars.

"You must be part goddess," Nopsan says, passing me a mug of water. "There are not many who can endure the throne."

"I endure worse every day." I pass him my cup for a refill and gulp down the chilly water. "I am well trained."

Nopsan laughs and leans into me, hot flesh grazing hot flesh. "You are tough, like our women here. I had heard Ectarian women were soft, but you have proven that rumor false."

"Our women are not soft," I protest. I think of Rayna, Lena, and the women from my old tenement. I think of my mother. "And those who are, are not so by their own choosing."

"I meant no offense," he replies, inclining his head in mock deference, a smile playing about his lips.

"I know. You're just being amusing, as usual."

"I thought you enjoyed a bit of levity, Klarke Ascher."

"Not at the expense of those who don't deserve it."

I turn away, drawn, despite myself, to the towering pinnacles of the nearest of the Sleeping God's fingers. I make my way behind the wall of tents toward the dark pillars, their presence lit by seams of flickering fire. Behind me, I hear Nopsan turning to greet the Ainarians who spill, laughing and talking, from the tent. Placing my hand on the jagged rock, I stare up at the towering pinnacle, charting a possible route to the top.

"You will be paid well for this information if you succeed." A muffled voice comes from behind the pillars—barely audible in the noise of the emerging crowd.

With a start, I recognize the voice as belonging to Haydrich, and I press against the stone, straining to hear the whispered words.

"They would have concealed the girl's identity well," another responds—a voice I do not recognize, but the accent is clearly Ainarian. "I've found no record of a Ramanata brought over by the Band of Sisters."

Haydrich lied, I realize grimly. He knows of Otto's sister, Ramanata, but he has yet to discover who she is or where she might be found. If the Dark Promise is looking for her, the urgency of my search has just increased exponentially.

"There is always a record," Haydrich whispers. "I trust you can track it down. Enlist whatever help you might require, and the Schaeter will reward you with riches beyond what you can possibly imagine."

"What is your plan once you have the girl?"

There is a momentary lull in the conversation, as if Haydrich is unwilling to share additional information.

"I might be of further help to your master," the Ainarian persists. "I have connections in high places, as you are aware."

"My master seeks two such candidates," Haydrich finally says. "One, to provide access to the beast; another, access to a kingdom."

"Then you intend marriage?"

"We intend an indestructible dynasty more powerful than all the gods."

My thoughts rush in a fevered tangle. Haydrich seeks the same woman I seek, that much is clear. And while I intend to protect her, he desires to make her a queen. Leaning back against the pillar, warm with a mysterious internal heat, I struggle to catch my breath. Are we on the same quest, I wonder, and should we join forces? But to make her queen, he would have to remove Otto. And me. Not that either of us has any great desire for the throne or for the power it wields. But Haydrich would have no way of knowing of our lack of political ambition. Indeed, it is likely impossible, I muse, for an ambitious man to comprehend that others might not be so driven. I hear the soft footfalls of the two men as they circle around the pillar—where I press back against the darkness—and rejoin the company.

An indestructible dynasty more powerful than all the gods.

To seek a power beyond the reach of mere mortals, beyond that wielded by the gods, what new horror is this? Such power in the hands of men… I shiver at the thought. King Adolar's nefarious deeds would be but the antics of a child in comparison. Whatever meeting Kiel attended in Kietsch, beneath the alehouse, was of a different gathering entirely—perhaps a deliberate ploy to throw people off the scent. As tumultuous as the night's events have been, at least now I have some answers—Haydrich and this Schaeter need to be stopped; I need to find Ramanata before he does, and both of these concerns suddenly seem far more urgent than bringing King Adolar's tyrannical reign to an end.

There is another, Gio had said. Was he referring to this Schaeter?

14

We depart from Paradox Valley early the next morning. By the afternoon, we have left the codal forests behind and climbed a winding cliff path to the Yavar Plateau. The land is bleak here—a windswept frozen desert dotted with short shrubs and spiny broad-leafed ground cover. I pull my coat tightly about my torso and wrap my scarf across my face; the wind whistles in my ears and flings stinging needles of sleet against our raw skin. Ahead, I see the rising mass of the Journo Mountains, a range grander than any I've seen before. We hike along a narrow, muddy trail, passing merchant trains of donkeys and cow-like creatures hauling vegetables, salt, colorful fabrics, bricks, and a variety of other goods for sale.

The people we pass carry equally heavy loads—heavier, I acknowledge, than the rocks I still carry in my pack. We move aside to allow traders room to pass, carrying baskets filled with produce or slender planks of codal timber balanced on their heads. The trail meanders from the vast wastes of the plateau to a scrubby forest of windswept trees with large leaves and hard purple fruits covered in spikes. Gradually, the path ascends into the foothills of the mountains, cutting through fizhte pines and knotted shrubs with gray bark peeling from blood-red stems. Snow dusts the surfaces of the vegetation and gathers thickly in the shadowed hollows along our path.

At night, the Ainarians erect leather tents that smell of smoke and animal dung, unfurl bedrolls, and dish out steaming plates of noodles, lentils, or rice for our dinner. The air outside is crisp and clean in my lungs, and I marvel that these places exist, free from the smog and rain of Ectair.

And always the mountains rise before us, guiding our path. I am astonished by the height of each successive peak we encounter—each seems to beat the previous one as the highest in the world, even though they are, Naisae tells me, nothing to Mount Opasno. I now understand why Naisae felt drawn back to Ainar from Kobo. One could spend a lifetime climbing here and summit only a small number of available massifs.

After a week of travel, we arrive at the Frozen Sea of Ard, where we take our rest in the ruins of King Miter's old palace, once called the Bessil's Nest after the great soaring birds of the high mountains. Miter had built castles all over the continent, but the ancient edifice of the Bessil's Nest, nestled at the base of the mountains and overlooking the frozen sea, had been his favorite. In those times, Galvaith had been one unified kingdom, before Miter traded his daughter, Layal, to Laren for control of Hildegroth. Had she stood on the steps of this wintry place, staring out at the sea? Had she guessed that those frozen wastes might one day consume her?

The palace now is a ghost of its former self, with a few inner walls of hickstone still standing, shrouded in snow. A partially collapsed ceiling still offers adequate shelter to our group, and we take our meal beneath its protection. As I devour my rice, I glance over the murals that remain on a portion of the wall, a delicate tracery of blue and yellow flowers that flourish in warmer plains to the south. Four towers once surrounded the keep, Naisae tells us, but they have long since crumbled into the sea.

The Frozen Sea of Ard stretches before us like an icy mirror dusted with swirling gusts of snow. Icebergs dot the surface, floating in water of deep turquoise; for, despite its name, the sea seldom freezes here. Farther north, beyond the first ring of the Journo Mountains, the sea is solid. Before the damming of the Waste, the Frozen Sea of Ard and the Sea of Toole in Ectair formed one giant brackish lake fed by salty, nutrient-rich rivers flowing in from the sea. The dam has divided the lake in two, with the salty rivers, upon which so many aquatic creatures depended, dried up. The lakes are now swollen with fresh water, and the fish often float, bloated and stinking, to the surface for lack of salt.

Two boats, shaped like hubermelon rinds, are outfitted with oars and will serve to sail us across the Frozen Sea of Ard. A boatsmaster stands poised at the bow, port, and starboard sides of the vessel, with a massive pronged hook, ready to shove ice out of our path. The greatest danger, Nopsan tells us with some glee, is not the icebergs we see but those we do not. It is the submerged ice chunks that present a danger to the ship's hull, and should the hull be breached, we could survive less than two minutes in the frigid waters.

I pull my fur coat tightly about my body and make my way to the bow in search of Naisae. Haydrich leans against the bulwark, intent on writing in his notebook. I wonder what he is writing—does he write of plans and agendas? Does he write of the Dark Promise and the Schaeter that governs it? What intelligence might I learn by reading his words? I suppress the urge to seize his book as I pass. The conversation overheard at the Sleeping God's finger made it perfectly clear—Haydrich is dangerous in the way the colorful gil-beetle is dangerous; even when it is inert on a rock, soaking in the Cleoslight, it emits a poisonous vapor that kills all living creatures within a half-fret radius.

As if sensing my scrutiny, Haydrich glances up, holding my stare through light umber eyes. Strange, I think. I recall his eyes being darker.

I find Naisae poring over maps that have been unrolled across the surface of a small table.

"I will consider that," Aedan is saying as he rolls up the top map and tucks it under his arm. "I don't want to put my team in unnecessary danger. The oxygen training can be extended by an additional week. King Adolar has allowed me a little flexibility in this regard."

Naisae nods to him and then smiles at me as I approach.

Aedan grips my shoulder as he passes. "This is going to be the greatest achievement of our lives, Klarke," he says with an infectious grin. "Mount Bonen is but a sapling to the mighty fizhte that is Mount Opasno."

I cannot think of Mount Bonen without terror. But it is not the mountain that frightens me. It is the image of blood on snow and the sound of piercing screams from the ice. It is the work of men I fear, not the mountain. I force a smile.

"Can't wait," I tell Aedan. Which is true. I wish for nothing more than to prove myself on the slopes. Both Ellias and my father climbed Opasno before the Waste was dammed; it will be as if I am climbing with their spirits beside me, as if they are witnessing my feat from across the darkened sea. Will I be able to see Ectair from the summit? Will I be able to see my homeland, beneath its clouds of smog and rain, the land that has forbidden women to climb?

I join Naisae at the railing, frigid spray misting my face in the steady wind.

"Your team is about to make history, Klarke," she says with a warm smile. "It has been many a year since an Ectarian summited Opasno."

"It is a great honor," I acknowledge.

"I'd like you to be part of the first kletshot to summit. Aedan has agreed."

"An even greater honor than expected," I reply, excitement threading through me. "There are some who won't like that."

"*Some* would benefit from realizing they are in a land that cares not for their ideology," Naisae says, turning to look at me with one brow raised. "You are free to agree with that statement here."

"Yes," I whisper, biting my lip. "I agree."

"Good. Now that you know you may speak freely, tell me what has made you seek me out."

"You're the only other female climber I've ever met," I say. "I have so many questions and don't know where to begin."

She laughs, a deep, joyful sound that rises on the wind, as if taking flight, with a power of its own. "We, too, have a team of nine, Klarke. Five of them are women."

My mouth drops in surprise. "Only four men?"

"Three men and one who identifies as our Sleeping God does."

"But how?" I wonder aloud.

"In Ainar, Klarke, we grant our women access to their full power, a power guaranteed to us from the Sleeping God. For they are neither male nor female but both together. They are nothing and everything, each part equal to the other, and both essential for survival. The same is accorded to our people."

I imagine Tizian roped up with a woman and someone who is both male and female, relying on them to keep his life safe. Sneering at them, hating them, but being entirely at their mercy. I hope he does not embarrass us too much.

"I can't wait to meet them."

"And they you."

A boy brings two steaming mugs of dark tea and, together, we toast the climb ahead.

"I hope that after summitting Opasno, your king will allow the Ascenditures to join us in the upcoming world games in Kobo. You know of the games, yes?"

I shake my head, embarrassed at my ignorance.

"In the past," Naisae continues, "all three lands sent teams every six years, not just to compete in climbing, but also teams of horse riders, stone throwers, log dancers, and firemancers. Lately, Kobo and Ainar have been competing, with small teams from The Gate and the Isle of Bloque. We miss the Ectarian teams and hope King Adolar will allow you to join us for these next games. Failing that, at least, rejoining the League of Ascension."

"What is the League of Ascension?" I ask, wrapping frozen fingers around my mug.

"It is the organization that manages the climbers of Ainar, Kobo, and, years ago, Ectair. The League gathers and shares the latest advancements in climbing gear and techniques, then shares them with its member teams. In this way, we learn of new opportunities as we grow safer and stronger. Climbers who have been injured can solicit help from the League, which will, in turn, oversee each kingdom's team to ensure they are treated fairly by their rulers."

I feel dizzy from the speed at which my world is expanding and fear that the strain might tear the fabric of my soul.

"Who are the League, and where are they located?" I ask.

"The League consists of climbers in each land, forming their own factions. In Ainar, they are located in Hidel. In Kobo, they are in Gunato. In Ectair, years ago, there used to be a League headquarters in Kietsch, down in the westlich on Hagnar Street."

"Yes, I know Hagnar Street," I say eagerly.

"This peace climb was formulated with the express intention of reconnecting with Ectarian climbers," Naisae says. "We hope for a better understanding between our peoples, and we hope for the eventual reestablishment of the League of Ascension in Ectair. Ectair has a history of greatness, Klarke. The father of mountaineering, Lars Veber, hailed from your lands, and what a tragedy it is that his legacy cannot be honored in his homeland."

My soul stirs beneath the frozen wrap of fur. I fight the urge to scream into the wind, so loudly that Otto can hear me in Kietsch. I want to reestablish the League of Ascension, to honor Lars, Ellias, my father, and all who devote their lives to the climb. I have been thinking too small. I have been afraid that I would be unable to summit mountains in Ectair when all the world is waiting. The world games in Kobo span lands and cultures, and gather teams that cross the seas to compete; for many of us, crossing the seas happens only in death, and it is a one-way trip. The world is alive with possibility, and this, I am coming to understand, is what King Adolar most fears us discovering.

"How was King Adolar able to keep all of this from us?" I ask. "It's been only a few generations since the Waste was dammed. Our omies and opies know the truth, don't they? How did the king persuade an entire kingdom to lie to its children?"

"Fear and violence," Naisae says. "If one repeats the same lie over and over, eventually it becomes your truth."

My thoughts darken as I remember the corpses piled into the justice wagons, Rosalie swinging from the gallows on a pink rope, and my mother and the queen conveniently dying of Death's Whisper.

"I understand that some initially railed against the king's deceit. But you have seen the consequences of such bravery, Klarke, yes? Dissidents are killed or sent to the labor camps. Examples were made, and most thereafter kept their heads down. For many, it was no longer a truth worth dying for."

I think of all those people in Ectair, living out their miserable allotment of years under the smog and the rain, fearful of contracting pulmonosis, afraid of being foisted into unwanted, loveless marriages. A kingdom, which Adolar has further isolated so he may force his will upon a weak and ravaged populace. A tyranny built on stilts and fabricated in deceit. How could this not be a truth worth dying for?

But perhaps that, too, will be Adolar's downfall. He imagines us weak and powerless. I am anything but, I vow, gripping the railing with white-clenched hands. But to defeat the wiles of Adolar and to survive the cunning calculations of Haydrich and his Schaeter will require a cool head. I exhale in one long breath, the warm air from my lungs crystallizing in the sharp, cold air.

"Have you ever come across a woman by the name of Ramanata, about my age, from Ectair?" I ask with studied casualness.

"I have not," Naisae replies. "Why do you ask?"

"A friend is looking for her."

"I wish your friend luck, Klarke, but unfortunately, I can be of no help to you."

"And what of Obid? You know where he is, don't you?"

"King Gyalzen holds him in captivity in one of the mountain holdings. We had to give him over to gain access to your team. But do not worry yourself on his account; he is a resourceful man and will certainly free himself before long."

Ellias. My father. My mother. Queen Eleonora. Rosalie—all

of these were smart, resourceful people, and they met their certain fates.

Obid won't escape.

You don't escape in Ectair.

You bow and lick the ground, or you hang.

"Resourcefulness doesn't save lives in Ectair," I mutter.

"Oh, but it does," Naisae says quietly, her gaze on the horizon. "Not every life, certainly, not enough lives, but it does save many."

A blast of sea spray hits my cheek, and I leave it to burn cooly against my skin. My mother, the queen, Obid, and who knows how many others, saved Ramanata, as well as countless other women and infant girls. If they were brave enough to sacrifice their lives to save others, to pursue the truth, then I must find the courage and persistence to find at least one of them. Ramanata.

15

The city of Hidel sprawls beneath the foothills of the Parowan Mountains, with the long, jagged shadow of Mount Opasno and the front range peaks stretching over the city like the claws of an ancient winged beast. Cleos's light is fading, but the skies are clear, granting us a view of Mount Opasno's razor-sharp ridges and steep fields of vertical snow and dark rock. Spindrift trails from the summit in an icy mountain wind like a bird's feathery tail. The mountain, I know, is not my enemy, but it is not my friend. I am nothing to it, just as a breath of wind is nothing to me. I will live by the mountain or die by it, and the mountain will endure in solid equanimity either way. Nothing, in all existence, cares less about the qualms of mortals than a mountain.

"Laren's mighty arsch," Russet whispers, his eyes wide and fixed on the mountain.

Burkhart remains impassive, although I would swear his face has paled.

"Behold Orna's masterpiece," Nopsan says. "Behold the great natural wonder of Galvaith."

Kiel sucks in a breath beside me, his fingers grazing mine. I dance my own across his and match his breath. At least we will be together this time.

We enter the city through the eastern gate, following Naisae's lead. Unlike the red brick buildings of Kietsch, Hidel is built of round cobblestones, stacked one upon the other, cemented with mortar, and topped with log roofs. Smoke puffs through a thousand chimneys, darkening the sky and scenting the air with earthy and bitter aromas.

Pyramids of dried animal dung are stacked beside each residence.

"Karad dung," Nopsan says, noticing Russet wrinkling his

nose. "It is burned for cooking and to keep warm. We do not wish to decimate our forests, and karad droppings are an unlimited resource."

Numerous animals crowd the streets, loaded down with potatoes, bundles of dung, and sacks of wool; they resemble our kuhkas but are shorter and broader in their bodies, with coarse hair that trails in the muddy streets and four curling horns that rise from their heads. Some are red, like the sands of Kobo. Some are white, like mountain snow. Some are the color of dung piles, and some are the color of volcanic rock.

In Ectair, women wear mostly green or white to signify that they are married or single. Women in Hidel walk the streets in vibrantly colored skirts of red, pink, yellow, and green, overlaid with coats intricately stitched in gold thread. A variety of beads are woven into their hair. With smiles and waves, they greet us not as foreigners but as friends.

"Himando!" they shout. "Tashta!"

"Himando means *welcome*," Naisae says. "Tashta means *greetings*. We have long anticipated Ectair's return."

"How do you say thank you?" Dieter asks.

"Ow mai," Naisae replies.

Small bell-shaped temples dot the city, shaped like giant versions of the bell in Hadrian's Monastery and painted in stripes of gold, white, and green. Next to each temple I can see a Laren schrein, a holzenschrein for Orna, and a neat pile of stacked rocks with a large boulder on top.

"That is for the Sleeping God," Nopsan tells me.

Bells hang around the necks of kuhkas, and from the corners of hats of people thronging the streets. Tiny silver bells are also woven into the hair of the children who skip in the street and dangle in the doorway of houses. The slightest breeze sends all the bells jingling merrily.

"Himando, brother!" A man touches Dieter's arm as we pass.

"Ow mai!" Dieter calls, beaming. "Brother."

Dieter's joy warms me, and I acknowledge the gift of being surrounded by people who welcome you. Who see you. Who don't search for reasons to send you to labor camps or to keep you from marrying their women.

There are many here, it seems, of Ectarian descent—men and women with muddy-brown hair, pale skin, and dark eyes. Finding Ramanata will be harder than I had expected, and how am I to find out if she is in Hidel at all? How many Ectarians had been living here when the Waste was dammed? And how many fled after Adolar's brutality in search of a better life? How many of these Ectarian women, I wonder, were smuggled by my mother?

I am struck most of all by the colors of this city—and not only that of the clothes. The tables of vendors that throng the roadside markets are covered in rich spices, bold fabrics with vivid patterns, brightly colored ribbons and beads, tall candles and fragrant incense in shades of celadon and magenta. The merchants themselves seem just as varied as the products on their tables, with glossy skin tones ranging in hue from gleaming igneous to freshly fallen snow.

Ectair is a kingdom of green. Our world is green, and we lack the creativity necessary to imagine any other hue. So we dress in green, decorate in green, and collectively pretend that our options are duly limited. If we cannot see it, it does not exist. It cannot change. We are trapped beneath a cloying green canvas, unable to remove the sheet from our faces.

Ainar, by contrast, is a land of imagination. A land surrounded by white, jagged peaks, and yet the people are as warm and as bright as their candles, as open as their Sleeping God, as vibrant as the beads around their necks. It is little wonder that King Adolar fears them so—the great unraveller of tyranny is imagination.

Before the steps of King Gyalzen's palace, a line of women drape colorful shawls about our shoulders and press steaming mugs of flada tea into our hands. My shawl is striped in thick lines of purple, turquoise, and white. No green. I smile and pull the warm wool more snugly across my shoulders.

The palace rises four stories that grow progressively smaller toward the top. It looks like a mountain. Like a decorated and bejeweled little sister to Mount Opasno. In the center of each of the four palace steps, three small shrines are situated, one to each of the gods—a holzenschrein to Orna, a statue of Laren, and the Sleeping God's stacked rock pyramid with a boulder atop.

The holzenschreins are festooned with candles, and each, I notice, depicts a carving of one of Ainar's majestic mountains. The first two steps honor two mountains I am unfamiliar with, but the top two are dedicated to Himmelisle and Mount Opasno.

As with Orna's monuments, each statue of Laren is different but in all of them he is engaged in benevolent acts: holding the hand of someone crossing the darkened sea; lifting a ship from the turbulent ocean to save it in a storm; lovingly embracing King Miter's daughter, Layal; and commanding rain to nourish a farmer's crops. In Ectair, Laren is a fearsome god. A tyrannical father. A god who demands death and blood. I stare at the Laren embracing Layal, his expression a carved visage of tenderness and love.

The Sleeping God's shrine, too, follows this pattern. A boulder, uncarved and untouched by an artist's hand, rests upon a platform of stacked rocks. Each boulder is different, as nature created them. They are simple but powerful.

I stare from the boulders to the gentle images of Laren, to the women following us up the stairs carrying pots of tea, and beyond them to the sprawling city of Hidel and the mountains rising across the Frozen Sea of Ard. There are no cannibals and barbarians in this harsh land. The green shroud of Ectair's lies continues to slip from my eyes.

We follow Naisae up the steps and through carved double doors on the third level. I gasp as I take in the detail and rush of color. Patterns painted on the walls run into the floors, which are covered with rugs of identical design. Guards dressed in long red robes and leather helmets stand next to each doorway. Vases painted with images of mythical cats and ancient warriors stand as high as a man and are filled with dried flowers the size of dinner plates, the variety of which I've never seen before.

"Welcome, Naisae." A figure draped in a silk dress the color of the Rolag sea during an orkansturm greets Naisae and nods to our party as we gather in the palace entrance. Their feet and ankles, I notice, are covered in rust-colored tattoos that look like twisted snakes and rope. "Our Gado is ready to receive you."

"Ow mai, Dechen." Naisae touches the hand of our greeter, and we follow them both into the gilded space.

The palace cuts deep into the mountains. I turn my head constantly, craning to see into each room, to take in the detail of each carpet and mandala painted on the wall. I stare into the faces of each guard or servant who passes, greeting them with a smile, mirroring the one they give to me. The wrinkles on the faces here differ from those that grace the faces of our elderly in Ectair. Here, the lines curve upward instead of down, reminiscent of joy rather than sorrow. I want that for my people.

Eventually we reach a vast room with colorful cushions scattered about a delicately painted floor. A bearded man rises from a red throne at one end as we approach, smiling. His beard falls to his waist, the hairs knotted with braids, beads, and tinkling bells. Twisting branches interlaced with dried flowers and shimmering red stones, like that of a woven basket, make up his crown. His black robe is stitched through with gold thread, depicting various constellations in the night sky. He stands, and the golden stars cascade with the fabric to the floor.

"Himando, friends. It is an honor to have you in my home. An honor to once again welcome Ectarians in Ainar's embrace."

Naisae bows her head, and we do the same. I glance at Tizian and Burkhart and am relieved that they know enough to be respectful. Veit's hands clench at his sides, but he lowers his head.

Aedan steps forward and places a hand over his heart. "The honor is ours, your…"

"Gado," Naisae says.

"Your Gado," Aedan repeats. "We are grateful for your invitation and hospitality and aim to honor the friendship between our lands."

"We share a goal then, Aedan of Ectair. Come." King Gyalzen motions to the cushions on the ground before him. "Be seated. You must all be weary, and I would have words before we part ways and you take to warm beds for the night."

I touch Kiel's hand, and we share a deep blue cushion that cradles us like a bed of moss. I lean into him, knowing the danger—the danger that Tizian could return home and inform the king. Nopsan's smile falters as he glances our way. Is he a danger, too? I wonder. We take the risk anyway. Lady Gelta and arranged marriages don't exist here. Only us. Only mountains. Only freedom. At least for now.

The king sits back on his throne and accepts a cup of tea from one of his servants. Others appear carrying silver trays full of steaming glass cups, and we accept the hot beverages. I nestle into the cushion and the warmth of Kiel's side and fight against a sudden heavy drowsiness.

"As I said," the king begins in perfect Ectarian, "it is an honor to have you all here and a mighty step forward that your esteemed ruler allowed you to cross the Waste. You have been told many things about me, about Ainar, about our shared history. Before we begin this journey of healing, I would like to share my truth. The truth of Ainar. I consider you friends, but some of you may consider me the enemy. I would dispel those thoughts, so that you may climb with clear heads in the coming weeks. So that you might return to your people with a message differing from the one they daily receive.

"You all know of Laren's monster, Hildegroth, who came through the Unity Canal many years back and left destruction in his wake. The monster gained easy access to our humble city through the Frozen Sea of Ard, so, as you might guess, Hidel was laid waste. Unlike Kietsch, we are not protected by a geological feature like Pieter's Uplift. Our homes and streets were ravaged, our citizens left broken and bleeding in the streets; we desperately needed our friends to the south.

"And Ectair answered our call. We worked together to dam the canal at both ends where it bisected our lands and to keep the monster at bay.

"But then your king lied to his people, claiming that I controlled the beast. That I laid waste to his kingdom with the hope of coming back and finishing the job. That I wanted to see an end to Ectair's freedom and a return to Galvaith, with me as the supreme ruler. Did he also tell you that my wife and daughter were on the Qualing Bridge that day, when Hildegroth raised a mighty tentacle and smashed the bridge into the canal? Did he tell you that I lost them both to that fearsome beast? Does this sound like the actions of a puppet master to you?"

I squeeze Kiel's hand, horrified.

"Your king blamed me for the destruction wrought by Hildegroth because he wished to alienate us from one another and to conceal his own misdeeds. I tell you this now so that you do not fear me or my people. We wish no one—no creature who walks the Sleeping God's realm—harm. And because I would like the Qualing Bridge rebuilt, to honor my family and to restore that which should never have been broken."

Veit clears his throat, and I fear he might speak, but he remains silent. Perhaps he has enough sense not to be an arsch when he is so far from home and surrounded by guards who don't care who his father is. We are brought a fresh round of tea, and as I chew on a mint leaf I ponder the king's words. I've learned a similar truth over the past weeks, and even though I've spent a lifetime believing Ainar to be the enemy, I've seen enough true evil to know King Gyalzen is telling the truth. I wonder if he knows of my mother or if he was part of the plot to destroy her. I must find a way to speak with him.

"Now, friends, it is late, and you are travel-worn. Dechen will show you to your rooms, where dinner awaits. Take the night to rest. Tomorrow your training begins, and you will need a strong heart and mind to keep up with the Parvanatari. Good night, and may the Sleeping God grant you easy passage into his realm."

"This way, please," Dechen says, waving us from the throne room with a silk-draped arm. "I will lead you to your chambers."

I want to stay and speak with King Gyalzen. I want to ask him a million questions. To find answers. But I must remember my place here. He is a king, and I am nothing. Patience.

"Klarke, a moment," Nopsan says, a hand resting lightly on my elbow. "Don't worry, I'll show you to your room." I nod to Kiel, who reluctantly follows Dechen and the others down the hallway.

"Yes?"

"I'd like to show you something. Come," he says, a mischievous grin curving his lips as he takes my hand, but I hold my ground, refusing to move.

"Why me?" I ask. "There are nine of us you could befriend. Why me?"

"You're cuter than the rest of them," he declares.

"No."

"Funnier?" he suggests, a twinkle in his eye.

"Definitely not."

He sighs. "What do you want me to say, Klarke? I just like you."

"I want you to tell me the truth," I demand. "Like your king just did. Why did you throw fish guts at me at the vintazite festival and shout 'fischbomb'? Why do you try so hard to be my friend? Why do you care about making me laugh?"

Nopsan holds my gaze for a moment, his mouth dropping open as if he will speak; but he changes his mind. He smiles, then frowns, moving closer until he is within an inch of me. He grips my shoulders, leaning his forehead against mine.

"Nopsan. With me, please," Naisae calls from the doorway, her expression stern. "We must join the team and prep the gear for tomorrow's training. Let Fram Ascher rest."

I touch his cheek and stare into his eyes before he pulls away. "You are Losan, aren't you?"

"Fischbomb," he whispers, his eyes still on mine.

"Now," Naisae says again.

He casts a final glance my way before disappearing. I exhale sharply—I knew it. He's alive! But why does Naisae not want me to know? Why would she feel the need to conceal his identity? And why, after this speech from their king pronouncing his verity, are more lies flowing from the mouths of the very people who are supposed to be our leaders? I long for truth but wonder if it even exists.

16

We stand in the shadow of Himmelisle—the second largest mountain in Galvaith—which towers above Mount Bonen and Mount Eldras but cowers in the shadow of Mount Opasno. We will train today on the lower slopes, learning the life-saving skills of alpenstock arrest, crevasse self-rescue, proper rope techniques, how to use the new gear they've assigned us, and, most importantly, how to climb as a team. While we received basic skills training for our previous climb up Mount Bonen, notably absent was any thought of *team.* Eighteen of us stand together at the base of the Harang snow field, nine with tanned and leathered skin to prove their experience, nine with soft pale skin unfit for this environment.

We leave today to begin our trek to Base Camp. While I'd wished for more time at the palace to speak with King Gyalzen, to discover what I could about Ainar, my mother, and Otto's sister, to rest on cozy pillows while sipping flada tea, I know that this is not a vacation, and I have no say in our itinerary. We have come to climb, and only after that is done will there be time to speak with the king. For now, I must focus on surviving and growing strong.

We have been outfitted in proper cold-weather gear, and every time I glance down at my hosen, I cannot help but grin with delight. Thick canvas pants are tucked into leather hobnailed boots lined with hair from the karads. Short nails have been hammered into the soles in irregular patterns to help prevent slipping on the snow and ice.

High karad-wool socks, woven with small mandala patterns in rose and gold, stretch to my knees. I wear a silk shirt underneath a wool coat, over which rests a jacket the likes of which I have never seen before; it is thickly quilted with small, ganzen-feather-filled pillows and fur-lined hems. We mimic the animals who thrive in these environments. A felted leather cap covers my head, with flaps that protect my ears from the wind. We all wear some variation of this same outfit, distinguished only by the patterns on our socks.

Naisae clears her throat. "Welcome Ascenditures and Parvanatari, to the beginning of what we hope will be a friendly and strong bond of competition and support. I will introduce my team first, and then Aedan will introduce his."

Nine faces stare at us. Nine faces with varied colors of skin and hair. We—with our bland pale skin, brown hair and eyes—must look like an inbred bunch from Ectair. Except for Dieter.

"First, we have Norda, a strong climber with a big heart who leads our search-and-rescue special team. He commands our summit wardens, who will support our climb and help to carry gear, set up fixed ropes and ladders along the way, and establish our high camps. Norda will also oversee today's practice."

Norda inclines his dark head in a slight bow. The tip of his nose is missing, I notice. A casualty of frostbite? "Welcome to Ainar, friends," he says in heavily accented Ectarian. "It is my task to keep you safe."

"You already know Nopsan," Naisae continues.

I look at the rest of the Parvanatari to see if this false name registers with them, but I see no sign of it. Maybe he is Nopsan to them. Maybe even here he is hiding, so his identity must remain a secret. It doesn't matter. He has given me what I need, and we will eventually have time to talk.

Menson, the last man on the team, is dark skinned like Naisae and is a year or two younger than me; from beneath his leather cap, a braid falls down his back, wound through with red ribbons and small bells that tinkle when he moves.

"In case I fall and need someone to find me." he says with a laugh, shaking his head.

My chest tightens. Menson's smile, his jesting spirit, reminds me of Gio.

"This is Tashi," Naisae says, gesturing toward a tall individual with long hair dyed red that falls to their lower back. Tashi possesses a graceful elegance, and their muscles ripple as they step forward and bow, smiling warmly. "Tashi is a knotsmaster," Naisae continues, "and they hold the title from the last world games for the fastest knot tying."

I notice the pronoun and conclude that Tashi must be the one who identifies as the Sleeping God does, as neither male nor female. I feel Veit tense beside me and hear his quick intake of breath. I send a fervent prayer to Laren that my team doesn't make us all look like bigots over the course of the climb.

Tashi's gaze lingers on Dieter, who meets their eyes, then blushes and turns away.

"And now to our strong force of women." Naisae beams at the four women standing proudly.

"We have Diki and Mida, twin sisters from a small village in the Valda Pass, who started climbing before they could walk and are some of the strongest mountaineers in all of Ainar—"

"In the known world, you mean," Diki interrupts with an engaging grin. Dark hair frames a rounded face, with blunt bangs accenting high cheekbones. "I doubt there are any south of the Waste and few, if any, in Kobo who could climb faster and with as little support as my sister and me. I mean, we hold the record for the fastest winter ascent of Opasno."

"I stand corrected," Naisae says. "Diki and Mida, everyone. The strongest mountaineers in the known world."

"Aye, aye!" Norda and Tashi shout.

Mida blushes and nods. While her facial structure appears identical to her sister's, her head has been shaved, and an intricate mandala has been tattooed onto the polished skin. I wonder if twins of opposing genders are allowed to live here—surely they do not practice the infanticide so prevalent in the south? Twin girls—the strongest climbers in the known world no less! I smile so widely my cheeks hurt.

"And this is Chessa, who hails originally from the Isle of Bloque; she is a technical master on the fel, finding holds where none exist and making her way up a wall as if she were weightless. We are convinced she has felfee blood coursing through her veins, though she begs to differ."

Chessa has hair the color of snow, tied in two braids that twist into knots behind her head. Her eyes are a shocking blue, bright like the sky on the clearest of days. She looks like a felfee—like some kind of magical creature, although I do not know how they look.

"And finally, we have Keema, our newest recruit, though a climber to be reckoned with. This will be her first ascent of Opasno."

Keema has the dark hair and eyes and the pale skin of an Ectarian, I notice.

"I look forward to proving myself," Keema says softly.

She looks to be Otto's age. My age. Could this possibly be Ramanata, Otto's long-lost sister? I catch Dieter's gaze, glance pointedly at Keema, and shrug.

Aedan introduces our team, and when he mentions my name, the Parvanatari cheer. I fight the effort to shrink away; instead I smile, trying to appear as poised as Dechen.

"Glad they're happy to have you and couldn't give a scheiz about the rest of us," Veit sneers. "Makes me feel so safe."

"Imagine how safe I've always felt with Tizian, Burkhart, you…Gio." My voice trails off, and I cough to keep the emotion away. "It's good for you to experience discomfort every once in a while."

Veit only grunts in reply. I turn away dismissively; my focus now is on Keema and how I might get to know her further over the next few weeks. Perhaps we can share a rope on the mountain, I muse, before acknowledging that I should doubtless try to link up with more experienced climbers.

"Much of the climb will be done with fixed ropes, but there are a few stretches, notably between camps three and four, where we cross the Juvan glacier and the Unger Throat, where we will rope up in teams. Today we will train with the teams we will be climbing with," Naisae says. "Two teams of four and two teams of five, each with both Ascenditures and Parvanatari. Get to know your teammates. To trust them. These are the climbers who will be responsible for your life and whose lives you, in turn, carry."

We glance around, each no doubt determining who we'd pick if we could.

"You will also sleep with these teammates," Naisae adds. Dieter, I notice, glances at Tashi, and Tashi notes Dieter's gaze with a slight smile. *Uh-oh.* "If you weren't friends before the climb, you will be after. Unless there is bad weather and we are forced into tents for weeks at a time, then whoever shares your rope could just as easily become an enemy," Naisae finishes with a smile and wink.

Aedan begins to read from a list in his hand. "Kletshot four will be made up of Kiel, Tashi, Burkhart, Diki, and Haydrich."

Dieter drops his gaze, and I breathe a sigh of relief. The last thing I want to have to tell Otto is that his beloved fell in love with a dazzling climber from the north, and that he's chosen to stay in Ainar, a place that welcomes him and where he is free of conspiracy and death threats.

"Kletshot three will be Dieter, Chessa, Mida, and myself," Aedan continues. "Kletshot two will be Russet, Tizian, Norda, Keema—"

Please say my name, I think. *Please let me be on Keema's team.*

"—and Menson."

Scheiz. Even Dieter and Kiel are on other teams, so I cannot rely upon them to dig for answers either.

"And kletshot one will be Naisae, Nopsan, Klarke, and Veit."

Veit groans, and I bite my lip. I'm glad to be on Losan's team but apprehensive about being paired with Naisae. She can teach me a great deal, but her determination to keep Losan's identity a secret is perplexing. What else might she be hiding and why? And Veit. Oh gods, spending this much time in close quarters with Veit will be a nightmare. I can't imagine sleeping next to him and waking up with his scornful gaze boring into mine.

"Good luck today," Kiel murmurs in my ear. "I'm bummed we aren't together."

"Me too." I elbow him playfully and smile up at his frown. "Your unofficial job will be to protect Tashi and Diki from Burkhart. I'm not sure our brother is ready for Ainar's openness."

We glance over at Tashi and Diki, both confidently prepping heavy gear. I recall Diki's declaration that she and her sister were the best mountaineers in the world and laugh.

"Although I doubt either of them needs protection. I bet the first time Burkhart opens his mouth with a distasteful remark will be his last."

"I'm more worried about Haydrich," Kiel mutters. "He's been silent most of this journey, but he always looks at you. Always rests his eyes too long. I'm going to use this time to get what information I can on his plot."

"Good," I say. "But be careful. I don't trust him. My gut tells me he's the greatest danger on this climb. Find out what you can, but don't let on that you know too much. People who know too much often come to a bad end on the fel."

We hug, and he kisses my cheek, and for a moment I can forget that he is forbidden and will soon be completely outside of my reach.

Kletshot one has formed a group, and Nopsan—no, Losan, I remind myself; he is Losan—watches as I approach, then glances over at Kiel. I smile, though my heart flutters uncomfortably.

"We are one of the smaller teams," Naisae says. "Climbing with five adds extra safety, but I believe in all of you. I know Nopsan is a strong climber, and Aedan tells me that the two of you also number among his strongest—the only two survivors of the Mount Bonen ascent, yes?"

I swallow and glance down at my feet. Surviving on Mount Bonen had not been a matter of strength.

"I beat Klarke up that mountain. I destroyed them all." Veit jabs his alpenstock into the snow and leans on it. "If Opasno's anything like Bonen, I'm not worried."

"I'm no expert, but winning against corpses isn't difficult," Losan says.

Veit reddens and opens his mouth to speak, but Naisae cuts in first.

"Opasno is nothing like Bonen."

"Yeah?" Veit asks. "You climbed Bonen?"

"Many times. Climbing Bonen is like scrambling up a boulder compared to Mount Opasno. Bonen is hard. Opasno is impossible. Where Bonen is indifferent to your life, Opasno actively wants to claim it. Humility is your only ally on the slopes. Humility might keep you alive."

"We'll see," Veit retorts, rolling his eyes. "Lecture me again when we're done, and I've kicked the mountain's arsch."

"You chose well," I interject with a laugh, shaking my head at Naisae. "Ectair's greatest climber graces us with his talents."

"Ectair's greatest arsch," Losan mutters through gritted teeth.

"What did you say?" Veit demands, leaning in menacingly, his face inches from Losan.

"Enough," Naisae says. "We are a team, like it or not, for the foreseeable future. You will eat together, sleep together, answer nature's call while attached to the same rope. Move past ego and focus on the climb."

We nod and grow silent.

"Better. Now, Mount Opasno stands 7,000 feet higher in elevation than Mount Bonen. What that means is that every obstacle you faced on Bonen, you will face here, only you will struggle to breathe. Whatever altitude sickness you experienced before will be that much greater here. Mount Opasno is Orna's domain, her home in our mortal world. She triggers avalanches, opens mighty crevasses, tumbles seracs, or steals your breath on a whim. We will train to counter these attacks, but ultimately, she and Laren have a deal. She is allowed to create endless life, so long as that life always returns to him across the darkened sea. And she honors that deal on the mountain's slopes more than anywhere else."

Naisae reaches into a duffel bag and removes eight pairs of goggles. "Wear these always to protect your eyes," she says, handing two to each of us. "Even when it is cloudy. Snow blindness is real and can be permanent. Keep the spare pair safely inside your packs. If you lose your glasses, you lose your eyes. If you lose your eyes on Opasno, you lose your life."

The goggles, more sophisticated than any I have seen before, are formed of two rounded lenses of smoked glass set in a metal frame and lined with velvet. We each don a pair, tightening the bands at the back of our heads until they fit snugly against our cheeks. My eyes welcome the relief from the bright glare of snow.

We lay out sisal ropes, alpenstocks, slings, spiky crampons, and something called a Veber that is used for climbing the fixed ropes. My thoughts turn to Ellias, and I wish he were here. What would I not give for us to be able to climb together and celebrate at the summit? Or even just for one of his all-encompassing hugs.

"The hobnailed boots will suffice for most of the climb, but once we reach those steep upper snow slopes, you will need to add crampons to your boots." Naisae passes a set of crampons around, and I practice attaching them to my boots.

"As you see, the crampons have twelve points rather than the old eight, a recent upgrade, which allows us to climb near-vertical slopes." Naisae points to the two horn-like spikes at the front. "Jab these into the snow, and you can practically stand straight up without sliding."

"Why wouldn't we wear the crampons for the whole climb?" I ask.

"You can't climb rock in these baddies," Losan says. "Even though it looks like all snow from here, half of our route up Opasno is over rock."

"Why do you keep all of this fancy new gear a secret? Doesn't seem very unified to me." Veit tosses the crampons back into the gear pile and glares at Naisae.

"The purpose of the League of Ascension is to disseminate updated climbing information across the world. If I'm not mistaken, your father favored dismantling the League in Ectair.

Perhaps you could take up your quarrel with him if you return."

If. The word sends a shiver down my back.

The rest of the afternoon is spent sliding down a hill, Veit and I tied together, as we practice stopping the slide with our alpenstocks. The Ainarian alpenstocks, with their oak handles and steel heads, are shorter than those we use in Ectair—which takes a little getting used to.

"Stop moving so much!" Veit yells.

"I'm sliding down a fiekin' hill," I shout back, ice chips stinging my cheeks. "How do you think it'll be in real life?"

Real life? I know how it is in real life. I imagine my face hitting the snow when Gerd fell into the crevasse and pulled our rope team down with him. I recall the weight of two men's bodies tightening the rope around my chest to where it cut into my skin and stopped the air from reaching my lungs. Blood had filled my mouth, adrenaline my blood. My hands shake from the memory, and I drop the axe. It spirals down the ice, toward the line of red dye Naisae has left in the snow, signifying the precipice of a bottomless drop, until Losan stops its slide with a forcefully planted boot.

Losan strides up to where I stand and hands me the alpenstock. "You okay?"

I nod, grasping the wooden handle with trembling fingers. I hear again Gerd's scream ringing in my ears. My heart pounds like a jackhammer beneath my ribs, and I feel momentarily dizzy, as if struggling to stay upright as my feet slide over the edge of the crevasse… It's not real, I remind myself. This is not Mount Bonen; this is Opasno. There is only the mountain to fear, and that, I conclude grimly, looking up at the glittering peak, is quite enough.

Veit and I swap places, with Veit on the downward slide as I attempt the alpenstock arrest to halt our fall. "You're too heavy!" I yell, crampons biting into the snow, my alpenstock bouncing as I struggle to prevent our downslope drag.

"How do you think it'll be in real life?" Veit yells back, mocking me.

Fiek all, he's right. I saved Gerd and Tristan with an alpenstock arrest before.

Gritting my teeth, I summon all my strength and plunge the alpenstock deep into the snow, just managing to arrest our slide as Veit's knees cross the red line.

"Good. Keep going. Again and again and again." Naisae ties in with Losan, and they join us in the exercise. I watch enviously as they make clean and quick stops each time.

I mess up the next attempt, and Veit and I go spiraling across the red line in a twisted mess of rope, alpenstocks, and flailing limbs.

Losan's shadow appears over us. "The good news is, ninety percent of the time when too much pressure is applied, these ropes fray and snap, so your success in this activity is not crucial."

Veit and I exchange worried frowns.

"So, the League of Ascension has fancy goggles and twelve-pointed crampons but can't manage ropes strong enough to hold their climbers?" Veit asks scornfully, untangling himself from our pile. He tosses the heavy coil of rope at me as I come to one knee. I fall back on the ice, glaring at him.

Losan taps his nose and winks at Veit. "Obviously not."

After lunch, we learn to slide the Veber—a hand clamp that moves freely along an expanse of rope in one direction but clamps to a stop if one begins to slide backward. I cannot help but reflect how useful this tool would have been on Mount Bonen; how with it, I could have more easily rescued Gerd and Tristan from the depths of the crevasse.

"Mountaineering is twenty percent physical," Naisae says, "and eighty percent mental. This is a sport of the mind even more than a sport of the body." She turns to welcome a porter who leads two karads up the slope to where we wait, slumped and exhausted, leaning on our alpenstocks. I wonder wearily what she has in store for us now. I am tired from the day, from the lack of oxygen, from the grief that never seems to leave me.

"Take a pack each," she says, gesturing toward the canvas

packs slung over the thickly furred flanks of the animal. "Load the slings, Vebers, and other gear, then grab a rope. We have loaded your gear for you, and during the weeklong trek to Base Camp, you will have time to familiarize yourselves with it all. As we are a team, I've divided the collective gear among us."

"So the teams of five have lighter packs?" Veit asks.

"Good thing you are so strong, my man," Losan says.

Cleos has started to slip behind Himmelisle, and a growing cold and darkness descends upon the valley. I look from the packs to the heavy coils of ropes to Veit. He looks as tired as I feel.

"Now?" he groans. "We leave now?"

"We head for Opasno this evening," Naisae says, loading her pack. Losan loops the thick rope into a series of coils, then slings it across his torso.

"At night?" Veit demands.

"You have a light," Losan says. "This is the part where we exercise your minds."

I bend down, ignoring the ache in my knees where I'd hit the ice time and time again, and load my pack. Igniting my carbide headlamp, I position it over my hat, then heave the rucksack onto my back and drape the coils of rope across my chest. Veit follows suit, mumbling a slew of curse words under his breath. The other three teams join us, and we set off behind Norda and Tashi. We are a large group. Eighteen climbers, eighteen summit wardens, twenty porters, and forty karads and mules hauling most of the gear.

"You did great today," Losan says, trudging beside me.

"Thanks," I huff back, impressed at Losan's easy breath and steady stride. I want to collapse into the snow and sleep for all seasons of the mooncycle, but I grit my teeth and set my pace to his, one foot in front of the other. You can do anything for fifteen minutes, I tell myself every fifteen minutes. Eighty percent mental. I play the game.

"So, about what happened in the palace," Losan says quietly. "We can't speak about it. You can't know. I want you to know. I don't want to lie to you, but you must pretend you don't know. Just be cool. Can you do that?"

"Just tell me why. Why are you lying? Why are you hiding who you are?"

"Yeah, see that. That's not you being cool."

I trip, and he catches me before I stumble.

"Also not you being cool," he says.

We laugh, and I shoot him an understanding grin.

"I've missed you," I whisper. "I thought about you all the time those first few years. It was hard enough losing my father, doubly hard losing my best friend."

He blushes, his eyes softening with a smile. "I missed you too. I still do. I had such a crush on you back then. I was smitten."

"What?" I stop walking, my mouth dropping open in surprise, but he strides on without me. I trot to make up ground. "A crush?" I ask.

He laughs, and his eyes twinkle in the fading starlight. "Of course. Not only were you the captain's daughter, but a fram who threw fish guts at people and romped around in dirty pants. You were my dream girl. My father always reminded me it would never work—I was just a poor kid from Ainar, but I didn't care."

I can think of nothing to say.

"When Naisae told me you'd made the team and that we were heading south…I was so excited. I was going to see Klarke Ascher again. The Klarke Ascher."

His gloved fingers brush against my arm, but in confusion, I pull away.

"Why is Naisae lying about who you are?" I demand.

"To protect me."

"From who? Who would care about a poor kid from Ainar?"

"Ouch."

"It doesn't make sense to me."

"Do you know about your mother, Klarke? What she was really doing?"

"Yes. I mean, I think so."

"We weren't just carrying saltz and tar on that ship when it sank. We had something else. Someone else. Of great importance."

"Prince Otto's twin sister?"

"Who?" he asks, perplexed.

"Never mind," I mutter, my mind racing with the implications. If not Otto's sister, then who? Then, as if answering my unspoken question, he replies.

"King Adolar's sister," he says. "Lady Genalt—"

"Lady Genalt?" I ask. "Are you sure?" Otto had been told his aunt had died by her own hand.

"Yes, of course," he replies with a frown. "Lady Genalt was struggling in the water, and I managed to get us both to shore on a piece of floating timber. I was afraid that saving her life would put a target on my back. It would be safer to disappear. When I finally told Naisae who I was, she agreed it was best to keep my identity a secret. Especially given our intention to travel to Ectair and face King Adolar."

"Were there other survivors? I know Obid also made it out of the water. Who else?" I try to keep the pained hope from my voice.

"I don't know who. After hours at sea, we washed up on an island on The Gate; then we made our way to Burndle on the first ship to Ainar."

"And your father?" I ask tentatively.

An expression of grief contorts his face.

"I'm so sorry," I say, touching his arm. "And my father?"

"Sorry, Klarke," he says with a sigh, shrugging the coil of rope more comfortably across his chest. "It's been a long time. We've both lost a lot. But we haven't lost each other."

"No, we haven't lost each other." My heart races, and I find myself longing for the warmth and safety I used to feel around those I had loved.

"You're beautiful and as astonishing as you were as a kid, sadder perhaps, but who can blame you? Unique, strong, and stunning. Prince Otto is a lucky man. But so is Kiel, if I'm not mistaken?"

I glance up at him, then quickly look away from the intensity of his gaze. Then, before I know it, we are tangled together on the ground, my boot having caught in his alpenstock, his body beneath mine. I wriggle to get up, but my pack weighs me down, my rope tangled in his axe.

Grinning, Losan tucks a strand of hair behind my ear. "We should stay like this," he says.

Before I can respond, someone pulls on my pack from behind, lifting me to my feet.

"Careful," Kiel says with a short laugh. "Must be a felfee in the snow that reached up and grabbed your ankles."

I nod, with a quick glance between the two men. Losan hoists himself up as Kiel, taking me by the elbow, resumes our onward march, leaving my childhood friend behind us.

"How was practice?" Kiel asks.

"Good," I say, resisting the urge to glance back over my shoulder at Losan. "Veit was an arsch, but that's nothing new. How was it for you?"

"Yeah, good. Hey, so Nopsan's a bit cocky, don't you think? It must be hard having two Veits on your team."

I choke back a laugh—his jealousy is new to me.

"Better cocky and experienced than humble and ignorant," Losan interjects, appearing to my left.

"Ignorant?" Kiel's eyes light with fire, his mouth compressed in anger. "Who here is ignorant?"

"Whoa!" I stop, grasping each man's arm. "We're all tired. It's been a long day. Please don't do whatever this is."

Kiel snorts, and Losan shrugs. I slow my walk, falling back to leave them both to trudge through the frigid darkness in sullen silence. My heart is rattled, and so is my mind—Losan saved Lady Genalt. She'd been on my father's ship when it sank. Could King Adolar have had a hand in that too? I thought he'd just murdered my mother, but was it possible that vile man had taken both my parents from me?

"Otto will be proud to know his wife is such a hot commodity," Dieter says from behind as he jogs to my side.

"The lack of oxygen is making people loopy," I tell him with a grin.

"I think it's just you," he insists, giving me a friendly arm bump. "You intrigue them."

"Oh yeah? And what about you, Dieter?"

"What about me?"

"I've seen the way you look at Tashi. And I've seen them return that same longing stare."

"There's nothing there," he says with a frown. "I would never betray Otto."

"I know you wouldn't. Just as I wouldn't betray Kiel."

"But they are intriguing, aren't they?" he says. "I've never met anyone like Tashi."

"They certainly are," I say, my thoughts returning to Losan. "And somehow safe."

"Safe," Dieter whispers.

We sigh and grow quiet, with only the rustling of wind across the snowy slopes and the creaking of the karads' harnesses breaking the silence.

"It's true, though. What Dieter says," comes Haydrich's voice by our side as he passes, carrying his weighted rucksack on his back and two rope coils across his chest. "You are an intriguing woman, Fram Ascher. Aye, many of us would value your company."

Dieter raises an eyebrow, but Haydrich doesn't mean *company* in any affectionate way; he means he wants me to join his weird and dangerous mission.

"I keep my own company, tanks ye."

"We're all patient men," he says.

I grit my teeth in sudden anger, anger that they all think I am some prize to be won or pawn to be used. I march toward the feet of the greatest mountain in Galvaith, and yet I am still just an object, still just an Ectarian woman. I wish Cleos's fading light and the fuel in my carbide lamp would expire so darkness might conceal my frustration and exasperation. I've spent years being ignored on the streets, and now I have a husband, two men vying for my affection, and a wacko and his Dark Promise seeking my allegiance.

I don't have time for crushes and infatuations. Kiel needs to focus on finding out what Haydrich is up to. Losan needs to tell me what he knows about Keema's past and where I might find Lady Genalt or Prince Otto's sister. And I need to turn my full attention to surviving the coming climb, somehow putting all the pieces together in the process, and staying a few steps ahead of Haydrich.

17

"I can't believe my greatest dream is about to come true," Keema says, her face, within the circle of dark fur, alight with excitement. She is deep in conversation with Burkhart, who has taken a fancy to her, it seems, since he rarely leaves her side. I cannot imagine what they talk about—he's a man of few words. But I have heard her laughing. Is Burkhart funny? Or is she just being polite?

I have quickened my pace to come alongside them, but their conversation proves difficult to interrupt without causing suspicion. I glance over at Keema, trying to see some resemblance to Otto. I think I see it, but then I'm unsure if it's real or if I've convinced myself of it.

The past few days have been spent trudging in and out of the dark shadows of the mountain peaks. The jagged peaks soar high above us, and the valleys are nested in shadow far below. The light from Cleos during the day and Azura at night descends in patches of dark and light, cold and warmth. I live for the moments the heat of our star touches my face, and I plow briskly through the shadows lest my blood freeze. Burkhart, too, appreciates the warmth of Cleos's rays, and when he stops to relieve himself in a sunlit spot, I seize the moment.

"Me too," I say. "Our dreams, that is. They will either come true, or we will die."

"Aye." Keema nods. "Or that."

The wind slips its icy fingers beneath my coat, and I shudder at the sound of its mournful cry. The heavy coils of rope dig into my shoulder, and a crampon spike, lashed beneath my pack, jabs me in the side. My legs ache with the effort of our hike, and the howling wind blasts my cheeks.

"So, were you born in Ainar?" I ask Keema, shifting my pack to dislodge a canteen banging at my hip. She glances over at me curiously, her gaze narrowed. "It's just," I say, "you look Ectarian."

"Many Ectarians lived in Ainar before the damming of the Waste and remained here after."

"So, is that a yes?"

"My parents adopted me from an orphanage in Stracto," Keema tells me. "I could have been born anywhere. It doesn't matter. I am Ainarian and nothing else."

"Of course." I inhale, taking a deep breath of icy air. Stracto is situated north of the Ungersea, far from Obid's trade routes. Any babies Otto and my mother smuggled would more likely end up in Burndle or Hidel. Maybe Dristo.

"It must have been nice living here, where you're free."

"I've heard stories of Ectair," Keema says. "Is it really that bad? Do you still practice twinicide and marry off your girls?"

"Well, I don't," I say. "But the kingdom does. We hate it, but most Ectarians don't know any different. Some are fighting against it, but many…" I think of the women in my old tenement, the ones working in the brothels or wasting away from pulmonosis. They don't have the luxury to fight. "Many can't. Or won't."

"Are you fighting?"

"Every day."

"Good for you."

I smile and then feel like a fraud. I don't feel like a soldat or part of any well-intentioned war. I feel like a silly girl fumbling in the dark while well-organized monsters conspire against me. I didn't say I was good at fighting, after all; only that I refused to submit.

"Is it true you're married to the prince?" Keema asks. I nod. "But you're so young."

"In Ectair, women can be married off at seventeen."

Keema's eyes widen, and she shakes her head. "As I said, I'm Ainarian, wherever I was born. I want no part of Ectair, even if it's in my blood."

"Have you ever met a man named Obid?" I ask.

"Not that I recall."

"Big man. Huge. Works as a cook on ships."

"I don't spend time in the port towns."

I take a drink from my canteen as I think through what I have learned. Adopted from Stracto. Doesn't know Obid. It's not impossible that Keema is Otto's sister, but what are the chances? She is, after all, the first Ectarian I've met.

You're too desperate, my mind helpfully reminds me. *Keep looking.*

"So, were ye born a freak, or did ye choose to become one?" I hear Tizian behind us interrogating Tashi, his voice taunting.

I momentarily close my eyes. Is this how it sounds to others when he attacks me? Keema whirls around to confront Tizian, her eyes raging, her mouth open to issue a stinging retort.

"It's okay." Tashi raises a hand to Keema. "I am unaffected by this man's words."

"Gleibels don't have normal feelings?" Tizian demands. "Or are ye always both happy and sad? Both hurt and not hurt? Help me understand how it works." Eyebrows raised, he glances toward Veit, who gives an uncomfortable chuckle.

Keema smacks Tizian so hard his nose bleeds. My mouth drops.

Tizian wipes the blood from his nose and glares at Keema. "Ye fiekin' foze!" He storms forward, lifting his hand. Keema raises her alpenstock. Before my mind has time to process my actions, I have moved—I square my body in front of Keema, fists coming up to protect my face.

Before Tizian can reach us, an arm encircles him from behind and drags him to the ground. "Enough," Burkhart grunts, pinning Tizian in the snow.

I can scarcely believe my eyes—Burkhart stopping his best friend? Burkhart defending a woman?

"What the hüle, Burk?" Tizian shakes him off, clambers to his feet, then shoves his friend. "Who do ye think ye are?"

"Just stop, Tiz. This isn't the place."

"No?" Tizian snarls, spit flying from his mouth. "Ye just

decided to pretend to be someone else here, then? So ye can sleep with that traitorous foze? That cannibalistic whore? Ye just abandoned everything ye believe in? I don't buy it."

Burkhart turns to Keema, ignoring Tizian. "I was telling you about my fall on Kara Do. Would you like to hear the rest?"

"Please." Keema smiles sweetly at him, then glares Tizian's way.

"What in all the worlds was that?" Dieter asks as he and Menson approach. They both appear to be as shocked as I am by Tizian's outburst. Muttering under his breath, Tizian rights his pack, seizes his alpenstock, then, glowering, stalks ahead. Tashi smiles, seemingly unfazed by the altercation.

"Are you sure you're okay?" Dieter asks.

"I am. But thank you," Tashi says, resting a hand on Dieter's arm. "I climb the world's deadliest mountains. I know what genuine danger is. I do not fear or take offense to simple words spoken by a simple man."

"I could learn much from you," Dieter says.

"Would you like to?"

"So, we should probably keep moving," I say, interrupting their flirtation. "Don't want to get too far behind the others." I feel bad for Otto, but what can I do? Dieter is getting a taste of what life could be like without the threat of death looming over him for who he is attracted to. How could he not explore this new freedom?

I fall in step next to Menson. Tashi and Dieter walk to his other side.

"Earlier I was telling Dieter about Mount Erschmagge," Menson says. "Do you know it, Klarke?"

"No. Where's that?"

"It's only a legend," Tashi contributes, rolling their eyes. "Believe only half of what Menson tells you."

"I think Mount Erschmagge exists," Menson continues, "and someday, I intend to find it. It lies somewhere up north, in the lands beyond Dristo, beyond the edges of any map. Beyond the known world."

"Then how does anyone know about it?" Tashi asks.

"Now wait just a minute. Don't ruin my flow."

Tashi holds up their hands and grins at Dieter. Dieter grins back.

"So anyway," Menson says, "Erschmagge is twice the size of Opasno, and every hundred years, fire shoots from her summit, spilling lava down her sides and melting the glaciers. The molten rock hardens, and the mountain grows ever wider, ever taller. And then the glaciers return. But Erschmagge is not just any mountain, and the glaciers are not just ice and snow. They are magical beings called Eiskrits, who drift down the slopes, eating the rocks and snow left behind by the eruptions. The Eiskrits grow longer and longer each year until they reach the base of Erschmagge, where they crumble. Seracs are their warts and crevasses their wrinkles. Erschmagge is also the home of the unger, the hairy man-like creature with teeth the size of fingers and jaws so strong they could rip a head from a body in one bite."

"We have ungers in Ectair, supposedly," Dieter says. "Some say they live on Mount Bonen too."

"They came from Erschmagge originally. Which proves it's real."

"Your idea of proof intrigues me," Tashi says with a laugh.

"You have not told them about the meisers." Chessa approaches from behind. She has a thick accent, which sounds like a drumbeat echoing through a canyon—deep and edged, carved by wind.

"I'm only getting started! Meisers are small stone creatures about the size of a cat who eat rock algae and sometimes the flesh of other creatures. They hunt by throwing rocks at animals. If you find one, grind its stony body into sand, and then burn it, you are granted one wish."

"Allegedly," Tashi adds.

"You have even more fanciful legends than we do in Ectair," Dieter says. "Your omies must be full of stories."

"Our omies are made up of half the things that make up

most people, and half complete and total karad dung," Chessa adds with a laugh, her green eyes sparkling in the gleam of our lights.

"Wait, I thought you had blue eyes," I say, certain that the first time we met they had been a striking shade of cerulean.

Chessa winks and shrugs. "Wait until you see what color they are tomorrow."

"I don't understand."

"Ever heard of Menagal?"

I shake my head.

"No," Dieter says.

"It's a potion that changes the color of your eyes when you add a drop or two to them. The color depends on which floral extract you use. It's a fun way to express myself."

"Let me guess," Tashi says. "Menson thinks it comes from Erschmagge."

"No, that one was developed by the päters on the Isle of Bloque." Menson shoves Tashi playfully, and we all laugh.

Other than the occasional moment in the tenement, when the girls were in good spirits and we'd scrounged enough food to be joyful, I've never experienced the camaraderie I feel now. Climbing in Ectair always felt hostile. There was always more than one person who didn't want me in a room, and conversations always seemed to steer toward why I shouldn't be there. Trudging along the snowy path in the Azura-washed night, surrounded by climbing peers talking about magical mountains, I feel a deep sense of calm, of happiness, of freedom. To be free to think of algae-eating rock cats instead of worrying about being married off to an abusive wife-beater. Other than Tizian and Haydrich, who never speaks, everyone seems to get along.

"My favorite part of the legend, though," Chessa continues, "is the great treasure that lies deep within a cavern at the very heart of Erschmagge, which is accessible only through a crack in the summit. You must first navigate the mountain and her creatures, and then, once you enter the cavern, you must also contend with lava and fire beasts."

"And if you survive the journey through fire," Menson says, "you will reach a giant cavern filled with treasure and the last obstacle—Herakin, one of the minor gods who emerged from the first diemant."

"And then what?"

"No one knows. No one has ever lived beyond that encounter with Herakin."

"Then how do we know Herakin exists?" Tashi asks.

Menson punches Tashi in the arm and grins. "We just do, okay. I believe the story."

"We grew up on *Silnar and the Darkened Sea*," I say. "That was my favorite book."

"Oooooh, we had Silnar too!" Mida says. "I love the story where he allowed himself to be swallowed by a sea snake to survive the journey underwater by using the snake's air."

"I always identified with Silnar," Losan says, glancing at me. "I used to pretend to be Silnar when I was young because I, too, lost my love and always dreamed of crossing the darkened sea to find her. I told myself someday I would."

I look away, feeling the heat rise in my throat and burn in my cheeks.

"Aw, Nopsan. That's tragic," Keema says. "What happened to her?"

"I don't know," he says. "But I'm hopeful I'll find her. That I haven't lost her."

"I like Silnar too," Burkhart mumbles.

Dieter and I make eye contact, but I turn away before I can laugh. Who is this version of Burkhart, and what has he done with our arschole?

Haydrich remains aloof, plowing ahead, keeping a distance between himself and the group. I cannot help but watch him as the others continue talking and laughing about the stories we share and the things we have in common, feeling both a great sense of belonging and a growing sense of foreboding.

18

Mount Opasno Base Camp consists of a smattering of canvas tents crammed together on the snowy tongue of the Himball icefall, a chaotic maze of ice blocks and seracs cleaved off from the Himball glacier high above. Jagged peaks surround the camp, each of which would be a monster in Ectair, but in Ainar they seem unimpressive in the towering shadow of Opasno.

Under Norda's tutelage, we spent the first week at Base Camp organizing our gear, learning how to ascend and descend the fixed ropes, cutting steps into snow and ice with our alpenstocks, taking short hikes to acclimate, and giving the summit wardens time to establish our high camps and set our ropes. Norda has provided us each with a container of thick, smelly green paste to help prevent skin burn. After he recounted a tale of a climber whose face entirely peeled off after a nasty burn, we all dutifully lathered the stinking goo onto our skin each morning.

Tonight is the final ceremony where we honor the gods before handing our lives over to them. I wear an ilice around my neck made of polished volcanic stones from the Paradox Valley, interspersed with red- and pink-painted beads, and crafted by artisans in Hidel. Everyone's ilice is distinctive, like the patterns on our socks.

The air is thin in our lungs, despite our gradual acclimatization to the elevation. Every few steps, I find myself gulping down the scarce oxygen and trying not to worry about the daunting ascent ahead. Enduring even Base Camp, at this rate, feels unimaginable.

I step from our tent, hugging my bergbear fur tighter around my shoulders. Glancing up at the Himball icefall, I note the shades of blue and white, the places where the ice goes dark.

Hungry. Beyond the icefall, one hundred feet up, over dark crevasses and treacherous ice, lies our first camp. Eighty percent mental, I repeat to myself. I know I can reach Camp One. Nothing matters beyond that objective. Once I get to camp one, I can set my mind on camp two and the obstacles that lie beyond.

"No matter how big you know a mountain is, nothing prepares you for its magnitude like standing at its feet." Keema hands me a mug of tea, and we clink our glasses together before sipping.

"I don't think I'll feel prepared until I've made it up and back down," I say. "Until then, some part of me will feel like I'm about to die."

She laughs, a melodic lilt that echoes off the snow, and I understand why Burkhart is drawn to her. Does that laugh sound like Otto's? I wonder.

"Do you know any Ainarian women who were born in Ectair and who look like us?" I ask.

She cocks her head and looks at me coolly. "Why do you want to know?"

"I'm looking for someone." I risk partial truth. "A friend of mine—his twin sister was smuggled out of Ectair to avoid execution. He's asked me to find her."

"And you think it's me?"

"I think it could be anyone, and I don't know where else to start."

"People don't talk about where they come from. It's safer not to. Safer not to know. Even if someone were born in Ectair but grew up here, they wouldn't say it. Ainar is safe, but we have those willing to trade secrets for silver shindos. Good luck finding her. It'll be gods near impossible."

"How old are you and when is your urday?" I persist with a smile.

She pats my cheek and smiles back. "It's not me, Klarke."

I exhale in frustration, trying to settle upon my next plan. If not Keema, then who? Obid is captive here somewhere. Once our climb is done, I will find him. I will beg Naisae, King Gyalzen even, to let me speak to Obid before they send him back to King Adolar. Obid will know if Otto's sister ended up in Stracto. Perhaps, if he is about to be executed, he may be more willing to share what he knows. He wouldn't take those secrets across the darkened sea, would he?

"We have a saying on the Isle of Bloque." Chessa joins us, her light hair swirling around her face like flakes of snow in a flurry, her voice like rocks tumbling down a raging river. "He who stares too long at the mountain is like a rabbit staring too long at a volve." She laughs and pulls her hair into a tight knot at the back of her head. Her eyes, I notice, are silver today. "Do not let the predator see in your eyes that you are afraid. Come, let us join the ceremony and begin our foray into the jaws of destiny." She slaps each of us on the back, and I marvel at her tall, lanky frame as she moves away.

Our omies told stories of the risants who used to live in the Mountains of the Unknown to the south, but who were chased out by humans. Legend has it that they fled north to settle the Isle of Bloque. The risants are long gone, but their blood lingers in the men and women who call the island home. Chessa could easily carry such blood.

Keema and I follow her through the maze of tents to an open space where the flames of a bonfire rise into the shadowed air. The rest of the Parvanatari and Ascenditures trickle in. I find Kiel and stand close to him, Dieter to my other side. I take Dieter's hand and give it a reassuring squeeze. He doesn't have Otto here to support him, to cheer for him upon our return from the summit. He will never truly have Otto in any situation, I realize, and, as lonely as I feel, he must feel that isolation even more acutely. I squeeze harder, and he returns the pressure.

Between the fire and the mountain sits a holzenschrein, a statue of Laren, and a rock pile topped with a boulder. A number of bowls, filled with various colored pigments, cover a nearby tabletop. A Laren grail—eighteen small bundles cradled in a basin supported by metallic tentacles—rests at the feet of our sea god.

Three päters, identical in garb to those from Ectair, with white masks and long black robes, stand with three other religious figures. The black robes these three wear are decorated with intricate, gold-stitched symbology of the sun, moon, and Sleeping God and lack any opening for their heads. They stand like black-shrouded phantoms, their robes fluttering in the cold mountain wind. Eyeless. Faceless. I shudder. I never thought I would miss the white masks of Ectair's päters, but these figures seem frighteningly inhuman.

"Pija," Mida whispers from behind. "Priests of the Sleeping God."

"Why do they have no faces?" I whisper back.

"The Sleeping God has no face," she says. "They are everything and nothing."

"Right," I reply. "So, is the Sleeping God nice? Or are they more like Laren?"

"We do not know their personality. We believe them to be benevolent, though we expect them to be angry when they awaken, as much of the world refuses to honor them."

"Why are they still sleeping? And when will they awaken?"

"They sleep because it is not yet time to wake, and, unfortunately, we do not know when that time will come. Until it does, we worship as called."

"And the rock pile?" I point to the stacked pile topped by a boulder. "What does that represent?"

"It is to honor them. They do not wish for elaborate elegance, only the simplicity of nature."

A gong sounds once, twice, but unlike the gong used at Vether's Fel to mark our climbs, this one sings and lingers, the pitch rising and falling as a pija runs a wooden stick around its edges. Somewhere a flute begins to play, accompanied by an unfamiliar stringed instrument. I glance over at the musicians on the far side of the bonfire.

"It's a lakilute," Tashi tells us. "Made from a mountain gourd.

That particular sound comes from strumming the strings with a stone; the stone represents the same one atop the Sleeping God's shrine. All things lead back to them."

Burning incense twirls through our ranks. The three pija do not speak as they move to the rhythm of the music. The first raises a hand from beneath dark folds of fabric, then dips their fingers into the yellow pigment paint and streaks it across the boulder. The second and third follow, selecting other colors. Next, the päters follow, and then the Parvanatari line up.

"The colors represent gifts we wish to strengthen," Tashi whispers. I notice other Parvanatari whispering to other Ascenditures, similarly explaining the significance of the ritual as it unfolds. Keema holds Burkhart's arm while whispering in his ear.

"You select the color you wish the Sleeping God to bless you with. Yellow is for patience, green for courage, red for strength, and purple for honesty. Orange represents generosity, blue tranquility, black wisdom, and pink is perseverance. When you wipe the pigment across the stone, you seal your prayer," Tashi says.

"And which color for revenge?" I ask.

"The Sleeping God delivers only positive virtues," Tashi replies with a laugh. "They do not deal in revenge."

"Not yet," I say, "but when they wake up into a world where Ectair exists, they will."

Tashi chooses blue and wipes their finger across the color-streaked rock. I select pink because perseverance is a virtue required of most tasks, namely revenge, and because pink is the color I most trust to guide me. Kiel chooses black. From the Laren grail, we select a bundle, a sacrifice to spread at the top of Opasno. Finally, we move past the holzenschrein, and I drape my ilice over the pinnacle. Naisae, I notice, selects purple paint—for honesty, and I wonder at the secrets she is hiding. Aedan selects green.

One of the pija steps forward, chanting in Ainarian; they are differentiated from the others by a simple red band around the black shroud of their head. "They are asking Opasno if it is okay for us to climb," Tashi tells me. "We must receive the mountain's blessing before we may go."

The chanting rises and falls like a mournful song as we stand shivering in the frigid wind. Finally, the eerie black-robed figure nods, and the Parvanatari cheer and clap their hands.

"With the gods' blessing, we are now ready to climb," Naisae says. "Tomorrow, we begin an epic journey requiring great mental and physical fortitude. Some of you have trained a lifetime for this, some only a few weeks. This will challenge everyone and be too much for some. Ultimately, this climb is about unity, and from the strongest to the weakest, we will either make it safely to the summit and back, or we will all fail."

Her eyes rest upon me, and she smiles. I attempt to return the smile, but I cannot help but wonder what else Naisae of Ubana is hiding. Can it be that she is really just trying to protect Losan?

"We are honored to join the Parvanatari on this climb," Aedan adds. "The Ascenditures were once trusted friends of the Parvanatari. Together, we often used to ascend the slopes of this sacred mountain. Let us bring back that tradition and once again climb as allies." He pauses a moment, then continues, his voice heavy with emotion. "I would like to dedicate this climb to our late leader, Ellias Veber, who loved Mount Opasno above all others. He once described it to me as 'Orna's most treacherous and wondrous creation.' He would have loved to be here for this, especially to have had the chance to climb with Klarke."

My eyes fill with tears, and I nod to Aedan. He looks over at me, placing a hand over his heart. "To Ellias Veber," he says.

"To Ellias," the group repeats.

"To Ellias," I whisper again, relishing the sound of his name spoken aloud.

The music shifts from ethereal strings and bells to an upbeat, festive tempo. A porter starts to beat upon a drum and the lakilute player runs the stone evermore quickly across the strings. My body begins to sway, and my foot to tap. During the ceremony, colorful flags, mimicking the color of the pigments, have been strewn between the tents, and now they flap in Mount Opasno's frosty wind. Unlike our Ectarian flags that hang sadly in the perpetual rain, heavy with the weight of unending moisture, these flags are joyful, like the music, like the people.

The päters and pija depart into the dark surrounding the tents, and a porter passes around wooden mugs of plum wine. Climbers and summit wardens begin to dance around the fire, their feet and arms moving to the beat set by the drum. The sky darkens, Azura peering over the shoulder of Opasno, casting her blue haze over the revelers. In the moon's light, the fissures and seracs on the Himball icefall glow deep and forbidding, a shade of ultramarine so rich it is terrifying. It seems a color not from this world but one that seeped over from the darkened sea.

I walk from the party to the edge of the icefall, where I spot a small stone, tumbled smooth by the glacier. Picking it up, I am reminded of Rayna running her fingertips across the painting of the Celebern Fields, yearning to touch the grass and flowers. I tuck the stone into my pocket to take home to her. A piece of Opasno. I will bring the world to Rayna until she is free to go to it herself.

Kneeling down, I touch a fallen chunk of ice, closing my eyes as the chill penetrates my glove and numbs my fingers.

"Orna," I say. "And maybe I should also address you, Sleeping God, and you, Laren. Keep us safe on the coming climb. Please don't let this be a repeat of Bonen. Please don't make me say goodbye to another friend. Let us find the peace we all yearn for." I exhale and look up the icefall toward Camp One as lightning strikes the summit.

It feels like an answer from the gods—I just don't know if it's a good sign or a bad one.

The sound of crunching snow draws my attention, and I turn to see Tizian walking toward the glacier's tongue. He pauses when he sees me, then pivots to move away.

"Wait," I say. He stops but doesn't face me. "We've never had an actual conversation."

"For good reason."

"What have I ever done to you?"

He turns now and fixes me with eyes as dark as the ice. "Ye want a conversation? Ye want to talk? Here's all I have to say to ye. I hope ye fall up there. I hope the mountain swallows ye, that freak Tashi, and all the other fozies. What else do ye want to talk about?"

"But why?"

He laughs at my question.

"I don't think you know why," I say.

"Because I despise ye. I despise ye all," he replies scornfully.

His words do not surprise me—he has communicated as such with his silent glares—but I am surprised by how little I care. Tizian's hatred does not wound me, but I wonder at it. "Was it you?" I ask.

"Was what me?"

"Did you help Gio kill Ellias? Did you kill those boys on Mount Bonen?"

"Of course not," he says. "I wasn't on Fitzhan, remember? I had to sit out so ye could climb. You'll know when I'm involved because you'll be on the rope when it happens."

"Be careful what you say, Ectarian," Losan says sternly, materializing out of the darkness. "Speak like that again, and you might end up with an alpenstock in the back of your skull."

Tizian huffs, flicks Losan the fickson, and strides back to camp.

"Are you okay?" Losan asks.

"We don't have the luxury in Ectair of being sensitive," I tell him with a rueful smile. "I hear that scheiz all the time."

"You hear that someone wants you dead?" he asks dubiously, frowning.

"Frequently." I laugh mirthlessly.

"Klarke, I'm sorry that's your world. I'm sorry you were left there."

"Well, not many other options when your parents die within weeks of each other and you're only eight."

"I hate that you've suffered," he murmurs, taking my gloved hand in his. "You can stay here when this is all over. Stay with me. You'll be safe in Ainar. Free."

He leans toward me, touching his forehead to my own. I close my eyes, breathing in the frigid, clear air. *Safe and free.* The women here are everything I have always longed to be—joyful, powerful, equal to the men. I want this life so badly, and the fierce desire for it hurts more than any word Tizian could utter. But then I think of the women in Ectair. Of Lena, Marike, Rayna, the girls from my tenement. I press my hand against Losan's chest and gently push him away.

"As long as women in Ectair are numb to those that wish them dead, I will remain in my kingdom. Until we can all be safe and free, I must go back."

"And like Silnar, I will continue my quest across the darkened sea to find you. To bring you home," he says. "I've waited nine years. I can wait as long as it takes."

I kiss Losan's cheek, my lips lingering for a moment on the warmth of his skin. Lightning again strikes the summit of Opasno. Another answer, and another sign I cannot interpret.

19

The serac is as tall as a Sleeping God's finger and is tilted at a precarious angle over the metal ladder I am about to cross. Below the ladder, the crevasse disappears into a bottomless shade of blue—but it is not the serac that frightens me or the dark depths of the crevasse or the frayed fixed ropes we trust to navigate the deadly maze through the Himball glacier. It's the crevasses we cannot see that terrify us all—the ones buried beneath rotten ice. Today we are making our first push to Camp One to acclimate, and then we will return to Base Camp. *Climb high, sleep low*, Norda tells us.

I walk behind Diki and Mida, studying how they place their boots on the ladder rungs, where they put their alpenstocks, and how they shift their weight to balance on fragile snow bridges. We've reached a crevasse two feet wide or more, too narrow to install a bridge over.

"Just jump," Mida says. A wool cap is pulled low over her ears, and the glacier goggles block her eyes, but I can see her mouth curve in an encouraging smile. "It's like hopping over a creek."

"Except you won't just get wet feet if you fall," Diki adds. Where Mida is kind and soft-spoken, Diki is brash and direct. I knew women like both of them in the tenements. Life hardens you or makes you kind. Sometimes, you're lucky enough to be both.

The crevasse may be narrow, but my body is burdened by a heavy pack, and my hobnailed boots feel clumsy on my feet. I glance down at the deepening shades of blue in the crevasse wall.

"Don't look," Mida says. "Trust me. Just jump. If you fall, brace your body against the walls. We will help you out."

"If you fall on the Himball, you don't deserve to summit,"

Diki adds. "We must have been all of ten years old when we first climbed the icefall."

They say everything in pairs, these two—one positive, one negative, like two balancing forces. I've never met twins before, not even ones of the same gender who are allowed to live. I rock back on my heels to gain momentum and jump, landing in a clumsy heap on the other side.

Keema jumps behind me, landing on her feet. She offers a hand and pulls me up. "It's funny how different they are, isn't it? If you find your friend's twin, how different do you think they will be? Perhaps that's where you start," she adds. "Find someone who is the exact opposite of your friend."

"So then I am looking for someone who is power hungry, deceitful, and manipulative?" I shake my head with a laugh. "That could be just about anyone."

Keema shrugs and digs the end of her alpenstock into the ice. "Just a thought," she says before trudging up the slope. I shake my head again—I need to focus on surviving my first day on the skirt tails of Opasno.

The summit wardens have gone ahead to set up the higher camps and to place fixed ropes. We pass them on the slopes as they shuttle back and forth, and I'm inspired by their unfailing energy and kind smiles. Even carrying a load of fuel or a heavy ladder, they pause to greet each of us and ask if we need any help. I am amazed by the number of expert climbers in Ainar, outside of the Parvanatari. These support teams could be their own professional crew—and indeed they are.

Later that night, we stumble back into Base Camp utterly exhausted. I feel overwhelmed at the thought of crossing repeatedly through the ice labyrinth of death. We will ascend to Camp One three times, Naisae has told us, each time returning that night to Base Camp. These pre-climb trainings will help our bodies adjust to the lack of oxygen and build the strength necessary to haul gear to Camp One, then Two, then higher.

"You looked strong out there, Klarke," Naisae tells me after dinner.

We sit on a wooden bench in the large mess tent as our fellow climbers dance and sing. I, like the others, have been given a long, loose garment to wear; mine is deep crimson and lined with goat's wool. I snuggle into it, enjoying the warmth of the tent. "Thank you," I tell her. "I don't feel very strong."

"Remember, it's eighty percent mental." Naisae leans into me, knocking her shoulder against mine. "You're going to be great. And you're going to have good days and bad days."

"Head up," I say.

"Head up," she agrees. "Always head up."

"Did you know Ellias too, or just my father?"

"I…" Her dark gaze drops to the ground, and I wonder if I will get the truth or another lie. "I did. I knew Ellias well. We were…" She trails off again, and if I'm not mistaken, her voice chokes with emotion.

"What?" I ask.

"It was a long time ago."

"What was?"

"He was my partner."

"Climbing partner?"

"Yes, and more."

Ellias had a partner? He was always single. Always alone. His team was his family.

"For a time, when you were young, Ellias moved to Ainar to be with me."

"Ellias lived in Ainar?" I ask, astonished but grateful for any morsel of information—each new detail feels like a bridge to him, a bridge across the darkened sea.

"He did," she says with a sad smile. "We loved each other, and we wanted to have a life together."

"Why did he leave?"

Norda begins singing as other climbers shout and cheer him on. I fight the urge to stand on the bench, to yell at them all to stop, to be quiet. I want time to stand still and to be alone with Naisae. To hear this truth. Whatever lie she told about Losan, this is the truth.

In the heart of the wilderness, under the moon's soft glow,
there's a mountain standing tall, in its majestic flow.
With peaks that touch the himmel,
and valleys lush and green.
I found a love so timeless, a dream I've never dreamed.

Tashi, Losan, and Diki join in Norda's song. I wonder where they have found the energy for singing and dancing. Aching and exhausted, it is all I can do to raise the warm tea to my lips and listen to Naisae's words.

Oh, I'm in love with a mountain, it's a love so pure and true.
Every starrise and moonset, I find my heart anew.
With every step I climb, and every trail I roam,
I'm lost in this love, my mountain, my home.

"Why did Ellias leave Ainar?" I ask again.

Naisae places a hand on my knee and squeezes. "Another time. Let's enjoy this evening. It's been a long day."

"Please. I need this."

"Later," she says.

Losan appears at my side, takes my hands, and pulls me to my feet.

"I'm too tired!" I protest as Naisae, too, rises to her feet—but not to dance; she gives me a nod, then disappears through the tent flap to the snowy slopes outside. I want to follow, but Losan refuses to release my hands.

"This will loosen your muscles," he tells me, smiling mischievously, as he used to do before terrorizing Ectair's fishmongers. "And force you to acclimate."

I want to hear more about Ellias, about his relationship with Naisae, but tonight, clearly, she has no intention of talking. We have an entire mountain to climb together where I can ask her for more, I console myself. Then, before I can think any more about it, we are off, Losan spinning me around in a whirl of skirts and laughter. At first, I stumble and cannot find my feet, but then I get the rhythm of the music and allow him to lead me around the fire where the others dance. Losan winks and makes faces, hoots and hollers until I am grinning along with him.

Burkhart and Keema dance past us, and I cannot help but laugh as Burkhart—easily the grumpiest of man—trips over his feet and bumbles off-beat to the music, clearly trying to impress his partner.

Menson's arm is slung over Norda's shoulder, and the two tap their feet and sing merrily out of tune.

Kiel glares at Losan from his spot on the bench. I send him a reassuring smile just as Losan spins me away. I lose my balance, falling into his chest, his heartbeat a steady thud through his robe. This moment with Losan feels as if I am inhabiting another time, another place. A time when I had a family and a cozy bed with a view of the sea. With Losan, I can almost forget all that has happened since.

Oh, I'm in love with a mountain, it's a love so pure and true.
Every starrise and moonset, I find my heart anew.
With every step I climb, and every trail I roam,
I'm lost in this love, my mountain, my home.

The song ends, and before another begins, I excuse myself. My emotions feel entirely too complicated—as if life were not already challenging enough.

"I'm going to bed," I tell Losan.

"So soon? But this is so much fun." His twinkling eyes beg me to stay.

"It is," I say. He grips my hands, but I pull them away.

"Stay," he whispers.

"You know I can't."

I slip through the tent flap and make my way over the snow toward our team tent. Tonight is a night for running from the past, not living in it.

We complete our second push up the icefall with no issues, except for Russet slipping from one of the ladders that traversed a crevasse. Chessa caught his sleeve and hauled him back to safety. The high-pitched yell from Russet as he fell has been a source of merriment ever since. Chessa has nicknamed him *shriek*, and each time he comes to a treacherous crossing, she yells, 'You can do it, shriek!' He reddens but allows her her fun, even though I can see that he hates having garnered a title associated with weakness. We stay a night at Camp One, our small cluster of tents positioned at the base of a large slab of volcanic rock that shelters us from wind, falling rock, and avalanches. There is no fire and no dancing tonight. I miss the warmth of the fire, but am relieved not to be coaxed into dancing with Losan again. He seems always to be staring at me, and I find myself working just as hard to avoid his gaze.

The next phase of training takes us from Camp One to Camp Two. This section contains technical rock climbing, a skill I'm more confident in. We follow in the path of the summit wardens along fixed ropes, sliding our Veber clamping devices along for safety, until we reach Lars's Chimney, a hundred-foot rock chimney surrounded on both sides with chossy slabs of snow. Tashi has told us of Ainarians who have free-climbed the chimney—a dangerous undertaking; it can be difficult finding purchase on rock with an oversized pack, thick gloves, and nails hammered into your boots. I am relieved to discover that the support teams have placed ropes, and it is an easy scramble for us—technically easy, anyway. With decreasing oxygen levels, the higher we ascend, I feel as winded as if I'd never climbed a day in my life.

Above the chimney lies another slog through the snow to Camp Two. My brain cycles through thoughts of Naisae and Ellias, Kiel, Losan, and Haydrich, but I can't focus on anything for too long. Cogent thoughts morph into wicked daydreams of ungers stalking us and the gods plotting ways to take our lives.

"In a mountain crevasse, where shadows play their part," Tashi says under their breath as they pass me. We are on a stretch of snowfield without fixed ropes, a "no fall zone," as Norda calls it, following in the footsteps of the summit wardens who came ahead of us. I kick my boot tips into the snow and dig in the spike of the ice axe for balance, keeping it ever ready in case I slip.

"A canvas of blues, a masterpiece of art. In a world of ice and snow, I ventured forth along. Leaving childhood's gentle warmth, a journey of my own," Tashi continues.

"What is that? A poem?" I ask breathlessly.

"Yes," they say, slowing their pace to match mine. "I repeat these lovely verses over and over to the summit; it helps keep my mind off the physical challenges of the climb. My mother was a poetess, her mother too, so I grew up surrounded by verse. You should try it." Tashi glances back at me with a smile.

"I don't know any poems," I say.

"What about 'Edge of Orie's Abyss'?"

I laugh. "No, I am afraid not."

"You don't know the Abyss?" Diki says from behind me.

"Must be a cannibal thing." I hear Veit contribute from behind Diki. "We don't know it in the civilized world."

"If I were a cannibal," Diki says, "I'd fry your liver first, then eat your heart raw. Then I'd boil your brains and feed them to my sister. Too bad the Sleeping God won't let us eat meat."

"Yeah, too bad—" Tizian sneers.

"Anyway, 'Edge of Orie's Abyss,'" Tashi interrupts from ahead, raising their deep voice until it sounds like it rumbles from a crack in the earth. "Upon the edge of Orie's abyss, I stood—"

"A place of grief and shadows embraced, as should," Mida adds.

"Where loss had brought me to my knees," Diki says.

"In the depths of despair, I thought to appease," Tashi says, completing the first verse.

"I don't know it." I shake my head, although I know that abyss. I know what it is to stand on the dark drop of never-ending pain.

"The darkness like a shroud enveloped my soul," Tashi continues. "As sorrow's tempest swallowed me whole / But in the depths of Despair's cruel kiss / I found a glimmer of hope on the edge of the abyss."

"Thank you, Tashi, for sharing that," I manage, feeling a little shaken. Grief is a complex subject for me to hold. Sometimes it hurts too badly to visit in song or verse.

We stop for a rest break, and I gratefully take the opportunity to relieve myself behind a crag of ice a little distance from the group. I pull up my pants and shoulder my pack. Nothing is private on a mountain's slope.

"It's a beautiful poem, isn't it?" Haydrich asks as I rejoin the group.

"It is," I reply. "Haunting. Do you know it?"

"Yes. Many Ainairians journey to the southern lands and bring their poems and legends with them."

"Why do they go south?"

"Some to climb Eldras," he says. "Finish checking off the big four."

Opasno. Himmelisle. Bonen. Eldras.

"And the others?"

"To see for themselves."

"See what?"

"The truth." He shrugs, glancing away, his expression hidden behind the fringe of his cap and the gleaming expanse of his goggles.

"Why are you here, Haydrich? If you're really part of some bigger, more important mission, why leave Ectair? Why waste precious time climbing mountains? Is it some kind of ego thing?"

"Ego?" He turns to me with a laugh. "I don't have an ego. I don't belong to myself. Like you, I seek answers. I am after a woman."

"Who?"

"You."

"Well, you've wasted your time then."

"I don't think I have."

Everything at this elevation is slow. Especially time. We wait in line at each obstacle, bridge, ladder, or rope, and when our turn comes, we move like sloths, our bodies heavy with fatigue. My life becomes a series of ascensions and descensions from Base Camp to Camp One, then Camp Two and Three, and back. Over and over. All to enable physical acclimatization.

Finally, after weeks of training, we set out from Base Camp bound for our final ascent to Camp One.

"Opasno is to Orna as Hildegroth is to Laren," Chessa says as we cross a bridge over a gaping crevasse in the Himball Icefall. I keep my eyes forward, averted from the yawning icy darkness below. "This is her monster," she adds.

"Comforting," I say.

"Comfort?" Diki laughs from up ahead. "What's that?"

"I hate this part." Kiel gestures with his alpenstock toward the serac that towers above us. "It feels as if that thing is just waiting for me to pass under it so it can finally fall."

"The Himball icefall is one of the most dangerous parts of this climb," Norda says from behind Kiel. "The Himball glacier moves daily, and that kind of movement leads to shifting ice and cracks. That serac could topple any moment."

"I told you the Eiskrits are real," Menson says. "Himball is dangerous because it is a living, hungry being."

"Also comforting," Kiel adds wryly, and we all laugh.

We chose to be here, I remind myself. We choose the risk of death every time we traverse rock or ice. It is in our blood, in our souls, and there is no escaping it.

We reach Camp One without incident. Orna, the glacier, and the Sleeping God have allowed us safe passage. Will that continue, or are they saving the entertainment of our deaths for higher, more treacherous elevations?

The next day, we scale Lars's Chimney.

"Named, of course, for Lars Veber," Naisae tells us. "He was the first to climb Opasno and to establish the Dalaga

Ridge route, named for the Ainarian climber who helped him summit." She speaks of the Veber family without any visible emotion. Whatever she shared before has been locked away. I must find the time and opportunity to crack it back open.

Then my turn comes to scale the chimney. With the help of a wobbly sisal ladder, a mess of tangled, fixed ropes, and a technique aptly named chimneying—where I press my back into one side and my legs into the other using pressure to hold me in place—I move upward, trying to keep my hobnailed boots from sticking in the ropes or slipping on the rock.

Camp Two is situated above Lars's Chimney, in the shadow of a steep exposed ridge of rock that towers above us. I stumble into my tent, exhausted, but feeling stronger than I did on previous trips to Camp Two. My lungs feel as if they are working more efficiently, and my muscles are less fatigued. Over a meal of potato mash, oats, and nuts, I feel quietly pleased with myself—Camp Two on Opasno. Not bad for a new mountaineer.

That night I pull my sleeping bag tightly about my shoulders and attempt to still my racing mind. I need my rest, I know, because my most significant challenge yet lies between Camp Two and Three—the Stone Schrein, a 1500-foot vertical section of rock, coated with jagged sheets of fragile ice prone to breaking free and sweeping us across the darkened sea. The technical requirement is not as tricky as that posed by Lars's Chimney, but the strenuousness of the climb makes it the greater challenge of the two. The Stone Schrein is rocky, icy, and precipitously steep. Our support team fixed ropes during their first ascent, so, for us, it's mostly a mental game and a constant prayer.

The Veber device is attached to my harness and the fixed ropes so I can move upward easily. If I were to slip, the device would arrest my fall. We've added the crampons to the base of our boots to secure us to the slope. I step, kick the spikes on my boots into the ice, breathe. Step, kick, breathe. Step, kick, breathe. Aedan, in front of me, sets the pace, and I try to match his rhythm, focusing intently on the hypnotic pattern of his gait—anything to chase away fatigue and fear. Norda takes his place behind me. Even though he could easily pass us all, he waits patiently, giving me plenty of space so I don't feel rushed. From below I hear the shout, "Rock!" and my thoughts rush to the last time I heard that alarm, warning climbers of a rock fall—when Ellias and Fieko died. I grit my teeth and continue my ascent. Nothing can be done for a climber behind me. The only safe thing to do is get off this metamorphic death trap.

By the time we reach Camp Three, we are weary, our exposed cheeks starburned. Kiel had been the one to shout "Rock!" but, fortunately, everyone had managed to avoid the rock fall. Tizian and Keema struggle for air, gasping for breath, and Kiel complains of a pounding headache; the rest of us seem to be managing the ascent without too much trouble. Norda reassures Tizian, Keema, and Kiel that with some tea and rest, their symptoms will pass.

Camp Three is prone to avalanches and can easily be swept away by an onrush of falling snow. It is the only available spot upon which to pitch the tents, however, so we try to put such thoughts out of our minds. Norda and Menson have stashed additional supplies along the Stone Schrein in the eventuality that Camp Three is buried by an avalanche and we have to descend for supplies. No avalanches come, however, and we rope up the next day in our teams and cross the Juvan glacier without incident. I keep anticipating that something will go wrong, not because the gods are angry or because the fates will it, but because some person with evil intent is pulling the collective strings. I remind myself again that this is not Mount Bonen, and King Adolar and his minions are far away. Even Veit is in good humor as we cross the glacier, forgetting, it seems, to be a jerk.

We reach Camp Four beneath bright blue skies. Kiel's headache has worsened, and Aedan has vomited several times, but they both assure us they can continue. I can scarcely move three feet before having to gulp in air, and I have little appetite but otherwise feel healthy enough.

Camp Four consists of a narrow ledge of icy rock with no

room for the large tents of previous encampments. Here we erect a row of small two-person tents. Naisae has requested that I bunk with her, and my mind races at this upcoming opportunity to ask all my questions.

At each camp, we are given tasks, either to prepare for the following day or to provide for the evening meal and the security of our camp. Even though no one is hungry, we prepare the food every morning and evening and force ourselves to eat. My job at Camp Four, along with Haydrich and Russet, is to melt snow for water and to fill the canteens.

I approach Russet and Haydrich, interrupting their conversation, which comes to a hurried close. "We can talk later…" Russet mutters.

"It's okay, she knows," Haydrich says as he leans over to light the stove.

I drop an armful of snow at his feet. "What do I know?" I demand.

Haydrich packs a pot with snow, places it on the stove, and sits back on a square of canvas. Russet glances between us, then sits next to Haydrich, filling another pot.

"You know that I intend to overthrow the king. That I have someone else I'd like to bring to power. And that I'm looking for allies."

I cough as a blast of icy wind steals into my lungs. "Not him, Haydrich. Whatever you're planning, please don't involve Russet."

"But he wants to get rid of Adolar," Russet says. "Don't you? Why would you not join him? Why should I not?"

How do I answer that? How can I tell Russet that Haydrich might also be evil, just a different variety of evil than King Adolar? That Haydrich Malte and his plan cannot and will not be our salvation?

"You could be hanged just for listening to him, Russet. And he will not protect you. You are nothing to him."

"We protect those who follow us," Haydrich says. "If you gave me a chance, you would understand this."

"He's got magic on his side, Klarke," Russet adds.

"What do you mean, magic?"

"Our world used to carry more knowledge. We were aware of ourselves, each other, the gods, the world, and everything in it." Haydrich pours water from a pot into a canteen and fills the pot again with snow. "We lost that, but my leader has found it, has brought many of us together under the banner of truth, and we will use it against the king."

I know of only one magic our world had access to, and it was outlawed, buried, and destroyed for a reason—it could not be kept from the hands of twisted souls.

"The darken mages are gone—" I'm about to say more when I remember the päter in the castle, wearing a black diemant and carrying the purple ferns. Russet gestures toward my pot to let me know the snow has melted and the water is boiling. I take it off the heat and shake my head. "Gone," I whisper.

Haydrich laughs. "Who said anything about darken mages? I said *awareness*. There's no reason to be afraid. We've taken what the mages corrupted and remade it anew into something far distant from darkness."

I don't like it. I don't want to think about battling magic. I can barely stay ahead of my normal enemies.

"And what will you do to those who oppose your takeover of the kingdom?" I stare out across the high peaks of the Parowan mountains toward Ectair. I think of Lena, of Rayna. Of the women in the tenements who don't have the time or energy to care about who rules them, who can think only of staying alive, of finding their next meal, of dodging the blows of men? What will happen to them in the coming war? What will happen to them after?

Haydrich smiles, revealing teeth perfectly straight and as white as snow. It's a rare thing, his smile, and it fills me with foreboding.

"No one will oppose us when they see what we arrive with," he says.

Wind chill seeps beneath my coat, and the hair prickles on

the back of my neck. My breath stops in my throat. "A weapon?" I whisper.

"You are familiar with the creation story, are you not?" Haydrich asks.

"Of course," Russet pipes in, clearly eager to impress Haydrich. "Lightning struck a stone in the darkened sea, turning it into the first diemant. And from that diemant sprang Orna, Laren, and the other minor gods."

"Yes," Haydrich says. "The diemants can create life. Not just life, but gods. Powerful beings. They can also bring them back."

"The diemants were lost or destroyed," I say, striving for confidence but unable to forget the black diemant worn around the neck of the päter in Ectair, and the one Kiel saw in King Adolar's room while repairing the Nied tower. So two survived? And if Haydrich claims the darken mages are back, they could have already created a hundred new black diemants.

"You know that's not true," he says, his gaze intent on mine, a smile curving his lips. I open my mouth to retort but find I can say nothing. "Do you know the place where the first diemant was created?" Haydrich asks Russet.

"The Celebern Fields," Russet whispers, eyes wide as he hangs on Haydrich's every word.

Haydrich snaps his finger and points at Russet. "Exactly. We are not building a weapon, Russet. We are calling upon something far more powerful."

My thoughts race furiously. Dr. Helmut had told me that the päters were using the purple ferns to create something. Could the päters be working for the Dark Promise and the Schaeter? Or for King Adolar? I laugh, out of fear or disbelief—I can't tell. "You're telling us you've found a way to create a god?" I ask.

"A god? No." Haydrich snorts. "A monster, to be more precise."

I think of Hildegroth, the great sea beast, the only veritable monster I know of in our world. "Impossible," I say.

"Necessary," he responds, his expression becoming grim.

"King Adolar searches for a way to control Hildegroth, and has for years. He has cursed the world in this quest. He is weak and must be stopped. And we are preparing something that could destroy Hildegroth, should the king be successful in commanding his movements."

"Destroy Hildegroth?" I ask, astonished. Orna created Hildegroth—with its thirteen powerful tentacles and fanged whirlpool maw—for Laren. A force powerful enough to defeat Hildegroth could annihilate Ectair. I glance up, toward the summit of the most dangerous peak in our known world, feeling as if I have yet to experience true fear. "But how? How could you possibly create this monster?"

"I can answer every question you have—if you join me."

I swallow, thinking of my mother and Otto's sister. Haydrich is promising ash in my lungs.

"I know who killed your friend," he says. "I can tell you who cut Ellias's rope."

"Gio cut Ellias's rope," I seethe through the hot tears that fill my eyes. *Don't get sucked in*, I tell myself. He wants to weaken me. To force me to do his bidding.

"Fair." He smiles. "Then I'll tell you which teammate started the rockfall to cover Gio while he cut your friend loose."

Russet grabs me as I leap forward to tear Haydrich's eyes out. I lash out, desperately trying to reach him, to inflict upon him the same pain he's causing me.

"Your boyfriend is starting to understand. He asks a lot of questions."

"What do you mean?" I demand furiously.

"You might think Kiel is just sniffing around, but I know when skepticism begins to shift toward belief. I see it in his eyes."

I want to tell Haydrich he's wrong. That Kiel is too smart, too good to align himself with the Dark Promise. But I don't want to blow Kiel's cover, particularly given the fact that I am the one who told him to investigate.

"I'll give you something right now," Haydrich says casually, gathering up the canteens. "Kiel told me King Adolar has a diemant, but I already knew that. You know how?"

I bite my lip and curse my traitorous head when it shakes back and forth.

"We gave it to him."

My hands ball into quivering fists. "Why would you give such power to a wicked man you wish to destroy?"

"It is a fake," he replies.

"But why?"

"Answers," Haydrich says. "For your loyalty." He turns away, a half dozen canteens strapped across his shoulders.

I sink to the ground, unable to process all that I have learned. Russet drops beside me and nudges my shoulder. "I want the truth," he says, "and so do you. And we both want the king gone. Maybe Haydrich is not the perfect ally, but he's better than what we've got now."

I inhale deeply and hold the air in my lungs, counting down slowly as I exhale. Haydrich offers me servitude to a new master. Fealty to a different tyrant. Adolar is my enemy, but at least he bleeds. If Haydrich is right, I have no idea who I'd be up against. Adolar is a beast I can destroy. I'm not sure if I can say the same of a monster created by the darken mages.

Then I'll tell you which teammate started the rockfall to cover Gio while he cut your friend loose.

I glance across our narrow encampment. Kiel, Dieter, and Tizian are checking ropes and sharpening crampons; Burkhart and Veit prepare a nut-based stew for dinner, which at this altitude, most of us will struggle to eat; Aedan is in conversation with Naisae, presumably going over tomorrow's climbing plan.

Haydrich is lying. It can't be. Not again. Not here. It can't be that another one of these men is a murderer. Kiel catches my eye and gives me a warm smile, but it does nothing to melt the ice wrapping around my heart.

20

I am curled up in my sleep sack, nestled close to Naisae. Our tent is small, and we rely upon the heat of our bodies to stay warm. The canvas tent flaps and pops in the snapping roar of wind that blasts across the narrow ledge, and I wait for the avalanche that will sweep the entire camp onto the Juvan glacier.

"Do you know what happens to a body that slides miles down a mountain?" Diki asked me during the afternoon climb.

"Not really," I'd said.

"When they find your remains, you'll be mostly naked and missing a head, a leg, an arm. A blood smear on the white snow, that is how they will find you. Your nose, ears, and eyes will have been ground to paste. Teeth gone. They'll pick you up in pieces and pack you away in a box before loved ones can see you. And that's *if* they find you. There is a good chance that you will be ripped into a thousand pieces that stay buried in the snow or lie undiscovered in a crevasse."

I know I need to sleep. I need to keep my mind focused on the climb ahead. I need to stay calm. But I can't. Worse than Diki's detailed description of what will happen to my body if an avalanche comes tonight is the thought of Russet, or even Kiel, being drawn into Haydrich's cult on the false notion that it will help me. Clearly, Haydrich is working with the päters on this mysterious power he spoke of, and I had thought the päters were loyal to King Adolar.

Could it be that everyone around the king has a plan to betray him? If I sit by, stay out of the way as Haydrich suggested earlier, perhaps the difficulty of King Adolar will resolve itself, and my troubles will be over. But what will happen to Otto?

If Adolar is removed from power, they will certainly destroy his successor's path to the throne. The simplest way to ensure that: kill Otto and any others who might lay claim to power.

Haydrich is here, in Ainar, to find Otto's sister, to either remove her from the world or confirm that she is already dead. What if he, too, suspects Keema? Could she be in danger? Might Haydrich kill her based on suspicion alone? I sit up, panting, and gasp at the thin air. I fight the urge to run from the tent screaming.

"It's okay, Klarke," Naisae says, rubbing my arm. "The air is very thin here, especially at night. It might feel as if you are suffocating, but you'll be all right. Take slow, deep breaths and focus on something that relaxes you."

All I can think about is the bloody torso of a headless Keema smeared across the Juvan glacier. I gasp and clutch at my chest. Where did all the air go?

"Would you like to talk about Ellias?" Naisae's voice is soft and calming. She sits up and we move closer to each other, so that our shoulders touch. The wind continues to roar and howl outside, the tent flapping around us as the canvas strains against the anchored pegs.

"Yes, I would. Did you love him?"

"More than anything. When I heard what happened…" Her voice breaks, and I feel her body tremble violently in the dark.

"What happened, Naisae? Why did he return to Ectair?"

The tent lights to silver in a sudden flash of lightning, a crack of thunder following closely behind. I imagine the snow loosening its grip on Opasno's slope, our tents sliding down in a dark tumble of ice and rock and death onto the glacier below.

"We had a child together," she whispers. "Kizi was his name. Ellias was so proud of our little boy. Said one day he'd be the greatest climber the world had ever seen."

"Ellias had a child? He never mentioned him. Where is Kizi now?"

Naisae is silent, then I hear a muffled sob and a quick intake of breath. "Nobody was to blame, and we were both to blame. But I couldn't admit that until it was too late."

"What happened?" I whisper.

"The three of us were out climbing. Kizi was only three. Old enough to wander around and play with sticks, rocks, bugs. He knew to stay close, but not too close. He was a smart kid. So curious. So full of joy." She pauses to take in a ragged breath. "I was belaying Ellias. He was about twenty feet up on the face when the hold he was gripping crumbled. I was able to pull him taut on belay. He was safe. But Kizi…"

Nausea swirls up from my belly as I think of the frayed rope. Of Ellias's broken body on the moraine. I don't want to hear what she's about to say. Not again. Not this.

"Below, Kizi had wandered too close to the wall," she whispers, barely audible over the roaring wind. "The rock landed directly on him…he was gone immediately…he didn't experience any pain, I can be grateful for that at least."

Tears run down my cheeks and drip from my jaw. I close my eyes against the image of that broken little body. Ellias had had a child. He'd been a father.

"And I…I blamed him," Naisae manages, her voice rough with unshed tears. "For many years, I blamed him. How could such an able climber, one who knew rock so well, have chosen a rotten hold? I blamed him for Kizi's death, and I pushed him away, all the way back to Ectair. And that's when your parents brought him into your life. They introduced you to each other to help him heal. And when they passed, Ellias embraced you as if you were his own child because that's what you had become for him. You were his second chance. I am grateful for you, Klarke. You were salve to a grieving father."

"As he was to me," I say.

Naisae reaches for my hand, and together we weep as the wind groans and howls across the icy ledge.

I try to recall Ellias giving any hint of his dead child, of the pain and guilt he surely carried, but I can remember nothing. I had simply made the assumption that he loved climbing more than he could love any man or woman. Guilt sweeps over me for not seeking a deeper understanding of him, for being satisfied with casual assumptions. *You can climb your way out of a lot of dark places*, he'd once said to me. Is that, then, what he had done?

"Did you ever apologize?" I ask Naisae. "Did you ever reach out to him?"

"No," she whispers. "I was too weak."

"He didn't seem like a man burdened with anger," I say. "He was one of the liveliest and kindest people I knew. I think he must have forgiven you, Naisae. And I think he forgave himself."

She weeps again, and I squeeze her hand as we sit quietly with the wind, the thunder, and our grief.

"I've wanted to meet you for a long time," she says. "To thank you for helping Ellias to heal and find peace. For bringing him back to life. For giving him purpose. For being there for him when I couldn't. I wanted to meet Ectair's first female climber, but I also wanted to meet the woman Ellias had helped to raise. I thought seeing you might feel like seeing Kizi."

I do not know what to say and wish I had the words to bring her peace. I can imagine the heavy burden of her guilt, allowing Ellias to die unforgiven and to carry that pain on his journey across the darkened sea.

"He knew that you forgave him," I murmur, "even if you did not tell him so while he was living. And he, too, forgave you. I know this to be true."

Naisae is silent in the dark roar of the tent, and I do not know if she believes me or not. But I feel in my heart that it must be true. I knew, at least, of Ellias's kindness, of his generosity toward those he loved.

Life is complicated. Grief is twisted. The world is full of broken people searching for someone else with a broken edge that matches their own. We take our broken edges and piece them together into connections that keep us from feeling shattered. Naisae's broken edges meet mine on the forbidding slopes of Mount Opasno, and somewhere in the merging of our two fractured hearts, I feel Ellias, I feel Kizi, and I think she does too.

21

After a few fitful hours of staring at the tent's roof, I rise and dress for the summit push. Even if thoughts of death and grief hadn't hijacked my mind, I wouldn't have slept much. The air is shallow, leaving one with the constant feeling of suffocation. Azura casts blue hues over the slumbering snow and ice, darkening the jagged rock and deepening the icy blue crevasses to black. It is quiet. The wind was swallowed while the others slept, and now we exist in a foggy vacuum of fatigue and fear, anticipation and triumph.

I pull on my layers, tie my hair into a braid, weave the pink ribbon through the plaits, and light the carbide headlamp. Our next climb goes up Laren's Crest. Along Laren's Crest lies the infamous Unger Throat, a narrow couloir of ice and snow overhung with a massive ice cliff, thin in patches, and prone to splinter.

"We have a ten-hour climb ahead of us," Naisae says, her eyes red and puffy from a similarly sleepless night. "Here is where your mind will be your greatest tool. Stay alert, and call upon your inner resilience to guide you whenever you feel you cannot continue."

What a resilient woman she is, I muse, to have carried such grief.

"We can do this, team," Aedan adds. "Watch where you place your feet and alpenstock. You will struggle to breathe, but be patient. Pause when you must. Watch out for the safety of each other, and remember, we do this for Ellias."

"We will cross the Unger Throat today." Naisae's face is somber as she gazes at each of us in turn. "Mount Opasno has claimed the lives of forty-three climbers since Lars Veber's first attempt. Nineteen of those lives were lost on the Throat. I do not wish to scare you, but it is important to understand what lies ahead. This is where the gods deliver their justice. This is where you release control of yourself to forces beyond you."

"Suertgût." Kiel wraps me in a hug, and I return the embrace. "We're here. We're doing this. We will make it through and celebrate together at the summit."

"Suertgût," I respond, my head nestled against his chest. "I will see you on top of the world."

I have yet to tell him about Haydrich's revelations or about Kizi. There will be time for that later, and, like me, he needs to be focused only on the task ahead. When we're safely back in Base Camp, drinking wine and filling our lungs with heavier air, I will bring him in.

"Head up, darling," he whispers with a wink as he moves to his gear. "Always head up—"

"—for that is the direction in which the mountain grows." I smile back. *I miss you, Ellias. I miss you so much.*

I rope in behind Veit, with Losan behind me, and Naisae bringing up the rear. We will cross the Throat together, and if the ice wall falls, we will die together. I don't particularly want to die, and I definitely don't want to die tied to Veit.

We move slowly up Laren's Crest, placing one foot in front of the other, pausing every few steps to catch our breath. Each step feels as if my boots are encased with fifty-pound weights. Our fatigue keeps us silent. Our headlamps move up the slope like serpents weaving a sinuous path, like the worms that float along the sea's surface, glowing bright blue and green, even when Azura hides behind the clouds.

The cold cuts into my lungs. Even when I pause to catch my breath, the breath won't stay. It is as if this is the first time I have moved and my body can't keep up with the demands. Occasionally I feel the rope tugging where Veit is moving faster than I am able to do. I try to quicken my steps, but it is impossible. How can someone lift lead with noodles?

The wind whips constant tears from my eyes and streaks them across my cheeks. After what seems an eternity, we reach the Unger Throat, and as team one, we will be the first to cross. Cleos begins to rise, and our headlamps fade in the brilliance of our star. Light pierces the clouds, gilding the snow and ice in beautiful shades of orange and pink, washing away the threatening blues and blacks of the night. Alpenglow is like a starset on the snow. A sky on fire kissing the ice. Naisae allows us ten minutes to rest, hydrate, and enjoy the view before crossing the Throat.

Above us towers the ice wall, and I cannot help but stare at every crack, at every block of precarious snow that hangs over our path. I look across at the Throat—barely wide enough to allow one foot in front of the other. And then I look to the near-vertical slope and trace its expanse to the cliff edge fifty yards down that drops over an edge that leads to the Juvan glacier hundreds of feet down. Should one of us slip or should the ice wall break, there would hardly be time to drive in an alpenstock. It would take a miracle to save a team here. Why do we even rope up? I wonder. Perhaps to make us feel better.

"One man saved his teammate while crossing the Throat," Naisae says, as if reading my mind. "Ellias Veber."

My heart aches as I stare down the glacier toward the drop. Ellias could do anything.

"Ellias was on a three-man team, with a climber from Ainar and your father, Klarke."

I whip my gaze toward her. "My fa—?"

"Ellias saved his life. Years before you were born. The Ainarian climber wasn't so lucky. The falling ice severed the rope, and he went over right there." She points toward the forbidding drop. "But Ellias got his stock in just in time and pulled Anselm to safety. One of the greatest mountaineering rescues of all time."

I'm too tired to cry, though some part of me, deep inside, constricts and weeps. I wonder how many times Ellias saved me, kept me from going over, protected me from the world without my knowing. I wonder at the danger I face because he is not here to do it again.

"A woman also saved her team here," Losan says as he applies green starblock cream to his face. "Norda and Chessa wouldn't be here if it weren't for you, Naisae."

"It is a terrible feeling to fall on a mountain," Naisae says somberly. "We can all only hope there is someone there to catch us if and when it happens."

"Which is why you picked me for this kletshot, right?" Veit grins. "Big, powerful man to save everyone. I get it now."

I exhale in exasperation, my breath a billowing plume that immediately condenses into tiny particles of ice.

"We picked you because you are disposable," Losan replies, meeting Veit's grin with one of his own.

"Nopsan!" Naisae scolds.

"Sorry, Veit," Losan says. "I meant to say, we picked you because you are so pleasant to be around."

"How about we don't do this right before the most dangerous part of the climb?" I suggest, tucking my own starblock cream back into my pack. "We're all strong. We're all valuable. And most importantly, we're all so close to the end."

"Well put, Klarke," Naisae says. "Everyone ready?"

"Any last words for us?" Veit asks, glancing between the ice wall and the drop.

"Move quickly," Naisae says. "And keep your footing."

"Suertgût, Veit," I say, giving him a wary smile.

He nods and, for the first time I can ever recall, looks nervous.

I take a deep breath as Veit steps onto the Throat. I watch his footsteps and the rope behind him, praying he doesn't trigger a snowfall. He traverses safely, and then, when the rope grows taut, it is my turn to begin. With a pounding heart, I follow in Veit's footsteps, keeping enough distance between us that the rope doesn't pile up. Vertigo threatens to topple me, but I keep my eyes forward and my balance steady.

"Head up, darling," I repeat in a meditative mantra. "Head up."

I can't tell what's happening behind me, but Losan and Naishe must also be on the Throat. Four of us who, at any time, could plummet to our deaths. One foot. The next. Breathe. The Throat is only three hundred feet long, but at this moment it feels endless. We move as quickly as we are able, but we are as snails to the rapidly moving cart—slowed as we are by the thinness of the air, the exhaustion of our bodies, and the fear that grips our hearts. Blood pounds in my ears, and I mistake it for the cracking of ice. If I make one mistake, I die. If I make one mistake, I kill three others.

Veit reaches the other side. He digs his axe in, secures the rope, and watches us carefully. I'm relieved to see him taking his job seriously. I make it across and let out the breath I've been holding. I dig my alpenstock in and let out another breath when all four of us are safely across. We move up and out of the way as we watch the next kletshot—Kiel's team. Diki steps out onto the Throat, followed by Burkhart, Haydrich, Kiel, and Tashi.

A rising nausea threatens to steal my vision, and my legs quake, but I fix my gaze on every step Kiel takes. He is a strong and confident climber. I see it in his movements. The way he plants his feet and alpenstock. And yet, up here it doesn't matter how good you are. The mountain, in the end, can take us all.

Diki makes it over, digs her stock into the snow, and secures the rope. I feel a momentary relief before I recall Norda's words that, under added pressure, the ropes break ninety percent of the time. Burkhart arrives next and digs in next to Diki. He gives us a nod and shakes out his shoulders.

"Come on," I whisper, my gaze never leaving Kiel.

Haydrich is about twenty feet from us when we hear the crack. My heart stops as Haydrich drops to his knees, jabs in his alpenstock, and braces himself for the fall. Kiel and Tashi mirror his actions. A chunk of ice the size of a saltz cart breaks free from above, crashes to the ledge five feet behind Tashi, then slides down the steep slope to the drop below.

I let out a sob and instinctively grip Veit's arm. The ice missed them! Blood rushes back into my head, and I sway, unsteady on my feet.

"It's okay," Losan says, patting my back. "They're okay."

Haydrich, Kiel, and Tashi rise to standing and continue cautiously across the Throat. My heart resumes its beating, I find my breath again—*Kiel is okay. Kiel is okay.* Eventually, all four teams make it across, and it is all I can do not to sing and sob, scream and cry, and fall to my knees in the snow.

We move beyond the Throat, onto the final ridge, and are immediately assaulted by fierce winds and a cold that rips at our skin. Whatever breath I have left is swept from my lungs. The wind steals each inhalation. *Step. Breathe. Step. Breathe.* We plow up the ridge for another three hours. And then the ridge ends.

Veit stops and turns to me with wide eyes, his face white beneath his starblock green. I smile, overcome with exhausted exhilaration and joy. Without thinking, I move to Veit and wrap my arms around him. "We did it," he whispers, his breath hot on my cheek. "Fiekin' hüle. We did it, Klarke."

Drawing back from me, he raises his fist in the air. "Aye-ah-di-fahr!" he shouts. It is an echosong, the response a climber makes when another has called out to check on you. It means, *I am okay. I am alive.*

"Aye-ah-di fahr!" I shout with him. We laugh and forget, in that moment, that we don't like each other very much.

Losan and Naisae arrive next, and we circle up, embracing. "Way to go, team," Naisae says. "You were brilliant. And you've now completed the hardest challenge in the world. Whatever comes your way in life, know that you are champions."

Losan and I hug next. "We've come a long way from the docks," he whispers.

"We have," I agree. "Could you ever have imagined we would be here, on top of the world?"

"Together," he says. "After all this time."

"Yes," I acknowledge with a smile before pulling away.

It is a clear day, crisp and bitingly cold, and I can see all the way to where the Parowan Mountains taper off into the Fields of Lamore to the north. The gaping trench of Miter's Waste lies far to the south.

The last time I stood on such a summit, it had been with Tristan, who told me I was *basically a man*—and that was where my worth lay. His words had made me feel so unutterably lonely, disconnected from any sense of joy at my success. But then he'd said he understood my feelings, that upon our descent, he would try to help others understand too. Part of me believes he could still be alive, eking out an existence in a network of icy crevasses, subsisting on dripping water and alpine algae. I know this is impossible. But not knowing his fate is almost worse—that small ray of hope is sharper than grief.

Whatever the truth, I know King Adolar is lying. Tristan had nothing to do with the deaths of those boys. He is innocent—*was* innocent.

Naisae stares at the summit of Himmelisle. Veit pounds his chest and hoots and hollers as Losan spins in gleeful circles. In spite of the burdens we each carry, there is joy here. We have done something wonderful. Together. If only Ellias could be here. And my father. The great climbers I've had the privilege to know.

The tears threaten again, but I suck in a shallow breath and hold them back. "This one is dedicated to you both." I take off my glove, kiss my fingers, and raise my hand in the air, imagining that the wind carries the spirits of Ellias, my father, and my mother.

Kletshot four arrives next, and I race to Kiel, pulling him into a hug as I bury my face in his coat. "When I heard that crack—" I say, my voice shaky. "I'm not sure I've ever felt sicker."

He laughs and pulls me close. "I knew that couldn't be it. I knew Orna cared more for you than to add my death to your burdens."

"You can't tell me you weren't a little terrified."

"Oh, I nearly shat myself." He laughs again and pulls away to look into my face. "The thought of not seeing you again horrified me."

"Me too." Cleos's rays wash him in gold, then expand to include us all, providing a meager warmth. I see myself reflected in his goggles. I see myself standing on top of the world. "Can you believe it, Kiel? We did it."

He leans down and kisses me, and I kiss him back, furiously, without a care as to what others might think or say. His lips are warm, his embrace firm. I could stay forever in this glorious moment. Kiel releases me finally, pulling a small book from his pack. He slips something from its pages and places it in my hand—a pressed ulrind flower, the pink faded like old parchment. "Like the one you gave me on my first climb up Fitzhan," I say, looking up at him. "Do you give flowers to all the Ascenditures?"

"Only the pretty ones," he tells me.

I smile and shake my head. "Are you going to take me to the summit's edge to show me Ectair?"

"I love you, Klarke."

"Oh, Kiel, you can't—" I glance around, but nobody is paying any attention to us. They have their own victories to celebrate.

"I do," he continues. "I've loved you for a long time. And I don't want to marry Gelta. I won't."

"You have to, Kiel." I think of Lars Veber—hanged because he refused to marry the king's niece. "They'll kill you."

"Let them try."

"But—"

"I am no one's servant," he says fiercely, a fire dancing in his eyes that warms the chill in my bones. "Look at me. I'm on top of the world. Free. So free I could blow away with a small gust of wind. I can't go back to chains. Not after this."

"But I can't be with you."

"Yes, you can. Not in a traditional sense, but you can. Otto and Dieter will live a similar life. Together, the four of us will find a way to be happy. We can do this. I can't pretend anymore that I don't love you. It hurts too much."

I kiss him again, unsure why I can't bring myself to tell him I love him too. But Kiel does not expect it now, I see. It is enough for us to hold each other freely, on top of the world.

Eighteen of us reach the summit. We stand united at the top of Old Galvaith, higher than King Miter ever stood, higher than Hildegroth can reach. We are untouchable by all but the gods. The wind rips around us, screaming in triumph as small chips of ice fly at our feet. Burkhart raises the flag of Ectair high above his head, Menson the flag of Ainar. Unity—it has always just been a word, but now it feels real and burns in my chest, swelling like a prideful sea. We did it. My freedom here extends far beyond kisses with Kiel. It is all-encompassing.

"We must give our honors," Norda says, dropping to his knees. The rest of us follow, and I pull the bundle of dirt from my pocket.

"We pray differently here in Ainar," he continues. "Please repeat after me. An-ka-hai-la-moringa-sha."

"An-ka-hai-la-moringa-sha," we repeat.

"Las schla humber ungara."

"Las schla humber ungara."

Norda opens his palm, and the wind whips the soil from his fingers. We do the same and watch as the dirt is swept away across the summit. Orna has received her offering. Perhaps she will grant us safe passage down, or perhaps it is not entirely up to her. After all, she did not start that avalanche on Bonen.

Before rising, I reach around and remove the pink ribbon from my braid. I dig a hole in the snow, tuck the ribbon into it, and bury it. "For Rosalie," I whisper. "For my mother, for the queen; for Rayna and Lena…" I go through a list of the women's names from my old tenement. "For Ramanata," I finish. Do symbolic gestures matter? I'm not sure. But it feels good and right to leave a piece of the fight up here. Not just to let pink ribbons be worn in the streets of Kietsch, but to let them soar from the highest heights in the world.

A shadow passes over us, and I look up to see a great white figure, wings spread, soaring over the peak. Another comes and then another. Soon a flock of six bessils fly over us. I smile up at the ancient birds, whose wings are as wide as a canoe is long. They make no noise as they fly but are silent, gliding shapes, like clouds blown about by the winds. It feels like a good omen.

"Rope up, teams!" Naisae calls. "The air here is too thin. We can't stay longer." She clasps Losan on the shoulder and presses her forehead against his. "Be strong," I hear her whisper. Is Losan afraid?

"Remember that most mountaineering accidents occur on the descent," Aedan says. "Don't be lulled into a false sense of safety because your movements are less difficult."

"That is truth," Menson adds. "When a climber ascends, they face the mountain, hugging her rock, feeling the safety of her embrace. When a climber descends, they face away, ungrounded from the mountain's sturdy base. No longer wrapped in her arms. You face the darkened sea when you descend."

I look out across the clouds that have moved in, hoping to glimpse the far shore of the darkened sea, hoping to see Ellias, my parents, Gerd, and Tristan waving, promising to guide me down safely. All I see is an endless ocean of white, perforated by the summits of the Parowan Mountains.

I attach myself to kletshot one's rope and then search for my alpenstock. "I thought I put it here," I say, perplexed, "right next to my pack."

"Me too," Veit says, staring around. "I left mine next to yours. Okay, who is trying to be a trickster here?"

"Here." Losan hands us our axes. "I just gave them a quick sharpening."

I load my pack onto my back and turn, taking in the view, knowing it is doubtful that I will ever come back—even if King Adolar allowed it. The journey was too far, and though I love the challenge of mountaineering, my heart belongs to traditional rock climbing, on a sheer face without ice and avalanches. I will leave Opasno to Mida and Diki, to Keema and Chessa.

The rest of the teams form behind us. Veit is in front of me, and with a nod from Naisae, he moves to the crest that will lead us back to the Throat. It takes less time to get down the ridge than it did to ascend, and we reach the Throat quickly. Our footsteps have hammered a solid path across the three-hundred-foot neck, the glistening ice cliff towering high above. Veit pauses and glances back. I smile, though my insides churn.

"Proceed, Veit," Naisae calls from the back.

I give him a nod, and Veit moves out onto the Throat. He treads carefully and proceeds several feet across the Throat without incident, the ice wall silent and still. When it's my turn, I follow Veit, planning each move, planting my feet into the packed snow, stabilizing myself with the alpenstock. The ice wall blocks the wind, and the Throat is eerily quiet. I hear only the crunching of snow beneath my boots and the blood pumping in my ears. One step. Another. I see the downslope in the corner of my eye, but fight the urge to look.

Veit is almost to the other side, which means all four team members are now scattered along the Throat. I think of Ellias saving my father here, and I feel his protection over me even now. I see him in the glistening ice, hear him in the crunching of snow, feel his presence in my heart and in my bones. He's with Kizi now. He's free. He—

The scream comes, and my face hits the snow before I can register what's happening. Veit was almost across—how could he have fallen? I glance up in time to see my weight pull him to the ground.

No, no, no, no, no! Shouts ring out from all around, echoing on the ice wall. I didn't fall. My mind wandered, but my feet were sure. Naisae or Losan must have fallen.

Ellias, help me!

I dig my alpenstock into the snow to anchor myself, but to my horror, the head breaks off and bounces down the slope.

A sickening realization washes over me as I see something dark sliding past me—another axe head. Veit's stock must have also broken.

Your nose, ears, and eyes will have been ground down to paste.

No. No, no, no.

You will be ripped into a thousand pieces.

My body spirals on the ice, and I spin and start to slide. I pound gloved hands into the glacier, frantically digging my fingers into a crack, a hollow, anything that will allow purchase. I kick my boots against the ground, trying to drive in a spike, but the surface is slick and unyielding. Ice chips sting my face and the wind howls in my ears. I know the drop is coming. I glance up as I begin to slide faster and see Kiel screaming my name, reaching out toward me as if he could halt my descent. Veit, just above me, desperately flails his fists, his feet—everything in his body—to try to stop our slide.

And then the ground drops out from under me, and I brace for impact.

22

At least I will die on the mountain. At least it won't be at the hands of a vile king or a usurper and his monster. I hit something and bounce. It hurts only a little, like whiplash, and my eyes fly open. I have just enough time to roll out of the way before Veit crashes into me. Dazed and confused, I glance around, unable to process what I am seeing. I'm lying next to Veit in what looks like a giant fisherman's net, the kind they use in deep sea trolling for thund and tûndles. We hang and twist in the wind, and through the thick rope netting, I can see the hundred-foot drop to the glacier far below. How are we not dead? How is it that we happened to fall into a deep-sea fishing net?

As we swing gently in the icy gusts, I notice Naisae climbing from the net onto a rock shelf, one I now see loops around the side of the mountain in what looks like a maintained route—the snow is packed down, as if by many feet, and ropes are fixed into the ice wall. Losan crouches by Veit, and I see a flash of metal in his hand. With a gasp, I realize Losan is holding a knife to Veit's throat.

Shouts echo down the icy slope. "Aye-ah-cum-eee!" The rest of the teams are calling out to see if we are okay. Losan puts a finger to his lips. He won't meet my gaze. My eyes widen, and I look to Veit.

"Aye-ah-cum-eee!" I recognize Kiel's voice.

"Do not answer them, Hannar Obeldorf." Naisae's voice is colder than the ice.

"Why not?" Veit's voice is low, shaky, like a child's when it is about to cry.

We should be dead. Why are we not dead?

"If you value your life," she continues, "you will remain silent and follow me."

Veit glances my way, and I nod. We are still roped together, so Losan releases Veit and moves behind Naisae, climbing from the net and untwisting our team in the process. I follow next, and Veit brings up the rear, glancing up toward the drop, mouth open as if he is about to shout.

"Don't do it," I hiss.

"They're going to kill us anyway."

"I won't let them. We'll figure this out. Please."

Below, I see splashes of red streaking across the snow, leading down the ice in a bloody trail. Dizziness grips me, but I try to breathe, try to remain calm.

"It's karad blood," Naisae says. "No one was harmed."

I look at Losan, but he still won't meet my gaze. Shame on me for believing I ever have control over my life, I think fiercely. That I'm not being used and lied to. I stagger forward in a state of terrified shock.

"You sabotaged my alpenstock," I hiss at Losan. "And Veit's. Didn't you? Why?" I attempt to blink back tears, but the pain of betrayal is too much, and they spill down my cheeks.

"You will learn soon enough," Naisae says. "You are not in danger, Klarke. Please know that. We are on your side."

"My side?" I glance behind us, at the drop to the glacier, at the net someone had installed to capture us. "What is my side? Shouldn't I know what the fiek is happening on my side?"

"Right now, it is imperative that you follow me and remain silent. The climbers above must believe you are dead."

"Sweet gods," Veit curses under his breath. "When my father hears of this—"

"He's not going to."

Veit grows quiet.

What are they planning? She says I am safe, but what of Veit? He's not my best friend, but I will protect him. I won't let the only other Mount Bonen survivor die. "Fine," I say. "Lead the way. But I want answers."

"And you will have them."

Roped together with fresh alpenstocks that had been stowed

on the ledge, Naisae leads us down a precarious alternative route. Eventually, the calls of our teammates die away. Kiel thinks I'm dead, and the pain he feels cripples me. It's all I can do not to scream his name. But if I do, it will endanger Veit—and perhaps Kiel too. And I must be careful and cunning and wait for my chance. My thoughts race from one possible scenario to another. Could this be King Adolar's doing? Impossible. This scheme was coordinated among the Parvanatari. Did they all know? Or was it a secret kept between Losan and Naisae? Does King Gyalzen know?

We descend for hours, winding down and away from the summit. I try to pinpoint our location by landmarks, the position of Cleos, but can only gather that we are somewhere on the north face of the mountain. Fixed ropes and ladders mark the route, and I realize this sabotage has been long planned. Before Naisae and Losan even arrived at the vintazite festival in Ectair. This sham of a unity climb has been a plot all along. Another lie.

My blood simmers, but I try to breathe in and to steady my pulse, to maintain a calm. Emotions are dangerous on the mountain. The most treacherous part of the climb is the descent. Were truer words ever uttered?

"Is what you said about Ellias even true?" I ask Naisae bitterly.

"Yes." She, too, refuses to meet my eyes. "Every word."

"Every word." I laugh, a hollow laugh that sounds as if it echoes out of some deep icy crevasse. "I am surrounded by liars."

"You are surrounded by people who care about you."

"That's the biggest load of karad dung anyone's ever shoveled," I snap back.

Below us, a small village of tents appears on the downward slope, but it is not our Base Camp. I swallow and glance back at Veit. His face is red, and his neck veins bulge. Could this be Haydrich's doing? Is this a gathering of darken mages and religious lunatics?

We reach the camp and make our way to the largest tent. I see not a soul. It is a ghost camp. Silent. Waiting. Holding its breath. Outside the tent flap, we untie ourselves from the rope, remove our harnesses, and set down the alpenstocks. I am reluctant to let mine go—I want a weapon, but they won't allow it. At least I have Veit—a thought I never expected to have.

"I will never join your Schaeter," I yell at Losan and Naisae. "You will have to kill me because I will never join the Dark Promise. I won't help you bring a monster to life that will kill innocent people."

"Dark Promise?" Losan says. "We are no Dark Promise."

"You're a liar too!" I spit. "And I will never forgive you. I don't care if you used to be my childhood friend. Whoever you once were, you have now become a snake, a demon worse than Ignaz. You're all twisted, cruel people who lie and lie and lie—"

"Klarke, please," Losan says, reaching out a hand, "you must understand that everything we've done is to help you. To save you."

"Klarke, come inside to get warm and recover," Naisae says. "You will soon learn all that you need to know. Keep an open mind, and know that you are safe."

Naisae ducks through the tent flap, and I follow, still trembling with rage. The tent is warm inside, so warm I almost collapse into an exhausted pile, my legs suddenly weak and shaky. But the perimeter of the tent is lined with expectant faces, and I don't want them to sense weakness. I straighten, force my weary legs to keep me upright just a little longer.

"Geitsê, Klarke," a familiar voice booms.

A giant man the size of a small tolvalus steps forward, holding a mug of kimmeron. His beefy face is already red with drink. Shocked, I recognize the ship's cook that I have been set on rescuing from captivity.

"Obid?" I exclaim. "How?"

"It's not my place to explain, but we'll have plenty o' time for talkin'."

Obid steps aside, glancing behind him. I don't want to look. I'm afraid. I'm afraid of so many things.

"Klarke."

I close my eyes as tears stream down my face.

"It can't be. It's impossible," I mutter, shaking my head.

"Please forgive me and allow me to explain."

No. No, no, no.

I'm falling again. Sliding down the glacier to a drop with no alpenstock to arrest my fall. I collapse to my knees, sobs wracking my exhausted frame.

I am going to die.

Maybe I already did.

Maybe that's what this is.

"You're safe," he says. "You're safe, and you're home now." He gently draws me up to my feet, holding me up so that he can look me in the eyes.

"Pa?" My voice cracks as I touch his hand. His flesh is warm. Real. I close my eyes and open them. He's still there, gazing down at me with a tender gaze I thought I'd never see again. "How?"

"It's a long story, Klarkey." He draws me into his chest and wraps his arms around me as I sob into his shoulder. "We have a lot to talk about."

Warmth spreads through me, but icy rage follows rapidly upon its heels. My father is alive. He's alive, and he left me to rot in Ectair. Furious, I pull away, wishing I had the strength left to strangle him.

23

"Perhaps we should let her sleep first, Anselm," Naisae says, touching his shoulder.

I cannot take my gaze from my father's face—his brown eyes hold the same twinkle but with less joy. His hair has retreated from his forehead in the corners and is peppered with gray. I search each new wrinkle for answers, for truth, and feel torn between wanting to throttle him and wanting to crawl into his lap and cry.

"I think that's a good idea," the man who looks like my father says. "We all need rest, and then we can proceed."

"Nide!" I shout. "Are you people mad? My father, who I have spent nearly ten years believing to be dead, shows up on the side of Mount Opasno, and you want me to take a nap?"

"First, please secure him in one of the tents," my father says to several men nearby as he nods toward Veit.

I push myself off my knees and move to Veit, wrapping my arm through his. He is the safest person present. He's an arsch, but at least he's an honest one. Maybe the only sincere person in my life. And they want to imprison him as if he were the enemy. "He stays. He doesn't leave my sight."

Veit gives me a perplexed look, then tightens his arm against mine and nods.

"Fine. But know if you cause any problems, we lock you up," my father tells Veit sternly. Then he turns to the silent crowd who line the perimeter of the tent and raises one hand. "Thank you all for being here. Please feel free to take your evening meal and get some rest."

Then, turning to me, he gestures to a long table behind him. "Let's at least sit and eat. Obid?"

"Aye, captain," Obid says and moves out a back flap in the tent.

The spectators start to disperse, murmuring quietly among themselves as they leave. An attendant brings a few jugs of kimmeron and places them on the table as Naisae, Losan, Veit, my father, and I take our seats. We are joined by a man I do not recognize who is missing a forearm, his sleeve folded and pinned at his elbow. Veit reaches for a bottle of the smoky liquor and begins drinking from it. I do the same. The others can share the rest.

"You left me." I lean across the table and hold my father's gaze, feeling the rage deep inside begin to boil over. Ellias lost his child. He would have given anything to have Kizi back, I'm sure of it, but my own father abandoned me. "You left me in a place to fester. To become a brideprize. You left me on the streets!" I slam my mug of kimmeron onto the table. "You left me!" I yell, rising to my feet, the pain of years-long misplaced grief roiling through my blood like fire.

"That was never my intention," he says quietly.

"You were here all along, and you let me believe you were dead. You let me feel alone. You let me feel broken."

"Please, let me explain."

I tip back the mug of kimmeron, gulping, and sink back into my seat.

"Obid tells me you know of your mother's work smuggling girls out of Ectair. This was our calling, our duty, but it became dangerous. When Queen Eleonora was murdered and when we learned of the torture of the king's sister, Lady Genalt, something had to change. And fast. The plan was to fake my death so that I could become a ghost and help your mother smuggle babies without suspicion.

"But someone let slip to the king our plan to get Genalt to Ainar. He planted explosives on my ship. Those of us who survived went into hiding. I had hoped Mina's involvement wouldn't be discovered, that the king would pin the scheme on me. She was never supposed to die. I didn't think he could kill her. Not her..." He coughs, and his voice breaks. I wipe tears from my eyes but say nothing.

"When your mother died, it felt safer to leave you in Ectair. You weren't a threat to the king, and you had Ellias. I knew Ellias would care for you as his own. I knew he could give you what you needed. My work here would not allow me to be a good father."

My mouth drops, and a numb tingling rises in the back of my skull. "A *good* father? I would have taken a scheiz father over no father. Over tenements and orphanages. Do you hear yourself?"

"You have no idea what we've accomplished. Our sacrifice as a family, including your sacrifice, enabled hundreds of innocents to be spared."

"My sacrifice?" I whisper. "I was eight, Papa. I didn't sacrifice anything. I was robbed."

"I'm sorry, Klarkey. I'm so sorry for what happened to you and for all that you have suffered."

"Suffered?" I choke out the words, recalling the ever-present fear of death by starvation, pulmonosis, or violence in Ectair. One hand instinctively goes to my throat; I can still feel the tightening of Gio's garrote at my neck. "You know nothing of my suffering."

"You're right. I don't."

Angry tears stream down my cheeks, and I furiously wipe them away. "Why now?"

My father and Naisae exchange glances.

"He shouldn't hear this," Naisae says, nodding toward Veit.

"He stays," I say coolly.

"We heard about your marriage to Prince Otto," my father says. "That you were becoming an Adolar. We have a plan to remove the Adolars from power, destroy the monarchy, and implement a fair and just system of ruling in Ectair, one that does not require that we pull baby girls out of gutters."

"A plan to—"

"Assassinate the Adolars. Initiate a coup. Reframe Ectair into a kingdom we can be proud of. A free land. We did not want you to be harmed during the course of the assassination."

"You're planning to kill the king?"

"The king, yes. And his son. The entire line has to be destroyed for our plan to work. Otherwise, there will be the dissenters working to put the Adolars back into power."

I feel the blood drain from my face. Veit places a warm and steady hand on my back. "You can't kill Prince Otto," I say fiercely. "He's not like his father. He's a good man. And he will be a good ruler. He wants to make reforms, just like you. Kill Adolar. Please. But don't touch Otto."

"It's too late. The plan is already in motion. Otto must die."

I feel my heart racing in my chest and anxiety and anger rising again like molten rock within the belly of the mountain. "Is this another one of those necessary sacrifices you like to make? For the greater good? You sacrifice your daughter. You sacrifice an innocent man."

"You couldn't understand."

"You don't think I understand sacrifice?" I stifle a sound that is half laugh, half sob. "You are mad, deluded. And not so different from King Adolar."

Obid brings a steaming pot of soup, and even though I want to throw the contents at my father, I scarf down two bowls. The warmth spreads from my belly to my limbs. I sit numbly at the table, staring at the empty bowl. "I'd like to sleep," I say, rising to my feet.

"We will finish our chat tomorrow, then," my father says, also standing. "It is good to see you, Klarke. I have missed you."

I turn away and follow Veit and Naisae out the tent flap and across the moondusted snow to another smaller tent. Stacked blankets and furs line the floor. "Do not think of leaving, Klarke," she says gently. "The north face of Opasno is littered with crevasses, and if you don't follow the only route up and down, you will die." She pauses a moment at the entrance, her figure outlined by a perimeter torch. "I really am sorry, Klarke. I know you don't understand. But I hope someday you will."

"Your dad is a lunatic," Veit pronounces after she has left. He slides beneath the fur blankets and rolls to face away from me.

"I can't believe this is happening," he mutters, as if to himself.

I don't enjoy sleeping so close to him, but I'm glad he's here. "We have to escape, Veit. They're going to kill Otto."

"I don't give a hairk's arsch about your prince. They're going to kill me. That's what I'm worried about."

"Whatever your reasoning, we can't stay here."

"What do you suggest, *princess*?" he replies. "You heard Naisae. There's no way out of here."

"I don't know yet." I bury myself beneath the blankets, knowing that my priority now must be sleep. Only after I have rested will I be able to clear my mind sufficiently to come up with a plan. My thoughts turn to Prince Otto—another casualty of politics and war, of cruelty and power. Another death to be piled on top of Gerd and Tristan. Ellias and Rosalie. Pawns. We are all just pieces in a game where those playing envision themselves as heroes who can do whatever they want regardless of the consequences. And those players—King Adolar, Haydrich and the Dark Promise, and now my own father, risen from the dead to take back a kingdom, but at what cost? And who will pay the price? Three powers are vying for a kingdom, and whoever is victorious will only be so at the expense of those I love.

I have to stop them all. Righteousness has corrupted my father, and he is now as dangerous as King Adolar. Tears spill from my eyes and dampen the fur beneath my head. It's not fair. None of it.

But what is?

It's not fair that Gerd died. That I was not allowed to train Marike. That a loose rock killed Ellias's son. That Rayna's father drowned at Pohle Pier. That she was forced to marry Eugen Martus… Why should I expect fairness in a world that grants it to no one? I am not special.

My father died nearly ten years ago. The man who raised me. Who loved me. Who brought me chocolate from Kobo and read me stories of creatures that lived deep within the seas. I mourned him. I mourned him for years. And then I said goodbye. This man is not him. This man is no more to me than my evil king or the Schaeter.

I will save Otto. I will save the people I love who love me in return.

And if I must destroy my father in the process, so be it.

24

Veit is still asleep when I wake, and I throw on my overcoat and pull my cap down over my ears. I, too, am convinced my father has no intention of allowing him to leave here alive. I find my father, Naisae, Losan, and the man with the missing arm in the large tent, in muted conversation at the table.

"Good morning," my father says, offering me a cup of tea. I accept the tea and move through the tent to the back flap, ignoring them. From the adjacent tent, I hear Obid's familiar swearing and slip inside. Obid bends over a stove, stirring a bubbling pot of mashed oats and bartlenuts.

"This whole time, you knew he was alive, and you didn't tell me."

"Wasn' my place," Obid mutters, keeping his back to me. "Tried ta get ya out, didn' I? Offered more'n once."

"That's not the truth."

"I gave ya more truth than anyone in yer life."

That, at least, was true. Obid had hinted to me about Death's Whisper. About my mother and father. There's a reason I've sought him out ever since I learned of the conspiracy—he felt like an ally, like someone who cared about me. Other than Veit—a thought that still makes me laugh—Obid is the person I trust most in this camp.

"I know about Death's Whisper," I say. "You were right. It's no accident."

"We're almost certain it's what killed yer mum and the queen," he says.

"It is what killed them. Obid—" I move into the dim tent and around the hearth so I can see his face. "I know where it comes from." I dig into my pocket and bring out the small crystal Gio gave me before he died. "They call it flüstodapul.

It's from a cave up in the Celebern Fields. Where the purple ferns also grow. Gio had been secretly collecting these crystals for the king, but he told me that there's also another that does the king's bidding."

"So it was Gio? We'd heard rumors, but it was hard to believe. Seemed like a nice kid."

"They have his sister. King Adolar blackmailed him."

"Scheiz."

An idea comes to me, and I kick myself for not thinking of it earlier. "You must still have a network in Ectair for getting babies out."

"'Course."

"Could they find Gio's sister? Liselotte. The king holds her captive somewhere. I promised Gio, in exchange for that crystal, that I would find her before he died."

"I'll see what we can do."

I sip my tea and watch the porridge thicken and simmer. "There's a climber on my team, Obid. His name is Haydrich. He says he's working for a man from the southlands to find a monster that can destroy King Adolar and his regime. They want to bring back magic. Have you heard of this?"

Obid stops stirring, and his eyes narrow as he glances up at me. "Only whispers," he admits.

"So they aren't allied with you?" I laugh drily. "Well, that means I have only three enemies to contend with."

"I'm not yer enemy, Klarke. I've only ever been on yer side."

"If you are in on a plot to kill Prince Otto, then you are my enemy, and I will do everything in my power to defeat you."

Obid laughs. "For that pompous son of a weasel?"

"Otto is a good man. He cares about me. He cares about making positive reforms in Ectair. After hearing Adolar, Haydrich, and my father speak about their intentions, I think Otto is the only decent ruler Ectair can hope to have. You all speak of change, but your methods for bringing it about are as murderous as the regime you hope to replace, without thought for the innocents. My father wants a new regime for a land he left long ago?" I shake my head. "You don't get to abandon a place and then have any say in how it is ruled."

"I understand yer angry," Obid says. "And I think it's all valid, but ye gotta see that the work we've been doin' is far bigger than all o' that."

Bigger than me. More important than me. I want to rage, but I have walked through fire and ice to find Obid, and I plan to escape as soon as possible. I don't have time to feel sorry for myself—I need answers and he is the only one who can provide them.

"I need to ask you a few things, and I need you to tell me the truth."

"Yes?"

"I have two people I need to find," I begin. "And I bet you know where they are. Dr. Vitus and Prince Otto's twin sister."

"What do ye want with them?" Obid asks.

"You don't get to ask questions anymore. Where can I find them, Obid?"

"Well, last I saw Vitus, he was high as a bessil and crawlin' around Pohle Pier. His brain is burnt toast, Klarke. He can give you nothing."

I recall the veisel-addicted man I encountered at the pier, who told me I "was meant for the sea." He was there, again, in the crowd in front of Revolution Square. Could it be Dr. Vitus? He seemed to know me. If his brain was truly fried, how did he recognize me?

"And Otto's sister? Where is she?"

"I don' know nuthin' about that."

"Don't lie to me. So help me, Orna, I cannot handle another lie."

"All I did was what the queen and your mother told me to do."

"And what was that?"

"'Round three in the morning, I took the baby from the queen and gave it to Mina. There were three babies being smuggled that night. Wrapped up so tightly, little wee ones they were;

couldn't tell one from another and Mina wouldn't identify the babes. Safer that way, she'd said. We took three girls to Burndle that night. I don' know nuthin' beyond that."

Three girls in Burndle. They could be anywhere in Ainar now. My heart sinks—finding her now seems an impossible task. "How many girls have you brought to Ainar, Obid?"

He shrugs and wipes sweat from his broad forehead. "Dunno. Over a thousand, I'd say."

"How many don't get out? How many don't find you in time?"

"It's not a number ye want to think about."

My gaze drops to the canvas floor of the tent, and I feel nausea rise in my throat.

"That's why what we're doin' is so important," Obid insists. "That's why ye need to forgive yer father."

I close my eyes, and for a moment I feel as if I am in the warmth of the ship's galley with Obid, talking around a pot of bubbling stew, not in a traitor's camp on the side of Mount Opasno. I want desperately to heed Obid's words—what reserves of energy must I summon to fight another battle, and one with my own father? But his is a betrayal I cannot abide. A little girl's grief did not have to be part of the plan. He did not need to make me collateral damage.

"Who is that man with the missing arm?"

"Name's Casso. He's been yer father's right hand for a few years now. Hates Adolar more'n most."

"Why? He's Ainarian. What contact would he have had with the king?"

"Not my business to say."

I sigh and pocket the crystal. "I hate that this is where we now find ourselves. I thought we were allies."

"I don' think it's as simple as ye want it to be. We are allies. In my thinkin'. What makes ye the ultimate decider of what is good an' what isn't?"

Feeling conflicted and no less confused—or angry—than before, I make my way back to my father in the main tent and take a seat at the table across from him. I will never be ready for this conversation, so why not now?

"I knew you were okay, Klarke, because you had Ellias," he says.

I want to silence him. To tell him I don't want to hear his poor excuses. I wish I didn't need this. But I ache for his words. I hate him, but a child's love runs deep, however hard we wish to root it out. I chew the corner of my lip and say nothing.

"Ellias promised to care for you. He told me how good you'd gotten at climbing. How strong you'd become, both on and off the fel."

Another punch to the stomach—Ellias knew. The man I grew to love and trust above all others was also lying to me. Ellias let me grieve.

"Why did you quit the Ascenditures?" I ask.

"We'd just finished damming the Waste—"

"I want the truth."

"And you shall have only that. We'd just finished damming the Waste when Adolar began spreading the lie that King Gyalzen controlled Hildegroth. We knew this to be a lie because the person who controlled the monster, the true descendant of Layal, came, nearly dead, to your mother one night."

"Lady Genalt," I say.

"Lady Genalt, King Adolar's sister," my father continues. "King Adolar had resurrected a sect of darken mages who tortured Genalt, hoping to remove her powers and bestow them upon her brother. The monster, driven mad by his mistress's pain, destroyed our worlds—not because she commanded him to but because he simply wanted to save her."

Obid enters through the back tent flap and deposits a bowl of nut-porridge before each of us.

"Around this time," my father continues, "your mother was, as you know, working secretly to rescue baby girls, but King Adolar, too, expanded his security forces tasked specifically with searching out newborn twins. Your mother's efforts were becoming increasingly dangerous. I quit the Ascenditures to work on the sea to provide cover to the rescue operations. Only adels or those with elevated status may captain ships. Being an Ascenditure and marrying into your mother's family gave me the required status. I relinquished my dreams to do what is right, to help mitigate and address King Adolar's atrocities."

I bite my lip harder and withhold my retort. I want him to keep speaking. The truth is a salve. And I believe what I'm hearing to be true.

"What really happened to my mother? How did it happen?" My voice breaks, and I swallow a sob.

"King Adolar discovered not only what Mina was up to but that she had helped his queen smuggle out a baby girl, the prince's twin. He destroyed everyone who knew of the urday—your mother, the queen, and the doctor who'd delivered the babies. He had to conceal the fact that he'd had a twin, a daughter, and that his line was doomed. They had been friends in their youth, your mother and Adolar; she had even been promised to him. She was destined to be queen."

"What?" I ask, startled.

"But playful youth always matures into who we truly are, and she recognized him for the monster he is. We married secretly the day before her birthday, before she was eligible to be declared as Adolar's brideprize. He never forgave her for that. He never forgave me. But the final outrage came when he found that Mina had smuggled his baby girl out of Ectair. She had doomed his line."

I recall my conversation with the king in the throne room, where he'd told me my mother had taken everything from him, and now I begin to understand what he meant. That painting of a beautiful dark-haired woman that Kiel and Otto had seen in Adolar's chamber—could it have been my mother? Was it possible he held, still, a twisted love for her after all this time? Even after he condemned her to death?

"So," I ask, "do you intend to find Adolar's daughter and kill her? If you must destroy the entire family line, then surely she, too, must die."

"Unfortunately, she did not survive," Naisae says.

"How do you know?"

"She became very ill on the transport north and died in Burndle before we could find a home for her. In the end, King Adolar got his wish."

"Obid said my mother mixed up the babies so no one would know which was Adolar's. How do you know it wasn't one of the other girls who died?"

"Your mother knew all along which one was the prince's sister. The rest of us didn't, but she did. She was with her in Burndle when the baby died."

Inexplicably, I feel terribly sad. What, then, did the stitched message on my mother's handkerchief mean? Why would she have instructed me to find someone she knew to be gone?

"So Ramanata is dead?" I say.

"What?" the one-armed man exclaims, clearly startled by the mention of her name.

"Please, Casso." My father rests a hand on his arm, almost as a warning, it seems, to say no more. What could it mean?

"Where did you hear such a name?" Casso asks me sharply.

Reluctant to reveal the stitching on my mother's handkerchief, I come up with a quick lie. "Otto told me it was his sister's name."

Casso frowns, his gaze intent on me. Something about the name Ramanata has rattled them, and I want to know what.

"Otto was mistaken," my father says forcefully. "Ramanata was just another orphan your mother helped to save."

So why stitch her name on the handkerchief? I wonder.

"Why do you hate King Adolar?" I ask Casso. "Why are you helping my father murder his son, an innocent man?"

"King Adolar took my love from me," Casso mutters, his fist clenching on the table. "And he hurt her."

Another woman betrayed and injured in Ectair—what a common story that is, and all to be laid at the feet of King Adolar. "I'm sorry," I say.

"Things must change in Ectair, Klarkey. You understand

this. Our actions may seem drastic, but it is only because we wish the suffering to end." My father reaches across the table and takes my hands in his.

As much as I strive to hate him, the feel of my father's strong calloused hands over mine brings me to tears. Tears stream down my cheeks and drop off my chin, falling into my oats, into my tea. I want to curl up in his lap while he strokes my back, telling me it's all been a bad dream, that the monsters aren't real, and that he is here for me and always has been. I gasp as the tears flow, trying to catch my breath, and steady my composure. I rest my forehead on our clasped hands and sob.

I've missed him so much. I missed him when I was homeless, hungry, and alone, when I led my first climb, and when I broke my first bone. I missed him when I climbed Fitzhan, and when, too, I got married. I missed him because he left me. Willingly. And he didn't come back. He wasn't there because he chose not to be. But Otto has stood by my side and protected me and cared for me—and now his fate rests in my hands. I don't get to fall apart today. I don't get to forgive my father. Even if what they tell me today is the truth, and even if this truth is important to me, they are not my friends. I have to get out of here, and quickly. I must warn Otto.

I sit up, pull my hands away, and wipe my face. "How do you plan on killing the Adolars?"

From his coat pocket, my father brings out a vial filled with translucent powder.

Horrified, I recognize the granules of Death's Whisper poison. "Where did you get that?"

"A smuggler out on The Gate."

"So you will kill the king the same way he killed my mother?"

"It seems fitting."

"It seems barbaric."

"Tell me you don't seek revenge for your mother's death, that you haven't dreamed of seeing that man's body lifeless on the ground?"

"I have seen enough dead bodies to last a lifetime," I say

wearily, knowing, however, that it is not the complete truth. Yes, I have long wished for Adolar's demise. I have dreamed of a thousand ways to make him suffer. But not when that fate is tied to Otto. And, I realize with a start, how sickened I am by the ongoing murder and brutality that seems to define our world, where our only recourse for change is to kill one another. Would it ever end? And how, then, is my father any better than the murderer he seeks to supplant?

"What about Veit?" I ask.

"I know he's your friend—" my father begins.

"He's not my friend," I interrupt.

"He knows too much."

"He's an innocent and decent arschole."

"He's an Obeldorf," Casso says heatedly. "The world will not be worse off with one fewer Obeldorf."

"You're going to kill him?"

"It's for—"

"The greater good? For the best?" I laugh darkly, disgust rising in my throat like bile. "And what will you do with me?"

"You will stay here and be safe. And when this is all finished, you can return to Ectair and lead the Ascenditures. Or you can reinstate the League of Ascension in Kietsch and bring the full glory of climbing back to Ectair," Naisae says.

I close my eyes. Climbing was a dream for a foolish young girl. I no longer have the luxury to dream of peaks and summits, of rope and alpenstocks, of camaraderie and echosongs. "But I know too much as well," I say quietly, meeting my father's gaze.

"And you would never dream of hurting us," my father says.

"If you harm Prince Otto, I will dream of revenge every moment I am not actively pursuing it," I say intently. "Do we understand each other?"

All are silent, watching me as I dig the spoon into my tear-filled porridge and take a bite. "So, I am curious. Is the entire Parvanatari team in on this plan? King Gyalzen? Was his speech about unity also kuhscheiz?" I ask.

"They did not know," my father says. "Everyone who knows

of our mission is here, in the mountain camp, or in the field, fulfilling our objectives."

"I assume 'fulfilling our objectives' means enacting your plans to kill the king and Prince Otto?"

Our conversation is stilled by the arrival of Veit, who throws open the tent flap and sits next to me at the table. After a moment, Obid returns with a bowl of nut-porridge, but I grab it away before Veit can bring his spoon to his lips.

"Hey! That's mine," he protests. "You've already eaten."

"And what if they poisoned it?"

He gives a bewildered look as I pick up his spoon and defiantly bring a few spoonfuls of his porridge to my mouth. Nobody says a word and nobody attempts to stop me. I pass the rest to Veit to finish.

Am I really willing to die to save Veit? I wonder. Or do I just want to see the look on my father's face, should he have poisoned the porridge and killed his daughter? Do I just want to see if he cares?

"When can I leave, or when do you plan to kill me?" Veit asks through a mouthful of porridge. "That is the plan, right? Kill the Obeldorf?"

"Oh, they're going to kill you," I say. "Welcome to my world, Veit. Remember after Mount Bonen, when I tried to tell you someone was killing climbers?"

"Your pa killed Julius and those boys?" he asks, dropping his spoon with a clatter, his face white and his eyes wide, as if he only now realizes the extent of his danger.

"No, that was Gio and one other."

"Okay, good." He exhales in relief. "For a second there, I thought I was in the presence of maniacs. Could you pass the saltz?"

"I was wrong when I said *someone* was killing climbers." I pass the saltz. "It's not just one person or group of people," I explain, glaring, in turn, at my father, Naisae, Losan, and Casso. "It's everyone here at this table and back in Ectair."

I feel suddenly helpless. I am just one and they are so many.

How can I prevent them from killing Veit? And what will I do when word reaches me that Otto is dead, taken from this world by the cruel and mysterious culprit, Death's Whisper?

I will become what I despise most about my world—an agent of vengeance, one that seeks retribution in the only way I know how.

I will destroy them all.

25

The day passes and another dawns on the mountainside where I wake in the small tent, Veit snoring by my side. As I wash my face with melted snow, my eyes gritty from lack of sleep, I ponder my growing plan. I cannot simply wait for Veit and Otto to be killed. From the little intelligence I've gathered, my father plans to hide on Opasno for a few days as the Parvanatari and Ascenditures descend and begin their journey back to Ectair. My father does not want to risk exposing his plan or me. Kiel is constantly in my thoughts, and I feel a wrenching pain at his unnecessary grief. I lived with unnecessary grief for years, and I know full well how it cuts at one every day, little nicks to the soul that never stop bleeding. I am angry at my father for many things. The pain he is causing Kiel and the others is one of them.

Veit and I lack the experience to get ourselves off the mountain safely, nor do we know the route. Without a guide, we are doomed. I keep a close eye on Losan, knowing he is our only hope, that I must find a way to sway him to the cause. He must sneak us out of here. But what can I say to persuade him to turn his back on his co-conspirators? I can pretend to love him. Isn't that what he wants? My affections.

That morning, after the early meal, I find him peeling potatoes for lunch in the mess tent.

"How could you hide the truth about my father?" I demand heatedly, unable to help myself—anger and bitterness seem always with me, another legacy of my father's deceit. So much for my plan of pretending love. "You lied to me, again and again. And then you pretend to have affection for me? How dare you?"

Losan drops his peeling knife and approaches me at the tent

entrance. "I do have feelings for you, Klarke," he says softly, "and I always have."

I grab the front of his shirt and pull him to me. "I would rather be eaten by Hildegroth than share affections with a serial liar," I snarl, then release his shirt, disgusted.

Losan seizes my arm. "Please," he pleads. "I never wanted to lie to you. I wanted to be close to you, to protect you, and could only do that if I were part of their plan."

"Then you only thought about yourself, and you don't know what it is to care for someone else. No one here does. Caring for someone isn't about manipulating them. It's being honest and acting in ways that don't hurt them."

I shake my arm free. "You hurt me, Losan. I don't blame you for disappearing as a child. For being afraid. But I blame you for what is happening now. I blame you for letting me walk into an ambush. For letting me slide off the face of a mountain, thinking I'm going to die."

"I understand, Klarke," he says quietly. "I'm so sorry."

"I wish that were enough." I turn and duck through the tent flap before he can see me cry. Maybe he is sorry—but is he sorry enough to get us off this mountain?

"I don't agree with all that your father is doing here." Casso startles me from behind as I stand, gazing out at the glacier and thinking of the vast distances that separate me from those I love, those I needed to protect.

"Then get me out of here," I tell him fiercely. "Do something!"

I don't know him. I don't trust him. But what do I have to lose? There was something about his expression when I mentioned Ramanata's name—an interest distinct, somehow, from that of my father's.

"I can't," he says. "I owe much to your father. And he has promised to help me find my child. Their mother took the child back to Ectair before they were born. Before I could see them."

"Them?"

"I'm not sure if my child is a boy or a girl or, like the Sleeping God, neither the one nor the other," he says.

"If you will not help me, why are you telling me this?" I ask.

A gust of wind rushes up the glacier, blasting us in a rush of air that almost knocks me off my feet. I drop to my knees to stabilize, and he does the same. The wind assault continues for a few minutes and then abates.

"You're from Ectair…" he says. He opens his mouth, as if to say more, but watches me through narrowed eyes. We are both determining if the other is trustworthy.

"Ectair is a big place. I know only a small bite of it."

"You live in the palace, though."

"I do."

"Then you must know."

I shake my head. "I'm going to need more than that."

"The mother of my child is the king's sister, Lady Genalt."

Oh my gods.

"When your mother smuggled her out of Ectair, she came here, and we fell in love. She was broken, but so was I." He lifts the stump of his left arm. "A climbing accident that forced me to leave the Parvanatari. Genalt and I found comfort and peace in each other. At first, she was elated when she found out she was with child, but then she became increasingly anxious. One day she disappeared, and a few weeks later, we received word that she had returned to Ectair."

Lady Genalt had a child—a child that is possibly alive somewhere in Ectair, the niece or nephew of King Adolar. If Otto's sister was indeed dead, as my father would have me believe, perhaps this child might be the answer.

"You said my father wants to help you find your child?" He nods. "You know my father plans to destroy the Adolar line, right? That would include your child."

"I cannot find this child alone, Klarke," he says. "After we find them, I will do what I must to protect them."

"Again, why are you telling me this?" I gaze into his eyes,

trying to discern friend from foe, truth from lie.

"You live in the palace; perhaps you've heard word of Genalt or my child?"

Unnecessary grief. We all carry it. There is a word for it. Hope. Hope is a bloodthirsty creature.

"I'm sorry. I do not know if Lady Genalt or her child is still alive."

He sighs. The air swirls in a cold fog around our faces, nipping at our exposed cheeks and sending cold fingers down the back of our jackets. "Genalt ruled that beast, you know? Hildegroth. She never learned how to control it completely, but she did possess the power. She was a formidable woman. And they tortured her. I know what Ectair does to capable women, and I am sorry."

My thoughts race furiously. "If Genalt is still alive, then she would still control Hildegroth. And if not, her child would…" I say.

"Only if the child is a daughter," Casso says. "Laren had a sense of humor, you see. When King Miter gave his daughter to the sea god in exchange for control of the beast, Laren stitched a caveat onto the deal. Miter's blood would control the monster, but only through the lineage of women."

"So Miter could never command Hildegroth?"

Casso laughs. "Never. And his impotence over the beast became his downfall."

"And King Adolar was never able to wrest that power from Lady Genalt? Even with the darken mages?"

"A mortal cannot steal power from a god," Casso says bitterly. "Adolar tried to defeat Laren in his quest for power. Why else would King Adolar have been gifted twins? They came straight from Laren. As I said, he has a sense of humor. Why allow Adolar to drown in a boating accident when Laren could have the pleasure of observing this pathetic mortal grapple, powerless, knowing he will die and his line will end with him?"

I've never cared much for Laren. I thought he was a cruel god, and perhaps he is. But his decision to endow the power of Hildegroth in women alone, and in their daughters after them—well, it is not often we Ectarians see such, and I feel an unexpected gratitude to this god of death and darkness.

"Laren favors his daughters," Casso says. "That is why Ectarians cast them into the sea. They think it will please Laren, returning his girls to him while maintaining their male dominance. But it does the opposite. Laren is angry. And I fear his wrath will soon spill over and consume this entire continent."

Oh, the situation is getting better and better all the time, I think dismally. Now I have three formidable men vying for power *and* an angry god. And I'm stuck on the side of a fiekin' mountain, unable to stop any of them.

"I think if we find Genalt, if we find my child, we can set this right. We can stop what has been set in motion."

"And you know nothing of your child? No clues as to where they could be or who they are?"

"One," he says. "I have a name."

A name. There is power in a name. Agency.

"Yes?"

"A name you already know," he whispers. "The child is called Ramanata."

A frisson of chaotic energy races up my spine, stopping the breath in my throat. My mother didn't want me to find Otto's sister! She wanted me to find Lady Genalt's daughter. I turn my head slowly toward him, reaching into my pocket.

"It seems we have the same goal then." I pass him my mother's handkerchief.

Casso stares at the letters, fingering the stitching that spells out his child's name. "What does it say?" he asks, glancing up at me.

"Instructions from my mother. But the last bit says, *Find Ramanata.* My mother's last words to me were a command to find your child. I thought it was someone else, but apparently I was mistaken." I step toward him, taking his hand in mine. "If you help me escape, Casso, I promise to locate your child."

He shakes his head, glancing as he does so toward the main

tent. I can see the struggle in his eyes, the conflict raging within. Should he trust the established and capable group he's currently allied with or throw caution into the crevasse and entrust his fate, and that of his child, to the young woman offering ghosts and an old hankie?

"You do not want to be associated with murderers," I say urgently. "And that is what these people are, no matter how just their motives. They are planning to kill an innocent and good man. The prince. A man who is trying to help me find Ramanata. I know I might not seem like a powerful ally, but my husband is the crown prince of Ectair, and he is a good person. He will not kill your child. But my father will." I thrust the handkerchief toward him. "*This* is what Mina, my mother, actually wanted. Not what my father is doing."

I let the silence swirl around us with the cold snow and wind. A minute becomes two and then five. I remain still. I have hope. Damn that hope.

"Meet me by that serac tonight when Azura crests the left flank of Opasno. Bring your friend, Veit. We will need a team of at least three for safety. Leave what you can in your tent. We move light, and we move quick."

"Thank you." I place my hand on his arm.

"I will not be able to stay in Ainar after this," he says.

"I will keep you safe. I will protect you in Ectair."

"I am not an easy one to protect in your land," he says, gesturing toward his darkly complexioned face.

"You have my word," I tell him. "I will keep you safe and reunite you with your child."

"Then we have a deal, Fram Ascher. Speak of this to no one but Veit."

As I watch him walk toward the main tent, I wonder if he will betray me to my father. Was this all a ruse? A game to test my loyalty? I swallow hard and curl my trembling hands into fists. Perhaps Otto's sister is dead, as my father says. Perhaps this, too, is an impasse. But if Casso is right, and if Lady Genalt or her child is alive, then maybe we have something greater than the truth of Adolar's downfall. King Adolar, Haydrich and the Dark Promise, and now my father, have seemed formidable, even undefeatable, enemies, but perhaps I don't need power, magic, and secret plots to prevail. Perhaps I need only one specific ally to set the world right—the woman who controls Hildegroth. Perhaps, without knowing it, I have been on the path to securing the greatest weapon all along.

I shiver, wondering if I am truly capable of unleashing such a monster on my enemies, knowing innocent lives will invariably be lost. Would I do it to save Otto? To save Kiel? To protect Rayna? *Yes*, something in the depths of my soul responds.

Yes.

26

A layer of clouds fractures Azura's light, but it is still light enough to see Casso's form beneath the serac as we approach. The camp is quiet. They don't bother with guards, as there is no way for us to escape. Casso has laid out a rope and motions for me to tie into the back, Veit in the middle, and he signals that he will take the front. He hands us each an alpenstock and pats our shoulders.

"My child?" he asks, holding my gaze intently.

"I promise," I say, gripping his shoulder.

We don't light headlamps. Not yet. It would be too risky. I take my first steps down the deadly slope with only Azura's muted light, following in Casso and Veit's footsteps. As we hasten downslope, each step feels lighter as the air becomes easier to breathe. Casso knows the route and is sure of foot. We climb down rickety ladders, over delicate snow bridges, and across steep slopes of icy snow; we traverse the old ropes of a rock chimney. He does it all with one arm, and I see his strength as a mountaineer.

After picking our way through a maze of seracs and crevasses, we make it to the valley, exhausted and chilled, but otherwise unscathed. Azura is setting, and Cleos is about to rise. Soon, the camp will know we've fled, and they will be on the move. As much as I want to rest, I can't. I think only of reaching Otto as quickly as possible.

We untie ourselves from the rope, and Veit coils it and drapes it across his shoulders. We each carry a rucksack filled with slings, harnesses, and food, and between us we carry a stove, a tent, and blankets.

"I'm not sure what we'll need," Casso says. "So we take it all. We can shuck gear along the way if we need to."

"It's a long way to Kietsch carrying all this," Veit says.

"I don't plan to walk all the way." Casso gives him a warm smile and takes off through the valley. We follow dirt paths and roads lined with muddy snow and hanging ice. Jagged peaks and thick shrubs with small waxy leaves surround the trail. Occasionally, I spot bright red flowers clustered together among the gnarled branches. In places, thin trees twist up and over the path, creating a dim forested tunnel, their branches coated with slick sleeves of ice. As Cleos rises, the ice melts, and we are pattered with drops of sparkling water from above. My breath, a cloudy billow in the starlight, pulls me along.

Everything that has happened over the past week feels like a dream, and I'm not sure what is real and what an exhausted, air-deprived brain has concocted. But as I stride behind Casso, Ramanata's father, I remind myself of the reality of the entire nightmare. My father is alive. My father is alive and wants to kill my husband.

Eventually, we reach a small village—a smattering of huts, gardens, stables, and pyramids of dried karad dung. Casso enters one house and comes out with a woman dressed in red robes. She smiles at us with a mouth short of a few teeth and disappears into a neighboring stable, returning several minutes later with three horses in tow.

"We make for the Roudan," Casso says. "We will cross where the dam meets the sea. It's the fastest."

The Roudan. My father helped build the dam in his days as an Ascenditure, helped to build and repair it. Queasiness coats my insides, and I attempt to remove all thought of him from my mind. Before, my memories were laced with grief, which was bad enough. Now, they simmer with rage, and I'd trade them for grief any day. A dead father who loves me is better than a live one who doesn't.

We move fast on horseback, covering country I've never seen. The mountains shrink. The gorges are steeper and narrower. Snow clings to the sides of the canyons and in wind-blown clusters at the bases of rocks. Knotted knee-high shrubs give way to thicker forests of wide-leafed trees crowned with pink and white flowers. As I canter beneath a low-hanging branch, I pick a cluster of pink flowers and tuck it into my horse's saddle. Pink, the color of perseverance, according to Tashi. I need the Sleeping God's gift now more than ever.

Finally, we leave the mountain valley and find ourselves on a vast, snow-dusted plain, which descends slowly to the sea many miles to the south. The snow melts into slush as we ride, which then gives way to spongy bogs, festooned with algae and lichen in bright shades of green and yellow. Beyond the bogs, I see dark meadows of damp grassland. The mountains rise as sentinels at our back, but ahead the land is flat to the glimmer of sea that lies at the horizon's edge.

The first night, we seek shelter beneath a canvas tent Casso erects in a patch of dry ground. Our nights are short, our sleep fitful—we don't want to give our pursuers time to catch up. We sleep only enough to survive. On the fourth day, bleary-eyed and exhausted, we leave camp at dawn and reach the edge of Miter's Waste by noon. I keep glancing behind, expecting my father and an army of warriors to be at our backs, but we are alone.

A steep and narrow trail leads to the bottom of the Waste. We slowly maneuver the horses down the zigzagging path of loose rock and unstable soil. Our horses, their flanks dark with sweat, are as weary as their riders and they stumble and slide down the steep cliff to the bottom. Once there, we rest for fifteen minutes, allowing the horses to graze on tuckweed that grows in the crevices of the basin.

Towering to my right is the Roudan, a massive wall of stone and aggregate holding back the sea. I gaze down the length of it, marveling at its grandiose size. Surely the Roudan must be the greatest construction ever undertaken. And we built it together—Ainarians and Ectarians both. To protect each other. It once stood for unity.

We ride along the valley basin, in the deep shadow cast by the Roudan. To my left, I can see the yawning canyon of Miter's Waste, littered with boulders the size of houses that must have rolled there before the sea was dammed, when the tides could carry rocks from the Rolag Sea to the Sea of Pibar. Glossy-leaved shrubbery cluster amongst the rocks where small pools of water rest. My horses' hooves clatter over river stones, which cover every inch of the Waste. I wonder if these stones miss the taste of saltz and the power of churning water, or if they've adjusted to the mosses that coat their surfaces and the wind that blasts them smooth.

We camp the first night near the middle of the Waste, surrounded by boulders that form a near-perfect circle. I imagine Laren presiding over great council meetings with fish and minor gods here when it lay beneath the sea.

As Cleos gives way to the bright face of Azura, cold air pours in over the Roudan and settles in the basin where we have set up our tent. It is a damp chill that cuts through wool and silk and penetrates to the bone. Casso builds a fire from the fallen limbs of a fizhte tree, and we eat our oatmash.

"You sure it wasn't your father who killed those men on Mount Bonen?" Veit asks. "Could Gio could have been working for him?"

"Gio?" Casso says.

"No," I reply, warming my frozen fingers at the fire. "King Adolar is holding Gio's sister hostage, which is how he forced Gio's hand. Gio spoke of another, also working to further King Adolar's plans, but I don't know who they are."

Veit tilts his head back to gaze up at the star-washed night, pulling his fur blanket closer around his shoulders. "I thought you were full of scheiz, Klarke," he says, glancing at me. "Now I realize there are wackos out there. So King Adolar really tried to frame you?"

"Among other things."

"What a prick."

I laugh. "Among other things. Tristan discovered the truth on Mount Bonen, but he was killed before he could tell anyone."

"They never found him," Veit says thoughtfully. "Maybe he's still alive."

Hope. Again. That painful creature. "Maybe."

I want to tell Veit about Haydrich and the Dark Promise. I want to let him know about all the shifting pieces on this game board, but I don't fully trust him. I lean against a boulder, gazing into the leaping flames of our fire. Did Ellias know of the Dark Promise? Is that why they killed him? I thought he'd discovered King Adolar's schemes atop Fitzhan, but what if it had been the Schaeter's plot he'd uncovered? And were those two somehow linked? My body aches after days of hard riding and my mind feels leaden with exhaustion after turning over and over the same questions.

"Get some sleep." Casso throws another log on the fire and settles down into his bedroll. "We ride early."

We awaken well before dawn and head out beneath a clear sky filled with stars. Tonight, with a full day of hard riding, we will be back in Ectair—back with the enemy I know. I shudder, thinking of all the balls I must juggle. Even Rüdiger the Dumt, the famous jester who'd saved Miter's life, couldn't keep this many objects in the air.

"Do you hear that?" I ask, reining in my horse to a halt. "What is that?"

A low, deep rumbling sounds in my ears, like thunder muffled by miles of sea or the slow collapse of hundreds of buildings turning to rubble and dust. The sky is overcast, but it does not look like an orkansturm day. Casso and Veit pull up beside me, their horses splashing through the pools of water that gather across the Waste. The rumbling grows louder, and I glance up at the Roudan to see a thin spray of water leaking through the aggregate from the sea. Then, I spot another and a third, and with a sinking feeling I realize the dam is failing and we are directly in the path of the onrushing floodwaters.

"Oh, scheiz," Veit says. "I thought your boyfriend just fixed these?"

"How could the repairs have already failed?"

The rumbling grows steadily louder, as if the Roudan itself were moaning.

"Look there," I say, pointing out a line of pitons hammered into the dam, stretching from the floor of the Waste to the summit far above our heads. Small ledges had been installed to create an easy, multi-pitch climb or rappel—the route the Ascenditures use for repairs.

"I need to go up and assess the damage," I say. "We will need to let the Ascenditures know when we get back to Ectair."

"I'll go with you," Veit says.

We dismount, leaving Casso to tend to the horses. "Be quick," he says. "We don't know the extent of the cracking on the sea side. The dam could burst, and we don't want to be in the Waste when it goes."

Veit and I pull the rope from the bag, tie quick harnesses, and fashion a few slings. We lack the gear to add protection at every piton, so a fall here will be long and dangerous. I won't fall, though—the ledges ensure an easy climb.

"I'm leading first," I tell Veit.

He ties in to belay, and I place my hands against the Roudan. My father climbed this. Not so long ago, this thought would have brought me comfort, made me feel close to him.

"Klettag," I say.

"Klettag und," Veit replies.

The holds consist of small protruding pebbles, and, in some places, cavities dug out by tools. It's an ugly line. Slippery and chossy. A few times, the cement crumbles under my grip, but I catch myself before I slip. Attaching a sling and karabiner to a piton, I aim for the first platform. Veit can pull the slings as we go, so we can reuse them as we proceed up the route. I reach the platform and anchor myself in. Veit climbs, and I manage the rope as he ascends, carefully coiling it so it's ready for the next pitch. Veit leads the next route, and then I follow. We alternate the lead as we move up the dam. Multi-pitch with two climbers is efficient, so long as we manage the rope properly.

We reach the final platform, and it is Veit's turn to lead. I belay him as he climbs and watch him disappear over the summit of the dam.

"What do you see?" I shout.

"Nothing so far. The edge is about fifty feet away, so I can't—fieken hüle!" Veit screams, a high-pitched shriek that makes my blood run cold.

"What? What's happening?" I yell.

"Fiek the gods!"

"Veit! Get me up there. Can you safely belay me?"

"I'm set," he calls frantically. "Hurry, Klarke!"

I climb quickly, too quickly, and slip in several places before reaching the crest of the Roudan, where Veit is tied in. I look toward the other side of the dam. The base of the Roudan is approximately six hundred feet thick, and the top is fifty feet wide, so I cannot see the face of the dam. What I do see stops me in my tracks and stops the breath in my throat: a thickly muscled giant tentacle rises into the air, slapping against the aggregate wall. A second tentacle joins the first, then a third, the summit of the dam shuddering under the impact as they pound the rock wall. Veit and I untie from the rope and, crouching to avoid scattering debris, race to the edge. Hildegroth's maw is the size of Revolution Square. A dark whirlpool swirls at the center, surrounded by jagged teeth that resemble the baleen of a tolvalus. Hildegroth's mottled flesh is red, green, and in patches, a shimmering purple. A deep, rumbling roar sounds from the depths of the monster, like a thousand furnaces about to blow. Looking over the edge, I see all thirteen tentacles, longer than any tree is tall, flailing against the dam. I grab Veit's arm to steady myself.

"How?" he whispers, his face white with fear.

Hildegroth's body rolls, and I see what looks like an eye—the iris the color of fire, with a narrow black slit running down the center. I feel as if he is looking directly at me, promising to suck me and all the known world into his cavernous mouth. My blood runs colder than the winds atop Opasno. My legs tremble beneath me, and I worry I'll tumble forward into the sea. Fear courses through my veins, greater than that provoked by any mortal enemy.

"Why?" Veit asks again.

Yes, why now? The last time Hildegroth raged, King Adolar had been torturing his sister.

"Lady Genalt's alive," I whisper. "And Hildegroth seeks to protect her." Could King Adolar or the Dark Promise be attempting again to obtain her power over the beast? Last time, they failed. But what if they have now found a way to succeed? What if King Adolar or Haydrich wrested control of this fearsome creature from her?

"We have to go, Veit. We have to stop this," I tell him urgently.

"How?"

How? I have no idea how. But it must begin with Lady Genalt—I must find her before Hildegroth lays waste to everything and everyone.

"What could Hildegroth want with the Waste?" Veit asks. "If he wanted to inflict the most casualties, why not attack Bolson? There's no one in the Waste."

Veit's right—what could be Hildegroth's intention? Perhaps Lady Genalt hides somewhere here or in one of the cities surrounding the Sea of Toole. My immediate focus, however, must be to stop my father's assassins. First, I have to get to Kietsch to warn Otto. Then, together, we can deal with the monster.

Veit and I rappel to the bottom of the Waste and race to our horses, where we mount and make for Kietsch, breathlessly informing Casso as we go of the rise of Hildegroth. It is more than I can manage to keep track of my tasks, and of my enemies. Somehow, this must all tie together, but how?

I glance over at Veit, his face set and determined. I once perceived him as an enemy, but now he feels like one of my closest allies. That is the only path forward, I realize. I must turn enemies into allies. I must shorten the list of people who want me dead.

And I must do it before Laren's beast destroys us all.

27

I never imagined I'd be grateful to see the ten towers of the Rektburg, but as we gallop past Miter's Backbone toward the bridge to Kietsch, my heart races to the beat of my horses hooves. Otto is in there. And pray to Orna, he is still alive. We hurtle through the shadow cast by Kara Do, across the narrow bridge, and into the streets of Kietsch. Everything is rain-slickened and coated in thick moss. Clouds hang heavy and gray, mixing with the smog rising from the factory chimneys. The people, dressed in green and white, their hands and hosen tar-stained, keep their heads down, their backs bent by endless hard work. We make a stop down at the beach caves where I'd met Marike and her friend, and leave Casso hiding in one of the caverns with what is left of our food and a promise to return.

Veit and I reach the palace, leave our weary horses in the stable, and climb the steps to the Rektburg.

"What business do you have at the palace?" one of the guards asks.

"I am Veit Obeldorf, and I am here to see the king," Veit pronounces grandly.

"I am Klarke Ascher," I say, pushing past Veit, "and I demand to see my husband, Prince Otto."

"Yer all Klarke Ascher, ain't ye?" he sneers and positions himself more securely in front of the door. "The princess is in Ainar. So get away with ye then."

"Fetch Silias," I demand. "He will vouch for me."

"I ain't here to fetch things for you, foze."

"Crimmian, let Princess Ascher pass." Like the towers of the Rektburg, Silias's familiar voice is oddly comforting. He dismisses the guard, stammering his apologies, and takes me by the arm, propelling me forward into the palace. "Where is your team? Why are you back so soon? You shouldn't be here." His expression is one of concerned confusion.

"We need to speak to King Adolar immediately. And Prince Otto. They must both be present."

"The king is engaged with a...new friend at present."

I frown, hoping the new friend is at least old enough to wed. Why not just shuttle Otto to safety and let my father and his cronies murder his father? It's what he deserves. I worry, though, at the prospect of another lunatic replacing the old. My father...Haydrich...the Dark Promise—they all seem driven to seize power regardless of the cost to innocent lives. And what would they do once they got it? It is clear—Otto must take the throne.

"This is a matter of life and death," Veit says. "The lives of the king and his son are in grave danger."

"Is this true?" Silias looks at me. His expression falters, and I see something there I don't fully understand. Is it fear, doubt, or further confusion?

"Yes! And if the king doesn't believe me, he will believe Veit. His name carries weight here."

"Very well. Wait in the throne room. I will request an audience with the king."

We sit on one of the wooden benches situated along the edge of the throne room, and wait. In the dim light cast by the flickering candles of the overhead chandelier, I look over at Veit. "You look like karad dung," I tell him.

"Think you look any better?" he replies.

Veit's face is streaked with dirt, his hair greasy and matted with travel. His jacket and pants are damp with rain and dark with mud from the Waste. We look like stable hands, not like anyone who belongs in the palace. Veit fiddles with the laces on his boots, rises to his feet, walks around the benches, and then resumes his seat. "What is taking so long?" he growls. "We did say *grave* danger."

"The king likes to remind us that we wait on his pleasure," I tell him.

Finally, after another half hour of waiting, the massive wooden doors scrape open.

"What is the meaning of this?" King Adolar snaps. "Why are you back, and what is this nonsense about my life being in danger? Did King Gyalzen send you? And gods, how dare you enter my throne room smelling and looking like swine feces."

"I will waste little breath on what I am about to tell you. I am here for Otto and will reveal the following intelligence to you only because I care for him," I say.

The king's facc reddens. "I will not—" he begins, his mouth curling into a snarl.

"Klarke!" Otto enters the throne room and rushes to me. We embrace, and he kisses my cheek. Tears well up in my eyes, and I brush them impatiently away—*He's okay. He's still alive. We made it in time.*

"Otto. I'm so happy to see you." I hug him tightly, then pull back to look him in the eyes. "Listen to me, Otto. Both of you." I glance toward the king. "First, King Gyalzen is not our enemy. He does not wish you or any Ectarians harm. He pushes for peace. He wants a reunion."

King Adolar snorts. "You've come a long way to tell me such nonsense," he says sharply.

"Second, my father is still alive. He is the head of a resistance that plans to kill you both and obliterate the monarchy. I begged him to spare your life," I tell Otto. "But he refuses, saying King Adolar's lineage must be destroyed. So I fled and came as fast as I could to warn you."

"Anselm is alive?" the king demands, his face pale.

"Your attempt to kill him by blowing up his ship failed. I was just as shocked as you, at the thought that I might have enjoyed an alternate life, growing up in Ainar, far from the likes of you."

"Dull your tongue, or I will remove it from your mouth," King Adolar bites out, his eyes narrowing to slits in his growing rage. He paces before the throne, fists clenched, his breath coming in a rapid wheeze. "This is a lie. All of it. You're playing at something, Klarke Ascher, and I won't fall for it."

"And third," I interrupt, "Hildegroth is back. And he is currently destroying the Roudan."

"Hildegroth?" the king screams, whipping around to face me. "Anselm Ascher? You wish to resurrect these ridiculous notions to make a fool of me."

"I have neither the time nor the inclination to convince you. Either take heed or watch your kingdom burn. It matters not to me."

I drop Otto's hands and walk deliberately over to the king until we are eye to eye, our faces inches apart.

"I know about your sister," I say quietly. "I know Lady Genalt controlled Hildegroth, and that you tortured her for her powers. And failed. And that when Hildegroth tore through the kingdom, it was because of you. Because you hurt his mistress. It was not King Gyalzen who killed all those people. It was you. And I can only imagine Hildegroth is back because you are once again seeking power that is not yours. That you shall never have. So for the good of your people, if you care for them at all, let your sister go. Leave her in peace."

King Adolar opens his mouth to speak, but words fail him.

"Protect your son and protect your people. Strengthen the guard and release your sister."

"You are lying," the king sputters. "Hildegroth couldn't possibly be back."

"Your majesty," Veit says. "I, too, saw the beast. Klarke isn't lying."

"I never thought I'd see the day when an Obeldorf defended a foze. Your father would be appalled," the king sneers at Veit.

Veit shrinks back, and I want to shake him—where is his bravado now when we really need it?

"The Roudan is about to fall," I say. "Free Lady Genalt and stop this madness before it's too late!"

"I can't!" the king shouts. "She's dead!" He sinks to a chair, his hands trembling in his lap—he seems suddenly old. "After she fled to Ainar," he continues, subdued, "she returned and died...suddenly."

"You told me she killed herself," Otto said. "That she went mad. You lied to me?"

"You had her killed," I mutter. Why, I wonder, am I trying to protect this monster from my father? And if Lady Genalt is truly dead, who is controlling Hildegroth? I think of Casso hiding in the caves, waiting for us to return to help him find his child, their child—the one born of the union between him and Lady Genalt. If it is, indeed, her child that now controls the monster, then that child must be a girl. And if Hildegroth is again trying to destroy Miter's Waste, Casso's daughter is in trouble.

But she is still alive.

My thoughts race, but I still them long enough to come back to the present.

"Lady Genalt was pregnant. There is a child. Where is she?"

"Twins," King Adolar says quietly. "They're dead. They died at birth. With their mother."

That can't be. Who could be controlling the monster if all his mistresses were dead? While I know nothing of lineages or long-past promises, something is angering Hildegroth. If not Adolar's niece, then who?

"Who was the doctor who delivered Lady Genalt's twins?"

"You are not entitled to the world, Fram Ascher," the king blusters furiously, recovering some semblance of his prior composure. "You are the daughter of a failed ship captain and a whore. Nothing more."

"She saved my life," Veit blurts out indignantly. "She's not nothing."

My surprise matches the king's, and I almost laugh—this might be the first emotion the king and I have shared. Veit reddens, bowing deeply. "Apologies, your majesty."

If Veit weren't an Obeldorf, he'd be hanged. His last name now warrants only a stern glare and a warning finger.

"Go to the Roudan and see for yourself," I tell the king. "You need to prepare for war. On all fronts. And you must know the extent of the danger if *I* am trying to protect *you*."

I turn from the king and storm from the throne room, Otto and Veit following. At the door, I glance back at the king. "Death's Whisper," I say. "That's how they plan to do it. Poetic, isn't it? That my father comes for you in such a way." Again, the king is uncharacteristically at a loss for words, his face pale beneath his dark shock of hair. "Secure your kitchens, your majesty, and prepare your stock of solans."

In the hallway, I exhale a shaky breath.

"What now?" Otto asks. "And how is Dieter?"

"Fine, I understand he is fine," I say. "I'll fill you in on everything. Right now, though, it is imperative that we find your cousin. I do not believe what the king tells us is true, that both Lady Genalt's twins died at birth."

"My cousin?"

"Yes, your cousin, Ramanata, who is surely behind Hildegroth's destructive rampage. We must find her before my father and Haydrich do."

"Welcome home, Klarke." Otto laughs darkly. "Things were dull without you here."

28

From the window of my room, I can see Queen Eleonora's tower looming through the mist. I go over the pieces of the puzzle in my mind. Queen Eleonora had twins. Otto is one; his sister, the baby girl, was smuggled to Burndle, only to die upon arrival. My mother and father smuggled the king's sister, Lady Genalt, to Ainar after the king sought to obtain her powers over Hildegroth. She met Casso, fell in love, got pregnant, returned to Ectair to give birth—again to twins—then died. So much death leading to the same dismal end.

Is that what I'm chasing? Ghosts? I'm hanging my hat on the hope that Ramanata lives, and that she, and her power over Hildegroth, might save us all from Adolar, Hildegroth, Haydrich, my father. All I have to guide me is a handkerchief with a name stitched into the fabric.

"I have spoken with Silias," Otto says, interrupting my thoughts. "He has arranged for Casso to be taken to a shepherd's hut near the Dangof Forest that belonged to a relative who recently passed. He'll be safe there."

I nod and give a soft grunt in reply, some part of me wishing I could join him in hiding from the outside world.

"I can't believe your father is alive," Otto says from behind, one hand on my shoulder. "Are you…are you okay, Klarke?"

I sigh and turn my gaze to the prince, then to the painting of Lady Genalt that hangs above the mantel. She is thin and dainty, attired in white gossamer silks, like a wisp of glittering smoke. Like a felfee.

"I haven't been okay in years," I admit. "First, it was grief. Now, it is betrayal. And soon, I'm certain, it will return to grief. I am what I am."

Veit rises to his feet and walks restlessly before the fire; he seems uncomfortable with emotions, and I wonder if he has ever experienced true friendship and kindness. He is not an arschole by accident, but by design. And that design is unraveling.

"Both our fathers are scheiz, it seems," Otto says quietly. "Our moms were great. Only the hard and the ruthless endure in this world."

"We're going to change that," I say.

"My father's also an arschole," Veit contributes, turning toward us. "But my mum's a prick, too, so we don't have that in common."

"It's not easy living with a powerful parent who doesn't care," Otto replies. "I know your burden, Veit."

Veit's mouth tightens, and he gives a half nod. "I should warn them, I suppose. You know, about Hildegroth. They're in Amia. If Hildegroth breaks through the Roudan, the only thing protecting Amia is that flimsy old dam on the Sea of Toole."

"Yes, Amia and Iri must be notified," I say. "They should begin evacuations. The Sevier River is too shallow for Hildegroth to enter, so Merket, Lastil, and Kaiwa are safe."

"And what about Kietsch?" Otto asks.

"Let's hope Hildegroth can't find a way through Pieter's Uplift. It's proven effective before."

"And Bolson?" Otto whispers.

"May Laren take mercy on Bolson," I whisper back.

"I still don't understand why Hildegroth hasn't come south," Veit says. "Why the Waste?"

"I wondered if Lady Genalt's daughter lived somewhere along the Waste, in Iri or Amia; if there is no daughter, if King Adolar speaks the truth, then I'm at a loss."

"I should go," Veit says. "I don't want to cause needless panic, but I must warn my family. They have a home in the Tono Hills where they can hide out."

"Suertgût, Veit."

"Yeah, suertgût to you too, Klarke. And tanks ye. Ya know, for all of it." He moves toward me, perhaps for a hug, but instead settles for an awkward pat on my arm.

"Be safe, Veit. We're going to need your help when you return."

He nods, clears his throat, and leaves.

"He's come a long way, hasn't he?" Otto raises an eyebrow.

"He's one of the most honest people I know," I say. "Never thought I'd say this, but our world of liars needs more Veit Obeldorfs."

"It's funny, in a way," Otto says with a laugh, "that my father wants you dead, and yours wants me dead. And we just want people to be nice to each other."

"And honest," I add.

"And honest," he agrees.

"Were they always like this, our fathers? Or has old age made them fearful maniacs?" I ask.

"I don't see either of us becoming like that."

"Nor do I."

I close my eyes and wish I could crawl into bed, pull the curtains, and sleep for a week. But there are too many nightmares to contend with in my waking hours to allow time for sleep; it is as if I am in the middle of one of my omie's stories, one of beasts and monsters, of kings and power and greed. Although this story is one stranger than any my omie has read to me.

"Life doesn't follow the book," she would say. "Life does what it wants. Life is wilder than imagination, and the sooner you learn that, the better prepared you'll be when your story flies off the page."

My story has flown off the page, and I am woefully unprepared for it.

"Rayna came to see you," Otto says. "She said she has something important to share."

I open my eyes. I can do nothing now but wait for the king to confirm that the monster is at Ectair's doorstep, my father to send his assassin to kill my prince, or for the Ascenditures to return so I can tell Kiel his grief was wasted. Seeing Rayna, hugging Rayna, will be a welcome distraction from helplessness.

I retrieve my horse, Ixy, from the stables and ride to Martus Meats. Crumbling brick factories, homes, and shops hide beneath a thick shroud of fog and mist. People appear and disappear like specters floating through a graveyard. Ixy trots along the cobblestones, threading her way through the narrow, winding streets.

I have not seen Eugen since the wedding, though he had seemed civil enough at the celebrations; perhaps he has forgiven my accusation made so many months ago. A sliver of fear traces down my spine as I tie Ixy to a road post and approach the front door. If he wishes me harm, now would be the time to exact revenge.

A bell tinkles as I push the door open. The air is heavy with the stink of death and blood. Avoiding the carcasses hanging in the window, I ring the bell at the counter. What will I say to Eugen? What is my excuse for being here? He told me to leave his wife alone. Panic rises as I try to summon a reason for my presence.

"Klarke!" Rayna rushes down the back staircase and pulls me into a hug.

"Rayna!" I squeeze her tightly then push away, glancing around.

"He's not here. He went to the pier to buy thund fish."

"Oh, Rayna. It's so good to see you."

"And you! We've had no word on the Ascenditures since you left. I've been sick with worry, but here you are." Rayna has cut her long hair into an impish pixie cut which suits her well—and she looks like she's eating again. "Did you do it? Did you stand on top of the world?"

I reach into my pocket and place the stone from Opasno's Base Camp in the palm of her hand.

"I did."

She presses the stone against her heart. "And? How was it?" she breathes, with a giddy grin.

"Hard. Terrifying. Amazing…and incredibly hurtful."

"Why, what happened?"

"My father, Rayna. He is still alive. He has been in hiding all these years, plotting against the Adolar dynasty. He wants to save this kingdom. At the cost of me."

"Oh, Klarke." She seizes my hand and presses it to her heart. "I'm so sorry."

"He's coming here to kill the king and Prince Otto."

"Kill Otto? But Otto is nothing like his father!" Rayna exclaims, her eyes wide.

"I told him. He doesn't care."

"What are we going to do?"

Rayna's *we* sounds so good to my ears, and I realize how exhausted I am of conspiring with and against men. I miss Rayna. I miss my buddy. I miss a woman's energy.

"There's more," I say. "Hildegroth is destroying the Roudan."

"That can't be true!" Rayna protests. "Hildegroth is just a myth, isn't he?"

"I'm afraid not. I saw him, Rayna, with my own eyes. I've warned the king, but I doubt he will do anything useful. I am sure he will find a way to lay the blame on me after Hildegroth destroys the cities along the Waste again."

"Anything else you care to warn me about?"

"That's all my news for now, but what's new with you? You look…better."

"I am," she says hesitantly. "I've just returned with Eugen from Iri. Yesterseve, actually. I think I told you at the wedding that we've been traveling there a lot lately so Eugen can purchase kuhkas. I'd never left Kietsch, so it's been a grand adventure. Eugen purchased a hundred head this time, and I even got to pick out a calf for myself. He laughed at me and called me a silly woman, but I've named her Elke, and he promised not to hurt her as long as I behave. She is the sweetest little thing with big brown eyes and a tuft of black hair that sticks up in front."

"That's good, Rayna. I'm glad you've found something that makes you happy."

"Elke stays at a ranch south of here, so I don't see her often, but it's something to look forward to."

"Definitely." I look at Rayna's face. At her narrow eyes, dark hair, pale skin, and wispy appearance. Like a felfee. A felfee with blood from Ainar.

"There's something else," she says, excitedly.

Iri. *I've just returned from Iri. We've been traveling there a lot lately.*

A wild notion occurs to me, but I instantly dismiss it. Rayna is not an orphan—she knew her parents before they died. She couldn't be Ramanata, could she?

"I'm pregnant, Klarke. I'm going to have a baby. I wasn't sure how I felt about it at first, but now I'm happy. Please be happy for me, Klarke."

"Happy? Of course, Rayna," I manage, feeling stunned from the wild path my thoughts have traveled. How could Rayna and Ramanata be one and the same? And the fact that Iri is located along the Waste, surely that was just a coincidence. Thousands of women with Ainarian blood could be traveling there even now, and any of them could be provoking Hildegroth's rampage. Shrugging this off, I direct my attention to Rayna. "I am so happy for you, Rayna. I am. We will ensure your child is born into a world worthy of them."

"Thank you, Klarke," she says with a smile.

Still, I find myself wondering—Obid brought us together, Rayna and me. Ellias was responsible for moving her into the women's tenement. She is almost as touched by the conspirators as I am. I could find out the truth. There is a way to be sure. It's an absurd plan, but it's all I have.

"When will Eugen return?" I ask.

"In a few hours," she replies.

"Is he good to you? Does he hit you still?"

If relations were now peaceful between Rayna and Eugen, then it seems Hildegroth would be at peace too.

"I..." Rayna's mouth tightens and she turns away. "We don't all live in a world where good means the same thing, Klarke."

Recalling the bruises on her arms from months before, I

realize that Hildegroth's path—should she be Ramanata—will eventually turn to Kietsch. I have little love for my home, but I will not condemn innocent people to death. The clues are thin, but they are all I have.

"I need you to come with me, Rayna."

"I can't."

"You can. As your princess, I command it."

"If I close the store, Eugen will kill Elke."

Rayna's stupid cow. I want to tell her it doesn't matter, that there are more important things. But I cannot help but remember her accusation, before I climbed Mount Bonen, that I was selfish and cared only about what mattered to me. My father chose some grand scheme, claiming it to be for the greater good, over my well-being. Am I now doing the same to Rayna?

"I understand, Rayna. I will be back." I shove open the door and rush out into the drizzling rain. "I'm happy for you, Rayna!"

I untie Ixy, leap onto her back, and race for the palace. It could be nothing, it is probably nothing, but nothing is all I have. Rayna must go to the Roudan.

29

After stabling Ixy, I race through the rain to the palace, colliding with Silias in the portico as I round the corner. "Princess," he exclaims, startled. "Is all well?"

"I need your help," I say breathlessly. "On a matter of royal security."

In Walburga's library, we find Otto bent over a book. He straightens when he sees us, sparing a skeptical glance for Silias.

"I asked him to join us," I say. I feel as if I am on a knife's edge, and I want a guard with us, even if I don't fully trust him. "Otto, I think Rayna is Ramanata."

"Rayna? Are you sure?" he asks, astonished.

"I am not sure, but I have a feeling, Otto…it is hard to explain."

"We leave for the Roudan then?"

"Yes." I feel a surge of affection for Otto and am so grateful that we speak a language between words.

"The Roudan?" Silias asks. "I cannot just leave my post here to go on a picnic with the two of you."

"You can and you will," Otto says. "If Klarke deems your presence needed, then I command you to join us."

"Very well, my prince," Silias replies, with a slight bow. "I will prepare our horses." He strides from the library and disappears down the hallway.

"How did you come to suspect Rayna of being Ramanata?" Otto asks, taking my hands.

"It's a stretch," I admit. "Ramanata's father, Casso, is Ainarian. Rayna clearly carries blood from Ainar. She is the right age. Obid brought us together when she was young, and Ellias afforded her an unusual level of protection. Also, she and Eugen just returned from Iri, where they have frequently traveled. Hildegroth is attacking the Roudan in an effort to get to the

Waste. Your aunt's child, Ramanata, must have been along the Waste or around the Sea of Toole when we passed the dam."

"My father rode out yesterday with a military detail to check the dam."

"I am happy to hear that. Hildegroth may have started to turn south, since Rayna has returned to Kietsch—if my theory is correct, of course, and Rayna is Ramanata. If we ride north with Rayna, Hildegroth will likely follow our path. We need to get Rayna to the Roudan before the king leaves, so he can see the monster and know I am telling the truth."

The three of us canter through the misty streets to Martus Meats. Otto and Silias enter first, and then I follow. Eugen is breaking apart the bloody carcass of a pig, separating the hindquarters with a forceful thwack of his cleaver. His eyes are streaked green, the telltale sign he's on veisel.

"Your princeship," he says, glancing up at Otto. "Fram Ascher." He acknowledges me with a cool reserve.

"I must borrow your wife for a few days, Eugen," Otto says. "We are traveling north for business, and the princess requires a traveling companion. I cannot deny my fair bride her desires."

Eugen squints, his heavy brow drawing into a frown, glancing at Silias, and then at a startled Rayna, who wipes her hands on a bloodstained apron. "Who am I to deny the future king?" Eugen says with a cold smile. "Get your stuff, woman, and do your duty." Rayna backs slowly up the stairs, her face a pale shade of terror.

She returns with a small bag in her hand. Eugen slaps her rear as she passes, and she jumps. "You'll have to make up for your duties when you return."

"Of course, my love."

"Go on then."

"Your fealty is well noted," Otto says with forced cheer. "I will ensure the kitchen staff orders more of our meat supply from your esteemed establishment."

"That would suit me well, highness."

Rayna climbs behind me onto Ixy's back, and the four of us take off. We catch the ferry across the Sevier River, ride swiftly beneath the shadow of Miter's Backbone, and camp our first night near the mouth of a small river east of Bolson. Trees grow thick and tall around our tents, blocking most of the sky. I start a fire and Rayna prepares a stew of oatmash for our evening meal.

"I'm going to look around," Otto says. "I'll be back in a moment."

"Where are we going, Klarke?" Rayna asks, glancing up from the pot simmering over the fire.

"Yes, I would like some answers too," Silias says. "Does this have something to do with Ramanata then, Klarke? If you brought me along to protect the party, I should know what it is I am protecting us from."

Rayna whips her gaze to me. "Ramanata?" she whispers. "From your mother's handkerchief?"

"I…had a notion that…well, that she might be you," I admit reluctantly, glaring at Silias. I had hoped to have more time to prepare Rayna. *Liar*, a voice within says. *You twist the truth like the others you so despise.*

"Why in Orna's name would you think I am Ramanata? And what does that have to do with our destination?"

"I…I can't tell you."

"Klarke."

"There is a chance—just a chance, mind you—that you are the long-lost daughter of Lady Genalt, King Adolar's sister."

"What?" Rayna's mouth drops open. "But, Klarke, I had a mother. And a father. I had a family who I knew and loved."

"I know." I also know what it's like to be lied to and betrayed by those you love. "I don't want to go into all the details yet, Rayna, because if I'm wrong, I don't want to have caused you unnecessary pain."

"Where are we going, then? Can you tell me that?"

"We're going to the Roudan," I tell her.

"To Hildegroth?" she whispers, eyes wide with fear. "Why?"

"Klarke!" Otto calls from the fringe of forest that surrounds our camp. "I need to borrow you, please."

I touch Rayna reassuringly on the shoulder as I pass her and join Otto under the trees. He beckons me forward through a maze of limestone boulders that litter the bank of the estuary, then holds a finger to his lips for me to be silent. We move forward at a crouch until we are hidden behind bushes that line the main thoroughfare leading from Kietsch to Bolson.

I hear voices—and recognize one as King Adolar.

"It must be the child," he says. "The male twin died at birth, but the girl lived, despite all assurances that she had been taken care of. I blame Mina and my sorry excuse for a queen. Their betrayal runs deeper than I knew."

"What would you have us do, my lord?"

"Find that child. The girl must be destroyed or our kingdom is lost."

"The Roudan will collapse within the next few weeks," a man responds. "Which leads us to assume that she is here, in the Waste. Should she travel to Kietsch, the strength of the Uplift will again be tested."

"Then we must act quickly," King Adolar replies. "Find the child and send her across the darkened sea; and without the interference of The Band of Sisters, you have no excuse for failure."

Band of Sisters? I turn questioningly to Otto. He shrugs. I know I've heard that mentioned before, but I can't recall where.

"If we kill the daughter, Hildegroth will go mad," the man says. "What then?"

"Veton had better come up with results soon. The fate of the kingdom depends on it."

Veton? I muse. *Who is he?*

The voices fade as the king and his companion move away.

"There's nothing more to learn from them right now," Otto says. "But if my father wants to find and kill Ramanata, and if Ramanata is Rayna, then we need to protect her."

He's right. We turn to head back to camp and meet the stares of Rayna and Silias.

"So, you think I'm the person the king is sending mercenaries to kill?"

I look at Silias, suddenly terrified he's not on our side. That he will rat out Rayna. That his allegiance is truly toward an evil king.

"I only want the truth," he sighs. "My allegiance lies wherever the truth does."

"There's only one way to figure out the truth. We have to go to the Roudan. And you have to trust me, Rayna."

We awaken early the following day and ride for the dam. We reach the edge of the Waste in the early afternoon and ride out along the wall of the Roudan. I scan the water as we ride, but the sea lies quiet, with only an occasional breeze rippling its surface.

"Hildegroth must be here," Otto says.

Glancing over the edge of the Roudan, I see a multitude of small leaks spraying water into the Waste. Then I search the Bay of Unity, seeking any sign of a thrashing tentacle, a blood-colored eye, or the cyclone mouth of teeth. Nothing. Perhaps I was wrong. Perhaps Lady Genalt's heir is now in Kietsch or Omalau or someplace farther south.

I kick a stone from the dam and watch it drop into the sea, creating a cascading ripple of circles that splash lightly against the base of the wall. I find myself again at a dead end, wielding a pathetic level of power among the players in this most dangerous game. I hold nothing. Not even information. Perhaps I should flee to Kobo after all. Perhaps I was not meant to break this system of oppression that is Adolar's power; perhaps that role falls to some other hero.

I glance at Rayna, her short hair loose and blowing in the wind. With closed eyes she faces the sea, inhaling deeply the fresh scents of saltz and fish. She looks calm, more peaceful than I've seen her in years. She is tranquil like the sea, as if she is part of it. And that is when I know the horrible truth of what I must do.

Silias is some distance away; he could not get to us with sufficient speed. Otto catches my eye, and I cast him a pleading look, placing my hand over my heart—the gesture we created to let each other know we need to speak in private. He tilts his head, perplexed.

With cold dread coursing through my veins and an intense self-loathing, I approach Rayna, moving as if in slow motion. In those seconds, it is as if I see my father clearly for the first time. I understand the shame he must face every day, knowing he hurt someone he loved. Rayna opens her eyes, sensing my nearness, and her mouth curves in a sweet smile. Before I can think any more about it, I reach up and wrap my fingers around her neck—squeezing just hard enough to cause distress, enough to make me more of a monster than the one I am fishing for.

"Klarke!" Otto shouts. "What are you doing?" He rushes toward us, but I shake my head, warning him to stay back.

Rayna's hands grasp my own, attempting to dislodge my grip, but the strength of my fingers, my forearms, from years of climbing serve me well. And before I take another breath, thirteen massive tentacles rise up from the sea and slam against the dam, so that the very ground shudders beneath our feet. I release Rayna. She staggers to the ground as Hildegroth roars, his fury louder than the strongest orkansturm. I move to help her up, but she pushes me tearfully away.

"I'm so sorry, Rayna," I say urgently, my voice breaking with emotion. "I had to know. This was the only way. And now I have to protect you. And someday, I hope you can forgive me."

I know what she is thinking; I can see it in her eyes—*Anselm's daughter, through and through.*

Silias races toward us, his eyes wide, his face tight with terror. Over the edge of the Roudan, we all can see the ravening sea disappearing into the spiraling mouth of teeth.

"Here is your truth," I shout. "Rayna is the daughter of

Lady Genalt. When her birth mother was killed by King Adolar, the power to control Hildegroth passed to Rayna. Hildegroth lay silent for years because Rayna was safe, because together, Ellias and I looked after her. When Eugen started abusing her, Hildegroth awakened and set out to save his mistress. Rayna is Ramanata. Rayna is descended from Laren himself. From King Miter's daughter, Layal. Rayna has the power to make Hildegroth do whatever she wants. Despite this formidable power, Rayna is in great danger from King Adolar, from the mages, from Haydrich and the Dark Promise.

"I need you to protect her, Silias. There is someone we all must go see, and then you must take Rayna and this person into hiding. The king will search for her soon, and we cannot let him find her. If he does, she will be killed."

"If I ask who this other person is," Rayna says, "will you answer me truthfully?"

"His name is Casso." I breathe deeply and contemplate keeping the truth from her. Sparing her feelings. But she'll find out soon enough, and not telling her really only saves my discomfort. It is not kind to her.

And I am not Anselm Ascher.

"His name is Casso, Rayna. And he is your real father."

30

Marike's hand slips, and she crashes to the floor of the lava tube. Exhaling in frustration, she scrambles to her feet.

"It's all about strength," I tell her. "Your technique is good. You just need to get stronger."

"I hate being weak," she grouses.

"You are far from weak." I laugh and pat her head, just as an older sibling might do to a troublesome child. "Strength is a spectrum. We do not exist as either weak or strong. You are stronger now than you were yesterday. That is something to be proud of."

"I want to be the best." Marike grips the first hold of Eldridge and the Goat, a mid-level bouldering problem deep within one of the lava tubes of Veber's Split. Through the red glow cast by a hovering colony of lihtbugs, I watch her scale one rounded side, hang on to the ceiling, and then crash again into the bed of straw covering the floor.

Against my better judgment, we have resumed training. I feel safe in the lava tubes. No one from the palace would dare enter for fear of getting lost in the twisted tunnels. Plus, training Marike is something I can control. It is a step forward. Without climbing I am at a standstill. The Ascenditures have yet to return. My father and his assassins remain inexplicably quiet, and King Adolar has yet to find Rayna. Hildegroth has returned to the watery depths, and the Dark Promise, too, has been quiet. It is as if all are poised to strike, as if the world is holding its collective breath before all of Laren's demons break loose.

To keep from suffocating, from descending into a frenzy of worry and fear, I try to keep myself occupied. Marike is old enough to understand the risk of our secret sessions. If I want women to be respected, I must respect Marike's desire to keep climbing despite potential consequences. I am not my father. I do not get to decide what is best for anyone but myself.

"Do you think Gerd ever tried this route?" Marike dusts the straw from her rear and takes a swig of water.

"Maybe. I never climbed with Gerd, except on the mountain. We never got to be on rock together."

Marike moves to an easier route, crawling up and over the cave's ceiling like a delicate lizard moving up a tree. "I like to think he did. I like to think when my fingers touch the rock, they touch his hands too. Rocks don't die. So maybe they carry pieces of us with them forever."

I imagine touching the rock holds along Fitzhan that Ellias must have touched a thousand times. I'd never thought of the skin or blood he'd left on the fel. Rain, ice, and wind remove us from our lines quicker than we can process our grief. But some part of him must be there, if not physically, then at least his essence.

Ellias knew my father was still alive; he allowed me to grieve and mourn. But I cannot summon the anger for Ellias that I feel toward my father. Ellias loved and protected me while my father hid himself away. Everything Ellias did, he did because he thought it was right. And Ellias was grieving too. People don't make the best decisions when they are stricken by sadness.

Just as Marike looks to me to protect her, to teach her, and to make the world better, so had I looked to Ellias. I'd always assumed adults had the answers, but knowing now how lost I am grants me empathy for Ellias. Even empathy for my father. The truth is, no matter how old we get, we still know nothing. We still make everything up as we go and try not to succumb to the terrible pressure to make the world anew. Is that it? None of us are monsters? We're just fumbling in the dark, and sometimes, in that fumbling, we stumble too far over the line.

Clarity returns with a few deep breaths, and I move to the base of Veber's Split. "You want to strengthen your fingers, your arms, your back. All of it. But through practice, you will also grow your technique and patience. I know many male climbers who climb with brute strength alone. Smaller people, like us, don't have that luxury. We must truly become great. We must learn to rely upon our whole bodies. We must forge an intimate relationship with the rock."

I reach for the first hold on Veber's Split, suddenly wanting to try the difficult route I was working on before the journey north. How much I have experienced since then! I jam my hands into the crack, keeping my hips into the rock and my feet secured. I bar my arm, twist my hips, and tuck my toe or heel into a hold. I pass the crevice where the gluspider lives and spot the little red and gold creature scurrying into the darkness. Marike watches from below as I cross the ceiling, not with brute strength but with technical precision and patience. Just as I saw Haydrich do. I reach the crux, where before I had always fallen, where Haydrich sought invisible pinch holds and crossed with enviable technique.

The other players in this dangerous game are far more powerful than I, but they climb without technique; they climb with brute strength. I have no great beast, no gathering army, no intricate plan. But I don't need those things. Instead, I must approach the coming war as if it were a bouldering problem. With technical precision and patience. Let the others wear themselves out with aggressive bluster and poor form. I must stay steady and focused.

I spot a tiny hold, no bigger than a pebble, and I move to pinch it. My forearms scream, and my shoulders bulge, but I tighten my abs, pull my body to the ceiling, and follow the impossible hand- and footholds across the ceiling. I arc up and over, ignoring the dyno move that would require me to jump, and slowly climb down the back side.

"Wow!" Marike applauds excitedly. "Someday I'll be able to do that."

I tilt my head backward to stare up at the volcanic ceiling that has stumped me for so long. "You'll be amazed how quickly it will come, Marike. You will be an Ascenditure if that's what you want. I guarantee it."

"We all thought it would be Gerd," Marike says. "And I wish it had been. But since it can't be, I want to be the one who climbs and supports my family."

"I will do everything I can to support you. You have my word."

Marike's smile falters, and her eyes dart toward the dark tunnel behind me. "Do you hear that? Someone's coming."

"Go," I whisper. "Move around the bend and stay out of sight. I'll pretend it's just me here."

"What if it's trouble?"

"Then it is my trouble. Go!"

Marike grabs her gear bag and disappears into the darkness, and no sooner has she gone than a tall, imposing figure appears. I cannot help a scream when the lihtbugs illuminate his face in eerie red.

"Tristan?"

"Geitsê, Klarke." He stops before me, looking thinner than before and tired, but alive. Very much alive.

Tears fill my eyes, and I hug him, sobbing into his shirt. "You were dead. The avalanche came, and you were gone."

"I saw the man pushing bodies into the snow. I was afraid to return to camp, not until I knew what was going on. When I learned that King Adolar blamed me for the murders, I stayed away and let them believe I was dead. I'm sorry."

"Sorry?" I pull away and cock my head. "For what?"

"For abandoning you when I promised to tell the truth."

I laugh, and the joy thrums through my veins. I feel, suddenly, as light as air. "Never apologize for surviving in hairk-infested water. You're here now, and I am so glad of it."

"I had to come back. I swore an oath. *I will not fall. I will not fail. I will not betray my kingdom.* To ignore what is coming would be the ultimate betrayal."

"What is coming?" I whisper, desperately hoping he refers to the dangers of which I already know rather than some new terror.

"I've been hiding out on the Umlauf Peninsula, living under

an alias. I met a man from Dresdal, the best climber I've ever met. He was free-climbing stuff I could barely top rope. He was also a drunk, and more importantly, a washed-up alchemist. The man said he'd trained his nephew to climb, the best climber in all of Galvaith, he claims. A child with one brown eye and one blue."

The man with the two-colored eyes. The päter at Mount Bonen—could that be this alchemist's nephew? How is it that everyone else around me seems to know who this man is, and I am still scrambling through the darkness, ignorant and clueless?

Technique and patience, a voice inside me whispers.

"And not only could this man's nephew climb, he and his master have discovered how to bring back magic to Ectair. They have revived the mages, assembled the diemants. Apparently, they have already crafted two new diemants and are using them to summon a monster greater than Hildegroth. King Adolar believes they are aiding him, but they are, in fact, seeking to destroy him."

"Did this man mention the Dark Promise?"

"That's them."

"I know one of their members. He tried to recruit me. Said he has a leader from the South he's working to bring to power. They call him the Schaeter."

"The Schaeter is already here, Klarke, in the palace."

The Schaeter is in the palace? Is he also a päter? How easy it is to hide behind a white mask. Was it the Schaeter who left jagged shards of glass in my bed? My initial fright is replaced by a growing determination—perhaps the Schaeter is now out of the shadows. If he lives in the palace, I can find him.

"There was something, too, about purple ferns," Tristan continues. "Some garble about how they were a gift of life Orna provided to counter the gift of death that Laren offered. Orna gave us ferns, Laren gave us Death's Whisper. And all these things lie in a cave atop Fitzhan. The fundamental components of creation and destruction lie at the top of Miter's Backbone. And this man's nephew has been gathering these items and manipulating them. While we've been fighting over whether a woman is allowed to climb, this man has figured out a way to destroy us all. The nephew's name is Veton, and he killed Gerd and Julius. He killed them all. I came back to warn you, but I have also come for revenge."

"He killed Gerd?"

Tristan startles at the soft voice that emerges from the darkness. Marike appears in the tunnel, angry tears spilling down her cheeks. "I want revenge too. I want to help."

I place one hand on Marike's and one on Tristan's. "Tristan, this is Marike, Gerd's sister. I am training her to climb. I think I may know who this Veton is. And we will stop him. We will have justice. But first we must have patience. Many move against King Adolar. Men with great strength and power. We have neither. We must be smart and careful. So, Marike, go about your life as if nothing has changed. I will keep you in the knot. I will make sure you are part of this. And, Tristan, remain hidden, but stay in Kietsch. I need you. The battle lines are being drawn up, the war is beginning, but it's complicated. Technique and patience. That is how we win."

Veton. The Schaeter. Haydrich. The Dark Promise. It is finally coming together. Veton, the greatest climber the world has ever known, is posing as a päter in the palace, pretending to work for King Adolar while, in reality, he is working toward the king's undoing. The Schaeter and leader of the Dark Promise may also be posing as a päter. And Haydrich, working for them both, has infiltrated the Ascenditures. But to what purpose? I need to find Otto, and I need Kiel and the Ascenditures to return.

We pack our gear and leave the lava tube. Icy rain pelts my face as I step from the cave. The peaks of Miter's Backbone are enfolded in a thick winter mist. But up there, hidden among the clouds and rain, lies the truth of everything. I think of the lies I've told, the lies we all tell every day. We are all liars. Not just the wicked. And because of our lies, monsters have awakened, evil has returned, and of friends we've made enemies.

The truth is up there, in a cave of crystals and ferns, and though vintazite has descended with vengeance and the climb to the top is nearly impossible, I know I will need to make the climb. I know Veton is still summiting Fitzhan. And he is using the fundamentals of creation and destruction to take over our world in a way that puts King Adolar's schemes to shame.

If I am to stop him, to stop all of this, I must do the unthinkable. I must rise up against years of tradition and years of lies about what it means to be a woman. To save us all, I must become the best climber the world has ever seen. Everything I've ever trained for has led me to this moment.

I will not fall. I will not fail. I will not betray the truth.

Acknowledgments

Finding Ramanata is, perhaps, my favorite book I've written, and I hope you enjoyed reading the next chapter of Klarke's journey. So many people have played a part in shaping this series, but there are a few who must be thanked, as without them, this book wouldn't be as it is in your hands.

To my agent, Lizz Nagle, and also Alisha West at Victress Literary for helping so much with the initial editing of this (and every) project, and for being such strong supporters of my work and my career.

To Natalie Wright for being the friend who keeps me sane in this crazy industry. What can I say beyond "I couldn't and wouldn't want to do this without you." Your friendship and talent as a writer inspire me daily to push myself and to enjoy the journey of it all.

To my mom, Carey, who is also an author and writer, for always being the first critique partner on my novel because I trust her most with my words in their raw, unpolished form—both to be brutally honest and wonderfully uplifting.

To Stephanie Scott for being an incredible critique partner and friend. I appreciate your feedback and willingness to edit anything I send your way, and how you always push for more emotion and feeling.

To my editor, Jaynie Royal, and the entire team at Regal House Publishing, for working tirelessly to get this book into reader-ready shape and for putting it out into the world.

To Adam Bassett, once again, for creating wonderful maps to accompany my narrative.

To my friend Deenie Bowen for being available to hop in and help with last-minute editing and read-throughs.

To the authors who took the time to read and write blurbs for my book: Stephanie Scott, Adriana Allegri, Janet Goldberg,

Zackary Vernon, Jill Murray, Samantha Schinder, and Laura Reeves. Check out their stories. They are all incredibly talented writers!

To my husband, Andreas, who not only supplies endless pizza and emotional support to me, but who is also an incredible sparring partner and creative mind, whose background in psychology helps me always find the motivations for my characters and within myself to keep going.

To everyone out doing the work to further equal rights for women.

And finally, to all my friends, family, and readers who have bought the book, showed up to events, shared the story with others, left reviews, posted photos and videos, and helped me to spread the word about my fierce rock climber, Klarke, tanks ye, from the bottom of my heart and to the summit of Mount Opasno.

Klettag und.